Baby for the Greek Billionaire

SUSAN MEIER

Published in Great Britain 2015
by Mills & Boon, an imprint of Harlequin (UK) Limited,
Eton House, 18-24 Paradise Road, Richmond, Surrey, TW9 1SR

BABY FOR THE GREEK BILLIONAIRE © 2015 Harlequin Books S.A.

The Baby Project, Second Chance Baby and *Baby on the Ranch* were first published in Great Britain by Harlequin (UK) Limited.

The Baby Project © 2011 Linda Susan Meier
Second Chance Baby © 2011 Linda Susan Meier
Baby on the Ranch © 2011 Linda Susan Meier

ISBN: 978-0-263-25203-3
eBook ISBN: 978-1-474-00382-7

05-0215

Harlequin (UK) Limited's policy is to use papers that are natural, renewable and recyclable products and made from wood grown in sustainable forests. The logging and manufacturing processes conform to the legal environmental regulations of the country of origin.

Printed and bound in Spain
by CPI, Barcelona

Susan Meier spent most of her twenties thinking she was a job-hopper—until she began to write and realised everything that had come before was only research! One of eleven children, with twenty-four nieces and nephews and three kids of her own, Susan has had plenty of real-life experience watching romance blossom in unexpected ways. She lives in Western Pennsylvania with her wonderful husband, Mike, three children, and two over-fed, well-cuddled cats, Sophie and Fluffy. You can visit Susan's website at www.susanmeier.com.

THE BABY PROJECT

BY
SUSAN MEIER

CHAPTER ONE

"THE ANDREAS BROTHERS have arrived."

As the secretary's announcement came through the speaker phone, attorney Whitney Ross turned from the window in her father's law office. The gathering January storm clouds above the New York City skyscrapers concerned her, but the Andreas brothers' visit would be every bit as tumultuous.

Gerard Ross pressed a button on his phone. "Tell them I need five minutes."

"You're enjoying this."

"Not *enjoying* exactly." He grimaced, leaning his round body back in his office chair. He rhythmically tapped the blotter on his cherrywood desk. "How about if we say Stephone used his will to accomplish a few important things?"

Though Whitney had never met Stephone Andreas's sons, the man had been a close friend of her father's. He'd come to dinner at least once a month from the time she was six, and had talked about "his boys" incessantly. So she suspected she knew what was going on. The senior Andreas had always believed his three sons needed a kick in the pants and it seemed he'd finally found a way to give them one.

"You persuaded Stephone to use his will to force them to grow up."

"This is about more than growing up. All three are smart. All three are good businessmen. Any one of them could take over the family holdings. But not one of them has a sense of loyalty or family."

"And this is where the will comes in?"

"Yes. Stephone made his oldest son, Darius, chairman and CEO and left him the Montauk estate. Whether that divides them for good or forces them to unite all depends on whether Darius takes the reins like a true leader."

He rose and headed for the black leather sofa in the comfortable meeting area in the corner of his big law office. After he sat, he patted the spot beside him, indicating that it was where Whitney should sit for their upcoming meeting.

"But before I bring the brothers in, there's something you need to know. Missy had something put in her will for you that Stephone agreed would also go into his."

Whitney took the seat he'd offered. "Missy put something in her will for me?" She wasn't surprised. Missy Harrington had been her roommate from the time they were freshman at university the whole way through law school. With an alcoholic mom and a dad who'd left when Missy was young, Missy had adopted Whitney's family as her own, and they in turn had taken her under their wing. For seven years she'd shared every holiday and most of her vacations with the Rosses. Whitney had hardly seen Missy since she had introduced her friend to Stephone Andreas, but they had still shared a strong bond.

"She didn't exactly leave you something. In accordance with Stephone's and Missy's wills, you and Darius got shared custody of their son."

Whitney's stomach squeezed. "What?"

"Okay. Look. It's been three years since the accident that took Burn and Layla. And though I had never dreamed that Missy and Stephone would die so soon when I let them put this provision in their wills, it's still time you came back to the land of the living." Her dad pulled a small envelope from one of the files in the stack on the coffee table. "She left this note for you."

Whitney wrapped her hand around the envelope, and she paled.

"In the unlikely event of their deaths, Stephone wanted Darius to raise their son, but Missy was adamant about you having joint custody. The Andreas brothers are rich and spoiled. And they don't even know their father had another son. It's anybody's guess how they'll react when they find out. I believe that Missy made you co-guardian to ensure that Gino was also in the hands of someone *she* knew could take the reins and care for her baby."

"But I don't know Gino! When Missy and Stephone moved to Greece, we practically lost touch. I've never even met Gino. I'll be no better for this baby than his brother."

He caught her hand. "You might not know Gino, but Missy knew you. She knew you had a sense of family. A sense of right and wrong. You've also been a mom. You'll get to know Gino and, as young as he is, Gino will grow accustomed to you, too." He squeezed her fingers. "Besides, you need this."

She tried to bounce off the sofa, but her dad held fast to her hand. When she faced him her eyes were blazing. "No! I don't *need* this! I'm fine!"

"You're not fine. Otherwise, getting custody of Gino wouldn't make you angry."

He pressed a button on the phone on the coffee table that sat in the center of the circle made by the sofa and three black leather chairs. "Cynthia, bring in Gino, please."

Whitney's heart stopped. Her stomach rolled. Her head spun. For the past three years she'd avoided even being near a baby. The scent of baby powder, the feel of snuggly blankets, the sight of someone so tiny, so helpless and so beautiful would have been her undoing. And now her father wanted her to take a baby into her home?

The side door opened and Cynthia Smith walked in carrying six-month-old Gino Andreas in a baby carrier, along with a diaper bag and a duffel.

Her father squeezed her hand again. "Your mother and I have been keeping Gino during the Andreas funerals, but it's time you took him." He rose and accepted the baby carrier from Cynthia. "Thank you, Cyn."

She nodded and her blond hair bobbed. "You're welcome, sir."

As Cynthia left the room, Whitney's father set the carrier on the sofa, pulled Gino out and presented the dark-haired, dark-eyed baby boy to her. "He's yours, Whitney."

Knowing there was no arguing with her father, Whitney slid the envelope into her jacket pocket and took the six-month-old with shaking hands. He immediately began to cry.

"Don't cry, sweetie," she crooned, automatically pressing his head to her shoulder to comfort him. "It's okay."

Her instinctive response to his crying amazed her,

but she wasn't surprised by the pain that sliced through her—the memories that flashed through her brain. Her daughter had been a tiny blonde with huge blue eyes. She'd rarely cried, except when she missed her mother. She'd loved bananas and puppies. To Whitney, she'd seemed the smartest baby on the face of the earth.

Tears filled her eyes. Her stomach tightened.

She couldn't do this.

Maybe she needed more time with her therapist, Dr. Miller?

But before she could say anything to her dad, the office door opened. Wearing jeans, cowboy boots and a cable-knit sweater, Cade Andreas entered first. Behind him was Nick, the dark-haired, dark-eyed brother who most resembled the senior Andreas. And finally Darius. Taller than their father, but with eyes and hair as dark as his, striking in his expensive business suit, Darius was very clearly the leader of the group.

Their expressions were solemn, yet strong. Almost arrogant. The head of the Andreas family was dead. They now controlled one of the largest shipping conglomerates in the world.

Or so they thought.

She glanced at the baby in her arms. For the first time in three years she felt a swell of protectiveness only a mother could feel, and she understood why Missy had given *her* custody along with Darius. The Andreas men were strong. Maybe too strong. And babies needed love.

The question was did she have any left to give?

"Are you kidding me?"

Darius Andreas gaped at Gerard Ross, his deceased father's attorney, then at Gerard's daughter Whitney

Ross, a tall, cool blonde with gray-blue eyes who looked nothing like her short, round father. The pair sat on the black leather sofa. The Andreas brothers sat across from them on three black leather chairs. Beside Whitney was a baby carrier and inside the carrier was a baby boy who looked to be only a few months old. His black hair and dark eyes marked him as an Andreas as clearly as Gerard Ross's pronouncement did.

"I assure you, there's no joke." Gerard leaned back, getting more comfortable. "This little boy is your father's final son. There are four of you now."

He picked up the will and began reading again. "It is my wish that the remaining two-thirds share of Andreas Holdings be divided equally among my four sons— Darius, Cade, Nick and Gino."

Gino.

A baby.

His final half-sibling was a baby!

Darius sucked in a breath, forcing that to sink in, but it wouldn't. His brain had frozen. He was stunned, speechless and working not to lose his temper over something he couldn't change. Nick and Cade appeared to be equally shell shocked.

Finally, the business sense Darius had trusted his entire life came to his rescue. "I want a DNA test."

The smooth leather sofa sighed when Gerard sat forward. He looked down at his entwined fingers, then caught Darius's gaze. "Your father might not have married Missy Harrington, but he's named on the birth certificate as Gino's father. Had Missy not died with your father, you might be fighting her for the company right now."

"I still want DNA."

"I understand you're surprised—"

"Surprised? How about shocked? First our father calls us to the hospital after the accident to tell us that he gave one-third interest in the company to someone else. So we'll never fully own our own damned company. Then he tells us *we* have no sense of family and unless we pull together we're going to lose everything he built. Then he dies. Just like that." He snapped his fingers. "Now you're telling us there's a fourth brother?"

"Mr. Andreas, the very fact that you didn't know your father had another child is proof that your sense of family leaves a bit to be desired."

Darius nearly cursed. Who was his womanizing father to tell him that he had no sense of family? His father had abandoned his mother. Hell, Stephone had abandoned *him* until he was in his teens. And then he'd appeared in Darius's life only because he had wanted to ensure that Darius went to a good university so he could be groomed to work for Andreas Holdings.

"For decades our father preached that we shouldn't take family troubles to outsiders." He rose. "Yet it looks like that's exactly what he's done." He reached for the baby carrier. Now that the shock was receding, things were beginning to sink in and make sense. He didn't really need DNA to tell him this was his brother. His father had been living with a thirty-year-old woman. It was no shock she'd gotten pregnant. Gino had all the physical markings of an Andreas. With his father's name on the birth certificate and Gino's name in the will, this little boy was family. And his father wanted him to care for him. So he would. Unlike his two brothers, Darius had always done what their father had asked.

"We'll take our brother and go now."

Whitney held back the carrier. "Dad?"

Gerard said, "There's more."

Darius just barely controlled his rising fury. *"More?"*

"You, Darius, get custody of Gino, but you share it with Whitney."

He turned his heated gaze on her.

Her yellow hair was probably pretty, but she had it rolled in a tight, no-nonsense bun at the back of her head. Her gray suit hid any hint of the body beneath it. He caught the gaze of her blue-gray eyes. In spite of the fact that she dressed to downplay her appearance, Darius felt a click of attraction. And it was mutual. He saw the flicker in her pretty blue orbs.

"It's up to you how you divide Gino's time. If you want to have him three days a week and Whitney four, or if you want to have him for two weeks a month and Whitney two, whatever you choose is up to you two. But she will vote his share at your board of directors meetings."

This time Darius did curse. But he quickly pulled in a breath, struggling to rein in his temper, and glanced again at Whitney. The click of attraction he'd felt when he'd first looked into her eyes turned into a current of electricity that zapped between them. They were definitely attracted.

If this were any other day, any other time, any other circumstance, he would have pursued her. Peel off a few layers of clothes, take down her hair—he was just about certain he'd find paradise.

But those eyes, those pretty Persian-cat eyes, told him to forget it. It didn't matter if they were attracted to each other. They had a job to do. Raise Gino. Together.

Whitney stayed perfectly still under Darius Andreas's scrutiny, though warm, sweet attraction hummed through her. She ignored it. He was a gorgeous man with his dark, brooding good looks, his tailored suit made to accentuate his broad shoulders and trim hips, and his commanding personality. Any woman would react to him. Simply from the way his other brothers hadn't even spoken since introductions were made, it was clear that Darius was the brother in charge. And that was very sexy.

With his piercing onyx eyes boring into hers, she suppressed a shiver. But she wasn't worried about falling victim to the attraction. Attractions frequently grew into relationships and relationships made people vulnerable. The pain that had followed the loss of her husband had been indescribable. She'd never put herself through that again. She'd never even let herself get close. She couldn't be attracted to Darius Andreas. She refused.

Darius squeezed his eyes shut in disgust and popped them open again. "All right. Fine." He motioned for Whitney to follow him. "Let's go."

"Go?"

"If this baby's on the board, he's working for a living."

Whitney's dad laughed. "Very funny, Darius."

"I'm not laughing. My father left the company in a sad state. There's work to do. And nobody's excused. Since your daughter has his vote, she'll pull his share of the duty."

"That's preposterous—"

"Dad." Whitney interrupted her father. "It's okay. I've never been one to shirk my responsibilities." She straightened her shoulders and looked Darius in the eye, accepting his challenge. If he thought he'd intimidate her on day one, he was sadly mistaken. She could handle a little work. "If everybody's working, then I will, too."

"All right," her dad agreed, "but before anybody leaves there's one more thing."

Darius turned. His dark eyes were ablaze now.

Whitney's dad looked from Darius to Cade to Nick and back at Darius again. "With someone else in possession of a one-third share of Andreas Holdings, and four brothers sharing the other two-thirds, you don't have to be a math scholar to know that individually none of you has controlling interest in the whole company." He glanced from Darius to Cade to Nick again. "Your father has instructed me to allow the holder of the one-third interest to remain anonymous until she decides how to handle her position. She's in her seventies, so she may simply want to sit back and enjoy the profits. But if she decides she wants to be active in the company, you had better be united or Andreas Holdings will end up being run by somebody other than an Andreas."

"We'll need a few minutes." Past being shocked by the conditions and warnings coming out of his dad's lawyer's mouth, Darius spoke quietly, with the authority of command. "We'd appreciate the use of your office to discuss this."

Gerard Ross rose. "Whitney and I will take Gino to her office. Have Cynthia call us when you're ready."

Gerard and Whitney left the room through a side door and Darius faced his brothers. "This wasn't exactly how we expected the reading of the will to turn out."

Nick snorted a laugh, but Cade rose. "Frankly, with the exception of Gino, nothing that happened this morning surprised me. You got most of the goodies, Darius. The Montauk estate and the chairmanship, but I think it all evens out with you also getting the baby." He saluted and headed for the door. "Good luck with that."

Right. Cade. The rebel. He should have guessed he wouldn't hang around to lend a helping hand and probably neither would Nick. There was no love, loyalty or unity among the Andreas brothers. They'd gone their separate ways, managed their trust funds individually, made their own fortunes. And each of them had his own life. But after Attorney Ross's warning about the mystery shareholder, Darius was beginning to understand some of the things their father had babbled about on his deathbed. If they weren't unified when that shareholder came out of the woodwork they could end up dockworkers in their own shipyards.

"Come on. You can't just walk away." He motioned for Cade to return to his seat, but instead, Nick rose.

"Sure we can. You're the chairman and CEO. You're the one who has to run things. You might have bullied Ms. Ross into working for you, but we're not buying in. We'll be back for board of directors meetings and for our share of the profits."

"So you really are just going to leave? Even after Dad told us he wanted us to unite? Even after hearing there's another shareholder?"

"You'll handle it."

"This company belongs to *all* of us. I thought you'd both want a part of things."

"Yeah, and I thought Dad would be around when I was a kid. But he wasn't." Nick caught Darius's gaze. "You were the golden boy. The company, the baby, the troubles are all yours."

He left the room with Cade right behind him.

Darius fell to the sofa. Over the years he'd cursed his dad for being a philanderer who had created three very different sons...four now. Today he looked up at the ceiling, finally understanding what had troubled his father for the last ten years of his life. The Andreas brothers truly weren't family. Having three different moms and hailing from three different parts of the United States, they were as divided as they were different. They might share dark hair, dark eyes and a shrewd business sense, but there was no love lost between them.

The silence of the lawyer's office rattled around him. Both of his parents were dead now. He had no cousins or aunts and uncles. He had two adult half-brothers, but they wanted nothing to do with him.

He thought back a few weeks to Christmas. He'd gone to parties galore, but on Christmas morning he'd been alone. His footsteps had echoed in his cold, empty apartment. Unless he did a better job of raising Gino than his father had done with him, Nick and Cade, this would be the sound of his life. Silence.

In a weird way, he was glad he'd gotten custody of Gino. Gino was his family now.

Well, his and Whitney Ross's.

A sliver of excitement slithered through him when he remembered the feeling of attraction that had arced between him and Whitney. Oh, she was tempting. A challenge. A buttoned-down present, begging to be unwrapped. But that would be nothing but trouble. He had to raise a child with her.

He understood why Missy Harrington had recognized that Gino would need a mother figure. Anybody who spent two minutes in the company of any of the Andreas brothers knew they weren't the settling-down kind. So if Missy wanted a mother for Gino, she'd probably known she'd have to pick her. But he didn't have a clue how "shared custody" would work in the real world. Would sharing a child be like being married? Or maybe being divorced? Would they have to draw up a custody agreement that set forth who got the baby and when? Or would they pass the poor kid back and forth like a tennis ball or Frisbee?

He ran his hands down his face. He had absolutely no idea how this would go. Worse, he had no idea how to care for a baby. Hell, he just plain had no idea how to be a dad, since his own father hadn't come around until he was nearly an adult.

Which gave Whitney a second, maybe more important, role in this child-custody venture. Because Darius didn't know how a father was supposed to behave, Whitney was going to have to teach him.

CHAPTER TWO

As WHITNEY AND HER DAD left his office, Cyn caught his arm. "They need you in the conference room right now."

"But I'm still working with the Andreas brothers—"

"The exact words Roger said were, 'The Mahoney case is going to hell in a ham sandwich. The very second Gerry is out of his meeting we need him in here.'"

Whitney's dad faced her. "Will you be okay?"

She forced a smile. "Yes. You go on. When the Andreas brothers are through with their little powwow, I'll have you paged if we need you."

"Thanks." He kissed her cheek, slid the duffel and diaper bag onto her shoulder, turned and raced away from her.

Walking to her office, Whitney looked down at Gino. Sucking a green-and-brown camouflage-print pacifier, he peered up at her. Luminous dark eyes met hers. Her heart stumbled in her chest. Layla's pale-blue eyes had been a combination of her father's sky blue eyes and Whitney's gray blue. Her hair had been yellow. Baby-fine. Wispy. Whitney had never been able to get a clip to hold and she'd become one of those moms who used multicolored cloth hair bands to decorate her baby's head.

Her chest tightened. She'd give everything she had, everything she owned, every day of the rest of her life, for even one more chance to touch that wispy hair.

Gino spat out his pacifier and began to cry. Whitney set the baby carrier on the small floral-print sofa in the right-hand corner of her office.

"Don't cry, sweetie," she said automatically and her throat closed. Her chest tightened. Caring for a baby was something like riding a bike. Unfortunately, all the remembered skills also brought back memories of the baby she'd lost—

The nights she'd walked the floor when Layla was colicky. Her first birthday party when the abundance of guests had scared her. Bathing her, cuddling her, loving her.

Being her mom.

Don't cry, sweetie.

She squeezed her eyes shut, trying to pull herself together, but Gino cried all the harder.

She sat on the sofa, lifted him from the carrier and cuddled him against her chest. Sobbing in earnest now, the little boy buried his face in her neck.

He smelled like baby lotion and felt as soft as feathers from an angel's wings. She closed her eyes again, weakened by longings for her own baby. Remembering treasured events. The plans they'd had for Layla's future. The mom she'd wanted to be.

Shaking with sorrow, she pushed at those memories, trying to get them out of her head. But they wouldn't budge. Instead, they arched in her brain like a rainbow of photos, a cacophony of happy sounds. Baby giggles. Toddler laughs. First words. Mama. Da Da. Nanna. Pap Pap. Kitty.

She knew it was the sweet baby scents that caused her

total recall. So she grabbed a blanket from the diaper bag and laid it on the sofa, then placed Gino on top, putting three feet of distance between them.

She swallowed. The memories receded. Her shaking subsided. The thumping of her heart slowed.

The little boy blinked at her.

"I know you're probably scared," she said, talking to him as if he were an adult because she couldn't risk the baby talk that she knew would soothe him. "I know my mom was very good to you the past few days, but I'll bet you miss your own mama…" She swallowed. Miss didn't even halfway describe the feelings of loss this baby must feel. Even though he probably didn't understand that his parents were dead, *her* heart broke because she *did* understand. She knew exactly what it felt like to lose the two people closest to her. He was alone. Scared. And wanted his mom. Or someone to make him feel safe again.

In three long years, she hadn't felt safe. Everything she believed had been tossed in the air and come down in pieces the day her husband had committed suicide and killed their baby with him.

As she checked Gino's diaper to see if that was why he was crying, a rush of memories of Layla flooded her brain again. Except this time they weren't happy. This time, she heard her baby crying, calling for her, and suddenly she was face to face with her worst fear. The fear that morphed into guilt. The guilt her therapist had told her was pointless.

No one knew if Burn had deliberately put Layla into the car with him when he'd decided to kill himself by sitting in the vehicle while the garage filled with carbon monoxide. Speculation was that he'd put Layla into her car seat to go somewhere, but when he'd gotten behind the wheel he just couldn't force himself out into the world. He'd sat in their garage long enough for the fumes to begin to get to him and was soon mentally too far gone to remember he had the baby with him.

That explanation had soothed everyone but Whitney. If everyone accepted that Burn's depression and mounting mental illness were reason enough to forget he had their child in his car, then shouldn't she have realized he was too sick to care for her baby?

Layla.

Why hadn't she recognized Burn's growing troubles?

Why hadn't she protected her baby?

What had been so important in those months that she'd missed all the signs that Burn was tumbling over the edge?

Tears filled her eyes as Gino began to cry, drawing her back to the present. She wanted to cuddle him, to love him, but her memories of Layla were still morphing into memories of Burn's suicide, Layla's death and the horrible, horrible feelings of guilt.

She couldn't deal with the guilt.

She changed Gino's diaper but rather than hold him, she returned him to the baby carrier. He looked at her with sad dark eyes.

She blinked back tears, hoping for his sake that the trouble she had holding him was only temporary. It wasn't his fault her family had died. Plus, Missy had wanted her to care for this little guy—

Remembering the envelope her dad had given her, she rose from the sofa to retrieve it from her jacket pocket. After fumbling with the seal, she pulled out the slim sheet of white stationery. Pacing in front of her sofa, she read…

Whitney…

It's funny to be writing this because I don't think you'll ever read it. Actually, I hope you never do read it. But we're having wills drawn up today and we have a baby. Plans have to be made for who will care for Gino just in case something happens. Stephone said he wanted Darius to have custody, but I didn't think that was such a good idea. I know Darius will never marry and that means Gino will never have a mom. But I also recognized I couldn't talk Stephone out of naming Darius as guardian. All I could do was suggest making you co-guardian. So that's what we did. If something happens to me and Stephone, Darius will be Gino's dad and you will be Gino's mom.

Love him, Whitney. I'm not sure Darius knows how. Missy

Whitney swallowed and sank to the couch. The note was short and to the point. A mother's simple plea. Love her baby. Because she wasn't sure his older brother knew how to love. Hadn't she already guessed that?

She glanced at Gino. The baby blinked at her dubiously. This little boy had gone from his parents' home in Greece to Whitney's parents' home, and now he was being passed to her. It had undoubtedly frightened Gino to be passed from one set of strangers to the next. He had to get into a stable environment. *She* had to get him into a stable environment. Without her, there was no guarantee Gino wouldn't be raised by nannies or at boarding school. Worse, there was no one to prevent Darius from seeing Gino more as a vote at a director's meetings than as a baby.

She had to do this. She had to be a part of this little boy's life. She had to care for him. She had to *love* him.

She popped the pacifier into Gino's mouth again. "This has been a rough couple of days for you. But you're safe now. I'm going to take good care of you."

An arrow sliced into her heart. How could she promise she'd take good care of this little boy when she hadn't even been able to protect her own child from her husband...the baby's father?

Darius gave himself another minute to collect himself, then stepped into the hall and instructed the receptionist to let Attorney Ross know he was ready.

Pacing the rich red Oriental rug, he waited for Ross to return. When the side door opened, he spun toward it to see only Whitney enter. She held Gino in the basket-like carrier. A big duffel bag and a diaper bag were slung over her shoulder.

"I know I said I could begin working for you today, but I just realized there's no one to care for Gino. Plus, I have no baby things at my home," she announced casually as she stepped inside. "No crib, no high chair, no swing or rocker."

Darius's male senses perked up. Probably because he and Whitney were alone for the first time. He caught the scent of her perfume on the air, noticed her legs were long and shapely.

"I was thinking I should probably make arrangements to get all of that shipped to my apartment."

Darius almost said, "Sure," if only because his immediate reaction was to give her anything she wanted. But that was his attraction talking, agreeing so she'd like him. He had to resist that. He wanted this little boy in his life. He also needed Whitney to teach him how to be a father. The only way he could see that working out would be for her and the baby to live with him—at least for the first few weeks.

"I've been thinking about this deal and I'm not sure either one or the other of us taking him is the right thing to do."

She blinked at him. "You want to leave him at a hotel?"

He chuckled, hoping she was joking. Surely she couldn't think he was that inept. "No. I'm saying we need a plan."

"We'll hammer out an agreement of some sort eventually. But he needs somewhere to stay tonight. It's already close to five and neither one of us owns a crib. We should also hire a nanny." She caught his gaze. "Unless you've got baby experience I don't know about."

Heat whipped through him. This attraction wasn't going to be easy to ignore. But he was a very strong man. "Actually, I'm going to need a little help getting accustomed to him."

She turned away, fiddled with something in the diaper bag. "We both will in the beginning."

Rats. She wasn't getting what he was driving at. He didn't want her to know just how baby-stupid he was, and he couldn't tell her without putting himself at a disadvantage. He wasn't accustomed to negotiating from anything less than a position of strength. But sometimes the best way to win an argument was to use the element of surprise. Just come right out and propose the ridiculous.

"Or we could live together."

She spun to face him. "What?"

"Look, I inherited my father's estate on Montauk. There's a house big enough that we wouldn't even have to run into each other. This way we'd both see the baby every day and we could discuss any issue that came up the minute it came up."

She didn't say anything. Darius wasn't sure if he'd taken her so much by surprise that she was speechless or if his suggestion was so ridiculous she didn't know how to respond. So he pushed on.

"It doesn't have to be forever. Only the first few weeks. That way the little guy wouldn't be shuffled from one of us to the other before he got to know either of us. Plus, we'd have servants. We wouldn't be doing this on our own."

Whitney surprised him by saying, "How many servants?"

He shrugged. "Well, if I remember correctly there are several maids. My dad also always had a cook. And an estate manager, Mrs. Tucker."

Her expression went from strained to thoughtful to sort of happily surprised. Victory surged through him. But she hadn't actually consented. The battle wasn't over yet. He needed a deal sealer. Something that would put her totally on his side.

On impulse, he walked over to her and glanced down at the baby carrier. The brown-eyed boy blinked up at him over his pacifier.

"He's cute."

"He's very cute." She paused for a heartbeat then said, "Do you want to hold him?"

"Yeah. That'd be great." How hard could it be? Not only was he trying to get on Whitney's good side, but he had to be a dad to this kid. There was no time like the present to begin learning how.

She set the carrier on her father's black leather sofa, unbuckled the strap that held Gino in and lifted him in front of her. Eye-to-eye with the baby, she said, "Gino, I'm giving you to your big brother."

Darius laughed. "Was that an introduction?"

"No. That was me preparing him to be taken by a stranger."

"He'll know?"

Her gaze met his over the baby's dark head. "Of course, he'll know."

Her eyes were the most wonderful color of gray-blue. A sort of sexy, yet innocent shade that sparked his attraction to life again. Something sharp and sweet stabbed him in his middle. He was wishing that he didn't need her so he could follow this compelling urge he had to pursue her, when she presented Gino to him and fear immediately knocked every other thought out of his brain.

But before he had a chance to panic over his first-ever attempt at holding a baby, his hand brushed Whitney's as she gave him the baby and pinpricks of awareness lit up his skin. He'd never felt an attraction this strong, this gripping. A warning stirred in his brain, but Whitney let go and suddenly Darius was supporting Gino's full weight.

"Whoa!" He bobbled him a bit before he got control. "He's heavier than I thought."

Whitney smiled slightly. "Yes. Most six-month-olds aren't quite that…sturdy."

Feeling painfully awkward, but determined to get the hang of this, Darius laughed uncomfortably. "We are a family of big eaters."

She looked away.

Not sure if she was totally disinterested in him and his family or uncomfortable at being so close to him, Darius casually said, "How about if we swing by your

apartment and gather some things so we can spend the
weekend in Montauk? My dad and Missy might have
only popped by the house for a few weeks a year, but
after Gino was born they had to have created a nursery.
So at least he'll have somewhere to sleep tonight. That
way you can take a look around the place and see that
I'm right. The house is big enough that we could live
together for a few weeks without getting in each other's
way."

Whitney's skin pricked with fear, trepidation and
possibility. She couldn't picture herself alone with Gino
tonight. Well, actually, she could. She saw herself paralyzed with grief as he lay in the crib sobbing. Darius's
suggestion that they spend the weekend together would
have been the answer to a prayer, except he wouldn't be
any better with Gino than she was.

Of course, he had staff and eventually they'd hire a
nanny.

Still, it could take weeks to hire someone. Especially
since they had to find someone willing to go back and
forth between her Soho loft and Darius's estate. If they
didn't have a nanny tonight, there would be no hiding
the fact that she was having trouble being around the
little boy. Trouble holding him. Trouble smelling him.
Trouble just being in the same room.

Of course, if she had a breakdown in front of Darius
it might be bad for her, but it would be good for Gino,
because at least there'd be someone to pick up the ball.
No matter how inexperienced. With a few quick baby
lessons she could probably turn Darius into a moderately
competent caregiver.

As if to confirm that idea, Darius jiggled Gino on his
arm, as he cooed and gooed at him, and Gino playfully

slapped his face. They liked each other. They almost appeared to have some kind of natural family bond.

Blessed relief swelled through her. It wasn't a perfect idea, but it was better than her being alone with Gino. In the name of teaching Darius how to do his part for the little boy, she could hand over most of the tasks that might cause her to burst into tears.

Plus he had staff. Gino would be surrounded by people who could care for him until they found a nanny. And if Whitney played it right, she wouldn't even have to have a panic attack to get assistance. Gino was so adorable, every maid, cook and butler would want a turn at holding him, feeding him, rocking him to sleep.

She sucked in a breath, caught Darius's gaze, and said, "Okay. We'll spend the weekend at your house."

He smiled at her, reminding her of the other teeny, tiny thing she'd forgotten to add into the equation. They were attracted. And about to live together.

Luckily, his house was huge. And she wasn't stupid. She'd keep a cool head and everything would be fine.

CHAPTER THREE

ON THE DRIVE OUT TO Montauk, Darius called ahead to let the staff know they would be arriving.

Clicking off his call, he faced Whitney. "There's a nursery."

"Really? That's great."

"Yes. My father and Missy had been staying at the house when they were in the accident."

Sadness tiptoed through her at the loss of her friend, but she focused on the job she had to do for Missy. "So there wouldn't happen to be a nanny?"

"No. Their nanny was a young woman from Greece. She went home immediately after the funerals."

"Too bad."

He shrugged. "Not really. I'm sure we can easily hire someone."

Whitney smiled noncommittally, then her gaze fell to Gino who was asleep in his car seat. She should have started Darius's baby lessons the minute they got into the limo. She knew what to do and his hands could be the hands that carried out her instructions tonight. But now Gino was asleep and probably wouldn't awaken until they arrived. And when he awakened, he'd be crying. Then Darius would see her struggle and fumble.

Sucking in a soft breath, she told herself not to borrow

trouble. Everything would work out if she just kept a cool head.

The limo pulled up to an iron gate and the driver used a combination on a keypad to open it. As they drove up the wide, circular drive to get to the enormous house, Whitney's heart kicked into overdrive. With bare tree branches blowing in the January breeze the estate had a cold, deserted feel to it. An ominous mood that almost made her shiver. And definitely made her wonder if this was the right choice. Darius Andreas was a stranger and she'd agreed to live with him.

Whitney unbuckled Gino as the driver opened the door. He helped her out and Darius stepped out behind her, then reached inside for the baby.

Refusing to panic or let her imagination run wild over the cold, empty feeling that surrounded her, Whitney followed him to the front door, where he hit a few buttons on a hidden security panel, then opened the door.

They walked onto white marble tile in the echoing foyer. A curved stairway led the way to the second floor. A huge crystal chandelier awakened with light when Darius hit the switch as an older woman wearing a tidy black suit walked into the foyer to greet them.

"This is Mrs. Tucker," Darius said, turning to Whitney then Mrs. Tucker with a smile. "Mrs. T, this is Whitney. She's Gerard Ross's daughter."

Mrs. Tucker nodded once. "It's a pleasure to meet you, ma'am."

Whitney returned her smile. Though her parents hadn't had servants while she was growing up, and she herself had never had anything more than a cleaning service, her parents now had a full staff for their home on Park Avenue. "It's a pleasure to meet you, too, Mrs. Tucker."

"You're in the guest suite in the right wing upstairs. Geoffrey will get your bags from the limo."

"Thank you."

Mrs. Tucker turned to leave, but a thought struck Whitney and she stopped her. "Where's the nursery?"

"In the left wing beside the master suite and Mr. Andreas."

"Will the nanny also be beside the nursery?"

"Yes, ma'am. The nanny's quarters are on one side. Mr. Andreas's are on the other."

That just didn't sit right. Not because of the unexpected jealousy that slithered through her at the thought of another woman being a door or two away from Darius's bedroom, but because she felt as if she were being eased out. She hadn't questioned Darius talking her into living at the house in Montauk. Her fears had actually caused her to be relieved he'd thought of it. But now that he'd assigned her to a room across the house from the nursery, suspicions rose in her. He wanted the baby at his house, wanted her at the other side of the mansion. What was he up to?

"Why am I not near the nursery?"

Holding Gino in the baby carrier, Darius stepped forward, caught her arm and directed her to the stairway as Mrs. Tucker scrambled away, obviously glad Darius would field the question.

"I thought you'd prefer privacy, particularly since Mrs. Tucker has agreed to sleep in the nanny's room to help with Gino until we get a regular nanny."

He sounded sincere, genuine. But this was a skilled negotiator, a smart businessman, a charming man. And her fears about caring for Gino had blinded her to the way he'd been calling the shots. That ended here. That ended now.

"Isn't there another suite close to the nursery?"

"Yes, of course."

"I'd like that one, then."

Darius stopped walking. His black onyx eyes snared hers, she was sure, in a show of strength, ready to meet her challenge. But within seconds the expression in his dark orbs shifted from serious to sensuous.

As if he only now realized how close they were standing beside each other on the stairs, he pulled in a breath. Tension rose up, shimmering through her. This man was attracted to her. There was no better aphrodisiac for a woman than the realization that a powerful, sexy man wanted her.

Her.

And she'd just insisted she be in a room closer to the nursery, *closer to him.*

She almost told him to forget about her request for a room change, but knew that if she did he'd realize it was because of their attraction. She also remembered it was her responsibility to love Gino and maybe even to protect him from overbearing Darius, and by God, she intended to. If that meant she needed to be close to him too, she'd handle it.

She smiled, hoping to appear to be a woman who hadn't even been slightly affected by the way he'd looked at her. "I take my responsibilities seriously, Darius. Though I'm glad Gino will be close to the nanny we hire, I want to be close too. The will says we share custody. I was given a job. I intend to do it."

His serious eyes suddenly filled with mischief that sent her pulse scrambling. "So you want to be across the hall—" he smiled "—from me?"

She stared into his sexy dark eyes with every nerve ending in her body humming and the blood in her veins virtually singing. Her voice squeaked when she said, "Yes."

"So be it. I'll have Mrs. Tucker tell Geoffrey to put your things in the room across the hall from mine."

With that he pulled out his cell phone, turned and walked up the stairs. Whitney nearly collapsed on the stairway. She heard him speaking on the phone, instructing someone to ready the room across the hall from his, and guessed he was talking to Mrs. Tucker. She hastily climbed the stairs with shaky legs and followed Darius to the nursery. But two steps inside the door, she froze.

A mobile over the cherrywood crib zapped her back in time. She could have been standing in Layla's nursery. The colors of the wall were different, but most of the furniture and lots of the toys were the same. So were the scents.

Darius carried the baby inside. "I think he needs a change. I'd offer to do it," he smiled engagingly, "but I've never changed a diaper in my entire life."

Smothered by thoughts of her baby, Whitney couldn't get her legs to move or her mouth to form words. Memories rolled through her mind. In perfect Technicolor she saw the vision of Layla standing up in her crib, holding the bars, crying for her mother. She remembered the Christmas gifts she had bought and hidden in the closet as if little Layla would somehow know to look for them. It had been almost a year before she had been able to clear out the nursery, if only because she couldn't step inside without crumbling.

But Darius didn't seem to notice her paralysis. Pulling Gino out of the baby carrier, he said, "I'd be happy to do it, though, if you want to teach me."

Whitney cleared her throat. "Sure." Relief swamped

her. For as much as she didn't want Darius taking over Gino's life, with her grief perilously close to the surface she simply couldn't handle touching Gino right now. Whether she liked it or not, take-charge Darius was saving her.

She glanced around until she saw the changing table. She pointed at it. "Take him over there."

Darius carried the sleepy baby to the changing table.

Whitney frowned. "We left the diaper bag in the car."

"Geoffrey will get it. But there should already be diapers here somewhere. I told the staff to make sure the nursery was stocked." With one hand holding Gino in place on the table, he opened the doors of the cupboard beneath it. "Ah. There they are." He reached in and pulled one out with a smile. "The staff is very efficient."

She took a cautious step to the changing table. "So I see."

"Now what?"

Forcing back the memories, she pulled in a slow, cleansing breath. Her grief subsiding, she strolled closer. "Unsnap his pajamas and slide him out."

He unsnapped the one-piece pajamas but was a little rough in getting Gino's arm out. She laid her hand on top of his. "Gentler."

"Okay." He peeked over at her and smiled stupidly. "His skin is soft, like velvet."

She remembered thinking that very thing the first time she held Layla and swallowed back the grief, pushed back the memory of the nurse laying her brand-new baby girl into her arms. "I know."

When Gino was out of his pajamas and wearing only

his diaper, Whitney pointed at the tabs of his diaper and said, "Yank on those to open the diaper."

He yanked on the tabs and to everyone's joy, the diaper was only wet.

Darius said, "Whew."

Whitney couldn't help it. She laughed. "Okay, toss that in the container beside the changing table." She motioned to the available diaper pail. "Slide another diaper under him, fasten the tabs, put him into clean pajamas and you're done."

Darius followed her instructions, needing another reminder about being gentle with Gino's little arms and legs as he tucked them into pajamas. But again he only smiled when she told him.

Her suspicions about Darius came tumbling back. He was too nice. Too eager. Once again she wondered if he wasn't trying to edge her out. "I'm surprised you want to learn all this."

He caught her gaze. "Gino is my family now."

"Oh. So you're really getting into the daddy thing?" Her voice dripped with skepticism as she asked the question, but she couldn't help it. A single man—a single *rich* man—who wanted to care for a baby was more than an anomaly. It was downright weird.

"My dad didn't have a lot of time for me." He peered over at her. "Or my brothers, and I don't want that to happen to Gino. If I'm to be his male influence, I want to do my end of the duties."

"So you're going to learn how to do *everything?*"

To her surprise, he wasn't insulted. He laughed. "Hey, I just changed a diaper. I think my commitment has been proven."

Not even close. Particularly since she didn't understand why he was making such a hands-on commitment.

Sure, he didn't want Gino to grow up without a dad. She got it. But there was more here. Her lawyer's instincts had gone from suspicious to downright positive there was something here she was missing.

"Okay, then tomorrow morning, we'll hit the ground running with your baby lessons."

He laughed, but Whitney wasn't kidding. Not just because she was afraid to touch Gino too much, but because she wanted to push Darius to the wall, give him so much baby time he would own up to what was really going on.

When the baby was dressed, Darius pulled him off the table and gave him a quick hug and kissed his cheek. "Good night, little guy."

Then he handed the baby to Whitney. Preoccupied with his motives, she didn't realize what he was about to do and had to scramble to catch Gino.

But the second the yawning baby was in her arms, the feel of his ultra-soft pajamas and smooth skin kicked her back in time again. Especially, when she brought Gino to her and hugged him. The second the little boy was snuggled against her, sadness overwhelmed her. The hollow, empty feeling of loss. Echoes of Layla's giggles rolled through her brain. Memories of her lifeless body haunted her.

She pulled Gino away from her shoulder and swallowed. Then, for Darius's benefit, she offered the baby a wobbly smile. "Good night, Gino," she whispered hoarsely, hoping Darius didn't notice she was trembling.

Because she wanted to cry. She missed her baby. She yearned for the life she'd lost. Was that so bad? So hard to understand?

She stopped. No. That wasn't so bad. Or so difficult

to comprehend. In fact, the smart way to handle her situation with Gino might be to *tell* Darius about Layla and Burn. She didn't want his sympathy, but it was clear now that she would have difficulty getting adjusted to caring for a baby. Soon Darius would notice. It would be better to get the story out in the open and solicit his help than to have him see her stumble and question her ability to care for his little brother.

But tonight wasn't the night for that conversation. With his motives now in question, she knew she had to wait a bit, see what he was up to before she bared her soul. If he was trying to get the baby away from her, she didn't want to hand him over on a silver platter. She'd wait. See if he didn't tip his hand or, alternatively, convince her that his motives were good.

Once the baby was in bed, Darius caught Whitney's arm and turned her to the door. "It's late. I'll show you to your room then we can have dinner."

Exhausted, confused and aching for privacy, she woodenly said, "I'm too tired for dinner."

"Really?" As they stepped out of the nursery and into the hall, he closed the door behind them. "I instructed Mrs. Tucker to have the cook make chicken and dumplings."

She turned, startled. "Chicken and dumplings?"

He smiled. "Yes."

How could he know her favorite food?

"I called your dad while you were in your apartment packing for the weekend." he said, undoubtedly answering the expression of confusion on her face, and directed her to walk to a door a few feet down the hall. "I figured if you could be kind enough to let me have at least the weekend with the three of us at my home, I could be gentleman enough to assure you ate well."

She quickened her steps down the hall, wishing he hadn't done something so nice when she was so tired, but at least slightly more comfortable with him. "I'll have some for lunch tomorrow."

She wasn't sure why she expected him to argue, but her suspicions were allayed even more when he simply said, "Good enough."

He stopped at a door only a few feet from the nursery. "Your suite?"

Feeling a tad foolish, she retraced her steps and stopped in front of him. He smiled slightly. Sexily.

Strange schoolgirl nervousness swept through her, reminding her of the first time she'd ever stood by a door with a boy, knowing he was about to kiss her good-night. Awareness tingled through her bloodstream. Her breathing went shallow and her legs turned to rubber. It had been so long since she'd reacted to a man that she'd forgotten the wonderful discomfort.

But Darius caught the doorknob and twisted it, opening the door, revealing a soft green-and-yellow room to her. Beyond the sitting room furnished with a sage-colored sofa and chair, accented by a cherrywood armoire with matching cherrywood end tables, was an open door leading to a bedroom. She could see patches of a yellow-and-sage-green bedspread. See the closed yellow drapes.

Her heart skipped a beat. The suite was calm, soothing. So different from her cool aqua and brown bedroom in her condo that she felt as if she was entering another world.

"Is something wrong?"

She spun to face him. "No. It's—" Warm, inviting, comforting. She swallowed. "—Lovely. I'm sure I'll be fine here."

"Let me make sure everything really is ready before I leave you." He stepped inside the sitting room, casually looking from left to right as he made his way to the bedroom.

Confusion buffeted her as she followed him inside. From a cursory glance into the room, it was clear that while she and Darius had been in the nursery, Mrs. Tucker had sent the staff to ready the room. He had no reason to check their work, unless he was stalling. Or unless the staff was so new to him that he didn't trust them?

That had to be it.

When he stepped inside the room she'd be sleeping in, a fresh ripple of unease passed through Whitney. It felt odd, uncomfortable to have a man who'd clearly had a sexual reaction to her standing beside the bed she would sleep in. Her chest tightened. Stupid nervousness rose up in her again, reminding her that it had been a long time, maybe too long, since she'd been alone with a man.

But his gaze was casual, touching the queen-sized bed, the bare dresser, the pale sage club chairs arranged by the window for reading.

After he'd seen everything in the bedroom, his peek into the master bath caused his expression to turn puzzled, and she had no idea why. The vanity was white oak with a glass countertop. The floors were Calcutta marble slab. A separate custom-glass tile shower was utilitarian, but the oversize, extra-deep soaking tub almost caused her to sigh with joy. She could have a bath. A nice long bath to ease away the tension and grief of this long, long day. That tub would be her haven tonight.

He glanced at her then quickly away. His expression was so odd that she peeked into the bathroom again. Her gaze lit on the huge tub and suddenly her face flamed with color.

Of course, a woman saw the tub as a haven. A man saw it as a playground.

Their eyes met and the warm syrupy feeling she'd had when she'd first seen him returned. She reminded herself he was handsome. Reminded herself that being attracted to him made her normal. Even congratulated herself on finally, finally, being attracted to someone again after three long years of mourning her deceased husband. But she concluded with a reminder that she didn't want to get involved with anyone—ever. She'd never again give another person that much power over her life.

Plus, she had custody of Darius's baby brother. The little boy whose vote on his board of directors was hers. All this "attraction" could simply be Darius angling to get on her good side so she'd vote his way at directors' meetings.

Darius rubbed his hand across the back of his neck and pointed at her door. "Since you're tired and I have things to do, I'll be going."

"Oh." That surprised her. Wouldn't someone who intended to use their attraction stay? Flirt? Instead, it seemed he couldn't wait to get away.

Disappointment flooded her, which rattled her. She didn't want him to be attracted to her, but since he was, having him not act on the attraction was the second-best thing. She shouldn't be disappointed.

She forced a smile. "Okay. Great." She headed out of the bedroom too, walking with him through the sitting room.

At the door, he was even more nervous. When their gazes bumped, she knew why. They stood about a foot apart, at the door, saying goodbye. He looked down at her. She gazed up at him. Attraction shimmied between them. The urge to kiss goodbye was like a physical thing. So strong, yet so foreign, it paralyzed her.

For the first time since her husband's suicide, she wasn't thinking about her broken life. In fact, it wasn't even getting half of her attention. His nearness dominated her mind. She couldn't think beyond the fear that he'd kiss her.

Then she realized she didn't fear he'd kiss her. She *wanted* him to kiss her. What she felt was glorious, spine-tingling anticipation. Not fear.

Dear God.

Curiosity and confusion combined and rumbled through her. How could she possibly be so attracted to Darius Andreas that she couldn't ignore it? That she wanted more.

But he didn't kiss her. He didn't even try. Instead he grabbed the doorknob at the same time that she did and their fingers brushed. Though she jerked away, the mere touch sent a maelstrom through her. It had been three long years since she'd been married, and for months before that her husband hadn't been interested in her. She hadn't been touched by a man she found attractive in nearly four years. Sensation after sensation poured through her, almost embarrassing in their intensity.

Darius quickly headed out the door. "I'll see you at breakfast tomorrow."

The door closed behind him before she could even answer. Knowing it was coming, she quashed her confusing disappointment when it was just a wisp, before it had a chance to fully form, because it was ridiculous. Stupid.

She shook her head. After that little episode by the

door, she didn't have any doubt that Darius was attracted to her. After the way he ran, she also knew he didn't want to be.

And that was good.

Wasn't it?

She sighed with disgust at her foolish ambiguity. This weekend was not about an inappropriate attraction. It was about figuring out how they'd raise Gino together, about helping Gino grow accustomed to them as they got to know each other—

Worry gripped her. She couldn't tell Darius about losing her husband and child without making herself look like an empty, sad, still-grieving woman, who wasn't ready to help him with Gino. Though part of her knew that was true and she should be honest, the other part warned her to tread lightly with this man. He was rich, powerful. If she showed her weakness too soon, he could take her to court, seeking full custody, citing her incompetence. Then Gino would be raised by him. Alone. And she wouldn't be able to fulfill Missy's wish that she love her baby.

She couldn't let Missy's son be raised only by Darius. Hadn't he gotten her into his house and almost put her into a room on the other side of the mansion? He'd have poor Gino in boarding school before he was four.

The thought of sweet baby Gino in a boarding school shored up her defenses and she felt herself growing ready to protect him. She would fight to her last breath before she let him put that child in boarding school—ever. And that wouldn't be their only argument. She and Darius would have hundreds of fights over the course of raising his half-brother.

That thought caused her to fall to a chair in complete shock. In the confusion of the day, she hadn't carried this guardianship all the way through in her head. But it was suddenly abundantly clear that whether they wanted it or not, this child bound them forever.

They might as well be married.

Or divorced.

Good God.

What had Missy gotten her into?

Tonight was supposed to have been the night she did her laundry. Instead, here she was in the home of a virtual stranger, with a baby who made her relive the best and worst part of her life and a man she was so attracted to she sometimes couldn't breathe in his presence.

It would be a miracle if she survived the weekend, let alone a lifetime.

CHAPTER FOUR

WHEN THE BABY AWAKENED at about three, Darius bolted up in bed. For a few seconds he was disoriented, then he remembered he was in the hideous floral and lace master bedroom of the house in Montauk. By the time he remembered Gino was in the room next door, the little boy's crying had stopped.

He got out of bed anyway, grabbed one of the pairs of jeans he'd had his staff pack and messenger to the estate and jumped into them. Heading out of the closet, he opened another drawer and snagged a T-shirt.

In a few long strides, he was at the door that connected his room to the nursery. Mrs. Tucker sat in the rocker feeding Gino, who gulped noisily.

He tiptoed into the room, but Mrs. Tucker laughed. "No need to be quiet now. He's wide awake."

Leaning against the crib, Darius crossed his arms on his chest. "And by the looks of things he's starving too."

Mrs. Tucker snorted a laugh. "They always are."

"Always? You mean this isn't an isolated incident? He's going to be getting up at three every night?"

"Maybe not on the dot, but, yes, he'll be waking somebody up in the middle of the night every night until he learns to sleep for long stretches without needing a bottle."

Staring at the dark-haired, dark-eyed little baby, Darius said only, "Hum." Gino was so sturdy that he looked packed into the green one-piece pajama. His hair sort of stuck up in all directions, making him even cuter.

Gino stopped sucking and Mrs. Tucker set the bottle on the table by the rocker. She lifted him up and he suddenly belched loudly. Mrs. Tucker laughed. "Well, now that takes care of that."

She reached for a tissue in the box also on the table beside the rocker and wiped away white gunk from Gino's mouth.

Darius winced. "Am I ever going to get the hang of this?"

"Eventually." She caught his gaze and smiled. "And just when you do the rules will change."

Darius's face fell. "What rules?"

Settling Gino on her lap to rock him, Mrs. Tucker laughed again. "Not exactly rules, but the things you'll need to do. He's a baby now. In a few months he'll be a toddler. Then there are the terrible twos—"

"Terrible twos?"

"You don't want to know about that yet."

He did but he also didn't. Because right now, falling asleep in Mrs. Tucker's arms, Gino looked like an angel. Darius swallowed. Strong, protective feelings rose up in him, feelings more intense than anything he'd ever felt.

He pushed them down. He might intend to be a part of this kid's life, but these feelings were weird. They had to be wrong.

Mrs. Tucker rose from the rocker and settled the

sleeping baby in the crib. "Better go back to bed. Morning comes quickly when you have a baby."

Darius headed for the door. "Good night."

Heading for the opposite door, Mrs. Tucker whispered, "Good night."

In his room, he crawled back into bed. He didn't like the idea that Mrs. Tucker had to do double duty, as his estate manager and the temporary nanny, so he set his alarm for six, hoping he'd get up before the baby.

When it went off a few short hours later, he didn't balk or linger. He quickly pulled on the jeans from the night before and a fisherman-knit sweater and, paying no mind to his bare feet, raced to the nursery.

"Good morning."

Dressed in jeans and a pretty blue sweater that brought out the blue of her eyes, Whitney stood on the far side of the crib, watching Gino, who was still asleep.

"Do you want to learn how to feed him this morning?"

He took an instinctive step back. He and Whitney had shared a powerful few minutes at her bedroom door the night before, but she didn't appear to be any the worse for the wear. Like him, she seemed to want to ignore their chemistry.

And he did want to feed the baby. But before he could say that, Gino's eyes fluttered open. He yawned and stretched and then let out with a yelp.

"That's your cue," Whitney said with a laugh. "Change his diaper, while I get a bottle."

Whitney calmly walked to the small fridge in the room and retrieved a bottle, which she put in the warmer.

Not wanting to jeopardize the peace between them or have Gino wake poor, sleeping Mrs. Tucker, Darius carried Gino to the changing table and simply did the things he'd done the night before when he changed the baby's diaper and put him into a clean sleeper.

Gino wasn't really happy about the arrangement and he began to scream. Darius noticed that Whitney was preoccupied with staring at a bottle warmer that seemed not to need her attention. It confused him that she didn't react to Gino's crying, but he wanted to learn how to care for this kid. He also wanted Whitney's help. He wanted them to get along, be a team. He couldn't complain about the tasks she gave him to do. He had to do them.

When the light on the warmer went out, Darius was already on the rocker, holding screaming Gino over his shoulder.

Whitney winced. "Do you still want to feed him?"

In spite of Gino's screaming, Darius casually said, "Sure. But you're going to have to tell me what to do."

"Arrange him across your lap so that his head is supported by your forearm."

Peeling crying Gino off his shoulder wasn't an easy task. He stiffened his limbs and refused to settle on Darius's lap.

Whitney handed him the bottle. "Here. Take this. Let him see the bottle is coming and he'll calm down."

With both hands busy with the baby, Darius didn't have a clue how to take the bottle, but he secured Gino as best he could with one hand and managed to get the other free to take the bottle.

He would have criticized Whitney for not helping, except as soon as he had the bottle in his hand, Gino began to calm down.

"Now, just press the nipple to his lips and he'll do the rest."

To Darius's complete amazement, as soon as he nudged the nipple against Gino's lips he not only stopped crying, he also started suckling loudly.

He laughed with relief. "Wow. That was different."

"Babies *are* different. They can't talk so you have to understand their crying and sometimes watch their body language."

"There's a lot to learn."

As Gino greedily gobbled his milk, Whitney walked away from the rocker and paced the room. Darius watched her for a few seconds, confused. She was in the room, but detached. Not like someone who didn't want to help, but like…well, a stranger. That was when he realized she might not know Gino any more than he did.

"So why did Missy make you guardian?"

She faced him, her expression rye. "You mean aside from the fact that she wanted to make sure her baby had a female influence?"

He laughed. "Yes. Why you?"

"Missy and I were very close from university until the day she met your dad."

"Really?"

"Her dad had left her mom before Missy was six, and her mom was an alcoholic who went in and out of rehab. Because she had money enough to have a maid, somebody who by default took care of Missy, no one ever realized how alone Missy was. So after we met, she began to come to my parents' house with me on weekends and holidays." She shrugged. "We were like sisters."

"And then she met my dad and none of us saw either one of them again."

She laughed sadly. "Missy really loved your dad."

"And he loved Greece."

"And that's where they lived."

They fell silent again. When the baby was done eating, he showed Whitney the empty bottle. "Now what?"

"Now you have to burp him."

"Burp him?"

"You hold him like this," Whitney said as she lifted Gino from Darius's lap up to his shoulder. "And pat his back."

As she said the words, she demonstrated by patting the baby's back. He burped noisily.

Whitney smiled and set Gino on his lap again. "That feels better, doesn't it, little guy?"

This close, her smoky, sexy voice curled around Darius and he nearly squeezed his eyes shut. That voice would be trouble if he heard it for several weeks with her living under his roof. Even the way she'd refused dinner the night before had been breathy and sensual. And then there was that tub. And the look that had passed between them.

He bounced out of the chair. "So do we take him down to breakfast with us or what?"

"Is there a high chair by the table?"

He nodded. "Yes."

"Then I think we should keep him with us."

"Okay."

After all the time he'd already spent with the baby, Darius didn't feel uncomfortable holding Gino, but that in itself was odd. The powerful feeling he'd had the night before came back full force. Sacred, reverent, it squeezed his heart and made breathing difficult.

Since his father's death, everything had happened so fast that he hadn't had time to think anything through.

But suddenly everything seemed so real. He had a child to raise, responsibilities beyond money and food. This kid would take up his time, change his morning routine, break into his afternoons, want his evenings. The understanding of what he'd taken on was so overwhelming that he felt as though he needed a minute.

He held Gino out to Whitney. "Could you hold him while I grab some shoes?"

She hesitated and Darius nearly groaned. The last thing he wanted to do was give her the impression he didn't want the task of caring for the baby. He wanted her to see his commitment.

"You know what? Never mind. I'll take him into my bedroom with me."

To his surprise, Whitney smiled. "And what will you do with him while you're putting on your shoes?"

He sucked in a breath. "Good question."

She took Gino from him. "Go get your shoes."

Relief poured through him. He raced into his bedroom, slid into socks and shoes and was back in the nursery in less than two minutes.

Noting that Gino was in the playpen, he frowned. "Ready for breakfast?"

"Yes." She reached down and lifted Gino out of the playpen, then handed him to Darius casually, smoothly, but as he took the little boy, she wouldn't look at him.

He hadn't expected her to put Gino in the playpen or to immediately pass him back when he returned from getting his shoes. But her not being able to look at him was actually more perplexing.

The night before, he'd walked away from the opportunity to kiss her without any hesitation, even though she was throwing off you-can-kiss-me signals. He'd hoped that walking away would show her that even though he was attracted to her, he didn't intend to follow through. Yet she still behaved in an overly cautious manner around him.

She strode to the door as if nothing were amiss and held it open while he came through with the baby. Following her down the steps, he stared at her stiff back. He'd never met a woman who was so hot one minute and so cold the next. It was almost as if she could turn her emotions off.

Which, in some ways, was good. They didn't want to be attracted to each other. It didn't work for either of them. And he was turning off his feelings for her every bit as much.

So why did it bother him?

In the breakfast room, which was actually one of several sunrooms along the east wall of the house, she took the tray off the high chair and instructed Darius to set the baby on the seat.

"But don't let go," she said, rummaging along the edges of the seat until she found what looked like seatbelts. "We have to buckle him in."

"Got it," Darius said, eager to learn. Especially when she didn't even seem to realize she was giving him lessons.

Another good reason to persuade her to live here with him permanently, not just for a few weeks.

Cook entered the sunroom with coffee and asked what each would like to eat. Darius ordered pancakes. Whitney chose a bagel and cream cheese.

"And should I make the baby's cereal?"

Darius glanced over at Whitney, who winced. "Wow. It's been so long since I was around a baby that I forgot that some kids start eating cereal around six months or so."

Cook proudly said, "He's been eating cereal for a few weeks now."

"Then get us the cereal." She faced Darius. "Sorry about that."

"Hey, I didn't even know babies ate cereal."

Cook walked in with a small bowl and a tiny baby spoon. As if recognizing his bowl, the baby slapped his hands on the tray. Cook handed the bowl and spoon to Darius who set them on the table then edged his seat closer to the high chair.

He didn't even consider opting out of learning how to feed Gino. He wanted to know everything. "So you're ready for this, huh?"

Gino screeched with joy.

Whitney said, "Just put a little bit of cereal on the spoon and very easily guide it to his mouth."

Darius did as instructed. Gino greedily took the bit of cereal and smacked his lips. The second bite was a little messier, but Darius just used common sense about getting the spoon and the cereal into Gino's mouth. After a few spoonfuls, when Gino tried to blow bubbles with it instead of eating it, Darius knew he wasn't hungry anymore.

"If you're playing in it rather than eating, I'm guessing you're done."

As he set the spoon down, Mrs. Tucker walked in. "Cook didn't want to start your breakfast until you were free to eat it. So, I thought I'd take Gino upstairs and play with him a bit. I'll walk through the kitchen to let Cook know she can make your breakfast now."

Darius rose and helped her get the baby out of the high chair. "Sounds good."

When she left, the little room fell silent.

Finally, Whitney said, "It's beautiful here."

Darius looked out at the steel-gray ocean, the deceptively blue sky. Though the day seemed calm, he knew winds off the sea would make it freezing cold out there. "Yes. I'd forgotten."

"Did you come here often?"

"After I turned eighteen I did."

"Why do I get the feeling you were forced?"

Her perceptiveness made him wince. "Because I was. My father gave me access to a five-million-dollar trust fund when I turned eighteen. He told me it was mine but he wanted me to go to college and work for Andreas Holdings. He hadn't as much as visited after he left my mom, then suddenly he was in my life, ordering me around. Our time here wasn't always pleasant."

She toyed with a salt shaker. "I liked your dad."

He laughed as Cook brought in his pancakes and Whitney's bagel. When she was gone, he reached for the maple syrup and said, "Most people who didn't have my dad for a lover or a parent did like him."

"Yes, I suppose that's probably true."

Surprised by her answer, he set the maple syrup on the table. "I thought for sure you'd sing his praises."

She snorted a laugh. "I know what it's like to deal with a person who has a public personality and a private one. I had a husband everybody loved."

His brows rose. So she'd been married? He hadn't even considered the possibility since she'd kept the last name Ross. But having been married, maybe even having been hurt by a divorce, might explain why she was so nervous around him.

Better than that, though, she'd opened the door for him to question her about her past. He'd been so focused on the baby that he hadn't really given much thought to the woman who shared custody beyond asking why Missy had chosen her.

Pretending great interest in his coffee, he said, "Everybody loved your husband but you?"

"Oh, I loved him. He loved himself too." She reached for the cream. "So what are your plans for the day?"

He recognized a change of subject when he heard it and realized that though she'd opened the door to talk about her past, she hadn't done it deliberately. He was curious about her, but he also knew asking about a husband she no longer had was a tad intrusive. It had no bearing on their situation and was none of his business. And if he wanted to convince her he was harmless, it would be wise to follow her lead and let the subject change.

"Actually, I want to spend as much time with the baby as I can."

She set her bagel on her plate and studied him. Her narrowed eyes were both suspicious and skeptical. "So, you weren't kidding. You really want to be a good dad?"

"I want to be a *great* dad." The words rolled through him. Now that he'd spent time with Gino, they meant so much more than they had even the day before. Now, he knew the cost. He was taking responsibility for another person.

It didn't confuse him as it had the night before or overwhelm him the way it had in the nursery that morning, but he was smart enough that it still sort of scared him. Especially since he'd vowed that he wouldn't be a part-time, no-show dad the way his father had been. Deep down inside, he had to admit he wasn't entirely sure he could do that. The only role model he'd had was a poor one.

Still, that wasn't something he could confide to Whitney. Technically, she was still a stranger. So, taking his cue from her when the conversation turned to something she hadn't wanted to tell him, he also changed the subject.

"What are *your* plans for the day?"

"I'm working on a class action case with my dad. Depositions are in. He's read them. I haven't." She grimaced. "That's never happened before."

Knowing he could get Mrs. Tucker to help him with Gino that morning and eager to make Montauk a comfortable home to Whitney, he turned his attention to his pancakes. "There are three offices in this house. You can have your choice. And you can spend the whole day if you need it. Mrs. Tucker and I will take care of Gino."

Relief saturated her voice. "Thanks."

She worked all day, stopping only to have lunch around two, long after Darius and Gino had eaten so she didn't have to interact with either one of them. But she couldn't get out of dinner. She arrived in the formal dining room at seven, dressed as she had been all day in jeans and a bulky sweater.

Darius, who was already seated at the head of the table, rose.

He still wore the fisherman-knit sweater and jeans he'd put on in the morning. Holding out the chair at the place beside his, he explained, "I assumed you'd be too busy to change."

She sat. "Yes. Thank you."

"My father insisted everything be formal. I'm more accommodating." He shook out his napkin. "I hope you like Italian."

"Actually, I love most foods." She risked a glance at him and fought a quiver of attraction. That morning she'd noticed that he looked very good in the casual clothes, but tonight he hadn't shaved. The scruffy stubble on his chin and cheeks made him sexy in a disreputable, sinful way. The man was simply too handsome for his own good and she was vulnerable. She hadn't interacted with a man like this—single and attractive—since she'd met her husband. She was out of practice, attracted and needy. A deadly combination when three feet away from a gorgeous man. Especially when she didn't want to get involved with another man.

But she couldn't be a total grouch or, worse, an unappreciative guest. "You don't have to worry when it comes to me and food. I'd eat constantly if I didn't have work to keep me busy."

He laughed. Pinpricks of delight raced up her spine. It had been so long since she'd made a man laugh in simple conversation that she'd forgotten the joy of it.

"I don't believe it." His gaze rippled down the lines of her body and lingered on her breasts. "Your figure's too nice."

Good Lord! He was flirting with her!

The desire to flirt back shoved at her. It rattled through the recesses of her brain like a prisoner banging the bars of his cell, longing for release. Especially with the joy of having just made him laugh taunting her, reminding her of what it felt like to be normal.

But it had been so long since she'd done anything even remotely like flirt, and he was absolutely the wrong guy to experiment with—

Or was he? They both needed each other too much professionally to cross any lines. He'd walked away from the perfect opportunity to kiss her the night before, proving that he might be attracted to her, but he didn't intend to follow through. And she was too frightened of relationships to let anything she attempted go any further than flirting. He might actually be the perfect person to practice on.

She smiled, trying not to look obvious, trying not to look self-conscious, trying desperately to look simply like a single woman flirting with a single man. "I'll bet you say that to all the girls."

He laughed again. "Only the really pretty ones."

Joy exploded inside her. She'd done it! Or maybe *they* were doing it. Flirting. Getting her back into the real world. What was a simple conversation for him was turning into a monumental event for her. But she hoped to God he didn't realize that.

A younger woman served dinner, standing off to the side to attend to their every need, precluding any possibility that the conversation could become intimate. The flirting stopped, but the discussion stayed casual, neutral and she relaxed totally.

At the end of the meal, Darius rose. "How about a game of pool?"

"Pool?"

"You know balls, sticks, table with green felt?"

She laughed then marveled that she had. Maybe her dad was right. Maybe it was time. She wanted so badly to be normal again. Real. Honest. Just herself. And Darius seemed to have the power to help her take the steps.

Still, no good would come of pushing things.

"I don't think so, I'm—"

"Tired? Really, Ms. Ross? I'm about to suggest you take some vitamins."

She laughed again, feeling light, young, incredibly

carefree. Memories of her other life, her sadness, nudged at her, but she shoved them back. She needed this. She *wanted* this.

He directed her to the door on the right. "Come on. This house is filled with things to entertain us. It would be a shame not to take advantage. Particularly since we're going to be spending lots of time together over the next eighteen years. We should get to know each other."

Fear and elation collided, creating goose bumps on her upper arms. Getting to know each other didn't have to be something to be afraid of or even something sexual. He wanted the same thing she did. Nothing sinister. Nothing difficult. Just a simple evening spending time together. To get to know each other. Because they had joint custody of a child.

Inclining her head in acceptance, she ignored the fear and tamped down the elation and reminded herself that spending time getting to know each other didn't have to be a big deal. She didn't have to tell him about her family that night. She could wait for a more suitable time. Tonight, he was only asking for a game of pool.

"All right."

The room with the pool table was a huge den. Cherrywood walls and leather furniture gave the space a totally masculine feel.

"Your dad's room, I assume," she said, walking to a wall lined with sticks, as Darius gathered and racked the balls.

"Got it in one." He ambled over to choose a stick. "But before you begin feeling sorry for Missy, take a look around. They might have lived in Greece, but they spent time here. Her influence is all over the place."

"Really?"

"She's redone at least three rooms." He winced. "Including the master bedroom."

"You don't like her taste?"

"If you're asking if I like floral bedspreads and lacy curtains, then no."

She laughed, glad she'd agreed to spend some time with him. Over the next half hour they played several games of pool and he handily beat her.

"You're a ringer."

"Ringers make you believe they're terrible so they can persuade you to bet them, and then they take your money. I haven't done that." He shrugged. "We're just having a nice friendly few games."

"With me getting my butt beaten."

He racked the balls and broke, scattering the colorful orbs across the table with a clack and clatter. In an uncharacteristic turn of events, none of them fell into a pocket.

"Hey! Looks like I get a turn this time."

She walked around the table, sizing up potential shots. When she found one she liked, she angled her stick across the table, levering her body in sync with the stick.

"No. No. You'll never make the shot that way." He strode around the table to her. "Let me help you." He lowered himself over her, his one hand covering hers on the stick, his other circling around her so he could guide her hand on the handle.

Her nerve endings exploded at the contact. Rivers of molten need rode her blood. And she remembered why they had to be careful. Even about becoming friends. Their attraction was like nitroglycerin. One bump and they could go up in flames.

As if realizing how close he'd put them, he turned

his head and caught her gaze. Their faces were only millimeters apart. His warm breath fanned her face. Longing burst inside her. Her fingers itched to touch the stubble on his cheeks and cruise his throat. Just a brush. Just a touch to feel the warmth of another's skin. To feel the pulse of another heartbeat, to know that *she* was alive.

His hands shifted from the stick to her shoulders and he lifted her from the awkward position of leaning across the table. For a few seconds, they stood there, barely a foot apart. She watched myriad emotions play across his face, as if he were arguing with himself about whether he should kiss her. It crossed her mind to say something. It crossed her mind to run. This attraction they felt was nothing but wrong, but curiosity and need warred with common sense. This entire night had been an experiment of sorts for her. A return to life. To people. She didn't want to stop. She almost couldn't stop. She needed him to kiss her as much as she wanted it.

Slowly his head descended, as if he were giving her plenty of time to step back. She considered it, but stayed frozen, mesmerized, hoping, and in seconds his mouth met hers.

A tsunami of need flooded her, a yearning so strong she shook from it. His hands smoothed from her shoulders, down her back to her hips and nudged her closer. The longing to be held, to be loved, to be touched percolated through her. He satisfied it with another nudge that brought her fully against him. Her breasts nestled against his chest, pebbling her nipples. His mouth moved over hers simply, smoothly, and temptation turned into action as her mouth instinctively opened under his and he deepened the kiss.

Desire thundered through her. Warm, wet need. Her

limbs weakened. Her breath hitched. And her brain clicked on again, like a light switch being flipped in a dark, dangerous room.

This is wrong! This is wrong! This is wrong!

The words were a litany in her brain. Not only was she not ready for anything beyond a chaste, experimental kiss, but the night before she'd sensed there was something wrong in his behavior. Something he wanted from her. Or maybe that he was trying to trick her. She shouldn't be kissing him, clouding the issues.

The sound of someone clearing her throat entered the room and Whitney jumped back like a guilty teenager.

Joni Johnson, the girl who had served dinner, stood by the door. "I'm sorry to disturb you, Mr. Andreas, but Mrs. Tucker asked me to get you. The baby is sick."

CHAPTER FIVE

DARIUS AND WHITNEY raced behind Joni, who led them up the back steps. When they reached the nursery, Darius pushed ahead, not caring about decorum, and ran into the room.

Gino lay in the crib, crying. Darius reached down and scooped the little boy into his arms. "Hey, little guy. What's up?"

"I've already called the pediatrician," Mrs. Tucker said, wringing her hands. "He said he'd be here as soon as he can."

Gino snuggled against Darius and cried harder.

"I couldn't get him to drink his evening bottle and now he won't stop crying." Mrs. Tucker's voice was strained and anxious. "I'm not a nanny and my only child is over thirty. It's been so long since I cared for a baby that I have no idea what's wrong."

Whitney peered at Gino over Darius's shoulder. "Can I hold him?"

Darius caught her gaze and the instant he did, he regretted it. Thoughts of their kiss devoured his mind and desire arched between them. He couldn't believe he'd broken the promise he'd made to himself not to kiss her, but he had. Part of him wasn't sorry. They had chemistry that just wouldn't quit and if they were in a position to pursue it they'd probably set his bedroom on fire. He couldn't resist a taste.

But they weren't in a position to pursue it, and there would be consequences. Especially for this little boy if he didn't handle the situation correctly.

He swallowed and handed Gino to her. "Here."

After laying the baby across her arm, she studied his face, pressed her hand to his forehead, looked into his mouth. "I think he's getting a tooth."

Furious that she could be so flippant, Darius pinned her with a hard stare. "I think we should let the pediatrician decide."

"Oh, of course!" she said, handing the baby back to him. "I'm just saying that there's no reason for us to panic while we wait for the doctor to arrive."

Mrs. Tucker visibly relaxed. "I should have thought of that. But it's just been so long since I've had kids." She sank into the rocker. "If I may make a suggestion, sir, I think we should get a nanny here as soon as possible." She sighed heavily, as if having trouble getting her breathing to regulate, and Darius realized just how worried poor Mrs. Tucker had been.

But his eyes narrowed in on Whitney, the woman he shared custody with, and he suddenly wondered how she knew so much about babies. She'd said she'd been married, but she hadn't mentioned children. If she'd had them and her husband had gotten custody, there had to be a reason for that. If there was something god-awful in her past that made her husband a better candidate to have her children than she was, he wanted to know what it was.

"I'll just go back to the kitchen, then," Mrs. Tucker announced, rising from the rocker and heading for the door.

"Sure," Darius said. "We'll be fine." Plus, he wanted some time alone with Whitney. Since the day they'd met at her dad's office, he'd been so preoccupied with getting along with her that he'd let all the inconsistencies in her life slide. That ended here. That ended now.

Darius sat on the rocker. Gino snuggled against him, sniffling, but relaxing against his sweater as if seeking comfort. His heart warmed with emotion. He was falling in love with this kid. In only two days, the little boy was getting to him.

But that was all the more reason to make sure he knew Gino's "other" guardian. His dad might have approved Whitney, but his dad hadn't planned on dying. He might have simply decided to placate Missy and agreed to appoint Whitney as shared custodian. Given that she was the daughter of his friend and the friend of Gino's mom, he might not have checked into her past the way he should have.

"So, are you going to tell me how you know so much about babies?"

She walked away from him toward the window, but didn't answer his question.

"I can have you investigated, you know. Or maybe even guess. A woman who was married but lost custody of her children to her husband probably has a skeleton in her closet."

She sucked in a breath, refusing to look at him. Darius squeezed his eyes shut. Damn it! If he hadn't needed her help so much, he would have realized something was off with her before this. He wouldn't have silenced his instincts, and he would have confronted her.

"You know what? Don't tell me. Go back to your room and pack. Because I'm going to contest that damned will. I'm getting you away from my baby."

"Don't." She turned, her eyes filled with tortured pain. He could easily guess why.

"Why not? Don't want a courtroom full of people to hear why you shouldn't be around a child? Why you don't have your own?"

She swallowed. "It's not what you think."

"You expect me to believe that?"

Whitney's limbs began to shiver, then her entire body began to shake. She had absolutely no doubt in her mind that he intended to check in to her past. When he did, he'd discover she'd had a child who had died. She'd wanted to tell him, but she'd wanted it to be on her terms, so she didn't look incompetent or grief-stricken. But it appeared *this* was the time.

She opened her mouth, debating what she would say, how she would say it, but the only thing that came out was, "I had a daughter."

Darius said nothing, only snuggled his baby brother closer as if protecting him from her, and her heart shattered. "I would never do anything to hurt Gino."

"Really?"

"My *husband* hurt my daughter." Her shaking intensified. Tears filled her eyes. "My husband *killed* my daughter."

Darius stopped rocking.

"He intended to kill himself." Her tears spilled over her lower lids, trailed down her cheeks. Memories of that day and all the days after it when she'd wondered, berated herself, lived in an ocean of guilt, filled her brain, stopped her tongue, clogged her throat with tears.

She swallowed hard. Once. Twice. Three times before she could speak.

"No one knows if he'd forgotten he had the baby in the car seat when he realized he could simply sit in the running car in the garage to eventually kill himself." Her lungs expanded to painful proportions. Sobs screamed to erupt from her chest, but she held on.

"His company had failed and though money wasn't an issue, his pride suffered." She turned, faced Darius, opened her hands in supplication. "It was his third company. He'd bragged that number three would be the charm. But it wasn't. His father was angry with him for wasting his time. His brothers were making names for themselves on Wall Street and Burn did nothing but fail." A sob escaped. "He was the family embarrassment."

Darius swallowed, visibly shaken by what she had told him. "I'm sorry."

Her sob turned to muffled weeping. "Everyone's sorry."

He rose from the rocker. "Maybe no one knows what else to say?"

She turned away as her crying took her. There was a place she went, a soft, comfortable place, where emotion took control of her body. Problems weren't solved. Trouble didn't disappear, but tension eased. Tears and sobs provided a welcome release not just for the pain, but also for her tight muscles and limbs. And she wanted to go there now. She wanted to go to her own room, sink onto the bed and let the crying soothe her.

"You weren't at fault, you know."

She spun to face him as sadness morphed into anger. "Really? I couldn't have noticed my slightly depressed husband tumbling into full-fledged mental illness? There were no signs? You're sure?"

"No, but—"

"You wouldn't accept my diagnosis of Gino. You

insisted on waiting for the pediatrician. So now I'm telling you to stop diagnosing me. Back off."

The door opened and Mrs. Tucker entered with a short, gray-haired man behind her. "Dr. Sullivan," she announced as she stepped aside and let the man shuffle over to Gino.

"Hey, Gino," he crooned, taking the baby from Darius's arms. Obviously familiar with the little boy, he hugged him before he said, "I hear somebody might be getting a tooth."

He laid the little boy on the changing table and began to examine him.

Silently, Whitney slipped behind the group huddled around the baby and out the door.

Darius watched her go, cursing himself for pushing her and cursing her husband.

She'd had a daughter. A little girl. A baby who was probably the light of her life. He squeezed his eyes shut in misery. He'd brought all that back for her, made her relive the worst days of her life.

The doctor examined Gino and told Darius and Mrs. Tucker there was very little that could be done for a baby getting a tooth. He gave them some gel to numb his gums and advised them to get a teething ring.

Luckily, Gino fell asleep almost immediately after the doctor left, but Darius stayed by his crib, angry with himself for forcing Whitney to talk, but more concerned about the baby.

Finally, around midnight, he went to bed. But what seemed like only two minutes later, Darius heard the sounds of the baby waking and he popped up in bed. Glancing at his clock, he saw it was only just after two and groaned.

Still, not wanting Mrs. Tucker to have to deal with a cranky baby alone, he jumped into jeans and a sweatshirt and raced into the nursery. As he entered through the side door, Whitney bolted into the room from the main door, wearing a fluffy pink robe over white pajamas.

Their eyes met across the nursery and everything inside him stilled. He'd forced her to relive the worst days of her life the night before, but at least with that out in the open she had to know he didn't doubt her anymore. He wouldn't be making good on his threat to contest guardianship.

Gino screamed again, reminding him that if he didn't pick him up and tend to him, he'd wake Mrs. Tucker. Beating Whitney to the crib, he lifted the little boy out and hugged him, patting his back to soothe him.

Whitney stood a few steps back. Concern brought her close enough to see what was going on, but not so close that she was actually part of it.

Things would have probably been a bit stilted and awkward between them as they worked through the aftermath of that conversation and her memories, but ultimately they would have been okay—if he hadn't also kissed her.

He couldn't believe he'd done that, but the temptation had been so strong he couldn't resist. He'd thought that one kiss might take the edge off. Instead, the taste of her stayed on his lips all night.

Turning away, she said, "I'll warm a bottle."

She took a bottle from the small refrigerator, set it in the warmer and waited, all with her back to him.

Guilt suffused him. He should have been kinder with her, gentler.

Whitney walked over with the warm bottle, motioning for Darius to sit in the rocker. "Once he drinks this, we'll put the gel on his gums again so he can fall back to sleep."

Panic rose in him. He might have fed Gino before, but he really didn't trust himself to feed the baby when his mouth was sore.

Obviously seeing his hesitancy, Whitney said, "Arrange Gino across your lap, but lift his head a little higher than you normally do."

In three or four movements, Darius had the little boy across his lap and halfway between sitting and lying on his arm.

"Now, put the nipple to his lips and he'll do the rest. His hunger will supersede the pain in his mouth."

Darius did as instructed and Gino latched onto the nipple as if he was starving.

Whitney stepped away. "I understand how his being sick would make you nervous."

Of course she did. She'd had a daughter. He'd brought up those memories for her. In the silence of the nursery where he'd confronted her, the most natural thing to do right now would be to apologize for pushing her to tell him about her daughter.

So he did. "I'm sorry."

She ambled to the side window. Though it was the middle of the night and she probably couldn't see anything, she stared out into the darkness. "For not knowing how to care for Gino?"

"For pushing you into talking before the pediatrician got here."

Her eyes never left the window. "You had no idea. You were worried about Gino. I accept that."

Just as he'd suspected, his mistake was something she'd probably faced before. She wouldn't hold a grudge or make something out of it he hadn't intended. Things might still be awkward for awhile, but ultimately they'd be okay.

The baby nudged the nipple out of his mouth and Darius pulled the bottle away. He sat him up a bit then waited a few seconds before he offered it again. Gino latched onto the nipple, and the room became eerily silent. This time he couldn't blame it on the repercussions of his pushing her into talking about her baby. There was a second elephant in the room and he had to get rid of it, too.

With a glance at Gino to make sure he was still suckling, he said, "I'm also sorry I kissed you. It won't happen again."

She stared out the window, saying nothing, and he wanted to groan at his stupidity. Kissing her had been a ridiculous, in-the-moment impulse that he should have thought through. Instead, he'd let his hormones rule him.

But rather than tell him to go to hell, or that he was an immature ass, she quietly said, "How do you know it won't happen again?"

He had no option but the truth. "Because it's not a good idea for either of us. We have to spend the next eighteen years dealing with each other as we raise this baby. If we started a relationship that fizzled, one of us would end up angry or hurt and that's not good for Gino."

Whitney stared outside though she didn't actually see anything. It was the second or third time he'd given Gino preference in a conversation. It had surprised her the morning before when he'd said he wanted to be a great dad. But after the way he'd behaved while waiting for the pediatrician—protective, strong—she knew he wasn't faking it, wasn't saying these things to make himself look good or get her into his corner. He intended to be a good father to his half-brother.

She peeked over at him. He wore jeans and a baggy gray sweatshirt and looked absolutely gorgeous in a casual, athletic way. His short hair wasn't exactly mussed; it simply wasn't combed as it usually was for a day of work, and wisps fell to his forehead boyishly. His typically stern face was relaxed. Neither a frown nor a smile graced his mouth.

She'd kissed that mouth.

He'd held her against him.

She'd faintly felt his heart beating beneath the fisherman's sweater.

She could have tumbled over the edge the night before, could have done something really out of character, really wrong. But fate had stopped them. He'd said he didn't want it to happen again, and she believed him. Not just because his first priority was Gino, but because of the conversation afterward. He now knew she came with baggage. She might as well have dressed in dynamite. There'd be no way a man who could have any woman he wanted would go near a woman with her kind of past.

Which was good.

Sad, because she'd finally begun to relax around someone; but good because she'd panicked the night before. She hadn't known how to stop. She'd gotten in over her head. If Joni hadn't come in, she could have messed up royally.

Her priority was to uphold Missy's wishes and to do that she had to be objective. Not get involved with her co-guardian. She also wasn't ready for a relationship. Burn had hurt her. No, Burn had cost her her ability to trust. As nice as Darius Andreas seemed to be, as good as he clearly wanted to be with Gino, an intimate relationship was a totally different thing. God only knew *if* he had the ability to have one. And God only knew *when* she'd be ready to have one.

Glancing at Gino's bottle, she saw it was empty, and walked over to the rocker. "Here," she said, easing the bottle out of Gino's mouth and Darius's hold. "You have to burp him now."

Darius sat perfectly still. Didn't let her perfume affect him. Wouldn't let himself wonder if her skin was as soft as it looked. Wouldn't let his mind wander back to the kiss the night before. He'd made a promise of sorts to her that she would be safe in his company, and he intended to keep it.

"Lift him to your shoulder the way I showed you yesterday morning."

He did as she instructed, but kept his gaze averted. They really were like gasoline and a match when they got too close, and the best way to handle it would be to keep their distance. But if he wanted her to teach him about the baby, that wasn't possible. His only alternative was simply to control himself.

"Now, pat his back."

He brought his hand to the baby's small back and lightly patted twice. Gino burped.

Whitney stepped away. "He's a good eater and a good burper. That's usually a sign of a very healthy child. He'll probably have this tooth in before we know it."

Relief washed through him and he rose. But once he was standing, he realized had no idea what he was supposed to do.

"Does he go back to bed now?"

Whitney laughed softly. "Let's hope. Otherwise, it's going to be a long night. First let's put some of the gel on his gums."

Darius winced. "Sorry, I forgot."

"You're new and there's a lot to remember." She found the gel and gently applied some to the baby's gums. He spat and fussed, but she persevered.

As she stepped away, Darius asked, "Should I lay him in the crib?"

"Actually, the best thing to do would be for you to stay on the rocker. Position him the same way you had him while you fed him, so that he's not lying flat but is upright enough that he can breathe more easily, and just rock him until he falls asleep."

Darius sat and positioned Gino on his lap. "Hey, little guy."

As he set the rocker in motion, Whitney leaned against the crib. "Don't talk too much or he'll never go back to sleep."

"What should I do?"

"Just keep rocking him." She smiled. "You could also sing him a lullaby."

Darius winced. "Yeah. Not in this lifetime."

She laughed. "Eventually, you'll sing. Everybody does."

"Not me."

"Just wait. The day will come when you're desperate and you'll sing."

Chuckling softly, Darius shook his head.

In a surprising move, Whitney pushed off the crib and stooped down in front of him. He noticed that she didn't touch either him or Gino, but she started to sing.

"Hush little baby, don't say a word, Papa's going to buy you a mocking bird…"

Her voice was soft, lyrical. Gino blinked his heavy eyelids and rolled his head to the side so he could look at her.

"And if that mocking bird don't sing, Papa's gonna buy you a diamond ring. And if that diamond ring turns brass, Papa's going to buy you a looking glass. If that looking glass gets broke, Papa's going to buy you a billy goat."

As if by magic, Gino's eyelids drooped. Whitney's voice softened even more, and she slowed the song, as if lulling him to sleep.

"If that billy goat won't pull, Papa's going to buy you a cart and bull. If that cart and bull turn over, Papa's going to buy you a dog named Rover." Her voice softened again, the words she sang slowed to a hypnotic pace. Gino's eyelids drooped until eventually they stayed shut.

Her song finished, Whitney rose. She nodded at Gino. "He's asleep."

Mesmerized by the sweet expression on her face and the casual way she'd lowered her voice and softened the song to lull Gino to sleep, Darius only stared at her. "He is?"

"He is." She headed for the door. "Good night."

"Good night."

Darius rose and put Gino in the crib. Sadness seeped into his soul. He'd bet she'd been the perfect mother.

Sunday morning, when Darius heard Gino cry, he popped up in bed again. He jumped into the same jeans and sweatshirt he'd worn the night before and raced into the nursery just as Mrs. Tucker finished changing the baby.

"He's feeling a lot better this morning." She caught

Darius's gaze. "I'm sorry I didn't hear him wake up last night."

"That's okay. Whitney and I took care of him."

Before Mrs. Tucker could answer, Whitney entered the room. Their eyes met across the nursery and all he could think of was her singing to Gino the night before. The sweet motherly affection he'd heard in her voice. The easy way she'd used the song to lull Gino to sleep. And he suddenly understood why Missy had chosen her for her baby's guardian. Whitney was born to be a mom. She really would be Gino's mom. Not a substitute, not a guardian, but a real mom.

Just as he intended to be a real dad.

He could picture them two or three or even six years from now, as the perfect parents. He could see them standing with their arms around each other's waists, waving to Gino who rode his bike along the big circular driveway in front of the house.

He shook his head to dislodge that image. It was one thing to parent a child together. But they didn't need to have their arms around each other's waists. They had to be objective. They couldn't have a relationship. He had a conglomerate to run. A life that kept him so busy he'd barely have time to squeeze this baby in. But he would. Gino would become his family. And after that there would be no time left for anyone else. Which made him the absolute worst choice of men for Whitney to get involved with. Now that he knew her past, he also knew she needed someone to love her, to understand her, and he simply had too much on his plate already. He would ignore signs that she needed to talk, or signs that she was feeling sad, or signs that she simply needed to be held. And he would hurt her.

She broke eye contact and strolled a little closer to the baby. "Good morning."

"Good morning," Mrs. Tucker chirped. "Here's the bottle," she said, offering both the baby and the bottle to Whitney.

Darius raced over, understanding now why she hesitated. Being Gino's guardian was probably a living hell for her, yet she'd accepted the job and planned to do it. "I'll take him."

Mrs. Tucker put Gino in his arms and glanced at her watch. "If you don't mind, I need to go now. Two of the maids are new and we don't really have a schedule yet." She smiled like the happy employee that she was, causing Darius to notice just how weary, how sad Whitney was in contrast. "If you need me, I can be free again after breakfast."

With the baby and the bottle in Darius's hands, Mrs. Tucker turned away and walked out of the nursery.

He sat on the rocker and gave Gino the nipple as he had the other times he had fed him. Gino latched on greedily and sucked down the milk. Whitney walked around the nursery, glancing at toys and knickknacks scattered on the shelves. She didn't say anything and, try as he might, Darius couldn't think of anything to say either.

When Gino was finished with his breakfast, Darius burped him like a pro then rose from the rocker. "So what do we do now? Put him back to bed?"

Whitney smiled slightly. "I'm guessing he just woke up before we walked in. So he should spend some time downstairs."

Panic fluttered through him. "Downstairs? With his gums just waiting to put him in severe pain again?"

"Of course. He still needs his cereal and I'm guessing

he'll want to play a bit. In fact it's good to entertain him and make him happy for as long as we can."

Panic was replaced by fear. Yes, he'd rocked this kid, fed this kid, even changed a diaper—much to his horror—but he wasn't capable enough to be alone with a potentially sick baby all morning.

"Ready?"

He peeked over at Whitney. "You're coming with us?"

"Sure."

That's when he saw it. The sadness that hummed through everything she did was sometimes eclipsed by very normal behavior, but it was still there.

And everything she did for Gino undoubtedly reminded her of the baby she'd lost.

CHAPTER SIX

DARIUS WAITED UNTIL they were seated at the table in the sunroom for lunch, while Gino was napping, before he broached the subject they'd come to Montauk to discuss—how they'd share custody of Gino. The wall of windows brought in the broad expanse of the ocean, sloshing sloppily, with no rhyme or reason or organization, against the shore. The scent of warm clam chowder wafted around them comfortingly, but Darius felt more like the ocean. Disjointed. Uneven. Unable to get his bearings.

Not only did he feel uncomfortable about pushing her to tell him about her family, but he also felt awful for her loss. Technically, he and Whitney would be connected for the next eighteen or so years of their lives, maybe longer. Gino would love her as a mother, and, he hoped, love him as a father. But their lives were so different he wasn't really sure it was possible for them to find common ground.

She'd been married, been a mom and now lived in a loft in Soho and worked at a law firm. He'd spent his entire adult life running from marriage and being groomed to manage a huge conglomerate. He also had an apartment in the city, but Gino had a nursery at this estate, so Darius genuinely believed it was better for him to get rid of his apartment and live here. If Whitney really wanted to make the commitment to Gino that Darius believed she should make, then she should want to give up her loft and live here too.

The three of them living together was the only way to ensure that Gino saw both of his guardians and also lived something of a normal life. Still, he couldn't hit her with that yet—especially not after the way he'd pushed her the night before. The way he had this figured, the best thing to do would be try to get her to agree to stay another week, or maybe two weeks, and then continue to tack on a week or two at a time until she realized, as he had, that Montauk was Gino's home.

Because the following day was Monday, the end of the weekend, there was no time left for delay. He had to persuade her to stay an entire week or maybe two and he had to do it now.

He casually picked up his napkin. "I'm glad we decided to spend the weekend here, getting to know the baby."

She met his gaze, her pretty blue eyes cautious.

"It was good for him to be in a settled environment—especially since this is his home, or had been when his parents came to New York."

She didn't even hesitate. "Absolutely."

"So you wouldn't mind saying a little longer?"

"How much longer?"

With her being so agreeable, it seemed a shame to ask for a week or two, when a month would be better for Gino. "How about a month?"

"A month!"

"Or six weeks." Going with his usual tactic of surprising his opponent by asking for more rather than backpedaling, he forged on. "This is Gino's home. He needs to be somewhere he feels safe. Since he spends half his day sleeping, I also think it's important he be in his own crib. We're adults. I think we can make an adjustment or two for him."

"Okay."

She surprised him so much he forgot they were negotiating. "Okay?"

"Yes. We have to hire a nanny, and I need time to turn my spare bedroom into a nursery. So, yes. It makes sense to keep Gino here where he's happy until I can get some of that done."

Dumbstruck, he said nothing.

She ate a spoonful of soup. "Layla liked being in her own crib. Especially when she was sick."

Layla. Her casual use of the name shook him. But the very fact that she'd said it so nonchalantly told him he had to be every bit as casual. Not make a big deal out of it. Not ask questions that didn't fit into their conversation about Gino. Even though he was burning up with them.

How could a man not remember he had his child with him?

How did a woman deal with the grief, the guilt, of not noticing her husband was slipping over the edge?

Though he tried to hold them back, they tore at him until he couldn't stop himself from asking, "How did you deal with it?"

"What?"

Recrimination roared through him, telling him he shouldn't push her again, but he was unable to stop himself. "Your loss. How did you deal with such a monumental loss?"

She glanced up at him. "Therapy."

He shook his head. "Dear God. It must have been awful. I am so sorry."

She set down her spoon. "Actually, that's one of the reasons I held back from telling you. I don't want you to feel sorry for me. I want you to know. You *have* to know. You have to understand. But if I really want to get on with the rest of my life, you can't feel sorry for me. You can't treat me differently than you would have when you thought I was just a thorn-in-your-side lawyer."

He laughed. "I never thought you were a thorn in my side."

She smiled at him. "Of course you did. You probably always will. We're not going to agree on how to raise Gino. We might as well admit up front that there will be disagreements and maybe set some ground rules for how to handle them."

"I'm not sure what you mean."

"Well, for instance, there could be some deal breaker things. Like I don't think he should get a new car at sixteen."

He laughed, not just at the absurdity of talking about something that wouldn't happen for fifteen-and-a-half years, but also at the absurdity of depriving Gino of something he'd need.

"Really? No car at sixteen? In case you haven't noticed, I'm rich. I can afford to get him any kind of car he wants. And he'll want one. It's the only thing he'll talk about the entire time he's fifteen."

"Doesn't matter. Kids that age aren't good drivers. We should have as much control as possible about when and where he drives. The best way to do that is for him to have to ask permission to take a car."

He gaped at her. "I have ten cars. He could easily take one without my permission."

"Then you're going to be busy keeping track of them. Because, to me, the car is a safety issue. And a deal breaker."

He scowled, remembering his own driving at sixteen, and realized she was right. "Okay, but then one of my deal breakers is pink."

"Pink?"

"No matter that you call it rose or mauve or some other flaky name, I don't ever want him dressed in pink."

She blinked, then frowned, then burst out laughing. "That's your idea of a deal breaker?"

He turned his attention to his soup. "Give me time. I'm sure I'll think of more."

"So will I. But that's kind of the point. We should balance. You know I'm right about the car, so you didn't argue once you understood. I get it about pink." She rolled her eyes. "It's a pet peeve and I respect that. But most things won't be so black and white. We're going to have to learn to discuss issues as they come up and respect each other's viewpoints."

He put down his spoon and motioned with his hand between them. "So this kind of works?"

"The fact that we're both objective parties?"

He nodded.

She smiled. "Give us a few years. We won't be quite so objective. The first time he looks at us with real love, we'll both melt." She caught his gaze. "That'll probably happen within the next day or so, so get ready. You and I are about to become mom and dad to that little boy."

The truth of that swooped down on him, reminding him of the things he'd thought the day before. He sniffed a laugh. "I already figured that out."

"Well, good. That makes you ahead of the game."

"What about you?"

"I've been through this before. I know exactly what I'm in for in the next year and a half. I've even thought ahead to the next twenty-five years. Kindergarten, elementary school, middle school, high school... university...marriage."

Of course she'd thought ahead to the next twenty-some years. She was a planner. She'd probably thought of every special event in her daughter's life, previewed it, then suffered through the memories of her plans when her daughter was gone. He'd love to ask, not because he wanted to know her dreams for her daughter, but just because he suspected she needed to talk about some of this. But they weren't really friends. They were two people bound by someone else's wishes. He didn't feel he had the right to be so personal. Yet he also couldn't think of a way to change the subject or even what to change it to. Nearly everything to do with Gino would remind her of her baby. After that there wasn't much for them to discuss.

They were quiet for a few seconds then Whitney said, "This soup is wonderful."

Ah, food. She'd said she loved food. That was as good a topic as any. "Cook worked for my dad for the past few decades. Every time she tried to quit he doubled her salary."

She laughed. "I can understand why."

Her laughter pleased him and reminded him of how relaxed she'd been the night before at dinner and while playing pool. She actually seemed happy now. Relaxed.

So once again, he talked about food. "You should see what he paid the pastry chef."

Her eyes widened. "You have a pastry chef?"

He laughed. *"My dad* had a pastry chef."

His laughter scared her. She knew he was being kind, but the sound of his laugh filled her chest with syrupy warmth. It wasn't love. But closeness. Companionship. Ease. They'd known each other a few days. Yet they were not only comfortable enough to discuss Gino and his future rationally, but she'd also told him about Burn. About Layla. Now he was laughing with her and making her laugh.

And he'd kissed her.

She shoved that to the farthest corner of her brain. He'd promised he wouldn't kiss her again, so that couldn't come into play. She had to forget all about that, the way he'd promised he would.

"If we stay here a whole month, I'll weigh two hundred pounds before I go home."

"You could stand to gain a pound or two."

His comment reminded her of the way he'd looked at her the night before when she had been practicing flirting. Yearning seized her, but so did the memory of how much trouble that longing had gotten her into.

"No woman believes she can stand to gain a pound or two." She set her napkin on the table and rose. "I need to work this afternoon."

He smiled slightly and rose politely. "Okay."

Walking back to the office, she congratulated herself. She hadn't exactly run away, but there was no point in hanging around when they had no future. She'd sealed her fate with him by explaining her past. He'd even told her he wouldn't kiss her again. Yet she still had crazy feelings around him. Which, now that she thought about it, was preposterous. They didn't even really know each other. So, whatever she felt, it was based purely on animal attraction.

On the up side, the fact that her feelings were wrong gave her a reason or a way to control them. From here on out, every time the attraction rose up in her, she'd simply remind herself she didn't know him. So anything she felt was purely physical. Something to be ignored, not pursued.

On Monday morning, they drove into the city together, leaving Gino with Mrs. Tucker. Reviewing files from his briefcase, he didn't talk. Not even to discuss the job she'd be doing for Andreas Holdings in Gino's stead. She'd been quiet at breakfast, stilted, and he'd gotten the message. She might have agreed to live in the same house, but she wanted her space. Which was fine. Probably smart. He wanted her to be happy. If being left alone made her happy, then he'd leave her alone.

Eventually, she'd come around on her own terms, soften to the baby and to him. When she did, he'd see it. And he wouldn't exactly pounce, but he would capitalize on the moment and suggest that they make their living arrangements with Gino, at his house in Montauk, permanent.

When they arrived at Andreas Holdings, he directed her to follow him to his office—formerly his dad's office. Cherrywood paneling and a wall of bookcases gave the room an old-fashioned, stuffy feel, but there was nothing he could do about that. He hadn't yet had a chance to redecorate.

He walked past the brown leather sofa and chair, directing her to follow him to his desk. Keeping with the all-business tone they'd established that morning, he handed her a stack of files. "These are contracts I'd like you to review and summarize for me."

"Okay."

He pressed the button on his phone and paged his assistant, who was at the door in seconds. "Minnie will show you to your office."

She left the room on the heels of his assistant, and Darius stared at the door that closed behind them, hoping he was doing the right thing.

He met her at the limo for the ride home and immediately retrieved files to review, so they didn't have to talk just because they were commuting together. He even let her go up to her apartment on her own to pack the things she would need for the upcoming weeks.

They talked about nannies at dinner. That morning, she had called the service she'd used when she'd hired a nanny for Layla and they had emailed résumés of potential candidates. She'd narrowed them down and had scheduled interviews with all four the next day. Because Whitney would conduct the initial interviews at the headquarters for Andreas Holdings, Darius had consented to sit in on at least five minutes of each interview and, acknowledging how busy he was, she'd accepted that. Before dessert she excused herself, saying she needed to go back to the depositions from the case she was working on with her father.

At nine when he went into the nursery to say goodnight to Gino, Whitney was already there. He was neither surprised nor concerned when she kept the slightest bit of distance between herself and the baby. He knew why she hesitated.

Still, he and Whitney were the baby's guardians and because of work that day they hadn't spent as much time as either of them wanted to spend with the baby, so he excused Mrs. Tucker.

"We're okay here. So if you want to go to your room, that's fine."

When she was gone, Darius sat on the rocker, bottle in hand. "Hey, little guy."

From her spot beside the crib, Whitney said, "He's really getting to know who you are."

Darius couldn't help it. He smiled. "I know."

"And you're really beginning to like him."

Darius looked up at her. "You were right. It hits you like a ton of bricks."

Her blue eyes softened and became distant. "Yeah."

He hadn't meant to bring her child to her mind, but with the two of them caring for a baby, it was very hard not to. Of course, if he kept the conversation specific to Gino, maybe he could avoid that.

"Remember how we were talking about him not getting a car on his sixteenth birthday?"

"Yeah?"

"Well, that started me thinking about some weird things."

"Like what?"

"Like how am I going to tell him about our dad. Or whether or not I should even tell him about our dad."

Whitney bristled. "You can't *not* tell him about his own father."

"No, but I could be judicious. You know…tell him the good stuff and temper the bad."

She took another step closer. "That won't work if your brothers decide to tell him the truth."

"I've been thinking about that too. My dad wanted us to behave like brothers. And, as you can see, Cade and Nick more or less deserted me."

"So you're going to keep Gino away from them so they don't tell him about your dad?"

He shook his head. "No. I've actually been thinking of inviting them up to the house. Maybe once or twice a year, so they'll have a chance to get to know him. There are four of us who are brothers, not just me and Gino. They might not want any part of me. But they're Gino's big brothers. I think they should be in his life."

She nodded. In front of the rocker now, she stooped down. "In some ways, that's going to make his life tough."

Darius frowned. "Seeing his other brothers only a few times a year?"

She caught his gaze. "No. Having three adult brothers. I know you might not get this yet, but this kid is almost forty years younger than you are. And the distance between his age and that of his other two brothers is almost as great. There are *three* of you who will expect him to meet your standards." She passed her hand lovingly over Gino's soft black hair. "Three of you who will criticize his dates, expect a say in where he goes to university." She shook her head then ran her index finger down Gino's cheek. "I'm guessing he's going to rebel."

Cautious, hardly breathing, Darius watched her. She didn't seem to realize how lovingly she was caressing the little boy. She appeared mesmerized, as if she'd waited all her life for a child and now that she was with one, she couldn't stop herself.

"In one way or another all three of us rebelled."

She looked up at him with a soft smile. "Really?"

"I attended Wharton instead of Harvard."

She gasped as if mocking him. "Wow. I'm surprised your dad survived the blow."

"Hey, to him it was a big deal. Harvard was his alma mater."

"What about the other two?"

"Nick got married at seventeen."

Her eyes widened. "Now, that's more like it!"

"And Cade refused to go to school at all. He bought a ranch with his trust fund and worked it."

"Okay. Cade wins. *That's* rebellion."

"Yeah, but when his oil interests got into trouble, he needed our dad. That still sticks in his craw."

She laughed and rose from in front of the rocker. "'Sticks in his craw?'"

"He's a Texan. It's like they have their own language down there."

With the baby asleep, Darius rose from the rocker and laid the little boy in his crib. After covering him with a green blanket, he leaned down and kissed his cheek.

From the corner of his eye, he watched Whitney lick her lips. He pulled away from the crib. "Want to kiss him goodnight?"

She pressed her lips together and shook her head slightly. "I need to get ready for bed."

He let her walk out of the nursery, but he had seen the longing in her eyes.

Could it be that he'd made a mistake in running interference for her? Could she actually need to be around Gino, not away from him? Would that help her take the next steps in her recovery?

Tuesday morning, he got to the nursery before Whitney, and when she arrived he dismissed Mrs. Tucker again.

As he fed the baby his bottle, Whitney started off standing by the crib, but ultimately gravitated to the rocker. Again, she stooped in front of it, watching Gino as he ate.

He thought about that all morning at work. He didn't know if the change was because she'd told him about her family, or if she was simply growing more accustomed to Gino, but that child drew her. And for every bit she was drawn to the baby, he felt drawn to help her adjust.

If nothing else, they shared custody of Gino. She was his partner. And he needed to help her.

When they stepped into the house that evening, Mrs. Tucker met them to take their coats. "Chinese for supper tonight," she said then walked away with their garments.

"I see your love of food precedes you. I've never had a housekeeper announce the menu at the door, unless she knew somebody was truly interested."

She laughed. "I am!"

Darius pointed up the stairs. "Baby first. Food second."

She didn't hesitate. Not only did they always put Gino first, but she was actually eager to see the little guy. She wasn't entirely sure what had happened, but with Darius in the room, it was no longer excruciating to be with the baby. There were painful minutes. She still made comparisons in her head. But Darius was like a layer of protection.

They walked upstairs together and the second they stepped into the room, Gino bounced up in the crib and held his hands out to Darius.

"Look how cute!" Darius said, laughter bubbling through his voice. "He wants me." He strode over and Gino all but leapt into his arms. The baby squealed, a sound that was half-joy and half-annoyance as if he couldn't wait the two seconds it took for Darius to snag him out of the crib.

Whitney's chest squeezed. Not with pain or fear or even a remembrance of her own child, but with happiness. Staying at this house hadn't been her first choice for how they'd share custody, but it was now clear that being here had been the right thing for Gino.

She grabbed a tissue and gently ran it beneath Gino's runny nose. He squawked and reached for her.

Darius laughed. "Take him."

She shied away. She might have been able to touch him, to experience some of the joy a baby brings into any world it enters, but she wouldn't go overboard. She liked being able to be in the same room without being overwhelmed with memories. She had weeks here at Darius's house to get accustomed to Gino. She didn't have to push. She could take this slowly.

"That's okay. You keep him."

Gino squealed and stretched out of Darius's arms toward her.

Darius chuckled. "I'm sorry, but he wants you. He likes you."

"I know. But he likes you, too." She took a few steps back.

Gino screeched again.

"Right at this minute, I think he likes you more."

Motherly longing laced its way through her. The pure feminine desire to lave love on a needy baby rose up in her. Especially a baby who so obviously wanted her. Her heart swelled with affection so strong it tightened her chest. She *wanted* to love Gino. She might even need to love him. There was a hole in her heart so big that some days she wondered how it managed to pump enough blood to keep her alive.

And standing in the nursery where this little boy belonged, beside the man who shared custody with her, suddenly it all seemed okay. She took Gino from Darius's arms.

Darius smiled. "Look how much he likes you."

She took a soft breath, preparing for panic, as sweet baby scents and the feeling of him snuggling into her assailed her. "I'm glad we came here, glad we decided to share these few weeks so we could all get adjusted."

He shrugged. "It works."

She nodded and turned away to rock Gino a bit as he nuzzled against her neck. The panic she expected didn't come and she realized the memories of Layla floating out of her subconscious were wispy, insubstantial. Not bold and blaring, but still there, soft and sweet. She wouldn't forget her baby as she got on with the rest of her life.

"Yes. Being together does seem to be working."

"What do you say we take the baby down to supper with us?"

She nodded.

He smiled. "Do you want to change first?"

"Yes."

"Okay. You hold him while I change and then I'll come back and take him while you change."

Whitney nodded, feeling herself able to take another careful step. Holding Gino, alone.

Darius left the room and she smiled down at the little boy. "So how was your day?"

He tilted his head as if questioning her.

She laughed. "I get it. Not much happens in the life of a six-month-old."

He screeched as if protesting that fact.

"Then again, Gino, everything that happens is sort of new to you. I mean, you can't even talk yet. Just wait till that happens." She waltzed him around the room, making him giggle. "Then there's walking. You're gonna love that."

She spun around the room again, but stopped when she saw Darius standing in the open doorway between his room and the nursery.

"That was fast."

He ambled into the room. "I'm hungry."

"Me, too."

She handed the baby to him, but couldn't help noticing his still expression. "What?"

"I think we should live together."

"We are living together."

"I mean permanently." He ran his hand along the top of Gino's head, across the shiny black hair so much like his own. "The house is huge. We both love the baby. He loves both of us. Wouldn't it be a shame to divide up our time when we could both see him every day?"

She gaped at him. "You're serious."

He smiled charmingly. "It's the right thing to do for Gino."

All the little warning bells she'd heard the Friday before when they'd arrived at the house, all the little suspicions that had nudged at her, suddenly found their meaning. He'd been leading her toward this from the beginning. Being nice, getting her to agree to one simple thing after another until they were at the point where his real goal became clear. He wanted them to live together.

Well, he could ask, but that didn't mean she had to agree.

"It doesn't work for me."

"Why not? There's plenty of space. We have a cook. We're hiring a nanny." He pointed out the window at the serene ocean below. "You're by the sea. On a beautiful, peaceful estate. You can keep your condo if you want. Spend time in the city anytime you want. And Gino can be here, comfortable and happy with his nanny."

"You mean with *you*."

"I can't always be here either, remember? I have a job that forces me to travel. All the more reason for Gino to have a home base."

"You mean all the more reason for you to keep control. You're afraid that with your schedule, I'll have him more than you'll have him."

He shook his head and laughed lightly, as if they were having a casual conversation, not a monumental one. "That's absurd."

"Then why do you want to live here?"

"Because it makes sense."

"Not to me."

"I can't see why not. Whitney, I don't want this to come out wrong, but you need this as much as Gino does. You're still shaky around him."

Fury rose up in her. She couldn't believe he'd use her fears around Gino against her. Telling him about her baby had been the hardest thing she'd ever done, but she'd trusted him! And he was using it against her.

Mrs. Tucker stepped into the nursery. "The cook wants to know when it will be convenient to serve dinner."

Whitney headed for the door. "I'm not hungry. I'm going to work. Have Geoffrey bring Gino's swing to my office and I'll watch him while Mr. Andreas dines."

Alone.

Alone from here on out because she wasn't trusting him again!

CHAPTER SEVEN

AT EIGHT O'CLOCK THAT NIGHT, after two hours of reading depositions, with Gino splitting his time between the swing and the playpen across from her desk, Whitney asked Mrs. Tucker to bring a bottle to the nursery.

She didn't look for Darius or even let him know she was putting Gino to bed. The mood in the nursery was subdued, as if Mrs. Tucker knew Darius should have been called in at least to say goodnight. Still, good employee that she was, she didn't say anything as she fed Gino his bottle.

But Gino fussed as if he, too, knew something was off balance, and Whitney began to feel a tad guilty for being so angry. Then as she tucked the covers around Gino's neck and his soft baby blankets brought Layla to mind, she remembered that she'd trusted Darius. She'd told him the truth about the reason for her troubles with Gino and he'd used it to further his plan to keep the baby with him. Permanently.

Needing a break from thinking about all this, instead of returning to her office, she headed for the kitchen to make herself a cup of cocoa and maybe an omelet, since she hadn't eaten dinner.

It took her a minute to find the kitchen. Coming from the other side of the huge house, she got slightly disoriented. When she finally found it and pushed open the door, she stopped dead in her tracks.

The space wasn't appointed to be a regular household kitchen, but looked like the kind of kitchen found in a restaurant. Stainless-steel appliances and hanging racks of pots and pans surrounded a long stainless-steel prep table that sat across from a sixteen-burner stove. Only a few cupboards lined the back wall.

Still, big or not, the kitchen had to have cocoa and milk. She headed for the refrigerator and easily found milk. When she spotted the eggs and cheese, she smiled. An omelet was a definite possibility.

She pulled supplies out of the refrigerator and went on a quest for mugs, plates and utensils. Unfortunately, the cupboards didn't hold so much as one mug, one plate or one fork. As quickly as her mood had lifted at the sight of eggs, it plummeted. What good would it do to find the eggs and cheese, if she didn't have anything to eat them with?

Hearing the door open, she spun to face it and saw Darius enter the room. He looked cute and cuddly in a big sweatshirt and sweatpants. Then she remembered he wanted her to live here permanently and her fury returned full force.

She sucked in a breath, told herself not to let her anger rule her. It was better to find out now that he was the kind of guy who would use her confidences against her, rather than later. At least now she knew not to get too friendly with him.

But just as she was about to freeze him out of the kitchen with a cold shoulder and a frigid stare, she realized he might know where the utensils were, and if she wanted food—and she did—she needed him.

Though it galled her, she very quietly said, "Are there any mugs or plates or forks in this house?"

He took a step into the room. "Probably."

"But you don't know where they are?"

He shook his head. "Sorry."

She stifled a curse. "I just want a simple cup of cocoa." She opened and closed two more doors, working to control her temper and not start another fight. "And maybe an omelet."

"If you're hungry, we can call Cook."

"Or I could just make myself something." His spoiled, pampered, rich-guy attitude fed her bad mood. He didn't live a real life. Probably never had. He wouldn't know a genuine emotion, especially not trust, if it came up and bit his butt.

"You rich people." She shook her head. "You're so helpless."

He sauntered the rest of the way into the kitchen. "Hey, I am not helpless. My dad might have been rich, but my mother wasn't. She not only cooked, but she had a job. And she taught me to cook." He pulled a skillet from the arrangement hanging over the prep table. "What kind of omelet would you like?"

Though all that surprised her, the last thing she wanted was for him to wait on her. She wanted to maintain her independence. She didn't want to trust him. She certainly didn't want to depend on him. Hell, from here on out she wasn't even sure she wanted to be friendly with him.

"I'll make my own omelet."

"No. You smeared the good name of Andreas with your snotty comment that I was helpless. I have honor to defend."

Right. Honor. A guy who used her trauma to try to get her to live with him was not a man of honor.

"Okay, how about this? I'll hunt for everything you need and you make your own omelet?"

Unfortunately, she was so hungry that she couldn't turn him down. "All right. Fine."

He rubbed his hands together, as if he were enjoying this. "What should I look for first?"

His enthusiasm only grated on her nerves. "I found the refrigerator so I know where to get just about everything for the omelet. But I have no clue where to find the cocoa."

"I'm on it." Turning to the right, he headed off and disappeared down a short hallway. After a few seconds, he emerged with cocoa but not the mug.

She frowned at it.

He laughed. "Don't get huffy. We eat off plates every day. Drink out of cups. They have to be around here somewhere."

While she broke eggs into a mixing bowl, ignoring him, he glanced around again. Then he disappeared down the short hall to the left. A few seconds later he was by the prep table holding two mugs and two plates.

"Here you go."

"Two?"

"You're not going to share?"

With a sigh, she added an extra cup of milk to the pot on one of the sixteen burners, her ire simmering. If this weren't his house, she'd lambaste him for thinking he could join her when he'd betrayed her trust. But it *was* his house. And he'd helped her find the dishes. If she refused to share, she'd look petty. Childish.

"Sure. I'll share."

Apparently missing the sarcasm in her voice, he smiled, and, spotting the onion and green pepper she'd laid out beside the chopping block, he ambled over to them. While she stirred her cocoa, he cut both the onion and the pepper.

She sighed. "Stop helping me."

"I have to." Chopping the onion and pepper and not looking at her, he added, "Not only will the cocoa get cold while we wait for you to make the omelet if I don't get it started for you, but I have to make up for upsetting you when I suggested you live here permanently."

"Huh!" Damn. She'd said that out loud. Sucking in a breath she turned on him. Since he'd started the conversation, they might as well have at it. "Do you really think you can make up for using what I told you against me? I trusted you. I told you something I don't talk about with anyone else and you used it."

"I didn't 'use' it. I simply pointed out the truth. You're having trouble and the three of us living together helps you. But there's more to me wanting Gino here than just that. Did you miss the part of the conversation where I told you Gino loves us both? He could have us both. Every day. If you'd live here."

"Did you miss the part where I have a life?"

"And you can keep it. You'd just live it from Montauk instead of the city."

"I like my home."

He stopped, caught her gaze. "Now who's being spoiled and pampered and even a little bit prissy?"

Icy pain froze her limbs. *"Prissy?"* After almost two years of caring for a baby and three years of mourning the loss of that precious child, the word *prissy* rumbled through her like thunder announcing an impending storm.

He winced. "Sorry. That was sort of over the top."

Oh, he wanted her to think he was sorry, but he wasn't. She had his number. He'd apologized only so she'd focus on what he'd called her and not on their real issue. There was no way she'd let him get away with that.

"You apologize for your words, but you skate over the actual problem." Pain rippled through her again. Not because of her anger over being called prissy when she was anything but, but because for some reason or another she believed he should know she wasn't prissy. And the only way to avoid dissecting that would be to force them back to their actual problem.

He dropped the knife and strode over to her. She snapped off the burner under the cocoa. If he wanted a fight, she was ready to give it to him.

"I know you love Gino. I see it in your eyes. You might have agreed to take custody only wanting to fulfill your friend's last wishes. But you like him now."

Once again, he was skirting the issue and she refused to let him. "Of course I do, but that doesn't change the fact that you used something I told you against me."

"I only pointed out the truth." He sighed. Stepped closer. "I thought that since you trusted me enough to tell me, that I could speak honestly about it, too."

That brought her up short and she didn't know how to answer. Had he really only been speaking honestly? Had it been so long since she'd spoken honestly about Layla and Burn that she didn't know what an honest conversation felt like anymore?

The truth of what he'd said rippled through her.

She *did* need help with Gino.

And he *was* Gino's other guardian. He had a right to be concerned.

Her skin burned with shame. Especially since she didn't want to admit any of it. He'd only been speaking the truth, but she was so out of the loop, she hadn't realized it and had accused him of using what she'd told him. And the truth was that she still did need help.

She wanted to turn away, to run, but she couldn't. Behind her was a sixteen-burner stove that ran almost the length of the room. In front of her was six feet of angry man.

"Maybe I'm just not ready to talk about it yet."

He gurgled a sound of disgust. "You won't ever be ready if you keep avoiding it in every discussion."

His angry voice echoed through the room and she realized how upset he was. She could understand his annoyance if he were defending himself against her accusations, but he wasn't. Not really. He was talking about her. Angry about her.

"Why are *you* mad?"

He forked his fingers through his hair. "Because you're a nice woman." He snagged her gaze, his brown eyes sharp, filled with banked fury. "You're a smart woman. I know you didn't deserve what happened to you. But it did and you have to get through it to the other side. Yet you won't."

"Hey! You try losing everything! Your hopes. Your dreams. Your *baby*. Your sweet little blue-eyed baby girl who hadn't done anything to anybody." Her breath hitched. "You try losing that much, being responsible for that loss, and then putting your life back together."

"What do you think I'm doing here...with Gino... with my brothers...after my dad's death?"

She gaped at him. "You think losing your dad compares?"

"No. But when you add the fact that I lost my mom

only a few months before, I think I'm in the ballpark. She was fifty-three. Smart. Funny. Everybody's best friend. My dad's biggest defender. And one day she gets to work, has a heart attack and dies." He grabbed Whitney's shoulders as if forcing her to focus in on what he was saying. "I'm alone except for that little boy upstairs and two brothers who hate me, shouldering the burden of a company that's floundering. Do you think I don't look around some days and want to pack a bag for Tahiti, buy a hut and a bottle of tequila and just say, 'screw it all'?"

"It's not the same."

"No. It's not. But just like my troubles don't give me license to stop living, neither do yours. And they sure as hell aren't going to turn into the reason you expect me always to give you your own way." His eyes sharpened. The anger in them flared.

Instead of being frightened, Whitney felt something sharp and sexual click inside her. They were both strong, passionate, vital people. Though she didn't think his trauma was worse than hers, she did believe he at least had a partial understanding of what she was going through. She was sort of sorry that she'd pushed him, but not completely. The score now felt even. Everything was out in the open.

But they were also toe to toe. Stimulated. Attracted. He'd promised he wouldn't kiss her again, but suddenly that promise seemed to belong to another universe, another time, another two people.

He held her gaze. Their physical attraction vibrated between them. Their anger withered and her breath shivered in her chest.

He was going to kiss her.

She told herself to turn and run. She knew the

outcome of the last kiss. She hadn't been able to control herself. She'd wanted everything from him. Not because she loved him but because her body was desperate for release, satisfaction, closeness.

But making love with a man who was virtually a stranger wouldn't give her the satisfaction or closeness she sought. Sex would be a cold, hollow, empty substitute for affection.

She couldn't let him kiss her.

Yet she had no path of escape.

Even as she thought that, his hands slid off her shoulders. He took a step back, away from her, then turned and walked out of the kitchen.

CHAPTER EIGHT

HE'D WANTED TO KISS HER senseless.

Darius stood in front of the mirror over the double sink in the master bathroom. He'd splashed cold water on his face twice, but he couldn't get rid of the weird, compulsive instinct that he should have kissed her. Not because of their silly sexual attraction, but to shock her. To knock her out of the prison she'd built for herself and into the real world. Not for Gino, but for himself. So he could taste her, touch her.

That was wrong. Or it would be if that were his only reasoning. But it wasn't. He'd also wanted to yank her back into the real world because he liked her. And he just *knew* that beyond her fear was a wonderful, passionate woman. Someone he could really relate to. Somebody he could love.

That had scared him silly. The impulse to connect with her was so foreign, yet so strong, he knew the only way to control it had been to leave the room.

He pressed a towel to his face to dry it and headed into the bedroom. Yanking off his sweatshirt, he tried to ignore the emotions swirling through him. Wanting her for anything more than a partner to raise Gino was foolish. Dangerous. *Selfish*. He was the CEO and Chairman of the Board of a huge conglomerate full of people who depended on him. He'd barely have time to be a father for Gino. How could he expect to have time for a wife—especially a wife who would need a more sensitive husband?

He was not a sensitive man.

He would hurt her.

He had to stop wanting her.

The next morning Darius was already feeding Gino when Whitney walked into the nursery. She said, "Good morning," then stooped down in front of the rocker. "And good morning to you."

Their fight the night before had had a greater effect on her than she'd wanted it to. Not only had she come face to face with how attracted she was to Darius, but some of the things he'd said to her had rattled around in her brain.

He'd called her a nice woman.

Just the thought of it made her smile. In the past three years she'd been called cold, distant, frigid. No one had seen past her pain to the real Whitney hiding beneath the surface. And the mere knowledge that someone had actually seen the real her gave her enough strength to try to be that person again.

She sucked in a breath and caught Darius's gaze. "Let me feed him."

Darius didn't say anything, but his dark eyes asked a million questions.

"Hey, I've got to do this."

He sighed. Breaking his silence with her, he said, "Yes, you do."

"Okay. So I'm ready."

He rose from the rocker and took a few steps away

so she could sit down. When she was comfortable, he handed her the baby first, then the bottle.

Fear made her hand tremble as she slid the bottle into Gino's mouth. Nearly every time she'd touched him, memories had assaulted her. And, after the memories came hours of recriminations. Guilt. Beating herself up for not seeing the obvious.

But Gino took the nipple greedily and this time she didn't see her baby's face as he suckled. She saw dark-haired, dark-eyed, very hungry Gino.

She laughed.

Darius turned away.

Her heart tumbled in her chest. Darius's silence made her feel ashamed. Selfish. He'd mentioned his mother's death the night before. He'd said he was alone. He hadn't exactly reached out to her, but had only told her because it fit into their argument. Still, this morning she knew she had to say something.

Seeing Gino was happily suckling, she drew in a quiet breath, swallowed, then said, "I'm sorry about your mother."

"It's okay."

"No. It's not." She shook her head angrily. "This is what always happens with people when I try to talk to them. Nobody's tragedy is as terrible as mine so nobody really talks with me."

He turned around again. His face scrunched in confusion. "That's ridiculous."

"No, it isn't. Look at you. You won't tell me about your mom."

He busied himself with arranging the items on the changing table.

"See!"

Still occupied with powders and lotions, he casually said, "There's not really a lot to tell."

"But you said you were alone."

"That was a slip. A way to show you that you're not the only one who's suffered a loss." He shook his head, but didn't face her. "I shouldn't have compared my situation and yours. Our losses were totally different. Plus, I'm lucky. I might have two half-brothers who intend to ignore me, but I still have a baby brother, and if I raise him he'll be in my life for at least eighteen years. I have a family."

She glanced down at Gino. "You know, if you really wanted to have a family you should bring your brothers together. You shouldn't hang back, waiting for the right time for them to come up and meet Gino. You should take the bull by the horns and invite them now. Get them involved with him now."

He faced her.

"The longer you wait, the more distance you put between yourself and them, and between them and Gino, and the less chance they'll accept your invitation."

He crossed his arms over his chest. "And you're the expert?"

She shrugged. "Lawyers counsel people. We sometimes can't see what's in front of us in our own lives, but we have this uncanny ability to think really clearly about the lives of our clients." She glanced down at Gino, then back up at Darius and smiled slightly as she caught his gaze. "You're not really a client, but I'm sort of new to your life, so it's easier for me to see the obvious."

"And you think I should invite my brothers here?"

"Yes. I think you need a chance to bond."

He snorted out a breath. "Bond. Like a bunch of

girls at cheerleading camp?" He shook his head. "That's ridiculous."

"No. Bonding is finding a common denominator. Something all three of you care about. So that you can relate to each other."

The baby spat out his bottle and Whitney burped him. But when she tried to sit him on her lap again he squirmed and squealed.

Without hesitation Darius walked over and hoisted him up, into his arms. "You look like a guy who wants to play."

Gino giggled. Darius hugged him and headed for the toy box. Whitney's chest tightened and her heart squeezed. He loved Gino so much. And his reasons for wanting Gino in his life were good. He wanted a family. This time, the guilt she felt had nothing to do with her past and everything to do with right now. This minute. She'd mistrusted him, accused him without knowing anything about him.

Maybe the same was true of his brothers?

Maybe they didn't so much hate the eldest Andreas son as much as they simply didn't know him well enough to like him?

Darius opened the toy box and pulled out four big plastic blocks. He sat Gino on a brightly colored striped rug and lowered himself beside him.

The way Darius so easily, so naturally played with Gino tugged on her heartstrings, and once again she thought of his brothers, of how wrong it was for them to dislike their oldest brother.

"I'm not going to drop the idea that you should invite your brothers here."

Preoccupied with trying to get Gino to take a block,

Darius said, "I've already told you I don't want to 'bond.'"

"So don't look at it as bonding. Look at it as getting a chance to talk about the company, about your dad, about the things you have in common."

"And you think talking will fix everything?"

"No. I don't know for sure that there's a way to fix your family. But I think it's a start. And I think you owe it to yourself and Gino to try."

He shuffled the blocks in front of Gino, who batted at them before he picked up the yellow one and inspected it.

When he didn't answer, guilt from their argument in the kitchen rose up in her again. At a point when he would have spoken about his mom, she'd been so wrapped up in her own troubles that she hadn't reached out to him. Every day they'd been here, he'd reached out to her. She owed him.

"If you can get your brothers to come up for a weekend, I'll stay here with Gino until the Monday after that weekend."

He glanced up sharply. "Their schedules aren't going to be any easier than mine. It might take eight or ten weeks before they can come."

"I'm fine with that."

He studied her for a few seconds. Finally he said, "I guess I do have enough room here that we could easily invite my brothers for a weekend."

Darius spent the first few hours at work on the phone with his brothers. He didn't actually speak with each of them all that time. He used most of it calling various numbers he had for them before reaching secretaries who could have given him Cade and Nick's private numbers, but didn't. Each opted to have her boss return Darius's call. Luckily, and somewhat unexpectedly, both did. Immediately.

Though Nick and Cade were reluctant to accept his invitation, he reminded them of their childhoods without their father. He asked them if they really wanted the fourth brother to be raised that way—never really knowing the rest of his family. And suddenly the tones of the conversations were different. Both brothers agreed that Gino needed to know his half-brothers and both agreed to spend a weekend.

He hung up the phone satisfied, happy that his brothers would be at the house in three weeks, until he realized that not only did he have to spend three days with two brothers who hated him, but also that Whitney would be spending three days with them.

Cade the rich, rebellious cowboy and Nick the brooding Southern gentleman.

Jealousy speared him.

He actually stopped walking.

He'd never been possessive of a woman before, never been jealous. Plus, he'd already figured out he was all wrong for Whitney. He had to get over this.

Before he could take his thoughts any further, his phone rang. His first impulse was to ignore it, then he remembered Whitney would be interviewing nanny candidates that morning and he'd promised to spend five minutes with each of them to determine which of the four would get interviews at the house, with Gino.

He picked up the receiver. "Yes."

"I'm sitting here with Mary Alice Conrad," Whitney said happily. "If you have a few minutes, I'd like you to meet her."

* * *

After Darius's five minutes with Mary Alice Conrad, Whitney had a very good idea of the kind of nanny Darius envisioned for Gino. She didn't invite him in on any more of the interviews and simply chose Liz Pizzaro and Jaimie Roberts for interviews at the house.

On the drive home that evening, Whitney informed Darius that the following night they'd be conducting the home interviews with Liz and Jaimie. So, Thursday night, they set themselves up in the den. When Mrs. Tucker escorted Jaimie in, Darius sat behind the big desk in the corner. Gino chewed on a block in the playpen and Whitney stood by the double-doored entrance.

"Come in," Whitney said, shaking Jaimie's hand as Mrs. Tucker discreetly exited and closed the door. She pointed at Darius, who rose. "This is Mr. Andreas, Gino's half-brother and other guardian." She turned and motioned to the crib. "And that's Gino."

Jaimie, a tall redhead wearing tight jeans and a red leather jacket, gasped. "Oh, he's darling!"

Darius dryly said, "We think so, too."

He walked from behind the desk over to the playpen. "Would you like to hold him?"

Jaimie turned and smiled at Darius. "Yes!"

He directed her to take him out of the playpen and she eagerly did so. But he also watched her like a hawk. Through the one-hour question-and-answer session, Jaimie didn't miss a beat, but Darius still didn't seem to like her.

When tall, blond, gorgeous Liz Pizzaro arrived, Darius brightened.

"Come in!" he said, rising from the leather sofa where he'd been sitting to chat with Jaimie.

Whitney's chest tightened oddly. It was such a cliché for the woman of the house to be jealous of the nanny that she refused even to let her thoughts wander to the possibility.

"That's Gino," Darius said, pointing to the baby who was now growing restless in the playpen.

Liz didn't wait for an invitation. She reached in and lifted Gino out and into her arms. "What's the matter, little guy," she crooned.

Gino screeched. But Liz only shook her head and smiled. "He's tired. Yet he's not very fussy. I'm guessing he's a really good baby."

Darius laughed. "Well, we think so, but we're prejudiced."

Liz jostled Gino and made him giggle. "Daddies are supposed to be prejudiced, aren't they?"

Darius winced. "I'm Gino's half-brother. Not really his dad."

Liz blinked innocently. "Of course, you're his dad. I can tell by how protective you are that you take the job as his guardian seriously." She smiled. "And that's what dads do."

Whitney suppressed her own smile. She didn't even have to wait for Liz to leave to know what Darius's choice would be.

"Gino just seemed more comfortable with her."

She nudged his foot with the toe of her high heel. "It didn't hurt that she called you Gino's daddy."

Darius raised his eyes until he snagged her gaze. "Is that so bad?"

Whitney's heart expanded to painful proportions. "No." Guilt assailed her. It suddenly seemed abundantly wrong to take Gino away from Darius, even for visits. Yet it seemed equally wrong for her to simply drop her life and move in with a man she barely knew.

There didn't seem to be a middle of the road to this

problem unless Darius could mend the rift with his brothers and get close enough to them to ensure that Gino wasn't his only family.

CHAPTER NINE

SUNDAY NIGHT, when dinner was over, Whitney rose from her seat and motioned for Darius to follow her.

"I took the liberty of having my secretary gather some information about your bothers, just to get some background details."

Darius also rose from the table. "You investigated my brothers?"

"No. I just had my secretary run a quick search. I told her to get only background information. Nothing serious. Just enough that we would know some basic things."

His eyes narrowed. "I have no desire to poke into my brothers' lives."

"We're not poking. We're just looking. Lawyers never go into a courtroom or a meeting unprepared."

"CEOs don't go into meetings unprepared either."

She turned and smiled. "Exactly. So my secretary got enough background information that we won't feel at a disadvantage when they're here."

They stepped into the office. She directed him to sit on the sofa in front of a low coffee table. Carrying the thin file she retrieved from the desk, she followed him and sat beside him.

The second she sank into the smooth leather, his

nearness overwhelmed her. He'd taken a walk outside after spending time with Gino when they got home from work and he smelled like fresh air and baby powder. A week ago that would have sent her into a tailspin of despair. Today, it only reminded her that she was attracted to this man. It didn't scare her. It didn't make her crazy. It was simply a fact.

She licked her suddenly dry lips and forced her mind back on the info her secretary had found.

"Okay. We'll do Cade first." She glanced down and read aloud, "Cade Andreas, age thirty-one, net worth—" She paused, forcibly told herself not to gape, and read the number on the page.

Darius snorted. "I see that little oil thing worked out for him."

She cleared her throat. "Yes. I guess it did." She returned to her reading. "He's a loner who doesn't really socialize too much, except with the employees of his ranch."

"All of which I already knew."

"Okay." She rifled through the sheets until she came to the first page for the information on Nick. "How about this? I'll read Nick's sheet. You read Cade's. If either of us finds anything noteworthy we'll tell the other."

Darius leaned back, got comfortable and began reading.

Whitney almost mimicked him, until she realized that leaning back into the soft sofa they'd be side by side, almost touching. Sort of close and cuddly.

Arousal sparked, sharp and sweet, at just the thought. It leaped through her, awakening the more dangerous longings. To be held. To be loved. But, luckily, her common sense rose up. It might not frighten her anymore to be attracted to Darius, but a relationship between them wasn't practical. No matter how much they now understood each other, they still had a baby to raise together. If they tried a relationship and it didn't work, Gino would suffer.

So she leaned forward, away from him.

"Here's something interesting. Cade is married."

That perked up her senses. "Really?"

"Yes." He glanced up at her, obviously confused. "But he didn't bring a wife to the funeral."

"Do you think he's the type to leave his wife at home?"

Darius shrugged. "Who knows? A man who says 'sticks in my craw' could do just about anything."

"Should we plan for a wife?"

"Nope, if he didn't mention bringing a guest, I'm not planning for her."

"Okay." She went back to her reading, then had a change of heart. "Maybe we should plan for a guest."

"We have plenty of extras. If we need something Mrs. Tucker will find it."

"You're sure?"

He pierced her with a look. "Positive."

"Maybe we should check?"

"No. He should have told us he'd be bringing a guest. Since he didn't, I'm not going out of my way. If he wants to be inconsiderate that's his choice."

At his snippy tone, Whitney laughed. "I see that hits a nerve."

He set the paper down again. "It doesn't hit a nerve. I think he has the right to behave however he wants to behave, but if the tables were turned I'd be more considerate. That's why I don't expect a lot out of him. Frankly, I'm surprised he's interested in Gino. He's busy with his oil company. He's got a ranch so big I'm not sure even he knows how many acres he has. And he doesn't really like people."

"He's going to be our tough nut to crack then."

Darius merely snorted a "Humph."

"Says here in Nick's report that he owns a factory." She shuffled through the papers. "His net worth is about one quarter of Cade's."

"Yeah, considering Cade's net worth, that brings Nick in at around half a billion dollars." Darius caught her gaze. "Don't ever underestimate Nick. He'll come here all Southern-gentleman charm and manners and he'll leave with the silver."

Her eyes widened. "He's a thief?"

"No, he's a sweet-talker."

Whitney couldn't help it; she laughed. "So you have a sweet-talker and a grouch for half-brothers?"

"Yeah, great, isn't it? I've got a grouch, a sweet-talker and a baby." He snorted in derision. "Which makes me crazy to think I can unite them."

"Or a tower of strength."

"Right."

"Oh, come on. You know you're strong."

He gave her a confused look, then a grin bloomed on his face and he nudged her playfully. "You think I'm strong."

She sucked in a breath. Even casual contact with him sent her senses reeling. But she understood why. Not only was she needy, but he was awfully good-looking. Now that they were getting to know each other, it was sometimes difficult not to simply fall into what seemed to be happening between them.

But, remembering Gino, remembering how difficult it was just to be able to hold him without thinking of Layla, she knew getting involved in a sexual relationship would be every bit as traumatic. She couldn't risk this newfound peace between her and Darius.

She got up from the sofa and walked to the fireplace. "Don't get too excited. I'm just saying that anybody who runs a company as big as yours has to have his attributes."

"Like what?"

"Like you're vain and arrogant." She smirked at him. "Do you really want the list to go on?"

He rose from the sofa and ambled over. "I like the other list better. The one where you talk about the good things." He paused and studied her eyes as if he'd been thinking the same thing she had been while sitting beside him on the sofa—how easy it would be to fall into whatever was happening between them.

Trying to get them back on point, she said, "Okay, you're strong. You're a good leader. And when push comes to shove, you always try to do the right thing."

He grinned. "See. I knew you could come up with a better list."

"You're making me want to go back to the one that starts with vain and arrogant."

His features shifted, his expression became serious again. "Don't."

Awareness bubbled through her. She wanted to believe it was only their sexual attraction, something she could deal with by always staying a few feet away. But gazing into his eyes, that excuse didn't work. In a few short weeks, she'd come to see what a good man Darius Andreas was. Were she not wounded, were she not afraid, she would be falling head over heels in love with him because he was the kind of man a woman couldn't help loving.

She sighed playfully as if put upon. "All right. I'll

stick with the list that reminds me that you always try to do the right thing."

"I'd appreciate that."

His expression was so intense she suddenly wondered if he wasn't telling her something more. That he seriously wanted her to see his good points because he wanted her to like him.

Her heart leapt with hope. But she squelched it. No matter how good he was, she was weak. She was broken. He deserved better.

She swallowed. Scrambling to get them out of their personal conversation, she pulled away. "I'll bet it seems odd for you to have brothers who are so different."

Watching her walk back to the sofa, apparently accepting her return to their original topic, he said, "Yes and no. We never met until we were adults, so I spent most of my life growing up as an only child. When we did meet, we didn't like each other. I was the product of a marriage. They resented me because our father didn't marry either of their moms. And Nick's mom had a long-term relationship with our dad. It was a surprise when he walked away rather than marry her."

"That is kind of awful."

He took the poker from beside the fireplace and stirred the logs, creating a shower of sparks.

"If you dislike that story, you'll really hate Cade's. His mom was a one-night stand. Stephone simply refused to return her calls until she got a court order for a DNA test after Cade was born." He shook his head. "He didn't think enough of Cade's mom to call her back. I don't know Cade, but if someone treated my mother that badly, I'd hate him, too."

"No wonder they're bitter."

"And don't forget, our different mothers taught us

different things. Mine always loved our dad. She taught me to respect him." He shook his head. "I wanted to hate him." He caught her gaze. "Not for me, but for her. He loved her, yet he couldn't stop cheating."

She understood Darius's anger, but she'd handled enough divorces to be a realist. "For some men, fidelity is impossible."

He looked at the ceiling. "Do you really believe that?"

"Yes." She answered unequivocally, knowing that would bring some sort of meaning to his childhood suffering. It didn't exactly smooth it over, but it did somewhat explain it and take the burden off the women who bore the Andreas brothers and put it where it belonged. On Stephone.

"With some men an affair is the best a woman will get. Lots of women go into them with their eyes open." She shrugged. "I know Missy did. She hadn't expected anything from your dad but what they had in the moment. I'll bet she never spent a sorry day because her expectations were real, honest."

Darius turned to face her and his gaze slid over to hers. His dark eyes held hers, as if there was something else he wanted to say, but instead he turned away and headed for the bar.

"So we get beer and steak," she said, snatching the opportunity to return them to their intended subject because the silence in the room was strained. Awkward. And she wasn't sure why. Especially since they had been getting along, relating normally, for several days.

She couldn't risk losing that. "Since Nick is from the South, I'd say some Tennessee whiskey would probably also be in order."

"Some shrimp."

"And crab legs."

Darius laughed. "Are you still trying to please Cade's potential mystery wife or yourself?"

"Hey, if I have to be here, I'm making the most of your money and connections to get some really good fresh fish."

Chuckling, he pulled a bottle from beneath the bar. "How about a glass of wine?"

"Actually, if our work here is done, I want to go talk with Cook and then call my dad."

"Why?"

"I have a fabulous recipe for jambalaya and my father has the name of a whiskey I think both your brothers will like."

"You don't have to do that."

She smiled. "I want to."

The funny part of it was she did. She liked taking charge. She liked the spike of adrenaline that formed when she had a plan to work and was working a plan. She'd been hiding in the background for so long she'd almost forgotten what a formidable force she could be. After a brief smile, she left the room.

Darius watched her leave, not missing one sway of her soft hips, one step of her long, curved legs. He leaned on the bar and rubbed his hand across his mouth. He wasn't sure if it was wishful thinking on his part, but could she have just told him that she wouldn't mind an affair?

Could it be that in the same way she'd gotten comfortable with her role in his house, she was also getting comfortable with their attraction?

He replaced the wine on the rack and poured himself two fingers of whiskey.

There was only one way to find out.

* * *

Saturday afternoon, after the baby had awakened from his nap, Darius and Whitney set him on the nursery floor. Strong, happy Gino crawled to a stray block that had missed being put into the toy box.

"Did you see that? He crawled!"

Whitney laughed. "You need a video camera."

Darius pulled his cell phone out of his jeans pocket. "Until I get one, this will do."

He aimed the camera at the little boy who slapped the block on the floor by the toy box. Whitney slipped behind him, lifted the toy-box lid and began tossing other soft plastic toys to Gino, who giggled with delight. Darius moved his cell phone to her.

She held up her hand. "Don't!"

"Why not? You look great."

"Yeah, but I don't want to be in your pictures."

"Why not?"

"Because we're...we're..." She wanted to say they were only co-guardians. She wasn't family and didn't really have to be a part of his life. But that was wrong. They were working together for Gino. Both were committed to raising him right and well. Like it or not, they were connected. Maybe for the rest of their lives.

She threw her hands up in defeat. "Whatever. Get me in the video if you want."

He laughed. "Such enthusiasm, right, Gino?" He said, catching the baby's attention. Gino patted his thighs and spouted a bit of gibberish.

"Wish we could get him to crawl again."

Whitney stooped beside the toy box and tossed a colorful ball a few feet away from the baby. "Hey, Gino. See the ball?"

He slapped his chubby hands on his thighs.

Whitney tossed another toy over by the ball.

Gino screeched.

This time she tossed a little stuffed frog she knew was one of Gino's favorites. Finally, he rolled to his knees and crawled after it.

Darius's face blossomed into a broad smile. "Got it."

She lifted herself from the floor. "You need a real video camera. Come on. We'll take Gino to your office, get on the Internet and have one delivered."

Darius scooped Gino from the floor. "Sounds good to me."

They trooped to the second-floor office Darius used. Whitney was not surprised to see he had a second swing set up beside his office chair. When Gino wasn't napping, Darius usually kept his baby brother with him.

He slid the baby into the swing and turned the knob at the top that not only set the swing in motion but also activated the music box. Then he dropped to the chair behind the desk, hit a few buttons on his keyboard and brought his monitor to life.

At first they went on a generic search that led them to the websites of a few well-known brand names of cameras.

When bending down to view the screen became awkward, Whitney leaned her hip on the arm of Darius's chair, half sitting so she could see better. After reviewing the websites for the brands with five-star recommendations, Darius ordered the camera he wanted and clicked off the website.

"We should have it tomorrow."

He looked up at her and she suddenly realized how close they were. At first she was surprised their attraction hadn't sprung up. Then she realized something amazing. She was sitting so close their arms had brushed yet she hadn't panicked. Hadn't noticed, really. She was blessedly comfortable with him. Relaxed. Content. Almost... happy.

No. She *was* happy. She *liked* him. And not just as a friend or co-guardian. She *liked* him.

She bounced from the arm of his chair. "Okay. Now that that's settled," she said, trying not to sound confused or angry or even weepy and scared. Liking him, seriously liking him, meant taking steps, doing things.

Kissing for real.

Getting to know each other.

Making love.

The thought caused her heart to stop. She could see them making love. And why not? They were attracted and they were already getting to know each other. They'd flirted. They worked together. Hell, they'd already kissed.

How had they gotten beyond her barriers?

It didn't matter. She wouldn't couldn't get involved with another man again, especially not someone to whom she was committed because of a baby.

CHAPTER TEN

FOR THE FIRST TIME since getting Gino, Darius felt his world righting. He had grown more than comfortable with his role as Gino's father. Plus his feelings for Whitney had taken a sudden, unexpected turn. Now that he realized she might be agreeable to an affair, their attraction no longer seemed wrong. It was just part of the picture. Part of who they were. And if they continued to grow in friendship as they had been, pretty soon he was going to act on it.

As they drove home from the city the following Tuesday evening, he realized "pretty soon" might come sooner rather than later. There she sat, long lean legs crossed, her soft yellow hair tumbling over her shoulders as she worked, tempting him. Over the past few weeks, she'd slowly changed the way she dressed from oversize suits to simple sweaters and skirts. She'd also relaxed her hairstyle, as if she was returning to her normal self. And she was captivating. Gorgeous. If he didn't stop staring at her, he'd be in sad shape by the time they reached the estate. So he did the only thing he could to get his mind on something else. He started talking.

"Nick's flight has been moved up. He'll be at the house on Friday afternoon of the weekend he and Cade are staying, instead of Friday evening."

Whitney looked up. Her pretty Persian-cat eyes warmed with humor. "So are we going home early to meet him, or are you risking the silver?"

"I told you. I'm not worried about the silver, but I'm not so sure I want to leave him alone with Liz."

She burst out laughing. "Oh, come on."

"No, you come on. He's a womanizer."

Her head tilted. "Really?"

He scuffed the toe of his shoe in the limo carpeting. He'd just called his brother a womanizer as if it was a bad thing when *he* intended to try to get Whitney into bed.

"He's got thirteen years on her."

She nudged his shoulder. "Stop acting like an old man."

He glanced up, caught her gaze. "I *am* an old man."

"At thirty-eight?"

The question came out on an airy giggle and everything inside of Darius thundered to life. He hadn't flirted with anyone in weeks. Maybe months. But there was something about flirting with Whitney that was more fun than normal. Maybe because only a few weeks ago this kind of conversation would have been foreign to her. And he'd helped her get to this place.

Surely that meant he could be allowed to enjoy it?

"Maybe I'm not so old as I am experienced."

She snorted and glanced down at her papers again. "I'll bet you are."

He knocked the toe of her high heel with the toe of his oxford. "Wanna find out?"

She looked up, her eyes filled with fear. But in a blink the fear was gone, replaced by curiosity.

Oh, yeah. She wanted to find out.

The mild tingle of arousal in his gut suddenly became

a raging river. He could have ravaged her right there in the limo.

And not been sorry.

That shocked him. He really wouldn't have been sorry. In his mind's eye he saw nothing but pleasure with her. No sadness or fear for her. No guilt or recrimination for himself.

This really was going to happen.

Finally, she said, "Don't flatter yourself," and returned her attention to her paperwork, but he knew she was lying. She wanted him as much as he wanted her.

It was a milestone for her. One he wouldn't take lightly. He would make sure the moment was right when he seduced her. But he would seduce her. Not just for his own pleasure but for hers, and to bring her wholly back to the woman she was supposed to be. He couldn't bring back her child. Couldn't change her memories. But he'd been helping her take steps to recovery all along. He could help her take the next one.

After dinner, he would lure her into the den and they'd have 'the' conversation. He wouldn't risk any misunderstanding. They both had to be clear about this or it wouldn't work.

Because they were now getting down on the floor with Gino, Whitney changed into jeans before she went to the nursery to play for the hour before dinner. After they ate, Darius rose from the table and immediately walked to her chair, which he pulled out for her. "Can you spare a few minutes to talk with me in the den?"

"Sure."

He led her back down the hall. Once in the den, he pointed to the sofa as he headed for the bar. "Wine?"

Because she still had two hours of reading to do, she shook her head. "No. Thanks."

"I was kind of counting on you having a glass of wine before our talk."

"Really?" She laughed. "You want me tipsy?"

"Yes. No." He winced, then pulled out a bottle of wine and popped the cork. "I want you relaxed."

She laughed again. "I thought we were past being nervous around each other."

"Not quite. There's one more thing we haven't discussed. Something we need to discuss and then we'll have everything out in the open between us."

"I'm ready."

He sucked in a breath. "Okay, Whitney, I don't have to tell you that we're attracted to each other."

That was the last thing she'd expected him to say. Rather than sit on the couch as he'd indicated, she took a step back toward the door. "And?"

"And I know I told you that I wouldn't kiss you again, but I've changed my mind. I now think we should do something about this thing between us."

Looking at his full lips, the gleam in his dark eyes, she felt a longing that she hadn't felt in years. Oh, she was tempted, but she'd already worked all this out in her head and decided it was trouble. She laughed nervously and, as casually as possible, took another two steps back. "I'm not ready for a committed relationship."

Unfortunately, he came out from behind the bar and easily caught up with her. He stepped close, toyed with a strand of her hair. "Who says that's what I want?"

Her breath froze in her lungs. Temptation rose up like the morning sun, bright and full of promise. But they weren't the only two people in this equation.

"Have you forgotten, we're parents...raising a child together for the next eighteen years?"

"We're also mature adults who understand ourselves.

You were hurt, nearly destroyed by a man you trusted. I had a father who couldn't remain faithful if he tried. I saw how he hurt my mom. I won't hurt a woman that way."

"And you think having affairs doesn't leave women hurt?"

"Not if you go into the relationship knowing the score. You said yourself Missy was fine with what she had with my dad."

"I know but—" Though that was true, she hadn't meant it in the context he'd taken it. "That's different."

"How?" He snagged her gaze, his eyes bright and serious. "Why? Neither one of us wants a marriage. Why are we any different than my father and your friend?"

"It's just that you seem so sure." She frowned. "Weirdly sure." As if an affair, not a relationship was the obvious choice, undoubtedly because she was the kind of woman no man would ever want to settle down with. Burn might have wanted her, but now she was damaged goods.

She tried to step away, but Darius caught her hands. "Look, I'm the son of a man who couldn't be faithful. I'm pretty sure I inherited those genes. But even if I hadn't, I've had enough experience to know that being wealthy changes everything. I'm tied to my job. I'm tied to this life. I don't have time for a marriage. If you married me, I'd only hurt you more. But there's more to it than that."

Seeing the expression of sincerity on his face, she reeled back her own insecurities. "Like what?"

"My dad blamed sudden riches ten years into his marriage to my mom for making him unfaithful. So he gave me and each of my brothers five million dollars when we turned eighteen, so we'd have a chance to see what it was like to have money. His theory was that when the right woman came along, we'd have all our playboy-bachelor days out of the way, and we could settle down the way he couldn't."

"But it didn't work?"

"No." He snorted a laugh. "Actually, it made things worse. I didn't get my playboy-bachelor days out of the way because I didn't want to run around. I didn't want to gamble. Or skip school or do any of the things kids that age usually want to do. I went to class, worked hard and fell in love with a girl who was one of my study partners. She was from an average family and we were in Wharton, so I knew she was only eking by. It wasn't long before I realized living with me would make her life easier, so we moved in together and pretty soon I was paying her tuition."

"This ends badly, doesn't it?"

He blew his breath out on a sigh. "About a year later, I rushed home early one day to surprise her and I found her with another man. She claimed she'd loved me at first but her feelings had died." He shook his head. "She quite honestly told me she hadn't left me because she needed the tuition."

She could picture idealistic, smitten Darius being so coldly dumped and her heart ached for him. "Maybe she was a little too honest. Cold-hearted even?"

He laughed. "You really haven't been around the block a lot, have you? Lots of life is about money. Your own husband committed suicide because he didn't measure up. It's how we keep score. It's how we keep safe. It's certainly not the root of all evil, but if you've got a weakness it will bring it out in you or make it worse, the way it did with Jen."

"So you're telling me you want an affair for my sake."

"I'm telling you I want an affair because I think that's the best way for us to remain honest with each other. We've come a long way in a couple of weeks. And I believe we've come this far because at a certain point we stopped hedging the truth and looking out for our own agendas and started being honest. It's why I didn't simply seduce you. It's why we're having this discussion now. Honesty might hurt in the moment, but real honesty keeps people from going over the edge."

Surprisingly, what he said made sense. Burn had never been honest with her, and, as a result, he'd delivered the ultimate pain. Even now she didn't know the truth of what had happened with him and the baby. Why he'd killed himself. Why he'd killed their little girl.

"You need this. You need to come back to the land of the living. I can bring you back. I can help you become whole again. No strings attached. Nothing to scare you. Just a nice slow romance to remind you of what it feels like to be a woman again."

She swallowed and turned away. It was too easy to believe him when staring into his sincere eyes. "And what about Gino?"

"What about Gino?"

"You don't think he'll be hurt when our affair fizzles?"

"First, I don't think we'll fizzle. I think we'll morph."

A laugh escaped her. "Morph?"

"Right now we're hot for each other, and you think that will burn out. I think it will simply temper. We'll always want each other." He turned her around, caught her gaze. "If we play this right we could be something like friends with benefits forever."

"Don't you mean parents with benefits?"

He laughed. "Maybe."

When she didn't reply, he leaned in and nibbled her ear. "Don't you want this?"

When her entire body tensed then softened, it was useless to pretend she wasn't attracted—maybe even overly attracted—to him. "Some parts of me."

He chuckled.

"We can't hurt Gino."

"We won't hurt Gino." He pulled away, forcing her to look up at him. "And we won't hurt each other. You've been hurt. I've been hurt. And I had a dad who couldn't stick with one woman if his life depended on it. I can't see myself being faithful forever. I won't make that promise. But I can tell you I'll always be honest and I'll expect you to be honest. When the time comes to shift or morph or maybe even call it quits, you won't be surprised. Or hurt."

"You can't tell me I won't be hurt."

"You might be disappointed, but you'll never be stung or shocked or even surprised. Because you and I will be nothing but honest, up-front, fair. And because what we have feels strong."

"But not strong enough to last forever?"

"Nothing lasts forever. And not always because people can't be faithful." He caught her gaze. "You would have stayed with your husband forever, but you had no control over that. With so many things that can go wrong in a relationship, people are foolish to think they can make one last forever. You're smarter if you go in eyes open. Brain engaged."

She laughed. "Why are you making so much sense?"

He slid his arms around her waist. "I'll give you a

choice of two reasons. First, I'm right. Second, you want me enough that it's easy to agree with me."

She laughed again, but this laugh was tinged with expectation, anticipation.

"Plus we're smart enough to put on the brakes when it feels like we're making a commitment we can't keep. Or when we want something that goes beyond the scope of what we know through experience is nothing but an illusion."

"Yeah." That was why she believed him. Permanency was an illusion. That's the big lesson losing Burn and Layla had taught her. "So what do we do now?"

He pulled away. "What? You think I'm going to seduce you tonight?"

Part of her almost wished he would. Soft and pliant, deadly nervous and hopelessly attracted to him, she knew she wouldn't change her mind, or freeze and run away. "Sort of get this over with?"

"So I'm a get-this-over-with?" He chuckled softly and moved away from her, walking back to the bar where he'd left his wine. "I was thinking more in terms of sweet seduction. A little time. A little flirting." He swirled his wine in the crystal glass. "A little cat-and-mouse."

She swallowed. "You'll have me a nervous wreck."

"Or I'll make you so eager maybe you'll seduce me."

She laughed. "Not likely."

"Oh, you don't know my powers of persuasion."

Friday night, Liz had just finished changing Gino into a fresh sleeper when Darius and Whitney entered the room.

"You guys are either too early or too late. I was just

about to take him downstairs for cereal before I bring him back for a bottle before bed."

Whitney frowned. She knew Liz was a stickler for keeping Gino on a schedule, and she agreed. Babies were much happier when things were always done at the same time of day. But there was no reason she and Darius couldn't spend time with him tonight.

"How about if Darius and I feed him his cereal and rock him to sleep?"

Liz clutched her chest. "No! I didn't mean to sound like it was a problem for me to feed him."

Darius chuckled and took the baby from Liz's arms. "We know that. We also respect your schedule. But we know you have classes tomorrow and you probably want to study. Since we want time with Gino anyway, we're the logical choice to feed him."

Liz cast a wary eye in their direction. "You do know he's already bathed and in his pajamas."

"I've fed him before," Darius said, the voice of authority now that he had almost two weeks of caring for Gino under his belt. "We'll be fine."

Liz was still wary. "I don't want to have to bathe him again."

Whitney batted a hand. "We're fine. Honestly."

Liz grinned. "Okay! I do have some studying to do."

She skipped out of the nursery, eager to get to her books and Whitney and Darius followed her out. She turned to the left. They turned to the right and took the back stairs to the kitchen.

"She's funny," Darius said, heading into the room filled with so much stainless steel and copper pots that it had something of an echo.

"I see her point," Whitney said, going to the cupboard

that she knew contained the cereal. Since her night of struggle to find a plate, spoon and mug, all the things she and Darius might need for themselves or the baby had been moved to a front cupboard. She grabbed the box of cereal, a bowl and Gino's tiny spoon. "She doesn't want to have to do double duty."

"We're virtually pros at this," Darius scowled.

She laughed. "I'm a pro. You're still a beginner."

"Ha!"

"Just go. Get Gino into his high chair."

Shaking his head, Darius left the room. Whitney quickly prepared Gino's cereal and by the time she brought it to the dining room the little boy was already pounding on the tray.

"He knows what this means."

Whitney took a seat beside the high chair. "Of course he does. Sit any human being in front of the table where they've eaten their entire life and they'll want food."

Darius took the bowl and spoon from her. "Good point."

"I'll feed him."

He shook his head. "I'm doing this. Liz maligned my good name."

"Your good name is very sensitive."

He set the bowl on the tray in front of the baby. "I just like it when people trust me to know what I'm doing."

"Liz also likes being good at her job."

He frowned. "I never thought of that."

"She didn't question us because she thinks we're idiots. She just likes being the one who calls the shots with the baby—"

Gino screeched loud and long and Whitney realized they'd all but forgotten the poor kid. But when she looked down at him her mouth fell open in horror.

He'd taken the bowl of cereal Darius had set on the tray, pulled it close to him, and had slathered it all over his face.

Darius gasped. "Liz is going to kill you."

"Kill me!" She grabbed a napkin. "Twenty seconds ago it was your good name being maligned." She pulled in a breath. "This isn't anything to panic about. We'll just make a new bowl of cereal, feed him and then bathe him ourselves."

Taking the bowl and spoon from the tray, she said, "Can I trust you to watch him while I'm gone?"

"Now, you're maligning my good name."

She shook her head and went to the kitchen where she prepared a second bowl of cereal. This time, she didn't give Darius a chance to intervene. She simply sat, fed the baby, and then took the bowl and spoon to the kitchen.

When she returned, Darius stood staring at the baby, who was still in the highchair.

"I'm not sure how to pick him up."

"You pick him up normally."

"I'll get cereal all over me."

"You're going to have to take one for the team."

He laughed at that, drew Gino out of the high chair and winced when the baby's cereal-covered sleeper met his sweater.

Whitney pushed on the swinging door to get out of the dining room and into the hall to the stairs and looked both ways before she turned back to Darius. "Okay. Coast is clear. All we have to do is race up the stairs and down one short hall and we'll be behind closed doors. Liz won't have to know any of this happened."

"I'm right behind you."

They made it up the stairs and into the nursery

without running into Liz and were laughing hysterically when they closed the door behind them.

No longer out of his element, Darius took Gino to the changing table and stripped him out of his one-piece pajamas.

Whitney walked over and cooed at Gino who lay on the changing table playing with a rattle. "Looks like you've got your work cut out for you."

Darius stepped back. He didn't remember volunteering for this duty. Plus, he'd been the one to carry the kid upstairs. "Or you could have your work cut out for you."

She playfully punched his arm. "Hey, you said you wanted to learn everything there was to know about caring for him. Baths are part of that. You've probably never bathed him before."

"But he'll be naked."

"So?"

"So I'm not entirely comfortable with his bladder control."

Laughing merrily, Whitney lifted Gino from the changing table and headed into the nursery bathroom. Seeing how happy she was with Gino sent a surge of pride through him. He'd done that. He'd helped her through her fear and guilt and grief and now she was happy.

Cocky and proud, he followed her into the bathroom, which looked surprisingly like a normal bathroom except instead of two sinks in the vanity, there was a little tub beside the lone sink. Beside the tub was a bin filled with soaps and shampoos and washcloths.

Holding Gino with one hand, Whitney turned on the tap for the tub. As it filled with water, she removed his diaper and set him inside. Gino all but purred with joy.

"Oh, so you like the water?" Darius said, leaning against the doorjamb.

"Oh, no you don't!" Whitney said, laughing when Gino patted his hands in the water and splashed her. "We're both doing this! I need the soap, a washcloth and some shampoo."

Darius stepped inside and handed her the things.

"Thanks."

He took a step back.

"Uh-uh," she said, grabbing the bottom of his sweater with her wet hands. "It takes two hands to hold a big, energetic baby like Gino. So I'm going to give you the choice. Either hold him in the tub or wash him."

"I think I'd be better at holding."

She motioned for him to shift to her left and he did.

"Now, slide your hands around his waist from behind."

He did. Gino squeaked and slapped the water again, this time splashing Darius. Whitney giggled.

"I think you just wanted me to get wet."

"No," Whitney said. "I just want you to share the joy."

"Right."

The bath took little more than five minutes, but before Gino was clean Darius was totally wet. Whitney, however, was suspiciously dry.

When he asked her about it, she gasped in mock outrage. "I just have an instinct about knowing when to step back."

As she bundled Gino in a terry-cloth towel that looked something like a baby blanket, Darius said, "Right."

"I'm serious. Knowing when to step back and when to move in with the washcloth is an art."

She carried wriggling Gino to the changing table in the nursery and pointed at the door to Darius's bedroom with her chin. "You can go change if you want."

"Okay."

He turned and went into his bedroom, but decided against closing the door. It might seem like dirty politics or maybe even a little bit tacky to strip off his shirt in front of her, but he hadn't forgotten their conversation about becoming more than friends. He itched for tonight to be the night, but he hadn't done nearly enough flirting yet. Every time he tried to flirt, the baby would squeak or squawk or want to be fed or just need time.

Actually, he'd seriously begun to wonder how parents ever had a second kid if the first one took up this much time.

Then Gino laughed as if Whitney had tickled him. The sound drifted to him followed by Whitney's happy laugh and something tightened in his gut. He wanted to make love to her in a way he'd never wanted to make love to another woman. Out of joy. Weird joy. A joy that sort of celebrated their lives.

He checked that thought. Not that it was all bad. He still wanted to make love to her out of joy—the joy of finally doing something about their attraction. He'd meant what he said about keeping a certain distance between them. Not just for himself, but also for her.

He would keep that commitment.

He would make love to her.

They would have a relationship.

He would never hurt her.

But he didn't want either of them to have their feelings confused. He didn't believe in permanent relationships.

His dad had taught him that. It was a lesson he'd learned the hard way, by being one of the people his dad frequently ignored.

Days later, Whitney still tingled every time she thought about seeing Darius changing his shirt that night in the nursery, and that, of course, took her back to the discussion they'd had about becoming more than friends. She'd known all along he was attracted to her and she was attracted to him, but it wasn't smart for them to get involved. They had a child to raise.

But, oh, he'd made some really good points for a casual affair. And every day that he flirted with her, touched her hand or looked into her eyes, his arguments seemed even more compelling.

When they found themselves alone in her office again the following Saturday night, her senses scrambled to red alert. He'd told her he intended to seduce her and she knew he wasn't a man to make statements he didn't intend to keep. In a way, it was exciting. Like a game.

Would this be the night?

Would he sweep her off her feet and carry her to the master suite?

Or would he woo her? Seduce her with kisses until she felt dizzy?

In other ways it was terrifying. What if this was the night? Could she handle a relationship that was only about sex and friendship? She'd never had casual sex. She'd only ever made love with a steady boyfriend and a fiancé who had become her husband. She liked commitments.

So could she have a relationship that was only about today? No mention of tomorrow? Burn had promised her tomorrow then snatched it away like a lie. Did she really even believe in tomorrow anymore?

Was Darius right when he said permanency was only an illusion?

"Anyway, when my brothers get here, I think we need to make sure one of us is in the nursery at all times with them."

She set her pen down on her desk. "Refresh my memory. Are we making sure neither one of them snatches Gino, or are we protecting Liz?"

"Protecting Liz!" He sighed. "You're not paying attention."

She winced. "I was working when you came in." Lounging on the couch in his jeans and sloppy T-shirt, looking so comfortably sexy, he had to know he was a colossal distraction.

"Well, stop. My brothers will be here next weekend. We have to make sure we have a game plan."

He seemed so nervous about his brothers' visit that she rose from the chair behind the desk and headed for the conversation area to give him her full attention. She then realized she'd put herself in a terrible position. If she sat on the chair, she'd appear distant and cool. If she sat on the sofa, she might as well tell him she wanted tonight to be the night.

She decided to pace. She'd look perplexed, thoughtful. Actively involved in their discussion.

"What part of the plan do we not have? We've decided every menu and activities for every day. They're going to want to leave just to get some rest."

"I'm not talking about big things. I'm talking about little things. My mother always said you can't be too prepared."

It didn't surprise her that he'd brought up his mother,

but it did relax her. As long as they kept the conversation on concrete things, he wouldn't be thinking about sex. Or maybe she wouldn't be thinking about sex?

"It sounds like your mother was a smart woman."

He sat forward on the sofa. "Oh, she was great. Seriously."

"I'll bet she was proud of you."

"She was." He bounced off the sofa, walked over to her and turned her to face him. "And I get the distinct impression you're bringing up my mother because there's something else you don't want to discuss."

"No! I'm fine."

"Then why are you pacing?"

She shrugged. "I don't know. Bored maybe?"

"We have sort of been stuck here for the past several weeks." His solemn expression shifted into a grin. "Maybe tonight should be the night I seduce you?"

Her breath froze. Her limbs liquefied. As she looked into his sharp, dark eyes, her vocal cords went numb. She couldn't have spoken if she'd tried.

"I promised you flirting and we've been doing that every day. What we're up to is kissing." He brought her right hand to his lips, kissed it lightly, then smiled. "Soft. Just as I expected."

She swallowed as a million pinpricks of excitement raced from the back of her hand up her arm and straight to her heart.

"You're beautiful, Whitney. The day we met, your eyes intrigued me. Such a beautiful shade of blue." His soft, seductive voice trembled through her, heating her blood, fogging her brain. "But your lips are magnificent. Soft. Kissable." His head slowly descended. "I'm going to kiss you now."

She didn't even try to muster an objection. Her

breaths shivered in and out of her chest. Her limbs had weakened. Her brain had shut down. No one had ever spoken to her like this. Listing her attributes. Silkily, sexily telling her he wanted her. How could she possibly argue with that? Resist that?

His lips met hers and Whitney closed her eyes. Dark, delicious sensations tumbled through her. Warmth filled her middle and coiled through her. Unlike their first kiss, this time she wasn't just kissing someone. She was kissing Darius. Someone she knew. Someone she liked. Someone who liked her.

They were really expressing emotion.

But he didn't make a move to deepen the kiss. Instead, he pulled away.

Their gazes clung. She could see the debate raging inside him by the look in his eyes, but he didn't kiss her again.

"We should do that more often."

A happy laugh wanted to escape, but nothing could get past the lump in her throat, the wonderful shivery feeling that held her captive.

His hands slid down her arms until he could catch her fingers. Gazing into her eyes, he said, "Good night." Then he dropped her hands and headed for the door.

He was gone before she found her voice enough to remind him it was only eight o'clock, too soon to go to bed. But it didn't matter. Tonight might not be the night they made love, but it was the night she began to feel again. Really, genuinely, feel. She hadn't even thought of her past. She'd made no comparisons. She had been fully in the moment with Darius.

Was she scared? Absolutely.

Especially since he could want to take the next step at any time, and that would be the real test of whether or not she was moving on.

CHAPTER ELEVEN

THEY DIDN'T GO TO WORK the Friday Darius's brothers were to arrive. Instead, Darius spent the morning in his office fielding calls for work that absolutely had to be handled, while Whitney saw to the last-minute details for the weekend.

She reveled in the job. In the week that had passed, Darius had kissed her every time he'd gotten the chance. He hadn't pushed her to make love, but she enjoyed his kisses enough that she was more than accustomed to their growing feelings for each other. They took care of Gino together and now they were entertaining his brothers together. She'd never felt more at home. She belonged here, in this house, with this man.

When the driver called to inform Darius he had Nick and was ten minutes away from the house, Whitney rose excitedly. "Everything is ready."

Darius wrapped his arms around her waist loosely. "I've decided I was making too big a deal out of this visit, worrying about nothing. My brothers aren't that complicated. Cade's a beer drinker and Nick is such a charmer that you could set raw skunk in front of him for dinner and he'd praise you for it. He'd sweet-talk his way out of having to eat it, but he'd still praise you."

With a laugh, she pushed at his shoulder and eased out of his embrace. "We'll see."

She headed for the main entryway and Darius scooted after her. "I'm serious."

"No. You have a poor opinion of your brothers. I'm hoping this weekend changes that."

The words were hardly out of her mouth before the door opened and Nick walked inside.

Darius stiffened.

Nick's eyes narrowed.

Whitney held back a sigh. She'd give anything to have a sister. Hell, she'd give anything to have a brother. She was an only child who longed for a blood relative to share life's trials and tribulations with. That's why she'd gotten so close to Missy. She wasn't going to let the Andreas brothers ruin this chance to get along.

"You know, I don't expect you to hug. But you could shake hands."

Darius stepped forward, his hand extended. Whitney's mouth fell open slightly at his immediate obedience, then she smiled. Everything she'd been telling him must have sunk in. He'd not only listened to her; he was taking her advice.

Narrow-eyed Nick took Darius's hand. "This isn't a truce."

To Whitney's surprise, Darius laughed and slapped Nick's back. "Right to the point, huh?"

"There's no other way to negotiate."

"Dad's rule number thirty-six."

"Offset by rule number seventeen. Never let the other side know what you want."

Darius laughed again. "I thought I was the only one who realized his rules contradicted each other."

He pointed toward the den on the right. "How about a beer?"

Whitney gasped and caught Nick's arm, turning him toward the dining room. "Or how about lunch? Cade's not supposed to get here until six, so we waited lunch for you."

Nick faced her. His brown eyes narrowed again, only this time it wasn't in suspicion as it had been when he'd looked at Darius. His gaze drifted from her face down to her toes, as if inspecting her.

Then he smiled. "Ms. Ross, right?"

She nodded and stepped back. "Sorry, we should have made introductions."

His smile grew. "We met at your dad's office, remember? I never forget a pretty face."

Darius caught his arm and turned him toward the den again. "Wait until you meet Liz."

"Who's Liz?"

"Gino's nanny."

Nick stopped walking. "Oh?"

Whitney stared at them. First, she wanted to swat Darius for throwing Liz to the lions when he'd told Whitney his goal was to protect her from his brothers. Second, he kept yanking Nick toward a beer, when all three should be having lunch.

"Lunch, remember?" she said, all but stomping her foot to get their attention. "By then Gino should be done with his nap and Nick can meet him."

Nick faced her again then looked at Darius. "She's a lawyer, right?"

Darius said, "Unfortunately."

Nick cocked his head. "Pushy?"

"Absolutely. This weekend was her idea." He motioned for Whitney to lead the way to the dining room.

Nick chuckled and shook his head. "Wait till Cade gets here. It's gonna be an interesting weekend."

The whole way through lunch Darius fielded questions Nick intended for Whitney. Never before in his life had he been so possessive and jealous, but he and Whitney were on the verge of sleeping together, and he had a sixth sense that his brothers were somehow going to ruin all the progress he'd made in the past week. Whitney was a sensitive, only-now-healing woman. One wrong word, one wrong action on his brothers' parts could send her scurrying back into hiding.

This close, there was no way Darius was going to let that happen.

When they went to the nursery, Liz was just finishing changing Gino after his nap. Because he felt bad for the comment he'd made about Liz when Nick first arrived, Darius dismissed her and fed the baby himself. He hadn't intended to throw her under the wheels of the bus, but he'd been jealous of the way Nick was looking at Whitney, and he'd panicked. Dismissing Liz was his way of making up for that.

After watching Liz as she exited the nursery, Nick put his attention on the baby. "He's cute."

"Very cute," Darius agreed. "Once I feed him, you can hold him."

Nick stepped back. "Great." He rubbed his hand along the back of his neck, as if debating something, then said, "You do know about Cade's wife, don't you?"

Darius rolled his eyes. "Yes, if he brings her we're prepared for the extra guest."

Nick shook his head fiercely. "No. I was asking if you knew his wife had died."

Shock took Darius. "His wife is dead?"

"She got sick a few years ago. She fought and fought, but didn't make it." He paced over to the window. "I just don't want you to stick your foot in your mouth by saying something you'll regret."

The urge to thank Nick rose in Darius, but he stifled it. First, it seemed weird to thank someone for telling him Cade's wife was dead. Second, he knew Nick. There was a reason he'd told Darius about Cade's wife, beyond sparing Darius embarrassment. His brothers were cool and calculated. If he wanted to keep the upper hand, he couldn't show weakness.

Gino finished his bottle and Darius rose from the rocker and held out the baby to his brother. "Here."

Nick took the baby with a practiced ease that surprised Darius until he remembered Nick's mom ran a daycare. He let Nick goo and coo and talk baby talk to Gino to his heart's delight. Then at three, he had Mrs. Tucker show Nick to his room and gave him time to unpack.

The second he and Whitney were alone in the den, he caught her by the waist, hauled her against him and kissed her soundly.

"What was that for?"

"I've been wanting to do that all day."

She giggled, and intense, primal need punched at him. At first he considered it arousal, then he realized it wasn't physical as much as emotional. When she giggled she looked young, cheerful, as if he'd all but erased the horrible years she'd just gone through, and that knowledge brought a lump to his throat. She was beautiful, happy, wonderful and his for the taking. He didn't know how long they'd last, but he did know they were good for each other. He was as good for her as she was for him, and that made him proud in the weirdest male way.

A way he'd never felt before. A way that sent an odd niggling of something cruising through him. Not fear. Not doubt. But *something*.

Before he could think it through, Mrs. Tucker walked into the room and Whitney jumped back, the way she always did when they got caught.

"I'm sorry to disturb you, Mr. Andreas, but you received a call from your brother, Cade, during lunch. He didn't want to ruin your meal by forcing you to come to the phone, and simply asked me to let you know he'll be arriving earlier than he'd planned."

"Okay, that's great."

Mrs. Tucker left the room and Whitney laughed. "There wasn't a lot of enthusiasm in your voice."

There wasn't. Not just because his half-brothers were a trial, but because he and Whitney were right on the edge of taking their relationship to the next level and his brothers were ruining it.

He caught her by the waist and pulled her to him again. "Gino's asleep and Nick's occupied." He kissed her neck. "What do you say we go to the master suite and relax?"

She pulled away and smiled. "Relax?"

He pulled her back. "Making love is the ultimate relaxation."

This time when he kissed her, he didn't waste time on preliminaries. He wanted her. She wanted him. They'd already proven they were good for each other. It was time. He kissed her deeply, his tongue delving into the sweet recesses of her mouth, and she kissed him back. They were both more than ready—

Then Nick cleared his throat.

Once again, Whitney jumped away like a guilty teenager. Darius held back a curse.

"I thought you were taking a nap."

Nick laughed. "Not hardly." Having changed out of his trousers and oxford-cloth shirt, he wore jeans and a cable-knit sweater. He strolled to the pool table. Running his hand along the smooth mahogany rim, he said, "So, play much?"

Darius shrugged. "A little."

"A little," Whitney gasped. "He—"

Darius nudged her, telling her with his eyes to stop talking. "I beat Whitney. She thinks I'm a pro."

Nick smiled wolfishly. "Really? I'm not very good either."

Darius racked the balls. "Right."

Nick turned to Whitney. "Want to play?"

Whitney glanced from Darius to Nick, then back at Darius again. "I think I'll sit this one out. I have some filings to read to catch up on my work." She nodded at both men. "I'll see you at dinner."

Darius watched her go. When he faced Nick, his brother was studying him. "I'd have thought the nanny was more your type."

Darius walked over and chose a stick. "The nanny is nineteen."

"That's my point."

Rattled, Darius broke, sending the multicolored orbs in all directions. Four balls fell into pockets. "I'll take striped." He caught Nick's gaze. "And I don't chase babies."

"Just babes."

Darius set up another shot. "Something like that."

Nick leaned on his stick. "So you're staking a claim on Whitney?"

Darius took the shot. Another striped ball fell into a pocket. But he hardly noticed. Nick's question reverberated through his brain. Was that what he was doing? Staking a claim? It seemed so permanent, so settled. And he wasn't the kind to settle. He'd figured out a way to make this situation work for both him and Whitney, and he wouldn't deviate. He didn't give women false hope, or make promises he couldn't keep. That was the rule.

Yet, he didn't want his brother flirting with her, either. Even the thought sent his blood screaming through his veins.

He caught Nick's gaze. "Let's just say that for the weekend I'm staking a claim."

If Nick surprised Darius, Cade shocked him. Instead of bounding into the house in boots and trademark Stetson, he wore a tailor-made suit, white shirt, blue tie. When it came time to change for dinner, he simply took off his jacket and tie, and rolled up the sleeves of his white shirt. He raced to pull out Whitney's chair at dinner before either Darius or Nick could get to it. And he engaged her in genuine conversation, not asking about the baby, but about her job.

Darius had never asked her about her job. Yes, he knew more about her personal life, her history, than Cade did. But Cade had asked about her present and her future. What she wanted. Darius never thought beyond the day they were living.

"So someday you're going to be a partner?" Cade's question slid into the conversation as easily as the chocolate mousse slid down Darius's throat.

"Actually, someday control of the firm will probably be mine. Not only does my father own most of the firm, but I'm the oldest of the junior partners. I'll choose who rises up, who falls."

Cade laughed. "Oh, interesting. I love a woman who's not afraid of a little power."

Whitney blushed endearingly and Darius's blood pressure rose. Having both lost spouses, Whitney and Cade had a lot more in common than he and Whitney did. If Cade kept flirting, eventually he and Whitney would talk for real and they'd realize Cade was the better choice of Andreas brother for Whitney. And Darius would—

Would what? Lose her? He'd never cared if he'd lost a woman before. Why would he care now?

She dabbed her lips with a napkin and said, "It's just past eight. If we go upstairs now, we can all say good-night to Gino."

Though Cade was closer to Whitney and beat Darius to her chair, Darius was beside her in an instant. He slid his hand to the small of her back and led the way with her to the nursery.

The next morning, breakfast was peaceful. Whitney had eaten early and was out of the dining room by the time the brothers came downstairs. She knew her presence was a distraction, causing them to avoid talking to each other. Instead, Cade and Nick had kept bringing the conversation back to her and her life.

However, she wouldn't have been able to have the kind of serious, honest discussion that Cade had initiated if Darius hadn't pushed her out of her shell over the past few weeks. Standing in the kitchen, peeking through the crack between the door and its frame, watching the brothers, her heart swelled. Darius's half-brothers were rich, powerful, overconfident men who weren't making Darius's task of bringing them together easy. Yet he wasn't backing down. He might be on the brink of losing his temper, but he held it back and held his ground, trying his best to get to know his brothers without an argument ensuing. Still, it was easy to see he was tense. Tight. She wished Nick hadn't strolled into the den the day before when Darius had kissed her and asked her to go to the master suite with him.

He'd been teasing about making love relaxing him, trying to lure her upstairs, but she knew that if they'd gone upstairs, if they'd made love, they would have talked afterward. She would have leaned her head on his shoulder and brushed her hand through the hair on his chest. With their thighs entwined and their bodies sated, they would have talked. About Gino. About his brothers. About how he felt. And she would have soothed him. Because that's what she did best. She soothed him, just as he had calmed her about Gino and brought her back to the real world so she could love again—

So she could love again.

She *could* love again.

The picture of them together, tangled in sheets in the master bed, formed in her brain again, and not an ounce of fear whispered through her. Only joy. Bubbly, happy, joy.

She swallowed. A new fear trembled through her.

She loved him.

She *loved* him.

And that wasn't their deal.

When she came down to dinner that evening, Darius stood by her chair and pulled it out, not giving either of his brothers the chance to one-up him as a gentleman. She didn't know whether to smile or cry. He liked her. He absolutely wanted to sleep with her. But love? In the scant weeks they'd spent together, she doubted it. She'd fallen hard and fast because he'd brought her back from the black pit of despair. He'd shown her tenderness, kindness. She might soothe him, but that was hardly noteworthy. She'd given him no reason to *love* her. As far as Darius was concerned, except for their friendship, they were exactly where they'd been six weeks ago. Physically attracted.

Dinner was spent the same way it had been the night before, with her fielding questions. Somehow or another, both Andreas brothers seemed to know to stay away from the subject of her past. Which didn't surprise her. A few minutes on the Internet could net a person the basic facts of her life. And both were kind enough not to question her about her loss.

Cade's questions were conversational. He asked about her likes and dislikes. Nick was a lot more obvious, asking if she'd been to Europe, if she'd considered visiting the Orient. All but hinting that he'd take her anywhere she wanted to go if she only said the word.

So she bowed out of the pool game to take place after dinner. "Darius and I have spent so much time with you that I'm afraid Liz hasn't had ten back-to-back minutes to study." She made a move to rise and Cade immediately was at her back, pulling out her chair. "Plus, I don't really need dessert." She laughed softly.

All three men said their goodbyes, but Darius was looking at her curiously. Halfway up the stairs, she stopped dead in her tracks. She'd casually, happily, chosen to care for Gino. Alone. And she wasn't afraid. Memories of Layla didn't hammer through her brain. The ones that did come were soft, sweet. Easy. The kinds of things she wanted to remember. There was no pain, just sadness. She'd always feel the loss. She'd always miss her baby girl. She'd always wonder what

Layla's life might have been like. But blessed acceptance had finally come.

Tears filled her eyes and she swallowed hard. A new segment of her life had begun.

Thanks to Darius.

The man she now loved.

In the den, Darius wasn't happy when Cade turned the conversation to Whitney.

"So what's the deal with you and Ms. Ross?"

"We're co-guardians."

That made Nick laugh. "Don't even think about making a move. He's already staked a claim."

Cade laughed. "Really? You're dating?"

"No."

Cade walked up to Darius, close enough to be a silent threat. "So technically you haven't really staked a claim."

Darius's blood pressure rose again. Anger thundered through his system like fighter jets. Standing in Darius's personal space as he was, Cade might as well have come right out and said he was looking for a physical fight, not just a verbal one. And, tonight, after two days of watching Cade and Nick flirt with Whitney, Darius wasn't about to back down.

"Stay away from her."

"Why?

"Because she's only now healing from a loss. She doesn't need to hear about yours and be sad again," Darius snarled.

Nick pushed between Darius and Cade. "Hey, hey, hey! That's enough. Cade, you're here to get to know Gino. Nothing else. And, Darius, get a grip. I can understand why you're sappy—"

Darius stopped his brother with a piercing stare. "Sappy?" He was blistering mad, macho, territorial, *anything* but sappy. And he couldn't believe Nick had said that. "Is that how you see me?"

Cade chuckled. "If you mean jealous and angry and an easy mark, yes." He walked over to the wall and chose a pool cue. "If Nick or I ever need leverage, we now know that all we have to do is talk to Whitney."

Realizing the truth of what Cade said, Darius got his pool cue, cursing himself for being an idiot. Cade wasn't interested in Whitney. He'd been testing to see what pushed Darius's buttons.

"Don't make so much out of what you think you've seen. Ms. Ross and I will eventually sleep together, but you know us Andreas men. Nothing's ever permanent. If one of you stole her, I'd move on. That's our dad's legacy to us."

Taking aim at a shot, Cade said, "So she's a fling?"

Darius snorted a laugh. "What else?" The words tripping off his tongue sounded like him again, reminding him that all the jealousy, the funny feelings, the weird connections he felt with Whitney hadn't been him at all. He didn't know who he'd been when he'd said and thought that crazy stuff. But this was him. It had taken a visit from his brothers to remind him that the soft, syrupy guy he was becoming not only wasn't him, but also that guy wouldn't stand a chance with his two brothers. If he wanted to get along, he couldn't be a sap. He had to be as strong as they were.

Having changed her mind about spending the evening alone after Gino was asleep, Whitney stopped outside the den door just as Cade said, "The next time just say you want Whitney to be off limits."

Darius simply said, "I thought I had."

"Snarling and getting jealous doesn't count." Nick slapped him on the back and the pool game resumed, but Whitney stayed rooted to the spot. Darius had just told his brothers he wanted her to be off limits.

Ridiculously, her heart rose. All this time she'd been worried that Darius hadn't fallen in love the way she had, but now she wasn't so sure. The events of the past few weeks rolled through her mind. Not just the kissing, the conversations. The way they'd compromised over Gino. The way they were creating a family with Gino.

Yes, they had agreed to an affair, but today she'd realized they'd grown so much closer, gone so far beyond that, that she'd fallen in love. So maybe he was feeling it, too?

He had to be. Why else would he be jealous and snarl? She stifled a giggle. She would have loved to have seen him snarl.

She turned around and went to her bedroom where she rummaged through the things she'd brought from home, looking for something cute, something sexy, something that would tell him in just one look that she was ready. Tonight they would make love.

Unfortunately, she didn't find anything. So she settled for a silky camisole and pajama bottoms.

Opening her door, she peeked into the hall, saw no one around and tiptoed to the master suite. She hadn't heard him come upstairs yet, but when he did she would be waiting for him.

An hour later, Darius headed for the master suite. Though they seemed to have come to terms about Whitney, he and his brothers were no closer to getting along than they had been the morning of his father's death. It was frustrating and irritating, and made him so angry he wanted to ask them both to leave. They weren't really trying to get along. Each appeared only to have come to Montauk to get a closer look at Gino.

He snorted a laugh. What purpose did it serve to have them here except to raise his blood pressure?

But when he opened the door and saw Whitney sitting on the corner of his bed, like a sweet present waiting to be unwrapped, everything about his brothers fell out of his head.

She was making the move. *She* was going to seduce *him*.

"Hey."

She peeked up at him and smiled shyly. "Hey."

He wanted to rip off his sweater and jump out of his jeans on the way to the bed, but he remembered her sensibilities so he simply ambled to the bed, sat beside her.

"How'd your night go?"

"Aggravating as hell. My brothers are morons."

She laughed. "I think they both have their good points."

"Oh, you would! They fawned all over you. They're making mincemeat out of me."

She laughed. "They're testing you. That's all. It's like you're playing a real-life game of king of the mountain. You might be the oldest brother, but they've lived their lives without you. They want to make sure you know you can't push them around."

He ran his hand along the back of his neck. "Right." The urge to confide in her rose up in him. He wanted to tell her everything they'd said, all the pushing they'd done, all the ways he'd had to hold his ground.

But, with his brothers in the wing on the other side of

the house, the infernal need to tell her everything only served to remind him that they thought he was sappy. Weak. Vulnerable.

So if he really only wanted a fling with Whitney, he couldn't tell her everything. There were pieces of himself he'd have to keep to himself.

"They're cautious about the three of us becoming friends," he said simply, sliding his hand across her back. "But...I'd rather not talk about them."

He said this as he lowered his head and kissed her. Because he'd taken her by surprise, the kiss she returned was instinctive and sweeter than any he'd ever experienced.

He stopped. He didn't want sweet from her. Not tonight. All he'd ever wanted from Whitney was untamed passion. Something he could easily label. Compartmentalize. Forget.

Forget?

The word brought him up short. Angered him. He pulled away, rose from the bed and began to pace. Planning to forget Whitney pierced an arrow through his heart. Yet, how could he deny that was what he was doing? All short-term relationships were forgettable. That was why they were so easy. So uncomplicated.

But he knew Whitney was neither easy nor uncomplicated. Plus, Gino would keep them together for the rest of their lives. Still, they'd made their agreement to start an affair keeping those two things in mind. They'd planned for this. Carefully.

"I take it you're here because you're still good with a temporary relationship?"

"Yes and no."

He spun around. "Yes and no?"

"Yeah, I...um..."

Nerves took Whitney as reality sunk in. A man who'd changed his mind about an affair because he loved her wouldn't be pacing by the bed. He wouldn't be nearly crazy with nerves or confusion. He'd tell her he loved her, kiss her and seduce her.

Somehow she'd gotten all the signals mixed.

She combed her fingers through her hair. "You don't love me."

His face registered shock, then dismay. But he blinked both away before he sat beside her on the bed again.

"That wasn't our deal. But this isn't a cold, calculating thing for me either. Otherwise, we'd be naked and tangled in sheets right now. I care deeply about you. I feel so many more things than I usually feel for a woman that it scares me."

Another woman might have taken his words to heart, seen them as a stepping stone to love, but she knew Darius. He made decisions quickly, easily. If there was even a chance that he loved her, he'd know it. He'd say it.

"You have feelings, but you don't love me."

He said nothing. But the fact that he wouldn't speak spoke volumes.

Confusion overrode pain, mostly because confusion could give her the strength to walk out of the room before she burst into tears.

He caught her chin and forced her to look at him. "I thought you wanted what I wanted."

"I did."

His gazed locked with hers. "But now you don't?"

"I thought we were on the same page."

Realization sparked in his dark eyes. "You thought we were falling in love."

"I *did* fall in love."

"Oh." He squeezed his eyes shut. "Whitney, I...
I..."

She sucked in a shaky breath. "Don't stutter. Don't
stumble. Just say it. You don't love me."

He swallowed hard.

She shook her head and sprang from the bed, racing
to the door, eager to get away as tears rimmed her
eyelids.

He jumped up and followed her. "This isn't about you
or me. My father—"

She spun around. "Don't!" Her sharp voice stopped
him. "Don't come after me and don't blame this on your
family, your genes. This isn't about genes. It's about
choices. Your dad might have been a runaround, but
that was his choice. You said we were going to build
this relationship on honesty. Then you can at least be
man enough to say you don't like me enough to choose
me."

"You don't understand—"

"No. *You* don't understand. If you loved me, you
wouldn't be able to resist. A commitment wouldn't scare
you. So, no, Darius, you do not love me."

With that she walked out of the room. Pain dulled her
senses, but not her brain. She slipped into the nursery
where she quietly packed Gino's duffel and diaper bags.
She gathered his bottles and cereal from the kitchen.
Then she woke Darius's driver and Liz. Before the sun
rose, she and Liz were in the living room of her Soho
loft and Gino slept soundly in his carrier.

CHAPTER TWELVE

DARIUS WOKE THE NEXT MORNING feeling like a man with a hangover. His head ached. His eyes thumped. Every muscle in his body hurt. He knew he hadn't had enough to drink to make him feel like a man who'd been run over by a train. Lack of sleep most likely had caused the aches and pains and thumping.

After his fight with Whitney, after she'd stormed out, he'd gone to the shower, hoping to give her twenty minutes or so to calm down before they talked again. He stood under the cold water for God only knew how long. But he'd had to spend a lot more time than he'd anticipated for the arousal thundering through his blood to dissipate. By the time it had and he returned to his bedroom, the house was quiet.

Relief had fluttered through him. He'd hated having hurt her, but he knew that if she'd fallen asleep that easily she'd be fine. Of course, he'd also realized that she could be awake across the hall and he wouldn't hear her. So he'd paced, listened for sounds that she was awake, listened for any indication that she'd gone downstairs for cocoa. Hoping they could talk again. But he'd never heard a sound.

That's when he'd started dealing with memories. She'd been everywhere in his house, even his bedroom.

He could picture her laughing, frightened, courageously walking over to take Gino from Liz. And every memory seared his heart, made him feel like a bastard for leading her on. But he hadn't led her on. He'd been honest. Fair. She was the one who'd broken their deal.

Now, *he* had to deal with the mess that caused. All the while she'd be two steps away, or a few rooms away. And the pain evident on her face would be his fault this time. Not a dead husband's.

He slid out of bed and into sweatpants and a T-shirt and forced himself into the nursery. Liz was nowhere around and the crib was empty. He hated the relief that flooded him at the obvious reprieve he was getting, until he saw an envelope leaning against a stuffed bear on the dresser. He walked over to it and opened it.

I've changed my mind about living at Montauk. I've taken Gino and Liz to the city. You may, of course, visit any time. Simply call before you want to see Gino. We'll see my father to get a custody agreement drawn up.
Whitney

Darius expected anger to roll through him. How dare she take the baby? Instead of anger, though, something squeezed his heart.

Before he could even think about that, the nursery door opened. Nick stepped inside and immediately walked to the crib. "Where's the baby?"

The nursery door opened again. This time Cade walked in. "Hey." He glanced at the crib. "Where's Gino?"

Darius waved the note. "Apparently Whitney took him back to the city."

Both Nick and Cade glanced over at him. Nick's eyebrows rose. Cade frowned. "What did you do?"

Darius tossed the note to the dresser. "What makes you think I did something?"

"Because that line you fed us last night about only wanting to sleep with her was pure rubbish."

Nick laughed. "Right. That was really kind of priceless."

Cade all but rolled with laughter. "I know! Any idiot could see he was smitten."

Fury at both of them rumbled through Darius like thunder before a dangerous storm.

"I was not smitten."

Nick said, "You were."

"And what makes the two of you experts? We are all three Andreas men. I know how we are."

Nick shook his head with a chuckle. "You keep telling yourself that. You keep telling yourself that you can't love her or be faithful or whatever it is you tell yourself and see how far that gets you."

Whitney awakened around ten to sunlight filtering in through the wall of windows in her condo bedroom and the sound of Gino crying. She popped up and was at the drawer-made-crib beside her bed in seconds, hoping not to disturb Liz.

"Hey little guy," she crooned, reaching for a clean diaper. "Just let me take care of this and we'll get a bottle."

Liz groggily walked into the room. "I'll get the bottle."

"I'm fine. Why don't you go back to sleep?"

Liz looked at her compassionately. "We're both exhausted. So why don't we share duties until we can both get a nap?"

Whitney smiled. Now that Darius had helped her out of her grief, it didn't seem wrong to accept another person's help. "Okay."

Liz left the room and Whitney changed Gino's diaper. Knowing Liz would need a minute to warm the bottle, she lifted Gino out of the drawer and held him. Close. Because she could. Because she was stronger now.

But memories of the days she'd spent with Gino and Darius assaulted her. She couldn't believe a man who'd so sensitively brought her back to life could believe he wasn't capable of fidelity...of love.

It made no sense, but she wasn't a dewy-eyed school-girl anymore. Darius had been very plain and very clear in his intentions. She was the one who'd gone too far.

And now she was paying the price. She might be stronger. She might finally have the ability to love again. But being able to love had put her in the line of fire for another kind of heartache.

Different from having lost Burn and Layla, this pain rattled through her like a restless ghost with a chain, called her a fool, reminded her that loneliness took many forms, reminded her that when Darius could have chosen her, he'd stepped away, not even wanting to try.

CHAPTER THIRTEEN

SUNDAY MORNING, after walking his brothers to the limo that would take them to the airport, Darius stepped into his huge house and closed the door. The front foyer echoed around him. Empty. Hollow.

He knew the feeling because it mimicked the one in his chest. He swore that without Gino in the nursery and Whitney working in the first-floor office, there was a hole where his heart should be.

Which was foolish. He was damned near forty. With the exception of Jen, he'd never had a relationship that had lasted over four months. He was a scoundrel. A louse. He'd hurt Whitney because he'd selfishly assumed they were on the same page romantically. True, they'd had an agreement but he should have seen the signs that she wanted something more. He should have realized she was falling in love. He knew she was delicate. He knew she deserved something more. Yet, he'd selfishly barreled on, seeking only what he wanted.

He should be shot. Not coddled. So he forced himself to work that afternoon. He took his dinner in the office because after trying to eat lunch alone, with only the ocean view for company, he felt like a man who'd been beaten with a club. He didn't want to miss Whitney, didn't deserve to miss Whitney, but he did.

Monday morning in the limo, he thought about the day he kept bumping toes with her and he laughed, then his chest seized with pain. She brought out the stupidest damned urges in him. He should be glad she was gone. Glad he'd dodged the bullet. Glad he hadn't actually slept with her and really hurt her.

Instead all he felt was lonely. Hurt. Alone.

On Thursday, after having spent the week at the office avoiding her, he realized he could get Gino for the weekend. That lifted his spirits, but the fact that he'd have to talk to Whitney to get permission lifted them more.

He told himself that was stupid as he walked down the hall to her office. It was best for the two of them to stay out of each other's way until the whole heartache thing was over with. He shouldn't want to see her. Still, he wanted Gino for the weekend and he was halfway to her office.

So he continued down the corridor, but as he stepped into her office he saw her desk was empty.

Her assistant walked up behind him. "She now works afternoons for Montgomery, Ross and Swaggart."

"The deal was—"

Maisey Lenosky, a tall brunette who'd worked for his dad for decades, looked at him over the top of her glasses. "If you're not happy, take this up with her. I'm not your go-between. But trust me, had I been in her shoes I'd have gone, too."

Fear sliced through him. "She told you?"

"She didn't have to. I could see for myself you hadn't given her any work all week. So she went back to the job that did."

Relief replaced the fear in a dizzying wave. "Oh. Okay. I'll call her."

He didn't wait for Maisey's reply, simply headed for his office. He dialed the number for Whitney's cell phone and immediately went to voice mail. So he dialed the firm and asked to be put through to her. Instead he got her assistant.

If it were anyone other than Whitney, he'd wonder about getting the run-around. But she was too serious, too honest, to dodge him. She would know he was calling to make arrangements for Gino and she'd accommodate him.

"I'd like Ms. Ross to call me back."

"May I ask what this is about?"

He wanted to say no, if only because it annoyed him to be jumping through hoops with staff, but he said, "Yes. We share custody of my half-brother. I would like to take him to my house in Montauk this weekend."

"That's great. I'll give her the message."

Ten minutes later, Whitney's assistant called back. "She says you may pick up Gino at six on Friday night and keep him until Sunday at about six."

Affront charged through him that she hadn't called him back, but he remembered that he'd hurt her and decided that this was the treatment he deserved. But on Friday night he intended to talk to her. To tell her he was sorry. Truly sorry. So that she could move on. So *they* could move on.

Friday night, Liz answered the concierge call that let him up to Whitney's apartment. He tried not to be on pins and needles about seeing Whitney again, but it was no use. He desperately wanted to ease the pain of the hurt he'd caused her.

So when he stepped into the apartment and Liz immediately handed him the diaper bag and headed for the door, he stopped dead in his tracks. "Where's Whitney?"

"Dinner with her parents. She just left." Liz smiled patiently. "And I'd like to get going so I can get a few hours to study tonight."

He took the hint and left the apartment, following Liz to his limo. But the weekend without Whitney was strained. Though Liz was bright and perky and very happy to stay and play with Gino and Darius the way Whitney had, it wasn't the same.

At night, he stared out the window at the dark ocean, brooding, angry with himself. What made him different from his father was that he didn't hurt the women he romanced. And he hadn't intended to this time, but he had, and that knowledge kicked around inside him. His chest ached. His soul mourned. He wasn't the kind of man who hurt women. Knowing that he had hurt Whitney was killing him.

Sunday night, Whitney wasn't around when he returned Liz and Gino to her apartment. He'd expected that. If he were angry with himself for how he treated Whitney, then how could he expect Whitney to be any less so?

Monday morning, he dressed carefully. Dark suit, white shirt, red tie. It was the first time in his adult life he could remember being worried about his appearance, but concern over the way that he'd hurt Whitney was eating him up. He longed to apologize, to make things right, and this morning he would so that he could get rid of this awful pain.

But when he reached Whitney's office, Maisey sat behind her desk.

"Where's Whitney?"

"She switched her schedule." Maisey sat forward,

smiling at him. "In fact, even she isn't sure what days she's working mornings and what days she's working afternoons."

"She's avoiding me."

"No, actually, her father has given her lead chair in a civil suit. She's very excited."

So was he. He knew how much she loved her work. "Really! That's great."

"She's like a kid at Christmas."

That did not hit him as happily as the first comment did. She wasn't missing him. Didn't care that he was out of her life. Not that he wanted her to be suffering. So this news should have made him feel better. Instead, he felt worse. Rumpled. As if he were an old shirt she'd taken off, rolled into a ball and tossed into the laundry.

Which was foolish. He wanted her to be happy. So why did the news that she was moving on make him feel worse?

Tuesday, he didn't go to work. He took the important phone calls at home and spent most of his day reading financial reports. He didn't shave. He didn't eat. The dining room was now an unholy place of torment. There was no baby to amuse him, no conversation to offset the sound of the pounding surf.

Wednesday morning, he was again in his home office, supposedly reading, but actually alternating between staring at the fire and staring at the ocean. It took him completely by surprise when Mrs. Tucker entered the room.

"You have a phone call."

"I told you I'm not taking calls."

"It's your brother." She smiled. "The sweet-talker."

Darius sighed. "That would be Nick."

She left the room and he yanked the phone from the cradle. "What do you want?"

"Oh, touchy."

"I don't have time to horse around Nick. I have—" Actually, he had nothing. He couldn't focus. He didn't want to focus. He didn't know what he wanted.

"You miss her."

Of course he missed her. What an asinine statement. "I hurt her."

Nick had the audacity to laugh. "Oh, Darius. It sounds like she hurt you more."

"I feel bad because I know I made her feel bad."

"Really?"

"Yes."

"You don't feel bad yourself?"

"Of course I feel bad. I just told you. I hate that I hurt her."

"And that's what's making you stay home?"

"That and the fact that I don't want to shave."

Nick laughed merrily. "Darius! Have you never had your heart broken before? You sound just like me when my ex-wife Maggie left. I couldn't eat. I couldn't sleep. I stared at the damned ocean all day."

Darius said nothing.

"Is that what you're doing?"

Darius scowled.

"Darius?"

"Yes, all right!" Darius snarled. "I've been at home for two days, not shaving, not eating, staring at the ocean. Let's not make a big deal out of it."

"Why not?"

Why not? Darius was just about to slam down the phone or thunder a retort, until he realized he had no retort. He ached. He missed Whitney. Not the way he'd miss a girlfriend who couldn't make it to the house for a weekend. Not the way he missed a lover who'd brushed him off. But like…like part of his life. When she'd walked out the door, his future had changed. He hadn't realized it, but in the weeks they had lived together, he had begun to picture Whitney helping him raise Gino. He'd seen them as Gino's parents. He'd seen them together, happy, for years…without even realizing he was doing it.

He missed her, longed for her, because she was the part of himself he'd been missing. And he finally saw that maybe, just maybe, he hadn't been a philanderer because he liked women—well, that was part of it. But in reality, after Jen had hurt him, he hadn't wanted to go through that pain again, so he'd been biding his time, entertaining himself, until he found the right woman. Someone he could trust with his heart.

And he'd found her.

He'd found the right woman.

And he'd lost her.

"Go get her."

Nick's advice sounded so simple, so easy. But Darius knew better. Or maybe he didn't. After Jen, he'd never wanted a woman back, never tried to get one back. He had no frame of reference for what to expect. She could welcome him with open arms. She could slash him to ribbons. Worse, she simply might not want him. She'd said she loved him, but what if he'd killed that love?

Intense pain rumbled through him. Seized his lungs. Burned his soul. He'd never gone to a woman without the confidence of knowing she wanted him. He'd be laid bare. Defenseless. He wasn't sure he could do it.

"She's lead chair in a big civil suit. I can't just walk

into a courthouse and pluck her out. Especially since I haven't shaved."

"How about this?" Nick said, his voice unexpectedly kind. "Shower, shave and stop at a florist. Buy an armload of roses. Then go to her apartment. Liz is there with the baby, right?"

"Yes."

"Well, Liz will let you in and Whitney's got to get there sometime."

That was true. "If I know Whitney, she won't work late. She might bring two armloads of files home, but she'll get home on time, relieve Liz, spend time with Gino, then she'll work."

"So now you know what time to go. Don't spend the rest of the day brooding. Think about what you'll say, but don't over-rehearse." Nick paused. "And call me tomorrow and let me know how it went."

Darius blinked. Had Nick just asked him to call him?

It had never occurred to Darius that having his brother's support would lift his spirits or give him a weird kind of courage, but it did. "Okay. I will." He stumbled over the agreement, but when it came out it was surprisingly easy. "Thanks."

Whitney took a cab from the office to her home. She yanked out two briefcases full of work, set them beside her on the sidewalk and paid the driver.

When she turned, Jake, the young concierge, was lifting her briefcases. "Evening, Ms. Ross."

"Good evening, Jake."

There was a gleam in his eye. An unholy sparkle. The force of it hit Whitney in the stomach and sent little pricks of misery through her. Jake liked Liz. Liz liked

Jake. They were about the same age, both attending university. They were a good match. She should have been happy.

Instead, their attraction reminded her of how foolish she'd been.

"I'll ride with you," Jake said, when Whitney attempted to take the briefcases as they reached the elevator.

She smiled. "Of course. Thank you." She wouldn't punish Jake for being a good guy who'd found a girl he really meshed with. But she would continue to remind herself that it had been stupidity to think the likes of Darius Andreas would fall for her and commit. She'd genuinely believed he'd fallen. But he hadn't. She had to get over that.

And she would. After she wallowed in misery for a few weeks over Darius. But that was good. It would teach her not to be so naive again.

When she opened her apartment door, the scent of clam chowder greeted her. Her mouth watered. By the time she turned around to thank Jake, he was gone. Her two briefcases sat in the open doorway, but he was nowhere in sight.

She grabbed the briefcases and pulled them into the condo, toward the table where she would work. "Liz?"

No answer. She walked to the kitchen area and snapped off the burner beneath the bubbling soup.

"Liz?"

No answer again.

Panic struck her heart. There hadn't been food bubbling on the stove when she'd arrived home the night she'd discovered Burn and Layla in the garage. But she had walked into a silent home when she'd been expecting to enter a house filled with the noises of a toddler and her overworked dad.

Terrified now, she pivoted and would have raced back to the bedrooms, but as she turned, Darius came out of her bedroom, Gino on his arm.

"Sorry."

Her heart stopped. Her brain turned to mush. Intense relief flooded her, but before it fully registered, the sight of Darius turned her knees to rubber and her heart to a swampy pool of emotion. He looked tired. Awful. His hair went in four different directions. He hadn't shaved—for days, she would guess from the growth on his chin and cheeks.

"Don't worry. I showered."

His comment was so unexpected that a laugh burst from her chest. But she caught it after one quick giggle. This man had hurt her. True, it was partially her fault— okay, mostly her fault for assuming things he'd never said—but she didn't want to get hurt again. She wanted to recover. Which meant he couldn't simply come into her home and take over the apartment.

"I thought you were supposed to call and arrange visits?"

"I did. I called Liz. She actually needed some time to go to the library. She was happy I could watch Gino this afternoon."

"You've been here all afternoon?"

"And I brought soup from Cook as a peace offering." He strolled a little farther into the apartment. "She also gave me a pan of lasagna for tomorrow."

Her mouth watered, but she caught herself. Even if his motivation was good—happy, healthy Gino sat on his arm like a contented angel—and he'd brought food, she couldn't pretend everything was okay between them.

Yes, she knew eventually she had to get along with him. But it was too soon. She wanted the time to heal, and by God she was taking it.

"I'm sorry, but—"

"Nick suggested I bring roses," he said, talking over her as he walked to the stove. He winced. "Thank you for catching the chowder before it boiled over. I'm not good at cooking." He winced again. "My mom would be so mad that I forgot everything she taught me." He produced a small piece of paper. "Cook wrote out instructions for how to heat the lasagna tomorrow."

It finally struck her that he intended to be here tomorrow and righteous indignation roared to life inside her. Her heart hardened. She would not let this man worm his way into her life when she needed time to heal.

"Oh, no. No. No. No. You are not tricking me into letting you live here for the next year. I left Montauk for a good reason—"

"I know." He interrupted her tirade and came a little closer.

Her heart rate sped up. The breath in her lungs shivered. Every nerve ending in her body rose to the top of her skin and all but glowed with awareness. Still, her heart was hard, her determination to get over him strong. If he thought he was going to touch her and have her turn to putty in his hands—

He passed her and she spun around to see him sliding Gino into the swing behind her.

Color bloomed on her cheeks. Why couldn't her hormones realize this man didn't want her? Why did they always jump to wrong conclusions with him?

He faced her. His words were soft and sincere when he said, "I am sorry for hurting you."

Her heart melted a tiny bit. There was nothing wrong with accepting a sincere apology from a guy she had to deal with for the next eighteen years. But she also had to take care of herself. She couldn't let him work his way too far into her life or her good graces.

"That's okay. I—"

"It wasn't okay." This time when he stepped closer, she saw the hesitation in his approach.

Her head tilted in fascination. She'd never seen him fearful before. Even when he'd never in his life as much as held a baby, he'd jumped in and tried things with Gino. To see him wavering now was odd, a curiosity.

"I am so bad at this because I have never done anything remotely like it before."

Her heart melted a bit more. She'd loved him because he was strong, but she also loved him for his honesty. And right now that honesty was costing him. How could she not melt a little inside?

"I love you."

That took her so much by surprise that her heart totally stopped, her chest seized, her mouth fell open.

"I thought I couldn't love." He snorted a laugh. "I thought I was like my dad." He met her gaze. "Turns out I'd just never met the right woman."

She swallowed.

"Nick told me all this." He glanced at her. "He was married, you know? She left him. He told me I have all the symptoms of a broken heart, but that I was lucky." He sucked in a breath. "He thinks it isn't too late for me to apologize and ask for a second chance."

"Second chance?"

"We had a bad first chance. I did everything wrong."

"I wasn't exactly Mary Sunshine."

She saw the spark of hope blossom in his dark eyes. "You're agreeable?"

"You did say you loved me."

"So much my heart hurts."

She laughed. He opened his arms and she stepped into them. Giddy joy flooded her. Relief felt like a warm blanket. Tears welled in her eyes. She'd never believed she would feel this again. Never believed life would be so kind as to give her a second chance. But it was. A chance fresher, brighter, better even than her first, because she now knew the fragility of life upped the importance of real love.

She'd never take him for granted.

"So isn't there something you want to say to me?"

She leaned back so she could look into his eyes. "I forgive you."

"Thanks, but I was hoping for something a little better than that."

"Better than forgiveness?" she asked, teasing him because she still needed a bit of reassurance that this wasn't a dream or a trick, and that they weren't misinterpreting their situation again.

"A lot better than forgiveness. Something that stands the test of time, means we'll be there for each other... means we'll raise Gino together."

She blinked. Shock and joy crashed in her heart. "Are you asking me to marry you?"

"Depends. Are you going to tell me what I need to hear?"

Her lips trembled. She smashed them together. She refused to cry—didn't want to cry. This was without a doubt the happiest moment of her life, the precipice of a new beginning, a second chance at everything, not just love, but babies, a soul mate, a home…an adventure.

She sucked in her breath, raised to her tiptoes, and said, "I love you, too, as her lips met his."

EPILOGUE

THE WEDDING TOOK PLACE in June at the house in Montauk. Darius's two brothers stood up for him as groomsmen. Whitney's two closest friends were at her side. She wore white—a simple strapless silk dress that caressed her curves—and carried roses. Her blond hair had been piled into a careless stack of curls on top of her head with tiny roses scattered between the loops.

Liz and Jake sat in the front row with her parents. Gino arched from her mom to Liz and back to her mom again until he realized Darius and Whitney were only a few feet away from him. Then he screeched and howled until the preacher stopped the service.

Darius laughed. "I'll get him."

He took the few steps over to Whitney's mom, and Gino all but flew into his arms. At nearly a year old, he was a handful, especially when he preferred walking to being held. Dressed in a little tux that matched those of Darius and his brothers, Gino easily could have been the most handsome brother.

Except to Whitney there was no one more handsome, more attractive, more wonderful than Darius. As she thought that, tears filled her eyes, but Gino picked that precise moment to launch himself at her. She caught him just in time.

The hundred or so guests in the ballroom of the Montauk house laughed.

Darius turned to the crowd. "Does anybody have a cookie?"

Mrs. Tucker bounced out of her chair. Wearing a pretty yellow suit, with her hair tucked into a French twist, she looked more like an aunt than his house manager. She produced a cookie from her suit pocket.

"I'm always prepared."

The crowd laughed again. Gino took the cookie and Darius settled the little boy on the crook of his arm.

"We can go on now."

The preacher smiled. Whitney slid her hand into the crook of Darius's elbow. The papers had been filed for Whitney and Darius to adopt Gino. They'd no longer be custodians, but parents. As Gino contently munched on his cookie, Whitney and Darius said the vows that officially made them man and wife.

Gino's parents.

Gerry and Julia Ross's daughter and son-in-law.

Nick and Cade's brother and sister-in-law.

A family.

Darius would never spend another Christmas alone.

SECOND
CHANCE BABY

BY
SUSAN MEIER

CHAPTER ONE

"Your ex-wife applied for the job as your assistant."

Nick Andreas glanced up at his current assistant, soon-to-be-retired Julie Farnsworth. He'd just flown back to North Carolina after six weeks in New York City. He was exhausted and wanted nothing more than to go to his beach house, get out of his monkey suit and take a nap on his hammock. He'd only popped into the office because he had a huge bid due to renew the government contract that was the bread and butter of his manufacturing plant. He had to get an assistant in now.

He just wasn't sure hiring Maggie Forsythe as Julie's replacement was the best way to go. When he had a bid due, his assistant worked with him—*directly with him, at his side*—ten hours a day, six days a week. No man wanted to spend that much time with his ex-wife. Not even an ex-wife he hadn't seen in fifteen years. An ex-wife he barely remembered.

He tossed his pen to his desk. "You wouldn't be telling me this if she wasn't qualified."

"She's qualified. Overqualified in some respects."

"And she actually applied?"

"Well, we certainly didn't drag her in off the street."

He laughed and leaned back in his chair. So Maggie wanted to work for him? He smiled skeptically as weird feelings assaulted him. He hadn't thought about Maggie Forsythe in over a decade. Now, suddenly, he could vividly recall how the sun would catch her red hair and make it sparkle, her wide, happy smile, the sound of her laughter.

"Sorry if I'm finding all this a little hard to believe, but we didn't exactly part on the best of terms. Andreas Manufacturing should be the last place she wants to work."

His sixty-five-year-old assistant caught his gaze with serious dark eyes. "She needs the money."

She was broke? The way he'd been when they'd met?

Memories of his childhood and teen years cascaded through his brain like water spilling from a waterfall. Maggie at six, toothless in first grade, dividing her morning snack with him before they went into the building so no one in their class would see he hadn't brought one. Maggie at twelve, fishing with him so he and his mom could have something for supper. Maggie at sixteen, hanging out in the souvenir shop where he worked, entertaining him on long, boring afternoons before the tourist season picked up. Maggie at eighteen, swollen with his child.

A long-forgotten ache filled his chest and made him scowl. The woman he was remembering with such fondness had dropped him like a hot potato when she'd lost their baby. She hadn't loved him. She'd only married him because he'd gotten her pregnant one reckless night. Twenty minutes after they'd returned from the hospital after her miscarriage, she'd been out the door of his mom's house. Out of his life.

"She should have as many reservations about working with me as I have about working with her."

"Her stepmom died while you were in New York. Rumor has it, she came home for the funeral and decided her dad needed her. She quit her job and moved back permanently but in three weeks of looking she couldn't find work—unless she wants to commute to the city." Julie peered at him over the rim of her glasses. "Aside from tourism, you're the only real employer in Ocean Palms."

He picked up his pen again. "Hire her."

Julie gasped softly. "Really?"

"Sure. We were married as kids. Fifteen years have gone by." He wasn't such a selfish, self-centered oaf that he'd let someone suffer because she had the misfortune of having a history with him. He knew what it was like to have no options. He'd spent his entire childhood living hand-to-mouth. He wouldn't ignore the person who, as a child, had shared with him, helped him, even rescued him a time or two.

Plus, if Julie said Maggie was the person for the job then she was.

Julie rose. "Okay. She's in my office. She said she can begin today. I'll bring her in and we can get started."

Nick sat up in his seat. Today? He didn't even have ten minutes to mentally prepare?

Julie walked to his office door and opened it. "Come in, Maggie."

A true Southern gentleman, Nick rose from the tall-back chair behind his huge mahogany desk. Ridiculously, he couldn't squelch the pride that surged up in him as he took in the expensive Persian rugs that sat on the hard-wood floors of his office, the lamps from China, the heavy leather sofa and chair in the conversation area, the art from the broker in New York City. He was rich, success-ful, and his office showed it. He'd fulfilled the promise of his youth. He had brains and skill and he'd parlayed those into wealth beyond anyone's expectations. One look at his office would tell Maggie he wasn't the eighteen-year-old boy she'd deserted anymore.

The click of high heels on the hardwood announced her arrival two seconds before she appeared in his doorway. Her gorgeous red hair flowed around her, but it was shaped and curled in a way that framed her face, not straight as she had worn it when they were married. Her once sparkly green eyes now held soul-searching intensity. Her full red lips rose slightly in a reluctant smile.

Just as he wasn't the eighteen-year-old she'd left behind anymore, she didn't look a thing like his Maggie.

He relaxed as his gaze involuntarily fell from her face to her dress. A simple red tank dress that showed off a newly acquired suntan, but also couldn't hide her slightly protruding stomach.

She was pregnant?

He gave her tummy a more thorough scrutiny.

She was pregnant.

And suddenly he *was* that eighteen-year-old boy again. Seeing his woman, the love of his life, swollen with his child. More memories washed over him. The dreams he'd had for the kind of father he would be rose up as if he'd been lost in them only yesterday. Love for her, the woman bearing his child, burst in his chest.

But this wasn't his child. She'd lost their child.

And she didn't love him.

Hell, he no longer loved her.

"Come in," he said. His voice was tight with a bit of a squeak but he ignored that, motioning to the chair in front of his desk.

Maggie took a few hesitant steps inside. Now trim instead of lanky, she wore her pregnancy the same way another woman would wear a designer dress.

That was when he realized she was probably married.

Happily married. Not scared and hesitant, with no other options because her stepmom had kicked her out of the house. But happy. Having a child with the man she loved.

He swallowed the knot that formed in his throat, reminding himself that these emotions churning through him were ridiculous. He was over her. Plus, they hadn't even seen each other in fifteen years. The feelings weren't really feelings. They were residue. Like cobwebs that had clung to the walls of his brain and would disappear once he got to know the adult Maggie.

"Julie wants to hire you but I have a few reservations."

He didn't even try to stop the words that flowed from his mouth. Though he'd already told Julie to hire her, now that he saw she was pregnant, he had some concerns. Not about the "feelings" seeing her pregnant aroused, but about her ability to do the job.

She gracefully sat on the chair in front of his desk, smiled softly. "You mean because we were once married?"

He snorted a laugh, but Julie's hand flew to her throat. "You know, I think I'll just go get us some coffee."

Nick said, "She can't drink coffee," at the same time that Maggie said, "I don't drink coffee."

Julie said, "Then I'll get some coffee for myself." She fled the room, closing the door behind her.

Nick sat back in his chair, reaching deep inside himself for the calm that was his trademark. He had to treat her as any other employee and speak accordingly.

"For the next four weeks I need my assistant to work ten-hour days."

"Six days a week. I get that. Julie told me."

"Can you keep up?"

"Of course I can keep up. I'm pregnant not sick."

The room plunged into eerie silence. Memories of

the day she'd lost their baby haunted him like menacing ghosts.

As if recognizing where his thoughts had gone, Maggie sighed. "Nick, I'm fine. Really. And I need this job. If you don't hire me I'll have to get work in the city and commute an hour each way."

"An hour commute might be better for a pregnant woman than racing around the plant looking for documents I need, assembling information from different departments—"

He paused to catch her gaze and when he saw green eyes sparking with fire, everything he intended to say fell out of his head. He remembered that look very well, remembered how many times it had taken them straight to bed.

"I already told you I can keep up."

He took in a quiet breath, reminding himself that Maggie was a married woman who wanted to work for him. The last thing he needed to be thinking about was how her fiery need for independence had played out between the sheets.

"Yeah, well, maybe I want some kind of proof."

She smiled sweetly, calmly. "In a couple of months, I'm not going to be pregnant anymore. Then you're going to be sorry you lost the chance to hire me."

A laugh escaped. Dear God. This really was his Maggie. Fiery one minute, serene the next. And the common sense, logical Maggie could be every bit as sexy as the impassioned one.

But she was married.

And he was a runaround now.

Having a father who'd abandoned him had made him want commitments, but Maggie leaving him had set him straight on that score. And he'd changed. He wasn't simple Nick Roebuck anymore. The guy who hadn't taken his father's name. The guy who wanted commitments. A wife. Family. Nope. Nick Roebuck was gone. He was now Nick Andreas, playboy.

"Besides, my father needs me."

Shifting in his chair, Nick blew his breath out in a gusty sigh. Who he was didn't matter. Who she was didn't matter. She was off-limits. "I'm sorry about your stepmom."

"Thanks."

"I was out of town or I would have paid my respects."

Her gaze dipped. "I know."

"Was everything—you know—okay?" He nearly bit his tongue for his clumsiness. But what could he say? How could he ask if she and Vicki had mended fences? If they'd ever gotten beyond the fact that Vicki had favored Charlie Jr. over her? If Vicki had ever forgiven Maggie for getting pregnant? If Maggie had ever forgiven Vicki for kicking her out of the house?

"It was fine." She shrugged. "Losing someone is always hard."

Which told him nothing. Not that it was any of his business. He scrambled for something safe to say, but the only thing he could think of was, "Yeah. My father died last January. I know how hard these things can be."

She smiled and her eyes brightened. "Oh, so you met your father? You had a relationship?"

"Yes and no." He tapped his fingers on the edge of his desk, tamping down the sudden, unexpected urge to tell her everything. They weren't friends anymore. She might act like the girl he'd known and loved, but she wasn't. And he wasn't the lovesick boy she'd married.

Still, he couldn't ignore her question. "I met my father but we didn't really have a relationship. Unless you call having dinner every other year a relationship."

"That's too bad." Genuine regret colored her voice. "So how's your mom?"

He chuckled. "She's just like a little general at the daycare. Loves the kids, but keeps them in line."

Maggie's laugh was quick and easy. "God I've missed her."

"We missed you." The words slipped out and he knew why. He was getting comfortable with her. And that was wrong. If they were going to work together, he had to draw lines. Be professional.

She looked away. "No point in staying once I'd lost the baby."

Hearing her say that now hurt almost as much as it had the day she'd left. "Right."

"Before I got pregnant, we both had plans."

"Is that what you were thinking about while I was talking to my father's attorney?" For years he'd wondered. What kind of coincidence could it have been that the dad who'd ignored him his entire life suddenly wanted to give him a trust fund? Had it been a gift from fate to Maggie, or a curse of fate for him?

She caught his gaze. "Yes."

When his heart squeezed, he swore at himself inwardly for asking the stupid question. He'd already reasoned all this out in his head. Gotten beyond it. There was no point going over it again. Certainly no point rehashing it with her. Fifteen years had passed and he loved the life he'd built without her.

If they were going to work together, the past would have to be forgotten. His only goal should be to make sure she really did have the education and experience to do the job.

"So you have a business degree?"

"Yes." She shifted on the chair. Her shoulders went

back. Her expression became businesslike. "But I'm not looking down on this job. I think there are a lot of ways I can help you."

"What did you do at your last job?"

"I was an analyst for a firm that put venture capitalist groups together with struggling businesses looking for investors or a buyer."

"Do you know much about manufacturing?"

She laughed. "Most of the businesses looking for investors or buyout are manufacturing companies."

He tapped his pen on the desk. He needed somebody and, as Julie said, Maggie was qualified. Now he and his ex-wife would be spending ten hours a day, six days a week together.

He looked over at her just as she looked at him and the years between them melted away. Her eyes weren't as wary as they had been when she'd walked in the door. Her smile was genuine.

Doubt rumbled through his soul. In the sea of women that he'd dated since he'd hit puberty, she was the only one he'd loved. It had taken almost five years to really get beyond her leaving; years before he stopped hoping every ring of the phone was her calling; years before he stopped looking for her in crowds. One five-minute conversation had already brought an avalanche of memories. This was not going to be easy.

Suddenly the door opened and Julie walked in. "Human Resources called. Before Maggie can actually begin working, she's got to spend the afternoon with them, filling out papers. You won't get to work together until tomorrow."

Maggie said, "Oh."

Nick said, "I hadn't planned on starting on the bid until tomorrow anyway."

Julie motioned for Maggie to follow her and she rose and walked out the door.

He dropped his head to his hands. After weeks of running the multibillion-dollar shipping conglomerate owned by his family, he needed this day out of the office to relax before he jumped into the intense work of the bid.

But the hammock was out. Stirred as his memories were, he'd never sleep. His best bet would be to take a long drive down the coast.

When he was sure Maggie and Julie were halfway to the Human Resources office, he rose from his desk, grabbed his keys and cell phone and headed out.

Five hours later, Maggie Forsythe walked out into the scorching June day and took a quiet, measured breath to calm herself. She'd been so confident when she'd applied for the job as Nick Andreas's assistant. Fifteen years had passed. Plus, her ex-husband, Josh, had done a number on her. The absolute last thing she wanted in this world was to get involved with another man. Yet, when she'd looked at Nick her heart had stopped. Her breathing had stalled. It was as if she was eighteen again and he was hers.

She blew out a frustrated sigh and reminded herself that one person could not possess another. Nick had never really been hers. Just as Josh had never really been hers. Oh, her ex had made the commitment with vows before a clergyman, but he'd cheated on her. And when she'd confronted him, he'd simply left, saying he liked the other woman better.

The sting of the pain of the loss of her marriage rose up in her hot and fresh. She pressed her key into the ignition of her car. She should be immune to men. Forever. But spending a mere five minutes with Nick had caused her brain to fill with memories of happier times. In the fifteen years that had passed, she'd forgotten how much she'd loved him. How gorgeous he was with his curly black hair and nearly black eyes. How commanding.

Calling herself every kind of fool, she pulled her gear-shift into Drive. It didn't matter how attracted she was to Nick Andreas. If she couldn't keep a forty-year-old bald-ing lawyer, she certainly didn't have to worry that she'd somehow attract a thirty-three-year-old gorgeous Greek god. Especially since she'd dumped Nick. For all the right reasons, but she'd still dumped him. Broken his heart. There was no way his pride could get beyond that.

She reached her dad's farm and climbed the front porch steps. After a few seconds of searching, she found her dad in the kitchen.

"How'd it go?" His wet hair had been slicked back as if he'd just come from the shower. His plaid shirt and jeans appeared to be clean. The fact that he'd come in from the fields and showered was a good sign. But there were still shadows in his eyes. Just because he'd had a good day today, it didn't mean he would have a good day tomorrow. That's why she had to stay. His good days might be good, but his bad days were awful.

She smiled. "I got the job."

Surprise flickered across her dad's weathered face. "Well, of course you did. You and Nick have always been friends. There's no reason to believe you wouldn't be friends now."

She turned away. Her dad had always believed that she and Nick had only married because she'd gotten pregnant and when she'd lost the baby there was no reason to be married anymore. He didn't know—no one knew—that the day she'd left Nick, she'd overheard his father's lawyer offer him a five-million-dollar trust fund, as long as he ended their marriage, and overheard Nick refuse.

Emotionally overwrought over losing their baby, she'd made a decision she'd known would hurt him. At the time, she'd believed it for the best, and she actually still believed that. Nick had become the man he never could have been if she'd selfishly let him throw away his trust fund by staying married to her. So she'd packed her bag and gone.

Grabbing an apple from the bowl on the table, she pushed all that out of her mind. It was ancient history. Of no consequence and certainly not something she'd tell a man who'd just lost his wife.

"You should see his office. Everything's sleek, sophisticated, wonderful."

"That's the rumor." Her dad ambled to the refrigerator and pulled out fresh vegetables for a salad. "He's got more money than the rest of the people in town combined."

Pride swelled within her. He'd become as successful as she'd known he could be. Her only real regret was that she'd had to lead Nick to believe she hadn't ever loved him, only married him for their baby. Otherwise, he wouldn't have let her leave. She'd never had a doubt she'd done the right thing, but she also knew her choice meant he'd never again love her.

But she didn't want him to love her. Thanks to her ex, she knew the truth about love. Most of the time it wasn't love at all; it was lust. And even if it was real love, real love died. And when real love died, people were left alone.

Except she wasn't really alone. Her father and new baby needed her. She had a job. A real second chance at a life in the small town she'd loved.

It was smarter to appreciate those things, than to pine for what couldn't be.

CHAPTER TWO

NICK's cell phone rang just as he pulled his Porsche into the garage beneath his beach house. Though it was only a little after five, he'd taken a two-hour drive, made a stop at a crab shack for a late lunch/early dinner, spent another hour walking on a rough, undeveloped stretch of beach and then made the drive home.

And he still didn't feel any better about hiring Maggie.

He turned off the ignition and snatched the phone from the seat beside him. Glancing at the caller ID he saw it was his older brother Darius.

"Hey, old man. What's up?"

"I need you to fly to Saudi Arabia and meet with the prince."

"Me?"

"Since you took my place while Whitney and I were on our honeymoon, you're up-to-date on everything. Plus, you're family. The prince will only meet with family and I can't go right now. Gino is just getting accustomed to having me and Whitney home again. I can't leave him."

Climbing out of his car, Nick winced. He understood that Gino, their one-year-old half brother in Darius's custody, had missed Darius and Whitney, but he couldn't do anything for Andreas Holdings until he got his own bid done.

"You're going to have to call Cade."

"Cade?"

Nick smiled at the resistance in his older brother's voice.

"He hates me."

"Nah, he just doesn't subscribe to Dad's theory that the eldest should rule the family empire." He rifled through his trouser pocket for his keys and unlocked the door that led him to a short flight of stairs. "Being a pain in the ass is his way of keeping you in line."

"What? Raising our baby brother, being newly married and running a global entity isn't enough?"

Nick laughed and tossed his briefcase onto the counter of the butler's pantry that led to the kitchen. Black granite countertops offset by a shiny metallic backsplash and sleek oak cabinets greeted him.

"No one said deciding to be brothers for real would be easy."

Darius sighed. "Yeah, and I guess it's better than all of us pretending the others don't exist."

Nick grunted in agreement. Their dad had been a run-around. Unfaithful to Darius's mom with both Nick and Cade's moms. Only Darius had been acknowledged and that had made things very sticky when their dad had died. But they'd pushed through it.

"That's why I feel free to call you for help," Darius said, bringing the conversation back to his point.

"I can't get away now. The bid is due for the contract that keeps my company afloat. Plus, I just hired a new assistant."

"So you finally hired someone."

"Human Resources hired her."

Darius laughed perceptively. "You don't like her."

"I do like her. At one time I loved her. She's my ex-wife."

Darius coughed loudly as if choking, then said, "Only an idiot would hire an ex-wife."

"We were married as kids, remember? I was eighteen. She was pregnant. It was a long time ago. We hadn't seen each other since the day she left."

"Still, there's got to be baggage there."

He opened a cabinet, found his whiskey and a glass. "No kidding. But my back's up against the wall and she's qualified. I have to deal with it."

"Do you want my advice?"

"Do I have a choice?"

"If I were you I'd talk about the past with her. Get it out in the open and discuss it, so you don't have to waste time tiptoeing around feelings."

Pouring a glass of Jack Daniel's, Nick scowled. Just what he needed. A wonderful conversation wherein Maggie told him about finding the love of her life, getting married and now having a baby. Yeah. Right.

"Fifteen years have passed. We don't need to rehash what happened."

"It's your call, but if you find yourself doing things like drinking in the afternoon, you'll know you're in trouble."

He stopped the glass of whiskey halfway to his mouth. It was after five…sort of still afternoon but close to evening. Ah, hell. Who was he kidding? He was drinking in the afternoon.

Nick threw back the shot of Jack anyway.

Darius laughed. "You know I'm right."

Nick poured another glass of Jack. "Yes, big brother, I know you're right. But that doesn't mean I have to like it."

The next morning, Maggie was standing at a filing cabinet near the window when she saw a black Porsche pull into the front parking space and Nick climb out.

"He's here."

Julie came to attention. "Okay. Don't worry about a thing. You sort of stay behind me. Let me take the brunt of his mood today."

Maggie smiled at Julie. "You already know he's going to be in a mood?"

"An assistant doesn't work with a boss for ten years without knowing when he's going to come in in a mood."

Maggie laughed.

"He's been out of the office for six weeks. Our bread and butter contract is about to expire and we have to rebid it. I'm assuming he thought about that all last night so today he's going to be cranky."

The door of Julie's office opened and Nick walked inside. Sunglasses hid his dark eyes but that only accented his generous mouth and the scruffy day-old growth of beard he hadn't shaved. Dressed in jeans and a T-shirt with sleeves that cupped his rounded biceps—hinting to the muscled chest beneath it—he was as built as an adult as he had been as a young man.

He took off his sunglasses and his dark eyes narrowed as he looked at her. His gaze traveled from her head to the toes of her pumps. Heat suffused her. Especially when she realized he was probably looking at her because she'd been ogling him.

"You don't have to dress like that."

She cleared her throat. "Excuse me."

He waved his sunglasses at her tidy blue suit, flowered blouse and white pumps. "We're five miles from the beach. Half the staff goes surfing before work. I don't think you'll find another pair of high heels in an eight-mile radius. Wear jeans."

With that he put his sunglasses back on, pivoted and walked into his office.

Maggie turned to Julie who was having difficulty stifling a smile. "I told you he'd be in a mood."

Maggie scowled. "In Pittsburgh some women still wear panty hose to work."

Julie's face froze in an expression of pure horror. "Good God."

Maggie shook her head and laughed. "I've been Northernized."

"Well, let's at least lose the jacket. Honey, it's June. It's hot and this is a casual company. And obviously Nick feels uncomfortable with you dressed too formally." She picked up a steno pad and a stack of files and walked toward Nick's office. "Follow me."

After quickly shrugging out of her jacket, Maggie scrambled to get in step behind Julie.

"Those stacks," Julie said, pointing at six tall stacks of files on the conference table in the corner, "are everything you need to work on the new bid, but that's not the priority."

Nick nodded in acknowledgment as Julie took one of the two seats in front of his desk. Maggie quickly sat on the other.

"These," Julie said, waving her stack of files, "are the things we've ignored for six weeks. Today, they're the priority."

One by one, she handed the files in her lap across the desk to Nick. One by one, he addressed the issue. A few times he dictated emails. Once or twice he kept the file saying he'd dash off the email himself. But he never once took off the sunglasses.

When they got through the stack, Julie rose to leave. Maggie followed suit.

"Not you," Nick said, pointing at Maggie. "You stay."

Julie scurried out of the office and closed the door behind her. Nick opened the top drawer of his desk, grabbed a small bottle of over-the-counter painkillers and popped the lid. He shook some into his mouth.

"Headache?"

Raising the sunglasses, he peered beneath the lenses at her. She swallowed. In all the years they'd known each other, he'd never quite scowled at her like that. Which was good because it reminded her that they were now different people. And maybe she shouldn't be taking liberties by asking him if he had a headache.

He dropped the sunglasses to his eyes again. "Hangover. I had a—"

She held out her hand to stop him. "You don't need to tell me. I'm sorry. I'm not a nosy person. I'm not a pushy person. I don't know why I said that. It was rude."

He turned his chair sideways and leaned back. "If I didn't have a rip-roaring hangover, I'd probably lambaste you about now. It might have been fifteen years since we've seen each other, but we can't pretend we don't know each other. We do." He pulled his sunglasses down his nose and caught her gaze. "Intimately."

The way he said *intimately* caused her breath to shiver into her chest. Memories popped up like flowers in a bountiful garden and her cheeks heated. That was when she realized he'd probably said that on purpose. Trying to get a rise out of her.

"So what are you doing? Pushing us to the point where we'll yell at each other?"

"Maybe."

She gaped at him. "Really? I was being sarcastic."

"Yesterday when I told my brother I'd hired my ex-wife, he suggested we needed to talk everything out. I disagreed, but he's right. If we don't talk some of this out, we'll spend weeks being miserable, tiptoeing around each other." He leaned back in his chair. "I don't like it."

"What? You don't want to be uncomfortable so you're making me uncomfortable?"

"Think of it more like ripping off a bandage." He turned his head to look at her, but with the sunglasses on she couldn't really tell if he was looking at her or not. "You can either pull a bandage off slowly and be in pain the whole time or rip it off and be in excruciating pain, but only for a few seconds. I'll take the few seconds."

"And I don't get a vote?"

"Nope. I'm the boss. My rules. We have a bid due in four weeks. Clock's ticking. We can't afford to be miserable or even slightly uncomfortable."

"So we're going to talk?"

"I thought we'd start off with what you've been doing for the past fifteen years."

"I told you I worked for a firm that put venture capitalist groups together with struggling businesses."

"I mean personally."

Her mouth fell open. The last thing she wanted to do was tell him about her miserable marriage. But she had a feeling there was no way out of this. He was the boss. They did have a past. They couldn't pretend they weren't curious. The best she could hope for was that he had a worse story. "If I talk, you talk."

"That's actually the point."

A man who had a worse story than a miserable divorce wouldn't be so quick to agree. She glanced around at his exquisitely decorated office. "Right. I don't think you need to tell me what you've been doing. Your office sort of speaks for itself."

He grinned. "It does, doesn't it?"

Pride reared up inside her. Her marriage might have been a failure, but she wasn't. "I haven't exactly been unsuccessful. I gave up a great job in Pittsburgh to come home and be with my dad."

When she stopped talking, he made a rolling motion with his hand. "And?"

"And?"

"And what else?"

She scowled. Damn it. She didn't want to do this. Her most recent life details were not happy or even positive. She was going to look like an idiot compared to him. Maybe the best thing to do really would be Nick's bandage technique. Tell him about her life quickly, concisely and get it over with.

"Okay." She sighed heavily. "I went to college, got a job in Pittsburgh, married a lawyer—"

He winced. "Really, Maggie? A lawyer?"

Her chin rose. "Not all lawyers are cutthroat. Josh was a very nice man."

He pulled his sunglasses down again. "Was?"

"We're divorced."

His nearly black eyes searched hers, but he didn't say a word.

Still, she could see the wheels turning in his brain. The honest woman in her knew she couldn't race through the truth or even sugarcoat it.

"You want to ask how two people who created a baby could get divorced."

"Yes and no. I just sort of realized that we should have set some ground rules for this discussion. I suddenly feel like I'm prying. Overstepping boundaries." He rubbed his forehead. "I'm going to kick Darius's butt for this idea."

"It's okay." And it was. If only because it forced her to realize that she was foolish to try to pretend she could hide her bad divorce. This was a small town. People would talk. If she didn't give them the real version, they might just make up something worse. Sometimes it really was best to stick with the truth, the whole truth—

Actually that wasn't a good idea either.

Because the bottom line truth between her and Nick was that she had loved him, but led him to believe she didn't. When she'd left him, he'd asked her if she loved him and she'd avoided the question. She hadn't lied. Simply let him draw the conclusion for himself that she didn't love him.

No wonder he was having trouble dealing with her. She'd broken his heart—hurt him—by making him think everything they'd shared in their two-week marriage had been an act.

But they'd been so young.

And he'd been so broke.

They'd just lost their baby. She'd had no more reason to hold him down—hold him back.

She'd genuinely believed she was doing the right thing.

She glanced around his office again. He'd done very well for himself with the five-million-dollar trust fund his father had given him. She wouldn't apologize for making the choice he'd refused to make for himself.

"No. It's not okay." He tossed the sunglasses to his desk, an indication that the painkillers were probably beginning to work on his headache. "I'm going to call tech support and tell them to set you up so that you can go into the accounting system." He swiveled his chair until he was facing front again and picked up the receiver of his phone. "Julie will give you directions to their office. Once they get you set up, just do whatever Julie tells you to do."

He punched a few numbers into the phone. "This is Nick. I'm sending my new assistant down for passwords and access into the accounting records."

He hung up the phone and she rose.

But she paused. Her heart clenched with the achy pain of realizing that he might trust her with passwords, but personally he was wary of her. He'd given her his heart and soul and she'd rejected them. Actually by misleading him into believing she hadn't loved him, she'd made herself look like an opportunist. Making him think she didn't love him was the same as saying she'd only married him because she'd needed a place to live. That wasn't true, but that was how it appeared to him. And now he was wary of her.

Even if she told him she had loved him that wouldn't fix anything because she'd be admitting she'd deliberately misled him. If she didn't, there would always be an odd void between them.

But she had done what she believed was for the best.

She turned and walked out of his office.

Nick worked cloistered behind his closed door all day, but he couldn't concentrate. The last thing he'd expected to hear was that Maggie was divorced. Not because he'd created the image in his head that she was happily married. But because she was pregnant. When she'd told him she was divorced, his first thought had been what kind of husband—what kind of man—leaves a pregnant wife? And he hadn't been able to contain or hide his anger. So he'd hustled her off to tech support.

But almost immediately after she had gone, he remembered that Maggie had left him. He couldn't rule out the possibility that Maggie had been the one to leave her marriage. But why? Even though she hadn't loved Nick, she'd stayed with him for the sake of their baby. Hell, she'd only married him for their baby. He didn't want to believe she'd leave her husband when she was pregnant. Unless her husband had done something—

Damn it! He had to stop thinking about her! It was stupid. Ridiculous. And he shouldn't care. She was now only his assistant. Nothing more.

When Julie popped her head into his office at five and announced she and Maggie were leaving unless he needed some help that evening, he simply said goodbye. There were tons of things they could have worked on that night. Projects to get the facts and figures together for the new bid, but he hadn't been able to get himself out of the emotional frenzy he'd created. He hadn't organized anything enough to be able to assign any of the tasks.

Darius was right. Working with Maggie was going to be hard. Every little step of her past that he learned had the potential to drag him back in time and destroy the focus he needed to work. He should have kept the conversation going. He should have endured her entire story. Hell, the entire story probably would have reminded him he had no right to feel anything for her. Good or bad. Fifteen years had passed. He shouldn't even be angry with her anymore.

But he was.

Damn it.

He was.

Forty minutes after Julie and Maggie had gone, he stepped out of the building and headed for his Porsche. But he saw a tow truck loading a Chrysler Sebring. The poor sap who owned the car would be walking at least a mile because Nick had located his plant as far out of town as he could. But, in a way, finding a stranded employee was good. Doing a favor for somebody was exactly what he needed to get his mind off Maggie.

He slid inside his Porsche, tossing his briefcase behind him. After putting down the top, he drove over to the stranded driver.

"Hey," he yelled over the low hum of the Porsche's powerful engine. "Can I give you a lift?"

Maggie peered around the tow truck driver. Nick almost groaned. This is what happened when a man hired his ex-wife.

"You wouldn't mind?"

He leaned across the seat and opened the car door. "No. Come on."

Maggie said a few things to the tow truck attendant who gave her his card, then she slid onto the seat beside Nick. He waited the time it took for the driver to get into the tow truck and pull away before he followed him out of the parking lot.

"Wow. Nice car."

Stuck behind the slow tow truck, the Porsche wasn't going fast enough for the noise of the air swirling around them to impede conversation. He'd not only heard her comment, he had to answer it.

"Thanks. It was a present to myself for my thirtieth birthday."

"I hope you thanked yourself."

"Driving the car is thanks enough." He sucked in a breath. Questions bombarded his brain. And so did Darius's advice. He and Maggie would have a terrible time working together if they didn't get comfortable with each other. Fate had intervened and handed him another opportunity to be alone with her. He could either take it—and attempt to help them ease beyond their past and the awkwardness between them—or he could spend the next several weeks unable to focus or concentrate. With a bid due that wasn't an option.

"It looks like you could use a new car yourself."

"I could, but I can't afford anything like this."

"So what can you afford?"

She winced. Because they had picked up speed, she had to shout to be heard above the wind whipping by them. "Whatever I can get a loan for."

Julie had told him that Maggie was broke, but that was before he'd found out she was pregnant and divorced. Now the word *broke* took on an entirely different meaning.

"How does a woman who was married, and probably had a house and a two-income family come out of a divorce with nothing?"

"House was mortgaged. Everything else had been bought on credit or leased. Plus, my ex had run up private credit card bills. So we had to sell the house and use the equity to pay off the balances. Technically I'm not in debt, but I don't have any money, either. I'm sort of at even."

The casual way she said it teased an unexpected laugh out of him.

"Why do you think that's funny?"

"I don't think it's funny." He picked up speed. Air punched through the car now. His voice rose the way Maggie's had. "I think the way you said it is funny. You're awfully damned casual about it. I'd be spitting nails."

She caught his gaze. "I had my nail-spitting days. I really loved my ex and he didn't give two cents about me." She put her head back and for a few seconds soaked in the warm sun and the cool air that floated around her, reminding Nick of how she'd been when they were young.

Spontaneous. Full of life. "But that's over now. I'm not going to brood. My baby will be my family."

Relief rippled through him. If he was reading her correctly, she was perfectly fine. Divorced, pregnant and penniless, but fine. He had no reason to worry about her. And, even more amazing, now that they'd talked a bit, he actually felt comfortable around her. The cascading memories of their childhood had stopped. The fear that she might have been hurt and abandoned subsided. So much had changed in her life that she really did seem like a different person to him.

They wound along the stretch of road into town, then drove down Main Street. Seafood restaurants teemed with tourists eating an early supper. Souvenir shops displayed their wares on sunny sidewalks. Past the tourist district, brightly painted houses with blooming flower beds took them out of town. In what seemed like seconds, they were on the stretch of road to Maggie's dad's farm.

Sunshine poured down on them. The scent of the sea air swelled around them. They didn't speak and Nick's mind wandered back to the days when they'd ridden their bikes along this road. Happier days. When they were two kids who were friends. Real friends. Back before that one magical night when they'd gotten carried away and made love.

Love?

He nearly snorted, but caught himself. What did two eighteen-year-olds know about love? The fact that she'd left him had proven to him love didn't exist. That belief had led to a very comfortable dating life. He didn't make false commitments as his dad had. He didn't promise to be around forever and then scramble away when his current mistress got pregnant. He was honest, fair. No strings. No messy involvement. Just good times.

Which was why he'd loved being in New York the past six weeks. The boredom he'd been experiencing in a small town that didn't offer much in the way of nightlife had melted away. Thanks to Darius, he had access to a Park Avenue penthouse and an estate on Montauk. As soon as his bid was in he intended to take full advantage by flying up every weekend.

They reached the lane for the farm. He downshifted and slowly cruised to the house. As soon as the car stopped, she hopped out.

"Thanks."

He said, "You're welcome," but she was already halfway to the porch.

He frowned. She certainly was eager to get away from him. *She* was the one who had hurt *him*. Yet she was mad? Eager to get away from *him*?

He shook his head, telling himself that in a few short weeks he would be spending weekends in New York where there were plenty of women who would remind him of why he'd moved beyond the love of his life.

He rocketed out of her driveway back to the main road and the huge beach house that seemed oddly empty that night.

CHAPTER THREE

THE next day blurred into a stretch of boredom for Maggie. Nick began reviewing data for the new bid, but only called on Julie and Maggie to pull files and search for reports. Time should have passed unremarkably, except Maggie's father couldn't seem to wrap his mind around the fact that he was supposed to drive her to work and pick her up after. She'd had to trudge into the field to find him that morning, and she spent the day fearing he would forget her. At four-thirty, she called to remind him, but, of course, she got the answering machine.

But when she called again at five, she got really lucky and he picked up the phone. She arrived home at a normal time, made a quick supper of salads and hamburgers then suggested they go to the Ice Cream Shack for a treat.

As eager for a break as Maggie was, Charlie Forsythe started his old rattle-trap truck and they rumbled into town.

"Are you ever going to get a new truck?"

"No need."

"It's going to shut down completely one of these days and we won't even have basic transportation."

Her dad glanced over at her. The wind coming in through the open window tossed his graying auburn hair to the side. His green eyes sparkled. "Sure we will." He grinned. "When your car gets fixed."

She rolled her eyes. "I haven't heard from Jimmy yet. I get the feeling I'm bottom of his list."

"When did you take your car there?"

"Monday."

"You should get a call next Monday, telling you what's wrong. Then it'll probably take a week or two to fix it."

"A week or two?" Maggie groaned.

The noisy truck chugged into the overflowing parking lot of the Ice Cream Shack. Because it wasn't on the main drag, but in the back of town, tourists rarely found it and the place was packed with locals. Wooden picnic tables were set up in a cozy arrangement to the left, giving patrons an area to socialize in as they ate their sundaes and cones. In a grassy field to the right, parents and small children played Wiffle Ball, a game just like baseball except with a lightweight plastic bat and airy plastic ball. In a town filled with fun and games for tourists, it was a quiet, normal, small-town respite.

Maggie filled her lungs with the sea-scented air coming in through the open window and suddenly felt like she was home. There was no place that epitomized their small town more than the Ice Cream Shack. The sounds of kids at play on rich green grass. The sight of parents licking cones with one eye on their children. Teens hanging out, getting to know each other.

Pure, unadulterated joy filled her. She was home. Finally home. Really home. No nagging husband. No bills. Just a dad who needed her and a baby to fulfill her.

A real second chance.

She rolled out of the truck. Though she was only six months pregnant and her tummy was barely round enough to be noticeable, she felt like a whale. Knowing she really shouldn't be eating ice cream and adding unnecessary weight, she had a plan. Before she indulged in a vanilla cone, she'd play ball with the kids.

"Are you coming, Dad?"

"Are you kidding? I worked a twelve-hour day in the field. I don't need more exercise to deserve an ice cream cone."

As her dad made his way to the ordering window, Maggie laughed and headed off for the ball game. The sounds of childish giggles drifted to her, resurrecting her joy. Someday she'd bring her little boy or girl to this ice cream stand for a sweet treat and some fun with kids his or her own age.

Standing at the edge of the grassy field, she shielded her eyes from the sun with one hand as she surveyed the group, hoping to find a parent she knew so she could figure out which team to play for.

She didn't see a parent, but spotted Nick's mom, Becky Roebuck. Standing behind home plate, wearing pink capris and a simple white blouse, with her curly blond hair floating around her shoulders, she looked about forty of her fifty-five years.

A little boy stood beside her, getting ready for his turn at bat. Positioning his hands on the bright red plastic bat, Becky said, "Okay, so when the ball comes toward you, you just swing at it like this."

With her hands on top of the little boy's she demonstrated the swinging motion. He giggled.

"See. Simple as pie."

"Yeah, Timmy. Simple as pie. You can do it."

That booming encouragement came from Nick. Maggie followed the sound of his voice, and there he stood. No shirt, cutoff jeans and flip-flops.

The urge to turn and run competed with the urge to

simply take in every beautiful bronze inch of him. The joy of being home was instantly eclipsed by sheer unadulterated lust. His biceps flexed as he scooped up an imaginary ball, practicing while his mom coached the obvious newbie to the game. His tanned skin gleamed in the sunlight.

Her breath caught and pulse scrambled. Her Pittsburgh friends had warned her that pregnancy would send her sex drive off the charts, but she'd barely noticed that particular side effect until the day she'd seen Nick again. Still, she wasn't giving him credit for making her weak with longing. It was safer to believe it was wayward hormones.

But good excuse aside, she still quivered, and she knew getting involved in the game would be just a tad foolhardy. Like tempting fate by dipping your toe into shark-infested waters. Nick hadn't yet noticed her. She could slip away.

She turned to go just as Becky yelled, "Hey! Maggie! Is that you?"

Embarrassment flooded her at the same time that the sound of Becky's voice resonated through her, reminding her of the happy two weeks she and Nick had lived with his mom. The peaceful breakfasts, lunches and dinners. Fun evenings eating popcorn in front of the TV. As a family. A real family. Not a third wheel as she'd always been in her own home.

She stopped and faced Becky with a smile. "It's me."

"Did you come here to play some Wiffle Ball?"

She instinctively glanced back at Nick. His smile was gone. In its place was the wary expression he wore at the office.

Not giving her a chance to reply, Becky jogged over and enfolded her in a huge, motherly hug before she kissed her cheek. "Of course you came to play!" She pulled away and held Maggie an arm's distance so she could inspect her. "I have missed you!"

Tears filled Maggie's eyes. "I have missed you, too."

"So why didn't you ever visit?"

That was a loaded question. Where would she start? She could fall back on the truth that everybody knew. She and Vicki had never gotten along. Or she could state the obvious. She'd hurt Nick and hadn't wanted to face that, either. Or she could say the convenient. Her husband hated what he called her grubby little North Carolina tourist pit town.

In the end, she said only, "There never seemed to be time. I had a busy job. My husband was always at the beck and call of his clients."

Becky glanced around. "Where is your husband?"

"We're divorced."

That caused sweet Becky's face to fall in sadness. "I'm so sorry."

The freedom she'd felt when she and her dad had first pulled into The Shack wove through her again. Her marriage might have seemed okay, but in the past few days Maggie had come to realize her ex-husband was a spend-aholic narcissist who'd never been particularly affectionate and who had ruled her. The truth was she'd never been what anybody would call happy. The sweet knowledge that she had a chance to start over, in her hometown, as herself, with no one telling her what to do filled her again.

Her lips tugged upward into a smile. "Don't be sorry. The more I'm divorced from him the more I'm coming to see it might not have been such a bad thing."

Becky looped her arm through Maggie's. "Since it brought you back to Ocean Palms, I'm afraid I'm going to have to agree." She nudged Maggie's shoulder. "Now what position do you want to play?"

Considering that Nick had already seen her—so there was no hiding from him—and noticing that the kids were getting antsy, she didn't argue. She glanced at the field and saw most of the important positions were filled by parents with a smattering of little kids in between, probably learning the ropes of the game. "How about shortstop?"

Becky patted her arm. "Perfect. We haven't had a shortstop in decades."

Maggie laughed and walked to her position. Taking a quick look to get the lay of the field, she noticed Nick was only a few yards behind her and waved. "Hey."

What else could she do? He might be her boss, ex-husband, first lover, but this was a small town. They were bound to run into each other.

"Hey."

His deep, gruff voice drifted to her just as a big bruiser of a boy stepped up to the plate, took a swipe at the first pitch and sent the ball flying to Maggie.

She held up her hands. "I've got it!"

But two seconds before the little plastic ball would have slapped into her hands, Nick cut in front of her and snatched it from the air.

"You're out, Timmy," he called, tossing the ball back to the pitcher, a freckle-faced girl who wore her dark hair in pigtails.

Nick turned to flounce away, but Maggie caught his arm. "That was my ball and I had it."

He glanced at her hand holding his magnificent biceps. Myriad emotions passed through his eyes. The anger blew right by her in favor of the little glimmer of attraction that sparkled in the dark depths of his nearly black eyes. She sucked in a breath. That one little glimmer lit a match under her overactive libido again. Her tummy tightened. Her blood sang in her veins. Her muscles melted. A very familiar sizzle arched between them.

She dropped his arm like a hot potato.

Stepping back, she calmed her voice, as she said, "You shouldn't have jumped in front of me."

He snorted and turned to go back to his place in the outfield. "Right."

"Hey!" She nearly grabbed him again to keep him from dismissing her, but she remembered the sizzle and fisted her hands at her sides. "I'm a good player."

"You're stale."

"And this is a pickup Wiffle Ball game, Mr. Macho! Not the World Series." Memories of how her ex had bossed her in the past two years filled her with righteous indignation. If she was here to be free, then she intended to be free. "You don't have to cover for me."

The next three kids hit low ground balls. Two whizzed right by the pitcher and both kids got on base. With two outs and two kids on, the next pitch could result in either the necessary out to end the inning or a run scored.

Maggie wiped sweat off her brow. Though it was after seven, heat still held the tiny town in a vise grip.

Nick called for a time-out and ambled over to her. "Are you okay?"

She looked around. "Yes." Her face scrunched in confusion. "Did you just call time to check on me?"

"You look awful."

She laughed. "Thanks."

"No. I'm serious. You look terrible. Like you're going to faint from heat."

Her gaze involuntarily fell to the sweat glistening on his pecs. She shook her head. "You should talk. You look hotter than I feel."

Too late she realized how that sounded and she clamped her mouth shut.

But everything inside of Nick stilled as he felt himself being slapped back in time. Back to when comments like that could set his blood on fire and make him want to take her right where they stood. It infuriated him that she still had that power, but when he saw her face heat with embarrassment, a thrill of male pride raced through him. Well, well, well. Sweet little I-don't-love-you Maggie wasn't so unaffected after all. If nothing else, she remembered how good they had been in bed.

He laughed and winked at her. "So I guess I've still got it."

She grabbed his shoulders and turned him around, giving him a shove to send him back to the outfield. He scooted off, pretending to be unaffected and not wanting to make a scene or call too much attention to them, but the skin she'd touched tingled. His body had tensed in anticipation. His blood shimmered in his veins.

He rationalized it away. He would always equate Maggie with sex, sex appeal. Because she was the first woman he'd touched, the first woman he'd tasted, no one had ever compared.

But he'd had lots of women since Maggie and intended to take advantage of the new group he'd begun meeting in New York City. He didn't need to flirt with Maggie. Not even out of boredom.

A little girl with a yellow ponytail got up to bat and hit a line drive right to Maggie. As naturally as if she'd been doing it every day for the past fifteen years, she bent and scooped up the ball. Unfortunately Nick was treated to a picture of her perfect butt and long, shapely legs.

He blinked a few times then spun away as she wailed the ball to the first baseman, who caught it effortlessly, getting the third out that retired the side.

Maggie jumped for joy, whooped and hollered, as she high-fived the dark-haired boy manning first base.

Unimaginable joy hit Nick like a freight train. Memories

of their past collided with the knowledge that she was home. Really home. He couldn't stop it. He couldn't fight it. He couldn't rationalize it away. The truth of it took hold and wouldn't let go. Not even when he reminded himself that he didn't like her anymore and had a good plan for his life that included meeting new people, going to clubs, entertaining in a penthouse. Out in the bright sunshine, doing the things they used to do as children, then teens, then lovers, he couldn't stop the memories, the feelings that erupted like a geyser.

Angry with himself, he took his time walking to the bench that served as a dugout. The team of six-, seven-, eight-, nine- and ten-year-olds continued to high-five Maggie as they grabbed their juice boxes and talked smack about how good they were.

Unofficial coach, Bill Taylor, Bobby Taylor's dad, wrapped her in a bear hug that speared Nick with unwanted jealousy and sent his anger with himself into the stratosphere. Calling himself an idiot, he took a juice box from the metal tub his mom provided and sat at the end of the bench.

Maggie scooted over to him. He pretended not to notice by taking a long drink from the child's juice box that seemed to get lost in his adult-size hand. But there was only so long a man could drink. When he pulled the box away, Maggie stood in front of him. Her long legs peeked out from white shorts. Her huge grin charmed him.

"I told you I didn't need help."

Annoyance skittered through him. She didn't seem to have the same problem he did with being together. While he suffered the torment of the sexually aroused damned, she appeared perfectly content to be around him as a friend.

Of course she wasn't the one who'd been in love. She

was the one who'd left. And maybe if he would continually remind himself of that he could get rid of the weird feelings that filled his gut every time he looked at her.

"I didn't really think you needed help."

Her green eyes sparkled and the fire in his belly sent a shower of sparks through him. "Then why bounce in front of me to catch that fly ball?"

This was not working.

He rose from the bench, inched away from her. "I didn't want you to get hurt."

She gaped at him. "Hurt?"

"You're pregnant," he said, stupidly, as if she needed a reminder.

Her face fell. The sparkle in her eyes morphed into a look of confusion. "It's Wiffle Ball. The ball is so light we don't even need mitts." She laughed. "The worst that could happen is that I'd get a sting."

Her laughter raced through him like a potent drug. The desire to flirt with her, to kiss her, just to enjoy her, exploded and sent longing skittering along his nerve endings.

"Right." He turned and walked away. But all his senses were engaged. His brain, too. He'd always loved sparring with Maggie. Tussling. Playing. Now, he didn't even feel he was allowed to talk to her and somehow it made the temptation even stronger.

He almost snorted a laugh, but caught it. Wouldn't he look like a pathetic sap if she realized he still had the hots for her?

He got into his car and headed down the coast, then slapped the steering wheel. This was ridiculous. He couldn't take an eighty-mile drive every time he saw her. Why couldn't he get ahold of himself? He whipped his car around and headed home.

As soon as he turned onto his street, he saw the big black SUV parked in front of his house. Leaning against the driver's-side door was his brother Cade. Wearing his usual Stetson, jeans and boots, he looked like an indolent cowboy, not the billionaire oilman that he was.

As Nick had pulled his car beneath his house, Cade slipped under the garage door and opened his Porsche door for him.

"I thought you were on your way to New York to talk to Darius before you flew to Saudi Arabia."

He slapped Nick on the back. "That's the thing about a private plane. I can stop where I want. And I wanted to kick your behind for telling Darius to send me to Saudi when you were the one he called first."

He motioned for Cade to precede him up the steps into the kitchen. This was exactly what he needed. A good scrap with his brother to work off some of the emotion simmering through him.

"Sorry. I'm busy."

"Like I'm not?"

"You probably are, but I just spent six weeks in New York, babysitting Andreas Holdings while you sat in your comfy chair in your ranch house probably watching reruns of *Lost*."

Cade snorted.

And Nick relaxed. They'd sit on old lawn chairs beneath the deck, watch the ocean, drink some beer.

"Yeah, well at least I didn't hire my ex-wife."

His dying irritation with himself for hiring Maggie burst into flames again. Still, there was no way he'd let Cade see that. He opened the fridge, pulled out two cold ones and tossed one to Cade. "I'll have to thank Darius for being able to keep a secret."

"Hey, when we decided to be brothers for real, we agreed there would be no more secrets."

"Right." When they were talking about Darius and Gino that had been a great idea. When it came to himself, Nick wasn't exactly thrilled with the no secrets policy. He pointed at the French doors that led to the deck. "That way. We'll pull the old lawn chairs out of the garage, stick them in the sand and watch the ocean and the stars."

Cade nodded and led the way. But the second they were comfortably settled with their chairs in the warm summer sand, Cade said, "So what's she like?"

There was just no changing the subject with a persistent half brother. He sighed and decided to be honest. "The same. Pretty. Tall, but sort of delicate."

Cade laughed. "Delicate? What guy in his right mind says delicate? I don't even use the delicate cycle in my washer."

Fresh annoyance rippled through Nick. Once again, she had him thinking of flowers and girlie words. Just like the sap he'd been at eighteen.

"You still have the hots for her or what?"

"Buzz off."

Cade hooted another laugh. "You *do*!"

"Great. Fine. Whatever. I'm still attracted to my ex-wife. Something like that doesn't just go away."

Cade took a slug of beer. "Sure it does. I have two foremen who cross the street rather than walk by their exes." He peered at Nick. "You should just sleep with her."

Nick almost spit out his beer. "You're crazy."

"I'm serious. Get her out of your system."

"Right."

"Okay, think it through. You have some sort of idealized picture of her in your head. Like she was the special love of your life or something."

Nick scowled, but what Cade said made sense. He hadn't thought about love or even commitments in fifteen years, and Maggie comes back and suddenly it was all he could think about.

"Over the years, you've probably forgotten all the bad stuff, all the stuff that makes her human and you only remember the good."

Nick peered over.

"So what you're remembering isn't true."

Sucking in a breath, Nick said, "I can't just sleep with her."

"Why not?"

"Because I'd be using her."

"How do you know she's not feeling the same things you are? Darius said she's divorced. Maybe she got divorced because her husband never measured up to *you* and now she's back, conveniently working for you—"

"And coming to the pickup Wiffle Ball game at the Shack."

Cade squinted his eyes in question.

"My mom runs the daycare. Knows all the kids. So every other night or so she goes to the Ice Cream Shack, gathers the local kids and entertains them with a game of Wiffle Ball so their parents can have a few minutes of peace."

Cade smiled. "And your ex was there?"

Nick nodded.

Cade laughed triumphantly. "I'm saying she's just as curious about you as you are about her." He took a long drink of beer, then said, "Test the water, bro, and you'll see I'm right. She's here to check you out."

The purely male part of Nick ate that up like candy. The male ego she'd battered needed to hear it.

"Chances are you both built the other into something

you're not," Cade continued, looking out at the ocean as if what he was saying was of very little consequence. A simple answer. An easy way to get both him and Maggie back to normal. "You sleep together once. You both realize you're not the wonderful demigods you've built each other into. And you move on."

CHAPTER FOUR

MAGGIE tossed and turned that night, upset because Nick was upset. She hadn't come home to remind him of things. She wouldn't even be working for him if there were other options. But she was working with him and they were both going to have to deal with it.

She woke late Thursday morning and couldn't seem to pull herself together in her usual forty minutes. Then she had to find her dad in the field and wait for him to change his boots so he could drive her to work in his old beat-up truck.

At the entrance to Andreas Manufacturing, she jumped out and raced to the building. When she plowed through the door into the office, Nick was waiting for her, leaning against the edge of Julie's desk. She saw his feet first, tanned toes wrapped in the thick straps of his leather sandals, then the long length of jean-covered legs, then his bright orange T-shirt, then his scowl.

Great. "Sorry, I'm late. I forgot I didn't have a car. Had to find dad in the field—"

He stopped her with a short, terse motion of his hand. "Julie called this morning. One of her friends has been taken ill and she flew to Vegas to help care for her."

A burst of fear raced through her. "She's gone?" *No go-between? No safety net?*

"She said she'd put in her time and was done."

"I don't get a training period?"

His gaze caught hers. "Do you need one?"

"No." She lifted her chin. She was fine with the work. It was the go-between they needed. But it would be a cold, frosty day in hell before she'd admit that to him. "No. I'm okay."

He pushed away from the desk. "Good."

Heading into his office, he turned away from her and she couldn't stop her gaze from skimming down his back and nearly perfect butt.

Good Lord. Would she ever be able to look at him without thinking of those two weeks they were married? Without thinking about making love, discovering sex... discovering each other? How proud she was to be married to him? How happy she'd been?

She shook her head. Being attracted to him was crazy. Not only had fifteen long years passed, but also she was living a second chance. Second chances did not come along every day. She did not intend to screw up by falling for a man who might be attracted to her but wouldn't really "want" her because she'd hurt him. So why she was having these thoughts was beyond her.

At his office door, he suddenly stopped and pivoted to face her. "Well, come on. Stow your gear then bring a pad and pen into my office and we'll get started."

Grateful that she'd brought her eyes away from his butt before he'd turned, Maggie nodded. She tossed her purse and sandwich into her desk drawer, grabbed a pad and pen and followed him.

He pointed at the conference table which was piled high with files and loose papers, including mail and messages. Julie had called them the information he'd need to write the bid, but though Nick had been reviewing information all week, he hadn't touched these stacks. So it appeared this was the day she and Nick jumped in.

"You sit there." He indicated a chair on the right side. "I'll sit here." He grabbed the back of the seat at the head of the table, pulled it out and sat, putting them catty-cornered from each other. Close enough to touch.

She almost groaned. She didn't understand the ridiculous temptation that continually rose up in her when he was around, except to blame it on pregnancy hormones unleashed the night before when she'd seen him shirtless. Actually, that made sense. Now all she had to do was stifle it.

Looking at the stacks, he drew in a deep breath. "Now the question is where to start."

"I'd go with the files. They're thicker. It'll feel like we're getting more work done."

He scowled, but reached for the files. He pulled a green one off the stack, opened it and began reading.

"Okay," he said, tossing the opened file in front of her. "This is our engineer's analysis of the differences between the product specs from five years ago and the current bid."

He rose and retrieved a cylinder of drawings from his desk. He unrolled it on the conference table. "The part we manufacture has been changed significantly."

She raised her gaze to meet his. "Which will change our bid."

He quickly looked away. "While I was gone, I'm guessing the estimating department already put together the materials numbers. They're waiting for us to call for them. So you do that."

She grabbed her notebook and pen and scribbled the instruction. "Who do I call?"

"Talk to John Sprankle. He's lead estimator. He'll have done the work himself since this is our primary bid."

She smiled. "Great."

He looked away again.

Okay. The first glance away she could think was normal. The second not so much. She didn't have to ask why he was uncomfortable around her. They'd had an awkward time at the ice cream stand. He'd left because of her. She could let it go, let him work through it on his own, but as he'd already said this project was too important for them to be tiptoeing around each other. They had to talk about this. At the very least she had to apologize.

She cleared her throat. "Uh…about yesterday."

He glanced over, his expression guarded. "What about yesterday? Did Julie say something needed to be done?"

"No. I just feel bad that you left the game last night."

He looked away. "Don't be. My younger brother Cade was waiting for me at the house when I got there. He wanted to surprise me."

Happiness bubbled up in her. Nick had always hated being alone. It was wonderful to realize he was getting close to his brothers.

"So what happened?"

"What happened when?"

"With your brother, you dolt." She playfully tapped his forearm. A current of electricity raced up her arm and she was transported back in time. This was how it had started the night they'd gone from friends to lovers. A touch that should have been playful had turned electric. They'd looked into each other's eyes and the spark of electricity had become an avalanche of desire.

He'd kissed her and she'd melted.

Wow. Not a good thing to remember when she was already overheated with pregnancy hormones.

"Is your brother here for a week or the weekend or what?"

Ignoring her, he read over the plans. She should have let him work. She should have been glad he wasn't having the memories she was, should have been glad for the reprieve. But her curiosity was like an overeager child jumping up and down inside her. Questions spilled out before she could stop them.

"Is he tall, is he thin, is he grouchy, is he fun?"

He rolled his head to the side to catch her gaze again. "Why? Want an intro?"

Pain speared her. How little did he think of her? "Are you kidding me? I'm just plain curious and I'm curious for you." She tapped his hand again then held back a groan. He was warm. Solid. His skin rough. Masculine. A magnet for her itching fingers.

He glanced down at her fingers, then back up at her face. Their gazes caught and clung. His eyes sparked with the same need that tormented her.

"Why are you here?"

Caught in his magnetic gaze, she could barely think let alone comprehend a question. "Here?"

"At my company. Working for me?"

"I couldn't get a job anywhere else."

"You wanted to know about Cade…well, he thinks that answer is baloney. He thinks you're here because there's still something between us."

The fire in her belly roared to aching life again. If she said yes, would he kiss her?

Stifling another groan, she reminded herself of the pregnancy hormones. Told herself she was too smart to long for a guy whom she'd jilted, a guy who shouldn't want anything to do with her. But she knew both excuses were, as Cade had so aptly said, baloney. She was attracted to

Nick. Always had been attracted to Nick. And working together had been a foolish, foolish decision.

Except neither of them wanted the attraction and if she nipped this in the bud now, she wouldn't lose her second chance.

"There's nothing between us."

"You're sure."

"I'm sure."

"You lie."

She burst off her chair and paced behind it. "Of course, I'm lying! Dear God, Nick! What purpose would it serve for us to be attracted to each other? None." She laid her hands on her stomach. "I have a baby who needs me. He or she needs me strong and smart. Not caught in a relationship that might only be us trying to recreate something that hadn't worked the first time."

Her reminder was like a bucket of cold water in Nick's face. What an idiot Cade had turned him into. He'd gotten him so stirred up that he'd forgotten the most basic fact about their relationship. *She'd* left him.

She hadn't loved him.

Sleeping together wouldn't solve or prove anything. Except that they found each other attractive. He'd never doubted that. In fact, that was what had shown him the way for his current lifestyle. He and Maggie were so good in bed, she left no doubt that people didn't have to be in love to enjoy each other.

But a smart man also didn't sleep with an assistant he needed.

"You're right. I was out of line. Let's just get back to work." He turned to the specs. "I'm going to dictate language to you that I want you to put into the narrative portion of the bid. Do you take shorthand?"

The relief on her face told him he was right. They

might be attracted to each other but she didn't want to experiment…didn't want him. She only wanted this job.

"No. But I can write really, really fast."

"Great."

He dictated slowly and concisely, his mind fully taken by the complex task. But when Maggie left his office, he ran his hands down his face.

Now he had a reason to want to kick both his brothers' butts.

Amazingly, Maggie's dad remembered to pick her up that night. Nick had been so busy that he hadn't even looked at the clock. But when Charlie Forsythe strolled into her office, still wearing his jeans and work shirt, his hat rolled in his hands, Nick glanced at his watch and saw it was a quarter after seven.

Glad to see her dad, especially since he hadn't yet had a chance to pay his respects, he rose from his seat just in time to hear the old man say, "Charlie Jr. called today."

The eagerness in her dad's voice caused Nick to sit back down.

As Maggie gathered her things from her desk, she said, "That's great."

"Yeah. Still the same old, same old with him, though. Busy. Busy. Busy. Work. Work. Work."

Nick frowned. The old man was picking up his daughter after she'd worked a ten-hour day, yet he didn't seem to notice that as he bragged about the son he'd always adored.

"He's busy," Maggie replied cheerfully.

Nick shook his head, closed his eyes, told himself not to get sucked into Maggie's problems. That was how it had started the last time. She'd always been there for him, so when the tide had turned and he'd realized how alone and abandoned she'd felt in her own family, he'd taken her into his.

He couldn't do it again.

Wouldn't do it again.

But despite his fierce denials, the urge to defend her, to care for her, to comfort her, rose up in him like an angry beast.

"Nick." She poked her head into the office and smiled at him. "My dad's here. So unless you need me, I'm going home."

No matter how much he wanted to take care of her, he couldn't. Hell, she'd yelled at him for stepping in front of her to catch a fly ball. There was no way he could run interference with her dad. He resisted the impulse. "Go." He waved her on, letting her know that her leaving was fine.

But after she had left, he raked his fingers through his hair.

Damn it! He shouldn't care, but the reminder of young Maggie, sad Maggie, needy Maggie, broke his heart.

It was ridiculous. She hadn't thought for more than two heartbeats about leaving him, after she'd lost their baby. She'd hurt him.

So why did he care that she might be lonely?

CHAPTER FIVE

NICK barely slept. He woke early Friday morning and took a quick shower, calling himself every kind of fool for being upset for her when she didn't care about him. Deciding that the sooner he got the bid done, the sooner he could go to New York, help Darius and enjoy the nightlife, he raced to work, and there she sat. Looking like a ray of sunshine at her clean desk.

"Good morning!"

He cleared his throat. "Good morning."

"I got in an hour early this morning and cleared up everything I hadn't gotten through last night so we could get started as soon as you arrived."

"That's good."

When she looked crestfallen at his lackluster response, little shards of pain, like glass, pricked his skin, demanding that he be nicer to her. So he reminded himself that as soon as he got this bid done he could go to New York and he smiled broadly.

"That's great. We have a lot of things to do today. So bring your notebook in and we'll get started."

"Okay." She grabbed her pad and pen and followed him into his office.

Nick tossed his keys and cell phone onto his desk, feeling better, stronger than he had all week. Now that he had himself anchored, nothing she said or did could break his good mood.

This was going to work, Maggie thought, happily scampering behind Nick as he walked into his office. Being honest with him the day before must have really worked. For the first time all week, Nick wasn't grouchy. He wasn't moody. They were finally getting their footing in dealing with each other and could now act like a real boss and assistant.

She happily scooted to the conference table when he motioned for her to sit. As he had the day before, he took the seat at the head of the table, catty-cornered from her. He said nothing. She said nothing. He picked up a file and began reading.

When a whole minute had passed with Nick engrossed in the contents of the file, she set her hands on her lap to keep from fidgeting. After another minute, she knit her fingers together. After the third minute, she glanced around the office.

Sitting close enough to read the framed degrees on the wall, she was surprised to see he not only had his masters but he also had a Ph.D.

"Wow."

He glanced up. "What?"

"You have a Ph.D?"

He turned his attention back to the papers. "Why does that surprise you?"

"Because you started a company at eighteen."

"And went to school at night."

"A lotta nights," she said, unable to keep the admiration out of her voice.

"You have to have knowledge to make a company successful."

"Yeah. Otherwise, it would have been a waste of your five-million-dollar investment."

He stopped reading again, glanced over again. "Excuse me?"

Too late she realized her mistake. He'd never told her about the trust fund his father had offered him. She'd overheard him talking with his dad's lawyer about it.

But what difference did it make? Fifteen years had passed. They'd both moved on. She might as well admit she knew where he'd gotten the money to start his business.

"Your trust fund. I overheard the lawyer telling you about it the day we lost the baby."

He set his pen down, caught her gaze. He said nothing, but his expression compelled her to explain.

"I heard you turn it down. I didn't think it was right for you to lose it."

His eyes narrowed, his gaze turned to stone. "Please do not tell me you left because you heard my dad's lawyer tell me that I couldn't collect the trust since I was married."

"You wouldn't have taken the money otherwise."

He shoved his back against the wall and leaped to his feet. "I didn't want the money!"

His face was a picture of disbelieving horror that sent a shot of uncertainty through her. She refused to give in to it. He might not have wanted it, but he and his mom had needed it. "Oh, come on, Nick. You and your mom had spent your entire life scraping to get by. I was supposed to just stand there and let you turn down five million dollars? I couldn't have lived with myself."

He snorted a laugh. "You couldn't have lived with me not getting the money? Well, live with this." He slammed his hands against the edge of the table and leaned toward her. "I didn't take the money."

"What?"

"I didn't take the money. I didn't want it. I wanted to prove to my dad that I could make it without him and I did."

Shock rendered Maggie speechless.

"So, consulting me before making such a huge decision would have been a good thing."

Unable to process what he was telling her, Maggie swallowed the lump in her throat. "You seriously didn't take it?"

"No." He shook his head as if in total disbelief of what she'd done. Then, without another word, he headed for the door of his office and barreled through hers. She heard the door slam then a minute later the roar of his car's engine, but didn't bother getting up.

Too many emotions roiled through her. Too many thoughts competed for attention.

She'd sacrificed their love so he could collect the money due to him—

And he hadn't taken it.

Nick was halfway through town when his cell phone rang. Shaking with fury, he wanted to ignore it but he noticed the caller was his mom.

He picked it up, sucked in a calming breath and said, "Hey, Mom. What's up?"

"The toilet in my office is overflowing!"

"Get a plumber—"

"I called one but he can't come this morning. Oh, my God, Nick! It's going to run over into the new hardwood and warp it—"

For a woman who had turned into a very shrewd business owner once he was able to give her some financial backing, his mother's lack of understanding of simple things usually made him laugh. Right at this very minute, he wasn't in a laughing mood.

Still, that wasn't his mother's fault. "Okay. Calm down. I'm in the car anyway, I'll be right over."

He made an illegal U-turn and headed for the daycare, the whole time telling himself that Maggie's admission meant nothing. Yes, he'd been too angry to stay in the office with her. And, yes, he hoped she'd leave a note on his desk saying she'd resigned. But the knot in his gut and the pain in his chest were ridiculous. Maggie had left him so long ago, and he was such a different person now, that it shouldn't matter why.

But it did.

And when he let his brain tiptoe into forbidden territory, he knew why it did. But he hauled his thoughts out of there. It served no purpose to consider the fact that she might have loved him. Might have always loved him. Might have left him *because* she had loved him.

He tightened his fingers around his steering wheel as he pulled into the driveway of the neat, redbrick building he'd bought for his mom's daycare when he'd gotten his first multimillion-dollar contract. He counted to four hundred as he walked up to the front door, calming himself, telling himself not to think of Maggie—

The door opened before he could grab the knob. His mom caught his arm and yanked him inside, her floor-length accordion skirt swishing with every move.

"Hurry!"

She dragged him down the hall, past the brightly painted rooms filled with toddlers, elementary school kids and preteens, separated for ease of discipline. Energetic music poured from the toddler room. Three-foot-high kids formed a circle in the elementary age room. Computer monitors blinked in the preteen room.

"Relax, Mom. The water's not going to reach the hardwood unless you've got about eighty gallons gushing out. And even if you did, I think by now you probably have towels sopping up the mess."

Stepping into her office, he could see he was right. She had a mountain of towels in front of the office door, protecting her beloved hardwood.

He stepped over the towels into the bathroom. "See? Everything's fine." He leaned down. "I'll just tighten this knob here that turns off your water and we'll call another plumber."

She leaned against the doorjamb, crossed her arms on her chest. "Why? Can't you fix this?"

"Probably. But I can also afford a plumber."

"And you have to get back to work?"

Not able to lie to his mother, he shrugged.

"Ah. Not going back to work. Hmm. Let's see." She ambled over to the open bathroom door, her skirt moving gaily around her. Bracelets jangled merrily on her wrist. "This is your first week back after being away for six weeks, so you need to be there. But you also hired your ex-wife as an assistant so that might be the problem."

"That certainly didn't take long to get around town."

"A good piece of gossip never does." She smiled. "Once Maggie left the Shack last night, Mary Bryant told us you'd hired her."

He carelessly lifted one shoulder, trying to look unaffected. "It's not a big deal. Maggie and I haven't seen each other in fifteen years. Working together won't be a problem. I'm fine."

She laughed. "No, you're not. I saw you leave the Wiffle Ball game the night before last. You played one inning with her then bolted. I'm not stupid. I figured you didn't like being around her."

Boy, he just couldn't keep anything from his mother. "All right, Kreskin. I'm not fine."

"So what happened this morning that you left?"

He rolled his shoulders, loosening the tightness. "She told me she overheard Dad's lawyer the day she lost the baby. She left so we'd get the money."

His mom blinked then she tilted her head. "But you didn't take the money."

"I know."

"Wow."

"Yeah, wow."

They were quiet for a few seconds. Nick stood perfectly still as his mom studied him, his face, his body language. Finally she said, "You're not just angry. You're surprised."

"I didn't know she'd overheard. So, yeah. I'm surprised."

"Oh, Nicky! Are you lying to me or yourself?" She shook her head, sending her curls bouncing. "It's not the surprise of finding out she overheard the lawyer that bothers you. It's the surprise of hearing why she left."

He squeezed his eyes shut in misery. As if it wasn't bad enough he had to face this, he had a perceptive mom who just wouldn't stop until she'd dragged every damned detail out of him. "Look, Mom. I've got to go."

She caught his arm. "We were in trouble, and Maggie had a big heart. You couldn't expect her to sit by and do nothing when she overheard you turn down five million dollars."

Nick's jaw tightened. "I *loved* her."

"And she loved you."

He forked his fingers through his hair. "No kidding."

She framed his face with her hands and caught his gaze. "That's what's really bothering you. That she loved you?"

The truth of that flashed through him like lightning illuminating a stormy night. He'd forced himself to go on after the loss of the one woman he'd ever truly loved by telling himself that only a schmuck pines for a woman who doesn't love him. Now, realizing she had loved him, everything changed. His heart broke again, only this time for an entirely different reason.

Still, he wouldn't tell his mother that. He wouldn't tell anybody that.

"We were a team. She should have consulted me." He stepped over the mountain of towels again, away from his mom and her penetrating glances and on-point observations. "Have Bernice keep calling plumbers until she finds one who can take an emergency call," he instructed, referring to his mom's office manager, as he walked toward the door. "Have the bill sent to me."

"I can pay my own bills now. But that's besides the point. You're hurt. You're furious. And you shouldn't be."

He rounded on her. "Really? I feel like somebody took my whole life, tossed it in the air and it came down in disjointed pieces that don't make sense."

"Oh, this makes perfect sense. Nick, Maggie had just lost a baby. She was grieving and tired and only eighteen years old."

He pressed his fingers to his eyelids. He hated thinking of Maggie being scared, alone, aching from the loss of their child when he should have been there for her. He *would* have been there for her.

"And now you're going to have to deal with it. Fifteen years have passed. You're a success. She's moved on. Life has gone on. You have to deal with it."

* * *

Maggie spent the morning sitting in her office chair, waiting for Nick to return. He didn't.

In the afternoon, she turned on her computer and cruised the various software, stopping to analyze the accounting programs since she knew that's where most of her responsibilities lay. At five, she packed up, hoping her dad remembered to pick her up. He didn't.

So she called, but no one answered the phone. Assuming he was outside, she waited until five-thirty to call again. Again no answer. Six. No answer. Six-thirty, he picked up the phone, apologized and headed out to get her.

She was waiting by the front gate when the shake-rattle-and-roll truck pulled up. It stopped in front of her, she climbed inside and they headed home.

"I'm sorry I forgot you."

She mustered a smile for her dad. "You're busy. I understand."

"It's just that being outside is so much better for me. Inside reminds me too much of Vicki."

Maggie swallowed and tears welled in her eyes. She'd kept her composure all day. All damned day. She'd sat at her desk, pretended nothing was wrong, prayed that though Nick had left angry—furious—he would spend the day thinking things through and realize she'd done what she'd done because she had loved him and it was the right thing. They were too young to be married, too young to be committed to one person or one course of action for the rest of their lives. He had to see she'd done the right thing.

When he hadn't come back or even called, her gut told her he didn't agree. And she'd faced the possibility that he'd be firing her the next day. And the worst part of it was, she knew Nick was right. They shouldn't be working together. She shouldn't have gotten a job with him. She should have sucked it up and stayed in Pittsburgh.

But her dad needed her.

"I know it must be hard to lose the love of your life." She swallowed. Why did saying that hurt? She'd lost Nick so long ago she'd gotten over it. She'd married someone else. She was pregnant with that man's child. Losing Nick was so far in her past it shouldn't hurt.

He sucked in a breath. "Harder than you'd ever believe. We were a team—"

The tears in her eyes spilled over. She and Nick had been a team. Until that one final decision. A decision she'd made on her own because she knew he'd never choose money over her. No matter how much he and his mom struggled.

Her dad glanced at her. "Are you okay?"

"I'm fine. Hot. Tired." She forced a watery smile. "Pregnant. I cry at the drop of a hat now. You know how hormones are."

"Alleluia. I sure do! I remember how funny Vicki was, pregnant with Charlie Jr. She cried at everything." He laughed as the old truck puttered down Main Street. "But I also know it's probably hard having to get a job while you're pregnant. Still, I think it was a real blessing that you got to work with Nick."

"Really?" That popped out before she could stop it. How could this be a blessing? Only five days in his employ and she'd not only been tossed into a sea of confusion, but she'd hurt him.

Again.

"Well, sure, he's a great guy. Everybody loves him." He glanced over again. "I've heard rumors about year-end bonuses large enough to pay off car loans. The money's great. And let's face it. You need money."

She swallowed. She did need money.

"And health care. You won't get on Nick's insurance before this baby's born, but you will have health care. You just need to save enough to pay the bills when this little one comes."

She did indeed.

"So you're lucky."

No. She wasn't really lucky. She was stuck.

CHAPTER SIX

SATURDAY morning when Nick arrived in the office, Maggie was waiting for him. His curly black hair had been blown around during the drive in his convertible. His red eyes told her he probably hadn't slept.

Their gazes caught, clung. A million questions arched between them. Silence stretched.

Finally Nick broke it. "It's Saturday."

"I know. Julie said we work ten hours a day, six days a week when you have a bid due. You have a bid due. So I'm here."

She didn't know why she'd been optimistic, but she'd honestly thought it would please him that she'd not only remembered he worked Saturdays, but that she'd come in.

Instead he looked away. "Is your car fixed?"

Disappointment trembled through her, followed by a wave of fear. If she said yes, would he fire her because she had a way home? Would she have to go searching for a job in the city? Hope somebody would hire a six-month-pregnant woman knowing she'd need a leave of absence in three months?

Her dad was right. It was a blessing Nick had hired her. She had to keep this job.

"My car isn't fixed. I caught my dad before he went out to the field."

He combed his fingers through his tangled hair then turned and headed for his office. "Okay, bring in a notebook and we'll get started."

Relief forced her breath out in a rush. She grabbed her steno pad and a pen and scrambled after him. As he tossed his cell phone and keys on his desk, she slid onto the chair at the conference table where she'd sat the day before. She glanced at the framed degrees and shame rode her blood. Memories of the expression on his face rolled through her brain, made worse by the disbelief in his voice when he'd told her he hadn't taken his dad's money.

The tension in her tummy jumped three notches.

He ambled over, sat at the head of the table. Reaching for the file he'd been reading the day before, he cleared his throat. "These are production reports." He flopped the open file down in front of her. "Every day we print out a report of how much each employee got done in his or her shift."

He grabbed the next red file and the next and the next, opened each and then stacked them on the table in front of her. "I use them to determine our labor costs and to estimate delivery dates for bids like the one we're working on."

"Okay." The reminder of the bid heartened her. With Julie gone and something so important due, he genuinely needed her. Her spirits brightened a little more. If she could help him, she could prove herself as an assistant and their past would become irrelevant.

"I like to review these in hard copy first." He glanced down at a tablet in front of him and crossed something off on the handwritten list on the top page. "So I want you to go through these files and make sure there's a report for every week."

"Why don't I just run the numbers?"

He didn't look at her, just sarcastically said, "You want to figure the labor costs and the delivery dates?"

She shrugged. "Sure. Why not?"

He sighed. "Just check the reports, print out what isn't there."

Panic tightened her chest. How was she going to prove herself if the only work he'd give her was barely even secretarial?

"Are you refusing to let me run the numbers because I'm a woman? Or because you're mad at me?"

"I take care of the numbers."

"Can't handle a little competition?"

He glared at her. "Competition?"

"Or maybe you just don't like the idea that your assistant can probably do everything you can do."

He set the file down and raised his gaze until it met hers. "Now who's pushing us to have a fight?"

Her heart tripped over itself in her chest. His dark eyes sparked with fury. His mouth was a grim line. The urge to turn and run gripped her, but pure nerve, the kind she hadn't had since she'd left Ocean Palms at eighteen, chased it away.

She was Maggie Forsythe. She was smart. She was strong. And she needed this job.

She leaned forward, invading his personal space. "I'm not pushing us to fight. I just want to do my job."

He leaned forward, too. His eyes a shiny, angry black now. "Sounds to me more like you're taking over."

She edged forward again, daring him to say what was really making him mad, so they could fight it out or just let her do the work she could do. "I always was better at planning than you were."

"You mean you were always pushier."

"If that's what it takes to get things done, then, yes, I'm pushier."

He yanked the rest of the red files from the stack and shoved them at her. "Great. Fine. You run the numbers."

Heart pounding, she rose from her seat, took the files and marched to her desk. She hadn't stood up for herself like that in fifteen years and, by God, it felt good. Not just because she'd won the battle, but because she could do this job. She shouldn't have to fear being fired. Her abilities, not their past, should be all that mattered. If it killed her, she would prove herself to him.

When she was gone, Nick rubbed his hands over his eyes. He was supposed to be furious with her, so why had he just found her bossing him around sexy?

Because it reminded him of *his* Maggie. That was why.

Just like at the ice-cream stand a few nights before, her hair was sleek, straight and youthful. She'd stopped wearing makeup and was wearing jeans and simple T-shirts. She bossed him around. Wanted to get to work. Didn't like foot dragging. Didn't like the tension between them.

Yeah. She definitely was his Maggie.

But his Maggie had left him. Maybe for good reason, but she'd gone. And now, when he was furious, only now learning and dealing with things she'd known for fifteen years, she was casual. Able to work. She'd moved on. He hadn't.

What the hell did it all mean? She'd left because she loved him, not because she hadn't? Was that supposed to make everything better? At least before she'd told him why she'd left, he could justify his lifestyle. He could blame his broken heart for the new man he'd become. The man who wouldn't commit, who refused to fall in love, who thought love was for losers and people like his brother Darius who needed a good woman at his side.

What had made perfect sense now seemed shallow, wrong.

And it shouldn't.

How could she come home, tell him she'd lied to him, and somehow make him feel like the one in the wrong?

Maggie spent the day reviewing the labor reports and the corresponding software, and by three o'clock had generated the numbers Nick needed. He barely thanked her. Instead he rose from his desk, ambled to the conference table and retrieved a yellow file.

"These are the résumés for the individual supervisors and admin personnel involved in the project, along with the education and experience stats on the machinists." He picked up an enormous white binder. "This is our final bid document from five years ago. Read the segment on education and experience and create a document that mimics what we did five years ago using the new information."

She looked at the file, looked at the bid document and looked at him. A real project.

She smiled. "Okay."

"Don't get cocky. There's a lot of work to do. I can't do it all. You're hired to help me and you want to do your job. So do it. Get to work."

Joy bubbled through her. "Okay."

Happier than she'd been in years, she read the appropriate section of the bid document then read all the résumés in the folder. At four-thirty she wasn't anywhere near ready to start putting together the new information, so she called her dad intending to tell him to wait for her call before he came for her. He, of course, didn't answer. At five-thirty she tried again, but again no answer.

At six, she turned her chair so she could watch for him out the window, as she continued to read. But she needn't have bothered. True to form, her dad didn't show up. At seven, he finally picked up the phone.

"Oh, kiddo! I'm sorry."

"Don't worry about it. We seem to be working later than I thought we would."

"Seem to be?"

"We're not actually speaking yet, so I don't know for sure. All I know is that I'm not leaving until he does."

"He's still mad?"

"Either that or he's turned into a real pain in the butt over the years."

She expected her dad to laugh. Instead he sighed. "Years ago you should have told him the stuff you told me last night about his trust fund."

"Uh, Dad. We didn't see each other for fifteen years."

"Then maybe you should have told him the day you left."

She squeezed her eyes shut. Hindsight was always twenty-twenty. But even if it wasn't, she knew in her heart of hearts that Nick never would have let her go if she'd admitted she was only leaving so he could get the trust fund.

Of course, he hadn't taken the trust fund.

She rubbed her temples. Picking apart something that had happened fifteen years ago would not make it any better. "I'll call you when we're done."

"How are you going to know when you're done?"

"When he leaves, I'll call you."

"Okay. Sounds like a plan."

She hung up the phone, proud of herself for staying, but still aching over the awkwardness between her and Nick. For fifteen years she'd considered paving the way for Nick to get his trust fund a noble sacrifice. Now that she knew her leaving had been moot, she had no idea how to handle it in her brain. She could no longer be proud of the decision that had seemed so right, but how could she be angry with herself when she hadn't known Nick wouldn't take the money?

The only thing she could think to do to make it up to him was work. Work hard. Work long. Save him some time and effort.

At eight Nick came out of his office, keys in hand. Surprised to see her, he stopped dead in his tracks.

"What are you still doing here?"

"We work ten-hour days. I'm staying as long as you are."

With any other assistant he would have admired her tenacity. But he just wanted Maggie gone. He knew it wasn't fair. He knew it wasn't right. Especially since she was such a hard worker—a qualified worker. But that was what he felt. Discovering she'd left him so he'd get money that he hadn't taken had turned his very sane, very comfortable life upside down. Every time he looked at her, knowing she'd loved him enough to give up everything she'd wanted, something horrible happened in his heart. It ached. It mourned. It started generating visions about what might have been.

Might have been.

He could have snorted in derision. There was no might have been in life. There was only what was—what had happened. And what had happened was that she'd made a decision they should have made together. She'd betrayed him by not talking to him. She'd made the mistake, but somehow he'd ended up paying for it and he was paying again. With questions that had no relevance. Questions that rattled around in his brain every time he looked at her.

He wanted her gone.

But she wasn't leaving. And he was going to have to learn to deal with this.

With a put-upon sigh, he said, "Gather your things and I'll take you home since we have now officially worked an eleven-hour day."

"That's okay. My dad—"

"Gather your things."

He hadn't meant for his voice to be gruff, but it had been and she quickly grabbed her purse and headed out the door.

They walked to the car in silence. Slid onto the seats in silence. And would have ridden the whole way to her dad's farm in silence, if she hadn't said, "I'm nearly done with the employee stats."

Frustration buffeted him. Did she have to be so good? Couldn't she drop the ball a bit so he could direct some of the anger racing through him to something tangible, something he could deal with?

"It took me about two minutes to find the files for the résumés in the computer. So I didn't have to retype anything, just organize the information." Strands of red hair that sparkled in the setting sun blew across her mouth and she pulled them away. "While I had the original bid, I took the liberty of perusing the whole thing. I saw the amount of work you have to do to get the bid ready and I know you need more help than you're letting on. So you can't fight me at every turn. You need to let go of the past and accept that I can help you."

The cheek! If she thought a little verbal lashing would

get him to forget that she'd betrayed him, she was crazy. He understood what his mom had told him about her miscarriage impacting her thinking that day, but making decisions alone wasn't how they operated. They had been a team and she'd broken their pact. Now she was virtually acting as if nothing had happened, which made him feel crazy, or as if he wasn't keeping up with the program. He didn't want her to be capable and smart. He didn't want her help. He wanted to nurse his anger. He wanted to be mad. He'd mourned her loss for five long years before he could push beyond it. He deserved his anger. He had earned it.

They finally reached her dad's farm. Maggie jumped out and he was just about to pull away when her father stepped out of the house and onto the porch.

Tall and slender, with a thick crop of hair that had darkened over the years from fire-engine red to auburn streaked with gray, Maggie's dad looked vibrant and healthy. He waved. "Hey, Nick!"

He waved back. "Hey, Mr. Forsythe."

"Come on up. Have a beer."

Eager to get away, he called, "No, thanks. It's late. I have to get home."

"Late? It's eight-thirty. Come on! It's been years. Give an old man a few minutes of your time."

It seemed downright wrong to ignore the request of a man who'd just lost his wife. Especially when Nick still hadn't paid his respects. He glanced at Maggie who'd stopped dead in her tracks on the grass. She didn't look happy at her dad's invitation. More like resigned.

Her dad waved again. "Come on! Please."

Nick turned off the Porsche's ignition, got out and headed up toward the house. Birds chirped. Flowers drifted in the breeze. In the distance a horse whinnied.

Maggie led the way to the porch. When she reached

the top step, her dad said, "Get us a few beers, would you, kiddo?"

She smiled slightly and nodded then disappeared behind the screen door. Charlie sat on the swing and Nick ambled over to the porch railing and leaned against it.

"What's it been?"

"Fifteen years."

Charlie shook his head. "Wow. I'm getting old." He shook his head again. "So damned old. Everybody I remember as a kid isn't a kid anymore."

Nick laughed. "We can all say that."

Maggie stepped out of the house and handed a beer to her dad and one to Nick. He refused to meet her gaze, but did say, "Thanks."

She said, "You're welcome," then headed to the door again. "I'm getting out of these jeans."

Her dad laughed. "Good idea."

She pulled open the screen door and walked inside.

"I'm sorry about Vicki."

Charlie nodded. "Thanks." He waited two beats, then peered around until he could look into the house. He quickly faced Nick again. "She married a louse."

In the middle of taking a swig of beer, Nick nearly choked.

"She won't tell you that because she's got a lot of pride. But she spilled the beans the day after her stepmother's funeral. Her ex had an affair with some bimbo at his health club and left Maggie. Then got her pregnant one day when he came back to pick up a few things. Maggie thought they were reuniting. He just wanted one last tumble for old-time's sake. When she told him she was pregnant, he told her he didn't want the baby. He'd pay support, but he never wanted to see it." He took a drink of his beer. "She's been through a lot. I'm grateful that you hired her."

Because he wanted to fire her, shame flooded Nick. The story of her marriage was abysmal, but from the sounds of things Maggie was lucky to get away from that guy. Even better, though, Maggie's dad might brag about Charlie Jr. but he also loved his daughter. And maybe he should focus on that, instead of her lousy marriage.

"You don't have to thank me. She's smart and educated." Wanting to make sure her dad understood Maggie was every bit as good as her half brother, he said, "She's helping me a lot more than Julie ever did." Though it pained him to admit it, he also added, "We're already over half done with the bid. Instead of taking four weeks, it's probably only going to take us three. With her experience, things may even run smoothly when I need to take trips out of town to help my brother."

"You do seem to be gone a lot."

"My dad neglected his companies in the last two years of his life. My brother needs me in New York to help him get the conglomerate back in shape."

Charlie grunted. "Doesn't make a whole lot of sense to me to fix one company by ruining another."

Upstairs in her room Maggie heard her father's comments through her open bedroom window. She fell to the bed, not sure if she should laugh or cry. Not only had her father told her biggest secret to her former husband and new boss, but he was also chastising Nick for being away too much.

"Things are fine."

"Right, I'll bet your dad said the same thing the years he was letting his company go to hell in a ham sandwich."

The sound of Nick's laughter surprised her. He was angry with her, furious. He didn't even want to be around her, but he was stuck with her. Yet he wasn't taking that out on her father.

"Hell in a ham sandwich?"

Her dad grunted. "I never really understood what a handbasket was. Figured a ham sandwich makes more sense, what with the cholesterol and all. The heart attack that gives you will send a person to hell quicker than some damned basket."

Nick laughed again. The sound of it filled her with warm, sweet delight and wrapped her in memories. In some ways it was good that Nick had matured out of the silly boy she'd married and become a serious adult. It helped Maggie keep her perspective. But in others, it seemed a shame that the happy Nick Roebuck was gone. Replaced by Nick Andreas, businessman.

"Anyway." Nick's voice drifted up to her again. "Thanks for the beer. I'd better get home."

"Why don't you stay for supper?"

A pause. "Actually I've got to call my brother, get the rundown on what happened at Andreas Holdings this week."

The swing creaked. "Okay, then. I'll see you on Monday morning when you pick up Maggie for work. Seems to me it's easier for you to pick her up than me to drive her in, since you're going there anyway."

Maggie's face fell in dismay. If she weren't in her bra and panties she probably would have leaned out the window and told Nick her father was a silly old coot who shouldn't be asking for favors. Instead she could only squeeze her eyes shut in misery.

"Unless you're picking her up tomorrow to work on Sunday? I don't like people working on Sundays, you know. Everybody needs a rest. You come by Monday."

Pure mortification turned her face to scarlet.

But Nick said, "Yeah, sure, I'll pick her up."

CHAPTER SEVEN

NICK thought about Maggie's crappy marriage the whole way home. She'd told him about her husband running up debts. Add that to the fact that he'd left a pregnant wife and the guy wouldn't rate high in anybody's book. But the situation hadn't entirely come together in his head until Charlie had told him he'd had an affair. Then the facts snapped in place like puzzle pieces and a picture formed of Maggie struggling, Maggie being at home alone at night, Maggie suffering in silence.

When he got out of his car, he punched the wall of the short stairway leading to his kitchen. He didn't understand the feelings swirling inside of him. He was angry with her. Furious. He shouldn't care that she'd married a cretin who didn't treat her well and left her pregnant and penniless.

But he did care. He didn't want to see Maggie hurt just because she'd hurt him. Only an idiot thought like that and he wasn't an idiot.

He called Darius and got a rundown on the week at Andreas Holdings, but he kept the conversation brief, telling Darius he still had things to read before he went to bed. He didn't want his perceptive brother asking questions he couldn't answer.

Sunday morning he raced to work, knowing he'd have the office to himself and desperately in need of something to think about to get his mind off Maggie. He stayed until eight o'clock that night and grabbed a hot fudge sundae as his dinner on the way home. He fell into bed and slept like the dead.

Monday morning he felt marginally better. Working alone all day Sunday in the silent office, he'd gotten a lot of organizational tasks done. He headed for Andreas Manufacturing ready to tackle some of the more difficult aspects of the bid with Maggie then remembered he was supposed to be picking her up.

As he drove out to the farm, the things Charlie Forsythe had told him flashed to the front of his brain again, and he groaned in misery. As long as he worked with Maggie, he would be trapped in an emotional vortex. He hated what she'd done, but he didn't mean to punish her. Didn't want to see her unhappy. He just wanted away from her. But because of the bid, he was in as much of a bind as she was. She might need the job, but he also needed an assistant. He was simply going to have to figure out a way to deal with her.

When he pulled up to her house, the front door opened and Maggie ran out. She jumped into his car so fast he'd barely rolled to a stop.

For the first time in days, he laughed. "You don't want to risk your dad talking to me again, do you?"

She turned wary green eyes on him. "Would you?"

"He's lonely. He wanted a few minutes of my time. That's all."

Blessedly the conversation stopped there. But remembering the things her father had said, he shifted uncomfortably on his seat. Lord, he wanted to be furious with her. She'd broken his heart because she hadn't consulted him before making a decision that had changed their lives. But he'd become a very rich man, dated lots of women, had a great life—

And she'd been hurt, taken for granted, cast aside.

"I'll be glad when my car is fixed."

All right, already! Fate didn't have to rub his nose in her troubles. He got it. Not only was she a divorced, abandoned pregnant woman, who had to take a job with her angry ex-husband, but her car had broken. Surely to God he could muster enough sympathy to engage in small talk.

He looked over. "I hope you're not angsting about me driving you to work."

"Yes and no. I'm embarrassed that my dad sort of cor-ralled you into this."

"It's fine."

She glanced out the window. "I know. Everything's *fine*. But you and my dad aren't the ones living without trans-portation. There's more reason to have a car than going back and forth to work. There are times that I'd like to be able to just go. Get out of the house. Get some fresh air."

He thought about his drives along the beach. "I hear that."

"Really?" She peered over at him, her eyes sad, tired. "You live alone. You can have all the privacy you want at your house."

His heart tried to crack open. He wouldn't let it. "Maybe too much privacy. Sometimes it's so quiet I think too much."

She laughed. "That would be the day."

"Oh, come on. It's just you and your dad. How much noise can one fifty-five-year-old guy make?"

"None most of the time." She shrugged then peeked over at him. "He's so preoccupied with keeping himself busy so he doesn't miss Vicki that sometimes we pass like ships in the night."

He forced his attention back to the road, but it was too late. One basic, all-important question had fallen into his brain. How could she want to take care of a dad who'd ignored her once his son was born?

With a sigh, he gave in. If he didn't get the answer, she'd preoccupy his thoughts and he wouldn't get a lick of work done all day.

"So are things okay with your dad?"

"Things?"

"No Charlie Jr. troubles?"

She laughed. "Charlie Jr. troubles?"

Her voice dripped with such incredulity that he grimaced. "I'm remembering the past. You know? How your parents sort of favored Charlie Jr."

"Ah. You're going the whole way back to high school." She smiled. "All that went away when I left for university. Because I worked, I didn't come home for breaks, so they visited me. I sort of had an identity. Was my own person. Had my own place." She shrugged. "I can't explain it. But it was like everything that didn't work at their house, suddenly worked at mine."

He eased back. "So all that stuff from our teen years is gone?"

"Yep." She smiled. "Vicki even made trips up to Pittsburgh without Dad so she could shop at our outlets."

They were quiet for a minute, then she faced him again. "So what about you? You said you and your dad only had dinner once every other year, yet you changed your name from Roebuck to Andreas and even used that name for your company."

Nick grimaced. "Actually it was supposed to be a slap in his face."

"Really? How?"

He glanced at Maggie. The wind tossed her hair. Her

eyes were soft, but serious. Old memories surfaced. Times they'd talked. Confided. He'd never done that with another person. He hadn't even really talked with his brothers about this. And now he couldn't stop himself.

"Think it through. You're Stephone Andreas, known all over the world because you run a multibillion-dollar shipping conglomerate, then suddenly you're not the only Andreas business that comes up when people look you up on Google. There's a tiny company in North Carolina…and guess what? It's run by the son you don't acknowledge."

"Ouch."

He shrugged. "I was young. Angry. I'd thrown my dad's five million dollars back in his face and I wanted him to know I hadn't needed it."

"You regret it."

A statement, not a question.

"Yes." He glanced at her again. "Not refusing the trust, but being such a lunkhead. In my twenties it felt wonderful to be a thorn in his side. But when my company really took root and became well-known in my industry, I started to see what an idiot I was. He might have abandoned my mom and never acknowledged me, but he was trying to make up for that."

"So you forgave him?"

How could he explain to Maggie that he'd become his dad—not completely, but in some ways—so he had no real right to be angry?

He couldn't. So he said simply, "I forgave him."

"I never did hear the story of how you got started without any money."

Eager to be off the topic of his dad, Nick answered without thinking. "I met up with a guy who knew a guy who knew a guy who was not only selling some old equipment, he also had the balance of a contract to finish. So we did the deal on a profit sharing basis—the seller wouldn't get money until the profits were official—and I was in business."

"Smart."

Pride lifted his mood as they reached Andreas Manufacturing. He was smart. He had made it. No one could take that away from him. He pulled his Porsche into his reserved parking space and followed Maggie into the building.

But as they stepped into her office, reality returned. A fierce pang burst in his chest, shoving his pride into another dimension, reminding him she wasn't his friend, only his employee, yet they'd talked. As if she hadn't left him, and there weren't fifteen years between them, he'd told her things he hadn't ever told another person.

Something like fear laced with a warning stole through him. What the hell was he doing? She needed this job. He needed her help. And he also didn't want to hurt her. Nick Roebuck had been the love of her life. Not Nick Andreas. Nick Andreas didn't want to be the love of anybody's life and he had better remember that.

After giving her time to put her lunch bag in a drawer and get settled at her desk, he called her into his office and quickly dictated a few things he needed to be done that morning. Then he went back to work on the bid. He closed the door, kept himself set apart and got back into Nick Andreas mode.

When Maggie returned to her office after eating her sandwich in the employee cafeteria, Nick wasn't back from lunch yet. Bored, she perused the labor files again and was surprised to notice something intriguing.

When Nick suddenly strode past her desk, her head snapped up.

"Hey! I just found the most interesting thing in the labor reports."

He stopped, hesitated then faced her. "What?"

His guarded expression told her that all the goodwill they'd built that morning in the car was now gone. He was back to being angry with her. She had to be okay with that. She had no right to his friendship, only to this job, and she intended to keep it by wearing him down with her abilities.

"This employee Jake Graessle?" She tapped the paper. "Look how the productivity of the person on the machine beside his goes up."

For that, Nick took the few steps over to her desk. He tried to read the paper upside down, but apparently was unable to because he walked behind her desk and stood beside her.

Woodsy aftershave invaded her nostrils. His pure masculine heat wafted to her as he leaned in and read the lines she'd pointed out.

"Interesting."

Forcing herself to ignore his nearness, she said, "If his supervisor is having trouble with another employee's production, he could try an experiment and put him beside Jake. If that employee's stats go up, then we'll know Jake's one of those people who just naturally exerts a sort of positive peer pressure."

With a "Hmm" Nick straightened away. "Call his supervisor in."

She reached for her notepad. "What time do you want to talk to him?"

"You found the data. You have the honor of telling him. And helping him figure out the best way to use it."

Pleasure warmed her blood. "Really?"

"Sure." He didn't look at her as he spoke and his words

were dull, lifeless. "This job can be whatever you want to make it. Julie preferred the secretarial end of things. You're trained differently. I'm not going to stifle you. Go with your gut. Do what needs to be done. Stretch yourself."

Reminding herself that his anger with her was justified, yet he was no longer holding it against her professionally, she let him walk away and called Jake's supervisor to her office. She spent a half hour going over the labor reports and her findings. Liking her recommendations, George Wyman left her office a happy camper. Unfortunately when he had gone, Maggie had nothing to do.

With a deep breath, she pushed herself out of her chair, picked up her steno pad and a pen and walked into Nick's office.

He didn't even glance up. "Yes?"

"I don't have anything to do."

He hesitated, but eventually looked up and pointed at the conference table. "Sit. I'll be right over."

She took her normal seat, but Nick didn't take his. Instead of sitting catty-cornered from her, he sat across from her.

A weird sensation enveloped her. The distance between them felt so wrong, yet what right did she have for things to be anything but strained between them? She shouldn't feel weird. She shouldn't be unhappy. She shouldn't feel anything but gratitude that he kept her in his employ.

He pulled the next file off the stack. It contained hard copies of reports that Julie had generated from the accounting software. He quickly explained that he got some of the reports monthly, some weekly, some daily. Printing all of them and having them on his desk was her duty. Filing hard copies where he could find them when he worked late was also her responsibility.

From there he dictated some correspondence, most of

which he wanted her to send as emails. His voice never wavered from a crisp, efficient monotone. He said nothing nice, nothing personal. In spite of her best efforts to accept that, the temperature in the room went from cool to frigid in the half hour it took him to get through the stack.

Finished, he rose from his seat. "That's all. I think you have enough to keep you busy until quitting time."

She said, "Yes. Thank you," and left his office.

At her desk, she dropped her head into her hands. She might have impressed him enough with her finding about Jake, but he was back to giving her only secretarial tasks again. The good impression she'd made had only been temporary.

She sighed. What did she expect—

Actually she'd expected him to take the damned five million dollars. She'd expected him to be smug about his success, while secretly she could be equally smug about her sacrifice. Instead he'd succeeded without her "help" and was angry that she'd made a decision without him.

She was the loser in all of this.

At five, she didn't even bother letting Nick know she was leaving. He might still be working on the bid, and working ten-hour days, but the work he'd given her that afternoon was his regular assistant day-to-day work. And she was finished. She had nothing else to do. No reason to stay.

She called her dad and left a message on the answering machine to remind him to come and get her before she gathered her things. She had her cell phone. There was no reason to wait twenty feet away from a man so cool icicles were forming on the doorway between them.

She ambled out to the warm, sunny parking lot. That's when she remembered her dad had asked Nick to be her ride to and from work. Even if he listened to the message she'd left on the answering machine, he'd think it was from the week before. She was going to have to go back inside.

She groaned and turned toward the building again but didn't take a step.

Couldn't fate give her a break here? Did she have to embarrass herself by going back to the office and either sitting there with nothing to do or tapping on Nick's door frame begging for work?

She waited a minute. Hoped someone from another department would be leaving and she could ask for a lift. But no one came out of the building. It had taken her long enough to gather her things that everyone from day shift was already gone. The parking lot was silent. Only the hot breeze stirred around her.

She waited another minute or two not sure if she was expecting a fairy godmother to show up with a coach or a coworker to return for something they'd forgotten. But no one appeared.

Straightening her shoulders she headed back inside. It was ridiculously unfair of fate to put her in this disgustingly humiliating position, but there was nothing she could do about it.

She breezed into her office. They were supposed to be working ten-hour days. So she was supposed to stay. And work. Not just sit at her desk waiting for Nick to emerge from his office and grace her with something to keep her occupied.

Angry, she rapped on his door frame. "Hey. I'm sorry, but I don't have anything to do again." She said the words in a rush before she could lose courage. "Could you give me something—anything—to do until you're ready to go?"

"We can go now." He rose from his seat and grabbed

his cell phone and keys from beside a stack of papers on his desk.

Embarrassment flared, fueled by humiliation. If she ever met fate in person, she swore to God she was going to kick its butt.

"You don't have to take me home right this minute. Just give me work to do until you're ready to go."

"I'm ready now." The truth was Nick had been watching her outside his window. He'd seen her stride out to the parking lot as if expecting to see her dad, then turn and look at the door as if finally remembering *he* was her ride. He should have simply left his desk right then and there and taken her home. Instead he'd sat in his office, watching her, because he just wasn't ready to deal with her.

When she'd asked him for work that afternoon, he'd barely been able to sit at the table with her. She smelled good. She looked fantastic. Her soft voice tickled along his spine. It had taken a monumental effort to stay in the same room as they sifted through the files on his conference table. And now he had to drive her home. In his little car, where she'd be six inches away from his fingertips. Somehow or another his hormones had not gotten the message that she was still the enemy. And that made him even angrier with himself.

"I didn't mean for you to drop everything for me—"

Her conciliatory answer turned his anger into disappointment in himself. Wasn't he a better man than this? He could understand not wanting to be friendly with her, but why was he so angry?

"It's fine."

"Thanks."

As he rounded the desk, she turned and, from the side, the protruding stomach that was barely noticeable totally changed her profile. Wounded male pride crackled through him like the sting of a whip. They hadn't just lost each other the day she'd left; they'd lost a baby. They'd lost plans and dreams and hopes...and everything. Had she stayed, there would have been other babies. He'd be a dad now. Not a womanizer. He'd have a houseful of kids and a devoted wife, something to come home to other than silence, something that would have him so grounded he wouldn't long to go back to New York City on the pretense of helping his brother, but actually to enjoy the nightlife.

He'd be a dad.

But she'd made their choices. And he'd made his. Changed who he was. Changed what he wanted. Now he had to live with them.

He motioned for her to precede him out of the office and followed her to his car. The sleek line of her back caught his attention. Just as with their pregnancy, she hadn't gained a lot of weight. The taut muscles of her back curved slightly at her waist then flared into perfectly rounded hips. She'd always worried that she was too thin, too much of a tomboy to be sexy, but he'd loved her exactly the way she was. Her skin felt like velvet, tasted like honey—

He stifled a groan. Really? Was he going to let his hormones rule? Was he going to let himself remember things that might be nothing more than an idealized vision he created because she was his first? Was he that confused or that much of a sap? Fifteen years ago, he might have loved her, might have wanted to be a dad, but after five years of mourning and ten years of being a very happy, very rich bachelor, that part of him was dust. He was who he was. Somebody halfway between his unfaithful dad and superfaithful, supertrusting, eighteen-year-old Nick Roebuck.

He was Nick Andreas. And Nick Andreas wasn't a sappy kid.

She jumped into the passenger side and he slid behind the steering wheel.

"I really appreciate this."

"It's not a big deal."

They were silent as he maneuvered out of the parking lot and through town. This drive, he wouldn't be so foolish as to engage her in conversation. He'd already told her too much about himself. He wouldn't give her false hope that everything between them could be okay and they could be friends. They couldn't.

When they arrived at the farm, she glanced over, smiled and said, "You know, I just really want to say one thing then we can never talk about personal things again."

He didn't reply. Let his silence tell her that if she wanted to speak that was fine. He'd listen. But there was no guarantee he'd answer her.

"I'm proud of you. You really did everything you set out to do."

Another man might have preened under her praise, but the final layer of his emotions peeled off, revealing the real source of his anger. Pain shimmered through him.

He nodded quickly, nothing more than an indication that he'd heard. Then she hopped out and Nick drove out of the dusty driveway.

Far enough away that she couldn't see him, he slapped his steering wheel. Now he knew why he was so angry with her. Why it still hurt so much that she'd left him even though fifteen years had passed.

She hadn't just left so he'd get a trust fund. She'd left because she hadn't believed he'd succeed. At least not without help.

And that was the real bottom line. She hadn't trusted him. She hadn't believed in him.

The one person he'd always thought would stand by him hadn't.

Because she hadn't believed in him.

CHAPTER EIGHT

THAT night, Nick made his typical call to Darius. But when his older brother didn't answer, he left a message asking him to return the call the next morning.

He didn't want to talk to Darius that night. He was too perceptive. He'd hear something in Nick's voice and he'd drag this part of the story out of him, too. Nick was getting just a bit tired of his entire gloomy past being revealed bit by bit for his brothers' entertainment. It wasn't a matter of keeping a secret; it had become an issue of privacy, of pride.

By the time Darius called the next morning, Nick was in control. Now that he understood the real bottom line to his hurt over Maggie leaving, it was easy to keep his anger under wraps. Also easy to put everything into perspective. He wasn't a sap who hadn't gotten over being left by the woman he'd loved. He was a hardworking, ambitious man who'd been blindsided. The woman he'd put his trust in didn't trust him to become the man he'd known he could be and she'd cast him aside.

There was a reason to be angry. But not stay angry forever. He wouldn't get involved with Maggie again. Not even as a friend. But he could work with her. Hell, he needed her. And with his new perspective, he wouldn't have to fight that anymore.

The balance of the week went smoothly. She didn't force them into any more private conversations and he didn't hesitate to give her work. Hard work. The good jobs she wanted. Not only did that free Nick to do the more complicated tasks only he could handle, but also that seemed to please her. Which meant there were no more questions, no more awkward conversations. Even Saturday flew by without a hitch. They were a happy assistant and a busy boss and life returned to normal.

On Sunday morning, when Darius called and said Andreas Holdings needed him in New York bright and early Monday morning, he didn't hesitate to call Maggie at home. With everything sorted out in his head, she was nothing but an assistant. The work for the bid was ahead of schedule. He could afford a day or two out of the office.

Her dad answered. "Hey, Nick!"

"Hey, Charlie. I have to be in New York first thing in the morning so my brother Cade's sending a plane for me this afternoon. I thought I'd come over and give Maggie instructions for what I need her to do in the two days I'll be gone."

"Well, sure. Come on over. I'll save some lunch."

"Don't save lunch. I'll have about two minutes to talk to her before I have to get myself to the airport."

He hung up the phone and, with a legal pad on his bed, he made a list of things for Maggie to do as he hastily packed.

Flying down the driveway to her dad's farm, he raised a layer of dust that barely had time to disburse before he jumped out of his Porsche.

Instruction sheet in hand, he headed for the front porch steps, but the sound of someone jumping off the diving board of the pool in back of the house caught his attention. He remembered swimming in that pool with Maggie when they were about six, after her mom had died but before Vicki came into their lives. Charlie always acted as life-guard and at least once did a belly flop, trying to dive. Now that he felt better about the whole situation with Maggie, he could spare two minutes to tease lonely Charlie about his dive.

With a happy snicker, he snuck around the side of the house and stopped dead.

Rather than see Charlie, Nick watched Maggie pull herself out of the pool. Water ran from her long red hair, down her arms and legs, and made rivulets down her chest to her breasts. The top of the bright blue bathing suit she wore fluffed out around her middle, effectively hiding her pregnancy. The bottom was cut high enough that every inch of her long, smooth legs was exposed.

His breath shuddered in and out of his lungs. Good God.

He hadn't forgotten how beautiful she was. How sexy. But he had forgotten that nobody did a bathing suit justice the way Maggie did.

She turned in his direction and surprise registered on her face when she saw him. She rubbed a towel across her head to absorb the excess water. "Nick? What are you doing here?"

As she spoke, she took in his black suit, white shirt and striped tie. When her gaze drifted down to his Italian loaf-ers, then roamed to the puddles on the blue and white tiles around the pool, she winced. "I'll come over to you."

"No. It's fine," he said, sidestepping the little bits of water. "I called your dad to let you know I was coming."

She grimaced. "He must have forgotten to tell me."

His gaze involuntarily fell to her long legs again but he immediately jerked his eyes up to her face. "He must have. I need to talk to you about some things for work tomorrow."

Dropping the towel to a nearby chaise lounge, then stretching out on top of it, she said, "Have a seat."

She pointed to the chaise beside hers, and, not sure what else to do, he walked over. Not wanting to wreck his suit or look like an idiot sprawling on a chaise dressed the way he was, he sat sideways, only to realize that put him only about a foot and a half away from her long, lean body.

She blew her breath out and closed her eyes as if enjoying the sun as she got comfortable.

Glad her eyes were shut, he ran his finger beneath his collar, stretching it away a bit so he could breathe. "I… um… My brother Darius called last night. I'm needed in New York."

She opened her eyes. Peered at him. "But you have a bid due."

"I know, but we got a lot of work done last week. We're ahead of schedule. Plus, you've got a really good handle on what we're doing. So I made a list of things that need to be done." He waved the paper at her. "At the bottom is my cell phone number, along with Julie's number in case you have any questions or can't find anything."

She took the paper from him, scanned it then smiled up at him. "Okay."

The hot Southern sun had turned her normally pale skin a soft brown. Her green eyes sparkled. Her full lips curved smoothly, naturally upward. And all he could think about was how he used to be able to kiss those lips. Run his fingers through her smooth, silky hair. Touch all that soft, soft skin.

Reminding himself she hadn't trusted him, hadn't believed in him, and she was nothing but his assistant—an assistant who really could handle things while he was gone—he cleared his throat. "You're sure? No questions?"

She nodded. "I'm fine." She waved the paper again. "And if I'm not, I can call you."

"Or Julie," he hastily reminded. "She's back from Vegas. If there's anything you need that you can't find, she's the one to call because she'd be the one who filed it."

"Great."

Rising, he inwardly cursed himself for sounding like an idiot. "Great."

Unfortunately she also rose, putting them toe-to-toe.

Heat and need roared through him. He didn't want it. He'd thought he'd dealt with it. From Wednesday through Saturday they'd worked together like a well-oiled machine, any thought of their attraction seemingly forgotten. But here it was. Heating his blood, scrambling his pulse, shifting his breathing.

In the past fifteen years, he'd had girlfriends and lovers. Plenty of them. But no one had ever compared to Maggie. He'd always believed that was because she was his first. His first love. His first lover. His first everything. But the desire currently stealing his breath was different, stronger—

Ack! Why the hell was he thinking like this? Sure, she was gorgeous, and, yes, he was attracted, but she wasn't somehow superior to every other woman on the planet. And they seriously needed to move on.

Hell, twenty minutes ago, he'd been absolutely positive he *had* moved on.

He pointed stupidly toward his car. "I'll just get going then."

"Okay, great."

Unfortunately she was directly in front of him. If he

stepped back, he'd trip over the chaise. Step forward, he'd bring them flush against each other.

The thought brought a vision of her soft breasts meeting his chest, their thighs brushing, their lips meeting and suddenly he realized what was going on. These feelings racing through him weren't about Maggie, but about sex. And why not? She was gorgeous. She was sleek. She was his first. So of course he had a special attraction to her. But it wasn't about feelings. It was about a fantasy. Nothing more.

He stepped sideways.

"I'll be back Tuesday afternoon or Wednesday morning. Not sure which."

"Okay."

He headed for his Porsche.

"And Nick?"

He turned. "Yeah?"

"Thanks."

"For?"

She waved the paper at him. "For having faith in me. I know all this has been hard for you, but I need this chance."

He cleared his throat as unwanted emotion clogged there. Every time he had the situation between them narrowed down to just sex, she reminded him that it had never been just about sex between them. Even if she hadn't loved him, they'd been friends. Best friends. Friends who took care of each other.

But in the end that had actually backfired. She'd taken care of him for so long that when a chance to let him stand on his own two feet had arisen, she hadn't trusted him.

He said, "You're welcome," and walked away.

When he was gone, Maggie snatched her towel off the chaise with a curse and went into the house. In eleven years of working in offices she'd never seen anybody who looked as good in a suit as Nick did. Nothing could add to his dark, brooding handsomeness, but the suit reminded her—and the world—that he was somebody. Somebody important. Somebody to be respected.

And she'd just behaved like a fool. Nerves had had her sitting on the chaise lounge and offering him the seat beside her. If she'd stopped there, she could have almost felt okay about it. But, no. She'd stretched out. Nervously closed her eyes. Then stood up too quickly when he'd tried to leave.

But that was because he hadn't been able to take his eyes off her.

That was the part that made her so nervous she'd acted like a damned fool. The part that made her want to shiver. No one but Nick had ever looked at her that way. As if he was starving and she was a feast. She'd forgotten how much she liked the shimmery, shiny look in his eyes when he couldn't stop his gaze from touching every inch of her.

She'd also forgotten the heady surge of power that coursed through her when his eyes simmered. She'd never felt that with any other man, so she'd always believed she'd imagined it. Or maybe that the burst of feminine power that had raced through her was the reaction of a woman being noticed by a man for the first time. Yet, here she was, fifteen years later, feeling it all again. The rush of adrenaline. The shivers of anticipation. The longing for his touch.

She groaned.

She had better get over this soon because from the way Nick raced away, he wasn't having wonderful, positive feelings about being attracted to her. If he was attracted at all. For all she knew he had only been looking at her to check out the differences in her from when they'd been married.

Or maybe the difference two short weeks had made in her tummy. Her stomach was more pronounced now. Though it wasn't the size of a basketball yet, it had grown. The changes might not be noticeable when he was around every day, but seeing her out of the office he might be noticing different things.

That had to be it.

Even if he had been attracted to her, he wouldn't follow through. Time had passed. And he was rich now. Rumor in town was that he dated constantly. While she'd married the first guy she met at university, he'd become a real playboy.

She glanced down at her tummy. What would a playboy want with her?

Nothing.

"So Cade tells me the whole ex-wife thing isn't working out."

Sitting in the backseat of Darius's limo, Nick looked from Darius to Cade, who snickered. "No secrets, remember?"

"I've thought that pact through and I've decided there's a thin line between not having secrets and giving a person his privacy. And we're crossing over into my privacy, so we need to stop talking about Maggie."

"You're just mad because you still like her and you're not sure how to make a move."

Nick gaped at Cade. "I do not still like her. I do not want to make a move. I want an assistant. I want to be able to go to work and be a boss again, not an ex-husband. Not an ex-lover. And I think we're getting there." He deliberately left out the feelings that had rumbled through him at her pool. There was no point to telling anybody about that since he had no intention of pursuing it. He'd rather tell his brothers about the good week of work they'd put in together. That made them both seem normal, sane.

"She's the best assistant I've ever had. Good enough that I left my bid in her hands without having to worry that my company will go to hell in a ham sandwich—" He paused, remembering that was what Charlie had said, then almost groaned when he realized how much the Forsythes were insinuating themselves into his formerly comfortable life. "I like being able to come up here to work without worrying about Andreas Manufacturing."

Darius's long black limo pulled up the circular driveway in front of the family's Montauk estate. As eldest, he had inherited it and the chairmanship of the company, as well as their half brother Gino, but the house was so big there was plenty of room for all of them. Cade and Nick never stayed anywhere else when they came to New York.

"So, it's working out well," Darius said as he climbed out after the driver opened the door. "Not poorly, as Cade had said."

"Cade wasn't off the mark. The day he visited things were bad, but the tide has turned. She's amazing. Perfect." There. He'd said it. Now his brothers could stop riding him.

Darius headed for the front door. "I'm hoping this means we can start talking about making your work for Andreas Holdings official. Get you a title, an office, responsibilities you can take off my plate."

Not waiting for a reply, Darius walked into the house and Cade caught Nick's arm, stopping him before he could follow Darius into the mansion.

"Okay. Here's the deal. Darius won't tell you this flat-out, but he really needs you here full-time. The chairmanship's enough for him. Add CEO of Andreas Shipping to that and he's working twenty-four seven. He thinks you only want to work part-time, so that's all he's offering, but he needs you here full-time and I think you should step up."

"Step up?"

"Sell your beach house and bring your butt to New York permanently."

"Permanently?" Something like terror gripped his heart. "Sell my beach house?"

"Or keep it for weekends. You're probably going to have to fly down once a month to check on your ex anyway after you put her in charge—"

Nick's head was spinning. "Put Maggie in charge?"

"Sure. I'm not saying you give up your job as CEO. I'm just saying that with fax machines and email, you don't need to be in North Carolina to run your company. You give your ex a title like general manager and let her run the day-to-day stuff and instruct her to send the really important things to you by fax or email."

Nick's head spun even more. First, it had never been his plan to move to New York permanently. Or to sell his house. Second, he couldn't see passing off that much responsibility to a pregnant woman—

"I can't pass everything off to her. She's pregnant."

"So? She's already working. You're just giving her the good office. Your comfy chair. The nice sofa. Hell, put a TV in there and she'd practically have an apartment."

"And what happens to the company while she's out on maternity leave?"

"You run it. You take a leave of absence from Andreas Holdings and I'll fill in for you here."

"Or we could just split the extra work at Andreas Holdings as we have been."

"That's not working out for me. I can shift my schedule

to accommodate a few months while your ex has her baby, but being away one week a month as I have been is wrecking my system. And I can't hire somebody to replace me. I run a ranch and an oil conglomerate. I'd need to find at least two people. Maybe four. You own one company. One person can replace you. You yourself just admitted you left your prime bid in the hands of your ex-wife. You trust her."

Nick rubbed his hand across the back of his neck. Not only had he made this mess by bragging about Maggie, but also he suddenly realized he did trust her with his company. Really trust her. What the hell had happened in the past week?

When Nick only stared at his brother, Cade sighed. "Come on. You love clubbing. You like being out and about. Plus, you love being around Gino. Why not do us all a solid and just make the move?"

Not anywhere near able to wrap his mind around Cade's idea, and absolutely, positively not wanting to argue with his younger brother about something that wasn't any of his business, Nick said, "I'll think about it."

"Think fast." Cade angled his chin to point into the foyer, nudging Nick to look at the happy scene just beyond the front door. Pretty blond-haired, blue-eyed Whitney kissed Darius before she handed one-year-old Gino to him. The little boy wrapped his chubby arms around Darius's neck and hugged him.

"We can't put all the pressure of Andreas Holdings on him anymore. He's got more responsibilities than making us money."

When Nick returned late Tuesday afternoon, Julie was sitting at Maggie's desk. His heart sank before he could stop it. Fear caused his pulse to race. Maggie had gone? She'd quit?

After two days of torment while he considered Cade's plan of leaving his business in Maggie's hands, it just didn't seem right that she'd simply quit. He was literally considering giving her the job of a lifetime. How could she leave? Why would she leave?

The answer to that popped into his head without hesitation. He'd been a crappy boss. A crabby boss. She'd been nothing but eager to please and he'd sniped at her. But they'd gotten along and worked together so well the week before—

Of course, he'd also ogled her by her dad's pool. They couldn't stand within two feet of each other without generating enough electricity to power a small city. And she was pregnant. Broke. Maybe juggling it all was getting to be too much for her? God knew he was having trouble keeping up.

He started to ask, "Where's Maggie?" but before the question was fully formed, Maggie came running into the office. "I saw Nick's car—"

She stopped, caught his gaze.

In his mind's eye, Nick envisioned her pulling herself out of the swimming pool, dripping with water, stretching out on the chaise. The feelings he'd had standing toe-to-toe with her slammed through him. His breathing stuttered. His pulse sped up. All his nerve endings went on red alert.

Oh, yeah. He could absolutely understand why she'd be tired of dealing with this—

Except she hadn't quit. She was right here, ready to work. And he was ogling her again.

Maggie took a step back. Her gaze dropped to the floor. "I couldn't find a few things and called Julie."

"That's fine." He had to stop this. She was a capable, dedicated employee, who was clearly uncomfortable with the fact that he was still attracted to her. Unless he wanted to lose her, he had better rein this in and treat her like the good employee she was. "Actually that's great."

Julie peered around Maggie to catch his gaze. "I sort of figure I owed you a week."

Nick didn't argue. "You did."

Bottle of water in hand, Maggie motioned for him to follow her into his office. Files and papers were strewn across the desk. His computer monitor blinked. Without a second's hesitation, she sat on his chair, hit a few keys on the computer and brought up a new document.

She looked so right, so perfect in his office, sitting at his chair that Cade's suggestion of making her general manager suddenly didn't sound so ridiculous. He set his briefcase on the desk.

"This," she said, proudly pointing at the screen, "is your finished bid."

He slowly rounded the desk. *"Finished?"*

"Sure. It was a piece of cake." She glanced back at him worriedly and quickly said, "Not that your system wasn't working, but you were asking departments to update the old forms and then you were matching the info to the new bid package. It was a lot easier to create the new forms in the computer and add our narrative and numbers from scratch. Especially since I had each department handle its own individual section of the bid."

"A lot easier," Julie said from behind him.

He turned. "You were party to this?"

She grinned. "I just monitored. Maggie's the one who gave out assignments, had the staff create the new documents and plug in their own numbers."

He faced Maggie. "So you're responsible."

Her face reddened. "Only if you're pleased."

"I'm flabbergasted." He caught her gaze. "But I won't say I'm pleased unless the bid is correct. I'm not going to take your word for it."

"Oh, absolutely," she said, jumping from his chair. "Here, you can start reading now."

Giving him the seat, she edged around him. But the space behind the desk was narrow and with her baby bump she couldn't slide through gaps as easily as she could if not pregnant. As he tried to get to the seat and she tried to maneuver away from the seat, they found themselves face-to-face again. Inches apart.

She looked up.

He looked down.

She couldn't disguise the spark that lit her green eyes or the hitch in her breath. The reaction caught him off guard. She was as attracted to him as he was to her?

He gazed into her eyes again.

She *was*.

Now neither one of them could deny it.

They held each other's gaze a moment too long and something strange passed between them. In some ways they were the Maggie Forsythe and Nick Roebuck who'd grown from friends into lovers. In others they were two totally different people. But the new people they'd become were still attracted. Very attracted. And connected. Which explained why he was so angry about the way her ex-husband had treated her. He'd always felt connected to her, responsible for her. Not just like the guy who was supposed to protect her, but also as if she were the other half of the whole they were supposed to create. In some ways over the past fifteen years, he'd always felt just a little lost without her.

But that was wrong.

Completely wrong.

Only a fool felt lost over a woman who hadn't believed in him. Especially a man in his position where confidence was sometimes the most important weapon in his arsenal.

He quickly shifted to the right as she shifted to the left and scrambled around the desk.

Julie headed for the door. "It's close enough to five that I'm leaving for the day." She turned and faced Nick. "Actually, with the bid done, I can't think of a reason to come back tomorrow. Unless you want me to work the other few days I owe you."

"No. That's fine." He smiled at her. "Thanks for coming in. For helping out. I think your debt's paid."

"You're welcome."

With that she left. Nick glanced over at Maggie. She smiled sheepishly and sat on the chair across from his at the desk.

Tension tightened his muscles. Understanding what was happening between them helped him to dismiss it. But it also resurrected his anger. He refused to feel connected to a woman who hadn't believed in him. What kind of a man even considered being attached to a partner who didn't share his vision of himself, didn't believe he could reach his dreams? She'd long ago left him. Her baby wasn't his. Her troubles weren't his.

Plus, his brother needed him. And he wanted a new life. As Cade had said, he loved clubbing. He loved nightlife. He wanted everything New York had to offer. If Maggie really had finished the bid, she might have proven herself qualified to take over as Andreas Manufacturing's general manager. He could leave and she could become the new day-to-day boss, saving only the really big executive work and decisions for him.

Everybody won.

That is, if she'd really gotten the bid done.

Turning his attention to the computer, he tried to read the pages on the screen, but he couldn't focus. He shifted on the chair. Peeked up to see Maggie eagerly awaiting his verdict. And then heard the door close behind Julie who was leaving them unchaperoned.

All right. So they were alone. They might not have a person between them, but they had a nice solid desk. And he had more reason to stay away from her than a man needed. Not just their pasts, but their futures. He was on the verge of offering her the job of a lifetime. In a way, he'd be satisfying the fury that rose inside him every time he thought about how life had cheated her, even as he tucked her away with a good job and a good income so he'd no longer have to worry about her. He wouldn't jeopardize that by letting their attraction get out of hand.

Everything would be fine.

Attempting to ease the stiffness of his muscles, he rose and shrugged out of his jacket. He hung it in a closet and walked back to his chair, unbuttoning the cuffs of his white shirt.

"You don't happen to have a paper copy of the bid, do you?"

She jumped out of her seat. "Sure."

She ran to her office and returned with a document about the size of a ream of paper. She walked over and handed it to him.

Once again they were toe-to-toe. But at least this time there was a ream of paper between them. When their gazes met, the air tightened. Synapses fired, but he simply reminded himself that he had found a way to take care of her, so he'd no longer have to worry about her. If he gave in to the hormones riding roughshod over his emotions, he'd spoil all that.

"Okay, great. So I'm just going to jump right in and start reviewing."

He headed for the conference table where he'd have room to spread out.

She picked up her notepad and followed him. "I'll sit here so that every time you find a mistake, you can tell me the section and page number and I'll make note. We can email our line items to the department that created the page and get it fixed."

He sank to his chair and peered at her dubiously. He'd actually been trying to get her to leave. He'd seen her car in the parking lot. She had a way home. Instead he'd somehow fixed it so they were reviewing the document together.

"It really worked to have each department write its section of the bid?"

"Supervisors were thrilled for the opportunity."

He snorted a laugh.

"I'm serious. Everybody said you do too much. That you could delegate and have more time for yourself."

He snorted again. Fate seemed to be pushing him out the door of his own company.

As she sat on the chair catty-cornered from his, he read the first few pages of the bid, the easy pages, introduction and narrative that answered basic questions about the company, and had to admit he was impressed. The answers were short, concise. No rambling.

He pointed at the sheet. "Who wrote these?"

"I did."

Well, no wonder they were short and concise. She didn't have the knowledge others in the plant did. Of course, that also meant she hadn't muddied the waters with unnecessary information.

He went back to reading. With her legs crossed, her sandal-covered foot swung a centimeter away from his shin. Awareness caused his toes to curl. This wasn't going to work, either.

He stopped reading. "Did the department heads give you backup documentation for their numbers?"

"Yes!" She popped out of her seat, ran into her office and returned with a stack of files—so many files, and such thick files, that it looked like he'd be in the office until the following morning reviewing all the data.

But that was good. He could use that excuse to send her home, telling her he'd make the notes of any problems he found himself because not only was this going to take a long time, but also he needed privacy and quiet to read.

Yeah. That was it. He'd tell her he needed silence to read the bid.

She set the files on the table in front of him and he rose. "Okay, then. Since I have everything I need to review this, you can go."

"Go? I thought I'd be taking notes on the problems you found?"

They weren't exactly standing toe-to-toe, but they were close. He thought to take a step back but refused to be that fussy. Surely he could stand a foot away from her.

"No. I don't want you here. You helped create this. You're prejudiced. I'm sort of an independent proofreader. So you can go home." He waved his hand. "You've obviously worked hard for the past two days and it's after five. Go. I'll be fine."

She looked up at him with big green eyes filled with fear.

His insides twisted. He hated to see her afraid. Especially since she had nothing to fear. He was considering promoting her. Trying to take care of her.

"You did an excellent job," he said, seeking to reassure her, but she didn't stop staring at him. Her green eyes softened, as she studied his face. And pretty soon he realized she wasn't afraid anymore. She was caught. Staring at him because she was as tormented as he was about them. About this thing between them. The attraction that just wouldn't quit even though they were the worst possible two people to be attracted.

He shouldn't like her. She hadn't trusted him.

She shouldn't like him. He was still angry with her.

But his head lowered.

She tipped her face up and stepped closer.

And their lips met.

Sweet memory poured through him. This was Maggie. Sweet, sweet Maggie.

Placing his hands on each side of her head, he tilted it back, deepening the kiss, drinking from her like a thirsty man took water. Her lips parted slightly in what could have been a moan of pleasure. He didn't notice, didn't care, but took advantage and slid his tongue into her mouth.

That time she did moan. The feminine purr drifted to his ears and filled him. Sensation after sensation bombarded him and each one flash-connected to a memory. The roar of the ocean. The brilliance of the sun. The heat of innocence.

He let himself indulge, enjoy. He let his thoughts go back to the idyllic time he'd thought would last forever. But when his hand drifted from her face to her shoulder and down to the opening of her simple blouse, common sense awoke in him. A kiss was one thing, touching quite another.

He broke away. They drifted apart slowly. Their gazes bumped. The sound of their breathing filled the air.

He didn't know what to say. What to do. He felt alive inside. But was he really? Or had that kiss taken them on a trip down memory lane? Was everything he felt simply a reflection of what he expected to feel from the past?

It had to be. He didn't know the new Maggie well enough to want her like this. Kissing her hadn't tested out their attraction. It had only proved they once had chemistry. It was a mistake that did nothing but screw up an otherwise perfect plan.

"I'm sorry."

She blinked. "Sorry?"

"You know we can't be attracted to each other."

"Because we work together."

He took a step back. He couldn't tell her about his thought to promote her until he checked out the bid and dug a little deeper into her credentials. So he clung to the reasonable excuse she'd just offered and even added to it.

"And because we really don't know each other anymore. And it might not be smart to get to know each other. You need this job and I need you. We have a past we probably wouldn't be able to overcome even if we did grow to like each other. So what do you say we just forget this happened?"

She studied him with sad green eyes, and he felt like a heel, a fool. He'd been the one to initiate the kiss. Then he'd dismissed it as if they'd been equally guilty.

Hoping to ease the sadness, he said, "Okay. The kiss was my mistake. I don't know what got into me but I was wrong. We need each other." He stepped away, rounded the conference table to get to the chair he intended to sit in and pulled it out. "Go home. I want to review this without interruption. We'll talk in the morning."

CHAPTER NINE

WEDNESDAY morning a torrential downpour sent rain cascading in sheets along the Carolina coast. By the time Nick made it to the office, Maggie had already shed her raincoat, put her sandwich in the desk drawer and started her computer.

"You might as well just bring your notebook in," he said as he breezed through her office into his. "I got through only half of the bid, but there are problems. Not big ones, just things that need to be addressed and we'll be doing that this morning."

She grabbed paper and pen and followed him inside. Taking the seat at the conference table, she watched him dump his keys and cell phone on the desk.

Confusion and sadness met and mingled in her middle. He'd kissed her the night before out of curiosity. They had so much chemistry crackling between them that it was difficult sometimes to not wonder about it. She'd expected the kiss. She'd also expected the fire that ignited her blood when their lips had touched. What puzzled her had been the sudden hope that burst inside her.

If only for the span of that kiss, she'd believed in miracles. She'd hoped and even prayed that it hadn't been curiosity that had pushed him to kiss her, but an uncontrollable impulse. She didn't care if that impulse had been spawned by memories. Now that she was home she was very much like the Maggie she'd been in her youth. If he'd loved her then he could love her now—

Except she'd hurt him. And that was why he'd pulled away. He'd never get beyond the fact that she'd left him. He was too strong, too proud, too *Nick* to simply forgive her.

The hope in her heart was ridiculous.

Wrong.

He took his seat. "When I got tired of reviewing the bid last night, I checked your résumé. You've never done anything like this bid before. How did you know what to do to pull this thing together?"

She shrugged. "I've analyzed hundreds of bids. Maybe thousands. If a company isn't winning contracts, nine chances out of ten there's either something wrong with the business itself or there's something wrong with their bid numbers."

Not exactly sure how to behave around him, she smiled tentatively. "Your bid was great. All I did was streamline your process. I can see why you win the contract every five years. Andreas Manufacturing is a fabulous company."

He coughed as if uncomfortable with her praise, reminding her so much of the old Nick that she didn't think through the nudge she gave him. It was purely reflex.

"You've got to know you're good."

Their gazes met. The wariness in his expression sent sadness trembling through her. He clearly regretted kissing her the night before. The flickering light of her hope dimmed a little more.

"I made a list of questions or problems I found last night. I want to speak directly with the department supervisors to get the answers but I'd like you to sit in on the sessions."

Her gaze snapped to his. *He wanted her around?*
"Really?"

He looked away. "This is a list of department heads
I'll need to see." Leaning in, he set a paper with a list of
names in front of her.

The scent of sea air and man drifted to her. Combined
with memories of their kiss, it filled her with longing.
Desire rose up as quick and as sharp as it had when his
lips met hers the night before.

"Your assignment is to call everybody and set appoint-
ments."

To get her mind off wanting Nick, she leaned in to look
at the sheet he held and their shoulders bumped.

He automatically pulled away.

The dying flame of her hope struggled to find footing,
but it couldn't. He might be attracted to her, but he didn't
want to be. And he was a strong, determined man. He
could ignore a stupid physical attraction.

But he still had it.

After fifteen years apart, *they* still had it.

"Schedule an hour with each department. Stop at noon,
then pick up again at one. That way we'll have spoken with
all seven supervisors before the end of the day."

At her desk, she picked up the phone, but as the first
extension rang, she peeked into his office. Head bent, he
labored over the papers in a file, looking smart, capable,
and so handsome. The bittersweet ache returned. Except
now that she knew he hadn't accepted the trust fund, the
ache made her wonder what might have been. If his father
hadn't offered him the five-million-dollar trust fund. If
she hadn't overheard him refuse to divorce her to qualify
for it. If she hadn't felt so guilty over Nick giving up his
legacy for her.

If.

If.

If.

Thinking about ifs was foolish.

But it was difficult not to. They were still attracted after fifteen years. Fifteen years. She could only imagine what their marriage might have been like if they'd stayed together, only imagine what they'd be like if they could set aside their differences and sleep together now—

"Yeah, Maggie? What's up?"

Maggie jumped as Mark Nelson's voice boomed to her through her telephone.

Placing a hand on her galloping heart, she said, "Nick wants to see you in his office." She glanced at her schedule. "He's meeting a department head every hour. Since you're the first person I'm calling, you get your choice of time."

"I'll take the first slot."

"Great," she said, penciling him in. She disconnected the call and her gaze slid into Nick's office again.

Why couldn't she get over him?

Because of the meetings, Nick stayed until eleven o'clock that night. He sent Maggie home at seven, telling her he would be leaving right behind her, though he knew it was a lie.

Cade was right. He was still attracted to her. The pull of her was so strong that soon he wouldn't be able to resist it. Eventually he'd seduce her—and then what? Hurt her? Lose her as an assistant? Lose her as a potential general manager?

He couldn't hurt her or take away the job she needed. He had to be the one who moved on. Darius needed him and as Cade had said, it would be much easier for him to find one CEO or general manager to replace him than it would be for Cade to find the small army it would take to shift control of his oil business and ranch.

Finally home, he sank into a leather chair in the game room and turned the TV to a baseball game before dialing Darius's number.

"Late night."

Relieved to hear Darius's voice, Nick relaxed. "Yes. I hope I didn't wake anybody."

"Gino's the only one asleep. Whitney's on the sofa across from me reading depositions."

"Hey, Nick!" she called, her voice loud enough to come to him through the phone.

"Tell Whitney, I said, hey, too."

Darius laughed. "Nick says hey, too." Then his voice turned serious. "So what's up?"

"Cade is right. I should come to work for Andreas Holdings full-time."

"Wow."

"I've been thinking it over since I was in New York on Monday. But more than that, I came home to find my bid is done. Except for proofing and final checks on the numbers, Maggie pretty much got the thing finished."

"She wrote it herself?"

"She had the staff write it."

Darius chuckled. "Well, I'll be damned."

"I know. Cade thinks she could replace me. At the very least, take over as general manager, leaving the executive stuff to be handled by me through phone, fax and email."

"So what's the problem?"

"She doesn't have any experience for this. She was a glorified analyst at her last job."

"But she did your bid."

"Exactly. She knows theory, but has no actual experience running the plant."

"So train her."

"I don't want to tell her that I'm considering her for a job if it doesn't pan out."

"There are never any guarantees with any employee. You've got to jump in and take a risk."

"I know. But this situation is delicate." He rose from his comfy chair, passed his hand through his hair. "I'm worried that I'm seeing things in her that aren't really there because I want so badly to promote her—to give her a chance."

Darius harrumphed. "That's funny. When you were here, you were telling us you felt nothing for her."

He squeezed his eyes shut. As much as he wanted to confide in his brother, he wouldn't. There were some things a man had to handle on his own.

"She's a penniless pregnant woman. I'd be heartless if I didn't feel something for her."

"Pity?"

The word tightened his gut. Maggie would hate it if she thought he pitied her. "No, more like righteous indignation. She didn't deserve what happened to her after we split. I'd like to see her succeed."

"So bring her up for Gino's birthday. I'll check her out. I can run her through her paces without her even realizing I'm backhandedly interviewing her."

That was true. Darius would be objective where he couldn't.

"That sounds great, except how do I get her there? Say my older brother who's never met you would like you to come to our baby brother's first birthday party?"

"Make an excuse about needing her to take notes at a brothers' meeting. Tell her my assistant can't do it because she works for Andreas Holdings and this is a family thing. It would be a conflict of interest because we'll be discussing our plans for our shares of Andreas Holdings."

It was a great idea. Plus, the thought of attending his one-year-old half brother's first birthday party cheered him. He was at a point in his life when he'd realized he'd never have kids of his own. That was the one drawback of his lifestyle. But with one-year-old Gino in the family, he had no worries about an heir or even someone younger to amuse him from time to time. He could teach the kid how to play basketball, teach him to fish, tease him about girls. In general get out all of his pent-up parenting needs anytime they arose.

He loved having a baby brother.

"Okay. Sounds good. We'll be there."

When Nick arrived at Andreas Manufacturing the next morning, Maggie was walking to the entrance. He hurried out of the Porsche to catch up with her and held the building door open for her.

"Thank you."

"You're welcome."

He followed her inside, making her just a tad paranoid. Should she wait for him? Walk beside him? Make small talk?

She wanted to. God knew the hope that sprang to life inside her every time she saw him. That hope wanted her to believe that if she just gave him time, he'd come around.

And then what? Was she ready for this? Was she over Josh?

In some respects, the answer came quickly. How could she pine for a man who not only didn't want her, but had also refused to acknowledge their child? It wasn't exactly easy, but it had definitely been possible for any love she'd had for Josh to die.

But was she ready to move on?

Her smarter self laughed. At this point it didn't matter if she was ready to move on. Nick might give her ten signs a day that he was attracted to her, but he gave her eleven that he didn't want to be. And today would be no different. He'd hold the door, maybe let his gaze linger a little too long on her face or unwittingly stare into her eyes, but he'd snap out of it. Cloister himself in his office. Not say goodbye when he went to lunch.

Any hope she had was foolish. So it didn't matter if she was ready to move on or not.

They entered her office. She turned and walked to her desk. He continued toward his office. But he stopped, faced her.

"I…um…was talking with my brother Darius last night."

"The older one?"

"Yes. The one who lives in New York and runs Andreas Holdings. He's having a birthday party for our one-year-old brother over the weekend and he'd like you to come."

Her heart stopped. Her breathing stuttered to a halt. His family was inviting her to a party? All the way in New York?

"We've having a brothers' meeting Saturday morning and no one from Andreas Holdings can take notes because there'd be a conflict of interest. Darius suggested I bring you up so you can be our stenographer for the meeting."

The pain of stupidity froze her tongue. When would she learn this man didn't want her?

"I…I…"

He glanced at her tummy. "Oh, God, I'm sorry. I forgot you might not be able to travel."

"I can travel."

"Oh."

She heard the awkward tone of his voice. He didn't understand why she hesitated. She was, after all, *his* assistant. An employee who could take the meeting notes without a conflict of interest.

She straightened her shoulders. She was his assistant. If he wanted her to go to New York, she would go to New York.

"I'd love to go. Thank your brother for inviting me."

"Great." He turned to his office door again. "We'll leave tomorrow morning and be staying at the family estate in Montauk. Pack for the beach."

The beach! That perked her up. She might only live a few miles from the shore herself, but between work and not having a car for the first weeks she was in town, she hadn't even gotten close to it yet. Maybe the weekend would be something like a vacation?

Wearing flip-flops, white capris and a sunny yellow tank top, Maggie met Nick at the small private airstrip a few miles outside of Ocean Palms. Only one airplane sat on the tarmac and Nick stood in front of it. She made her way over, carrying her overnight case.

Approaching the plane, she said, "Wow. So this is how the other half lives."

He took her small bag and handed it to a man dressed in a blue pilot's uniform, then motioned for her to climb the short column of steps. "This is how my brother Cade lives. He's the family multibillionaire. He put this plane at my disposal for the next year."

She stopped, faced Nick. "The next year? That's awfully generous."

He batted a hand. "He has seven planes. He won't even miss this one."

Seven planes? The magnitude of the changes in Nick's family situation never ceased to amaze her. Or to remind her that he was so different now that it had been totally wrong for her to think—even for the fleeting few seconds of one blistering kiss—that they fit together anymore.

She stepped inside an area that looked more like a comfy living room than a seating area for a plane. White leather sofas lined both sides. A shiny wooden bar took up the back.

Amazed, she stopped.

"If you're wondering why the space looks so small," Nick said from behind, "that's because there's an office and a bedroom in the rear."

She spun to face him. "Holy cow."

"I know. Only a guy who never stops working would think a plane ride a waste of time. I'll bet he's never once sat up here and just looked out the window. He probably either works or sleeps. Never wasting a minute."

They sat across from each other, each on one of the long sofalike lounges. They buckled up and fell silent as the plane taxied and took off.

In the air, Nick unbuckled his seat belt and headed for the bar. "Drink?"

She glanced down at her tummy. "I don't think so."

"We have orange juice, apple juice and water. Not just alcohol."

She still shook her head. "It's a long flight. I'd rather not be jumping up and down running for the bathroom."

He shrugged. "Suit yourself."

When he sat again, soft drink in hand, Maggie glanced around. After the quick brush with conversation about the plane, they'd run out of things to say. But she refused to sit silently for over two hours.

"So, you have a baby brother."

Nick surprised her by laughing. "It was the damnedest thing."

"I'll bet."

"Oh, you have no idea. Not only did we not know our dad had another son until Dad's lawyer handed him to Darius at the reading of the will, but also the kid owns an equal share of Andreas Holdings."

Because he chuckled when he said it, Maggie tilted her head in question. "That doesn't bother you?"

"Not really. I don't 'need' the money I get from Andreas Holdings. It doesn't matter to me how many ways it's split." He smiled stupidly, fascinating Maggie. She'd never quite seen that expression. "It doesn't hurt that the kid is adorable."

Ah. That's right. Nick loved kids.

"Of course, he's also pure Andreas. Dark eyes. Dark hair. But he's built like a little truck. Big shoulders and arms. If I wasn't absolutely positive we'll be training him to take over Andreas Holdings when we want to retire, the kid could easily be a football player."

Hearing the pride and love in his voice, Maggie smiled. "He sounds cute."

"You'll get to meet him. It's his party we're going to. Plus, since we're staying at the estate, he'll probably be underfoot." He pointed at her tummy. "Maybe you can persuade Whitney to let you get in some practice."

She smiled again. "Maybe."

It almost hurt to see how happy he was. How in love with the little boy. She thought back to their baby, to how she'd always known Nick would be a great dad, and sadness enveloped her. They lapsed into silence. After a few minutes, he opened his briefcase.

Seeing how he'd been forced to spread papers and file folders around him on his seat, she said, "You should just go back in the office if you want to work."

He peered over. "Are you sure?"

She shrugged. "Yeah. I'm fine. In fact, if you need me, I might only have the notebook I brought for the brothers' meeting, but I could probably still put some of your notes in it."

"With the bid done and in, I'm primarily reviewing things to catch myself up." He rose. "But if I need you I'll call."

"Okay."

Ten minutes later she fell asleep and didn't awaken until Nick jostled her shoulder. "Hey, you have to get up. We're about to land and you have to be in a seat belt."

She opened her eyes and found herself staring into his. Crouched in front of her, he was eye level. His hand on her shoulder was comforting. His dark eyes were warm. The softness of his voice was sweet, soothing.

As if he realized she'd caught him in an unguarded moment, he got to his feet and looked away.

Maggie told herself not to make too much out of the expression she saw on his face. Lots of people looked with love upon sleeping people—

That wasn't true. She was reaching, trying to make something that wasn't innocent seem innocent. She didn't know how long he'd been watching her sleep, but he'd been watching her sleep and it had put a soft expression on his face. And he'd invited her to his family's home. Yes, she had to take notes at a meeting, but they could have hired an outsider for that.

Maybe it was crazy-just-waking-up brain, but she

couldn't stop the feeling that something more was going on here.

Again, they landed at a private airstrip. A long black limo was parked close to where the plane stopped. A beautiful blonde dressed in a black sheath and a wide-brimmed black hat stood beside a tall, dark-haired man, wearing a black suit, holding a baby. All three of them wore black sunglasses. That made her laugh. Though she wasn't sure why. They looked rich, sophisticated, so far beyond her world that Maggie wasn't even sure she could comprehend it.

Nick got out first and held up a hand to help Maggie navigate the stairs. As they deplaned, the trio came over to meet them.

"Darius, Whitney, Gino," Nick said, "This is Maggie."

"Hi." She glanced at Gino. Chubby, happy, with the trademark Andreas dark hair, he was so cute she could have squeezed him. "He's...well, he's so adorable he's breathtaking."

Gino laughed, an airy giggle that warmed Maggie the whole way to her soul. That was what she currently lived for. The day when she'd hear baby giggles. Have someone to guide and love without condition.

"We like him," Darius said, jostling Gino, who jabbered something that contained the word *Dad*.

Whitney stepped forward, glancing at Maggie's tummy, as she took her hands. "You're pregnant."

"Yes. A little over two months to go."

Whitney slid her arm across Maggie's shoulders and began to lead her to the limo. "How exciting for you! Darius and I are talking about having a baby before Gino gets accustomed to being an only child and too spoiled."

Maggie glanced around at the quiet, private airstrip. The area was spotless, silent. There were no other people, no other planes. She'd bet her bottom dollar the Andreas family owned it.

"I don't think there's a snowball's chance in hell that Gino could grow up anything but spoiled."

Whitney laughed merrily. "Oh, you'd be surprised how good I can be at caring for a baby so he doesn't get spoiled."

The driver opened the limo door and Whitney entered with the ease of someone accustomed to luxury, but Maggie glanced around for Nick.

He was at her side in a second. "Everything okay?"

She blew out her breath, feeling a little crazy for having a near panic attack. She'd simply never been around so much luxury before. Her best capris and top felt like rags. Though Nick sensing her distress and racing over eased that odd sensation, it created another.

She hadn't even spoken and he'd come.

Were they getting that much attuned to each other again?

Yes.

The answer came quickly and her heart tumbled in her chest. They'd always had something. A click of recognition. Something.

And she was only kidding herself if she thought she could fight it. Whether she was ready or not, she and Nick were tumbling headfirst into a relationship. She, at least, saw it. Nick—

She glanced around. He'd invited her to meet his family. He'd been by her side every step of the way—

Maybe there was more to this trip than he'd let on? And maybe she was the one lagging behind, not sure she was ready when the truth was it didn't matter if she was ready. She and Nick were a force of nature and if he was falling in love with her again, then she wanted it.

Wanted him.

"Yeah. I'm fine. Just wanted to make sure I wasn't getting into the wrong limo."

He laughed and guided her into the car. "Funny."

She sat on one of the luxurious leather seats. The windows were tinted. The bar discreet. The seat so comfortable she could have happily drifted off into another nap.

As soon as the doors closed and the driver headed toward the front of the vehicle, Darius said, "So, Maggie. Thank you for agreeing to come up and take the notes from our meeting tomorrow morning."

"You're welcome. It's my pleasure." She winced. "Actually I can't wait to see your house." She hoped that hadn't made her sound too much like a penniless bumpkin. "I live five minutes from the beach myself, yet I never get there. I just want one really nice walk on a private beach tomorrow morning."

"Well, that's a given," Whitney said. "If you like, I could come with you."

"No. That's fine. A beach is a beach. I won't wander far enough that I'll overtire or get lost. It's not like I can make any unexpected turns on a shoreline."

Darius laughed. "Sense of humor. I like that."

She smiled, but she also noticed Nick sending Darius some kind of message with his eyes.

Okay. Now this was getting weird. Because Nick had never had much in the way of family when they were dating, she hadn't gone through a screening process. But she had with Josh's family. And she recognized it when she saw it. She might have ostensibly been invited to take a few notes and attend a birthday party, but these people were checking her out.

Oh, God!

These people were checking her out!

The truth of that burst inside her. Something Nick had said caused them to believe there was reason to be worried about her being around him—

Well, she had hurt him. So okay. She got that. But they couldn't be checking her out to make sure she didn't hurt him again. He'd consider that an insult and he'd deck them for that. And he was in on this.

Oh, God!

He *did* have feelings for her.

CHAPTER TEN

As THEY stepped into the Andreas family's magnificent mansion, people bustled back and forth, in and out and through the entry. Nearly everyone wore black or white and they looked like chess pieces scrambling across the black and white blocks of the foyer floor.

"What's going on?"

Whitney faced Nick with a beaming smile. "Prep for Saturday's party."

"You need a staff for a one-year-old's birthday party?"

"No, silly," Whitney said, taking a clipboard from a woman who had appeared at her side and signing off on something after she read it. "The kids' party is Sunday afternoon. On Saturday night, their parents make big donations in Gino's name to one of three charities we've set up to take gifts. And we thank them with a ball."

Nick watched Maggie's skin grow pasty-white.

He caught her arm. She peeked at him with an expression that totally defied explanation. He couldn't tell if she was scared, sick, shocked...or all three.

"There's a ball?"

"Only about two hundred people," Whitney said, her eyes skimming Maggie's face as she checked her out, obviously seeing the same things Nick had. "It's really not a big deal."

Maggie huffed in a deep breath and laid her hands lightly on her stomach.

Nick nearly had a heart attack. Fear that there was something wrong with her clenched his stomach. He remembered the night she had lost their baby. No warning. Just sudden pain.

"Maggie?"

"I don't…actually, I didn't…well…I packed for the beach."

Relief washed through him as Whitney turned to Darius. "You didn't tell them about the ball?"

He winced. "Sorry. I got everything crossed up."

Whitney faced Maggie with a sunny smile. "No worries. You and I will just go shopping."

"But I—"

"Do it for me. I never get to shop with a girlfriend." Whitney took her arm and began leading her up the stairs. "First, we'll get you settled. You can have a nap or take a long bath or even walk on the beach. When you're ready, we'll shop."

Ten minutes later Maggie was alone in her bedroom, unpacking the few things she'd brought for her stay. The entire room was ivory satin. Chunky bed pillows layered with more delicate throw pillows sat on top of an ivory satin bedspread. The simple hue counteracted the rich cherrywood headboard to make the bed elegantly inviting. Ivory satin drapes were pulled back to reveal a stunning view of the sea.

In front of the bedroom was a sitting room done in soft sage-green. A sage and ivory striped sofa sat by a solid sage Queen Anne chair. Cherrywood tables and an armoire made the room rich, luxurious. The sitting room, bedroom and bath were bigger than her first apartment had been.

Taking out shorts and tank tops, capris and T-shirts and one scrappy pair of jeans, she groaned. There had been no arguing with Whitney about the shopping trip, which in some ways was good because she couldn't exactly wear a scrappy pair of jeans to a ball. But bad because she was about to spend money she didn't have on a dress she'd wear once.

When was she going to get invited to a ball again?

She snorted a laugh just as someone knocked on the door.

Thinking it was the maid with fresh towels or lush scented soap or some kind of expensive, imported chocolate, Maggie sucked it up and said, "Come in," as she walked into the sitting room.

The door opened and Nick entered. "I am so sorry."

Knowing he was talking about not telling her about the ball and deciding to just take it all in stride, Maggie said, "That's okay. I'd have never assumed there'd be a charity ball attached to a one-year-old's birthday party, either."

"Whitney had a child who died. She's very big on charities that involve children."

She pressed her hand to her chest. "Oh, I'm so sorry."

"She's fine. The best thing to do is not mention her past, but she loves to raise money for children's charities. If I'd been on my toes I would have guessed this."

"No harm done."

"Except that you don't have a dress." He stepped closer.

And Maggie noticed something odd.

In a sea of people she didn't know, Nick was the one she did. The one she was comfortable around. And he seemed comfortable with her, too.

"Your sister-in-law has volunteered to rectify the situation."

He laughed.

Maggie smiled. Pinpricks of delight pirouetted across her skin. It was nice to be alone with him, in a neutral environment. He wasn't avoiding making an impression he'd have to live with if the town gossips got a hold of it. She wasn't worried about embarrassing herself in front of people who knew their history. Here where he could be himself, it was clear he really cared about her. She wasn't imagining it because she wanted it so badly.

She remembered the "scoping out" being done by his brother. Though panic tried to rear up, she stopped it in favor of reason. This was what she wanted. Josh was a distant memory. Her marriage to Nick fifteen years ago seemed clearer in her brain than her marriage to Josh. They might have a bumpy road ahead. Some things to iron out. But if he was taking steps to try, then she wanted it, too.

True, it wasn't exactly comfortable to know Nick had brought her here for his family to check her out. It also wasn't fun that she didn't fit in this environment, but she and Nick didn't live in this environment. They lived in a small town, by a beach, with people who said good morning even if they didn't know you and didn't dress in black and white serving uniforms.

If they could get close, admit their feelings, maybe it would hold when they got home?

"I'll be fine."

"Still—" He reached into his pocket and pulled out a money clip. He flipped through the bills until he came upon a credit card, buried in the cash. "Take this. I know Whitney's taste. You'll never be able to afford what she wants you to buy."

This time it wasn't panic that reared up, but disappointment. She wasn't sure which of them she was disappointed in. Him for offering her money—making her feel cheap—or beneath him. Or herself for not having the money to afford a simple party dress—

Well, all right, it wasn't just a dress. It was ball gown for an elite New York event. But she was an adult. She'd worked her whole life. She'd scrimped and saved and her ex-husband had squandered—

She tugged her fingers through her long hair. Yet another gift from her ex-husband. Humiliation in front of someone she wished she could impress. "I have a credit card."

"Yeah, but we don't want to run up any balances."

She laughed. How could she not? He didn't even realize he was talking about them as a "we" a team.

So many emotions tumbled through her. Regret for having married a cretin and for putting up with him for ten years. Fear about what she would be getting herself into if she and Nick really did get together. Pure love for him for being so sweet.

Pure love.

Simple love.

The kind a person only came across once in a lifetime.

She almost gasped. It had never left. She had always loved him.

And maybe that was the thing she needed to face. She loved him. There was no "falling" about this. She was already in love.

And he…well, she had no idea what he felt. He might be falling. He might be testing her. His family might be checking her out. Or she could simply be imagining all this.

She pushed away his credit card. She wouldn't take

money, gifts, *anything*, from him until she understood what was happening between them.

"I'm fine."

He frowned, glanced at his card, then back at her face. She tried a wobbly smile.

It worked.

He sighed and tucked away his credit card.

"All right. You handle this. But you have my cell phone if things get dicey."

"They won't."

In the first floor office, Nick flopped on the sofa.

Darius sat at the desk, talking on the phone. He finished the conversation in only a few minutes and rose. "Drink?"

"No. Too early."

Darius laughed. "Well, that's a good sign. The day Maggie started you were drinking in the afternoon."

Nick scowled. "It was after five."

"Whatever." Darius dropped to the sofa beside Nick. "I like her."

"Everybody does."

"A man could do a lot worse."

"Excuse me?"

"Come on. You know you like her. You fawned all over her in the limo."

Nick gaped at him. "She's pregnant and in a strange land. I'd do the same for any assistant."

Darius snorted a laugh and rose from the sofa. "If you're not going to talk about the fun stuff, I have three contracts here I'd like you to review."

He ambled to the desk and got the contracts, but Nick couldn't focus. He hadn't fawned all over Maggie. He'd done a few nice things. He *would have* done the same for any assistant.

Still, he'd given his brother the wrong idea and that could mean he was giving Maggie the wrong idea, too.

That would have to stop.

"So what's the deal with you and Nick?"

Seated in the limo, nearly in the city, having exhausted all potential conversation about where they'd gone to school, their parents, their lack of siblings—except for Maggie's brother who was never around—Maggie lounged against one bench seat while Whitney relaxed against the other.

"You mean aside from the fact that we were married?"

Whitney winced. "Sorry. Darius did tell me the two of you had been married as kids. I wasn't trying to sound like I know nothing at all about you. I know there's history. I'm more interested in the future."

Whitney's forthrightness caused Maggie to frown.

Whitney winced again. "Sorry. I'm a lawyer. Half of what we say sounds like a cross-examination."

"That's okay. I'm not the kind of person to keep secrets, but there really isn't anything to tell. I work for him."

Whitney harrumphed. "You bought that story about them needing you to take minutes?"

"Yes and no." She toyed with the glass of juice Whitney had insisted she drink before they hit the stores. Whitney was the kind of person who inspired honesty, and, being as confused as she was, she could use a friend to talk to. "I think Nick asked me up here so your husband can check me out."

Whitney tapped her long, slim index finger against her lips. "Interesting. They grew up without each other." She smiled. "Of course, you know that. You went to school with Nick, so you know he didn't even know he had brothers. But the thing of it is, last winter once they decided to be brothers for real, they hit the ground running. They really depend on each other. Trust each other. If Nick asked Darius to check you out, there's a reason. A good reason. A big reason."

"Like a test?"

"No, more like the way a guy brings his girl home to his family to see if she fits—"

Fear fizzed through her. Wasn't that the conclusion she'd drawn herself?

"—so that's good."

She shook her head fiercely. "No! It's not good! I *don't* fit! If that's why I'm here I'm toast."

Whitney laughed. "You're not toast. You didn't bring a ball gown. That's all. And apparently Darius's invitation was deficient, not your packing. So we're getting you a dress." She leaned across the space and patted Maggie's hand. "We're getting you one special dress because once you get in the right dress, you'll belong."

"Really?"

"Trust me. My parents were very solidly upper-middle class. Then my dad scored a few really big clients and suddenly we were on Park Avenue. I never thought I'd fit. Especially at my first formal charity event. Then I found the right dress and walked into that ballroom with my head high, knowing I was just as good as everybody else in the room, and—*poof*—I was fine. Sometimes all you need is a little bit of confidence."

"I hope you're right."

Whitney settled into her seat and smiled. "I know I'm right. Plus, the right dress might just be the push Nick needs to admit what he's up to."

"So we're getting this dress to impress Nick?"

The driver opened the door. Gorgeous, sophisticated Whitney stepped out into the hot July sun. This time, she wore white pants and a black shirt with her wide-brimmed black sun hat and black sunglasses.

The picture of sophistication and knowledge, she said, "The right dress can do many things."

That night Maggie felt stupid for spending hundreds of dollars she didn't have on a dress to impress a man. She could say Whitney had been overly persuasive, except she knew in her heart of hearts she desperately wanted Nick to take the next steps. He definitely cared for her. He unconsciously looked out for her. He'd out-and-out offered her money to help her. And he'd asked his brother to check her out.

He had to have some feeling for her. But if she didn't get him to admit it here, where they were just themselves, when they got back to Ocean Palms, where everything was stiff and stilted and too many memories blocked them, he'd go back into his shell and never admit it.

Because she'd packed so sparingly, dinner had been informal in a small dining room that looked out over the ocean.

Darius pulled out Whitney's chair. Nick pulled out Maggie's. She smiled over her shoulder at him. "Thanks."

He returned her smile. "You're welcome."

Maggie's heart swelled like the waves rolling up to the shore. She didn't think this dinner was the be-all and end-all of opportunities for Nick to realize his feelings and be able to voice them. But it was one step in many steps she'd have to take with him this weekend. Everything had to go well.

Darius set his napkin on his lap. "So did you girls have a good day shopping?"

Whitney's eyes sparkled. "The best. Maggie has excellent taste."

Darius laughed, but Nick picked up his water glass and said, "So what happened with the people from London?"

"The group that wants to buy into Andreas Holdings?"

"Yes."

"I shut them down. But we're not the only ones who own Andreas stock. We've got to get to Dad's old secretary before London does. Otherwise they could end up owning one-third of our company."

And with that, Darius broke into a long, detailed explanation of problems that would cause, and Nick listened intently. They talked business through dinner, while Whitney and Maggie discussed how Whitney juggled her life, raising Gino and working. Everything seemed fine. Almost normal. Two couples chitchatting at dinner. Until Darius suggested they retire to the game room to play pool or cards.

Suddenly Nick glanced at her, glanced at the door and said, "I think I'll just go to my suite. In fact, I think I should walk Maggie to her suite, too."

Happiness burst inside her. He wanted to be alone with her. If that wasn't a good sign, she didn't know what was. "Yes. I am a little tired."

He took her elbow and led her through the maze of halls in the downstairs and finally up the spiral staircase to her room.

At the door, he met her gaze. "Can I come in for a second?"

Nerves and joy attacked her simultaneously. "Yes. Sure."

"Great."

He opened the door for her and she walked into the sitting room.

He pointed at the sofa. "Have a seat."

She smiled. "Uh, since this is my room, isn't it me who's supposed to say that?"

He chuckled. His eyes crinkled at the corners when he smiled and Maggie's heart sang. He was the older, wiser version of the boy she had loved, but she loved him every bit as fiercely as she'd loved Nick Roebuck. If he was here, in her room, to spend time with her, to tell her he was beginning to have feelings or even just to kiss her again to test the waters, she wanted it.

She facilitated it. She sat on the sofa instead of the chair so he could sit beside her.

He did.

Her heart thumping in her chest, she set her hands on her lap to still them.

"Maggie, there's something I have to tell you."

"Yes?" She pried her nervous hands apart, giving him the chance to take them.

He didn't, but he did gaze into her eyes. "By now I guess you've figured out that I didn't just bring you here to take notes."

Telling her pounding heart to calm down, she smiled. "I'd have to be pretty thick to have missed the signs."

He winced. "Darius isn't very good at being sneaky."

She laughed. "No."

"I'm amazed he didn't tell Whitney what was going on."

"Don't underestimate Whitney. She has her suspicions."

He laughed nervously. "Right." He sucked in a breath.

"Anyway, since there's no point in hiding this anymore, I've decided to just come right out and tell you what's going on."

As a prelude to telling her he loved her, or even was only interested in her again, that left a lot to be desired. He'd been a lot more romantic as an eighteen-year-old.

"Sunday and Monday, I talked about you at length with my brothers. Cade, my younger brother, suggested that it was time I see the truth."

Her hands shivered with the need to take his. Her tongue nearly said the words he was taking so long to say. She had to clamp her teeth together to stay silent.

"I need to move here to New York to take some responsibility from Darius. And I'd like to make you my general manager of Andreas Manufacturing."

She managed to prevent her mouth from dropping open, but for thirty seconds silence reigned.

Finally Nick broke it. "I thought you'd be pleased."

"Yes!" She bounced off the sofa, desperately trying to shift her brain to work mode and to blink away the tears flooding her eyes. But frustration and disbelief rose up in her. He'd kissed her. He was attracted to her. Whether he knew it or not he'd brought her home to meet his family—

She spun to face him. She couldn't quell the disbelief that roared through her and demanded clarification. "This has all been about a job?"

"Not just any job. I want you to take over my company. This is a big step for me. For both of us." He paused. "What did you think it was about?"

She swallowed, turned away again. Dear God, if she cried, she would kick her own butt.

"Maggie?"

When she wouldn't face him, he put his hands on her shoulders. The warmth of them seeped through her simple T-shirt, and tried to warm her heart. He might not love her but he cared about her enough to make sure she had a really good job. More, though, he now trusted her.

He turned her around. "You wanted this to be about us?"

She wouldn't look at him.

"There is no us." His voice was a soft whisper. "There can't be an us."

She swallowed.

"I loved you fifteen years ago."

Definitely unable to meet his gaze for this, she mumbled, "And you're still attracted to me now."

"That's physical." He chuckled sadly. "I'm not sure that's ever going to go away. But you're right. It's always been about more than sex with us. You were the one person I was absolutely positive believed in me."

For that she caught his gaze, searched his dark, dark eyes. "I did."

He shook his head. "No. You didn't. You left. You might as well have said you didn't believe I would make it unless I got help from my dad. You broke that trust."

She frowned, confused that he was laying all this at her feet as if he'd had no part in things. "I was young and exhausted. I'd just lost a baby. I wasn't thinking about trust. Only about need. About you and your mom going without—"

"I needed you. Not money."

His voice was soft, calm. But anger had begun to brew inside Maggie. The arrogant confidence in his tone trembled through her like the first shakes of an earthquake. He might not have been the one to leave, but he was far from innocent.

She didn't stop the fury that seeped into her tone when she confronted him. "Oh, yeah. You needed me? So why didn't you try to find me? Why did you simply let me go? I was home for a week before I left for university. Yet, you never came after me. Never once recognized I might not have been in a good enough emotional state to make the choice I'd made. You simply let me go."

"Maggie, no man goes after a woman who doesn't have faith in him. Especially not the one person he always believed was his number one supporter."

"You think I don't have faith in you?" Shaking her head, she sniffed a laugh. "When I needed a job, who did I come to? When I was pregnant, alone, abandoned by the husband who simply walked away for greener pastures, who did I come to? I didn't think we'd get back together. I gave no thought to the fact that we might still have chemistry. I was in trouble and I knew the one person in the world who could help me was you...and that's who I trusted. Who I came to. You."

The truth of that hit Nick in the gut and totally disarmed him. "You came to me because you knew I could help?"

"I might have come for a job, but it was because I knew for sure I could depend on you to help me. You were always the only one I knew I could depend on."

Her admission didn't change the fact that she'd left him. But she was right. He'd never gone after her. He'd let his blasted pride stop him. Pride so thick it had taken him years to grow up and out of it. Still, he wasn't that boy anymore and she wasn't that frightened girl. She was a smart, successful woman, who when she'd fallen on hard times had turned to him. And he was a smart successful man, who, when she'd come, couldn't turn her away.

"Wow."

"I'm sick of paying for something that happened fifteen years ago," Maggie said, her voice thick with tears. "I'm sick of thinking about it, talking about it—"

"So am I." Hands already on her shoulders, Nick yanked her to him. The truth of the present didn't merely override the events of the past, it obliterated them. They were adults. Two different people. Two people who'd both made mistakes. Two people who could only find longed-for redemption with each other.

He pressed his mouth to hers and kissed her the way he'd wanted to kiss her when she'd first walked into his office. He slanted his mouth over hers, taking, not asking, not caring that he might be rough or crude. He'd waited fifteen long years to kiss her again. And he intended to indulge, enjoy.

She opened her mouth on a gurgled sound of pleasure that seeped into his skin and set fire to his blood. He couldn't get enough of the feel of her, the taste of her. When his hands skimmed down her arms and back up again, he redirected them to her waist. He cruised the slight indentation, then shifted upward until he met her breast.

Her breathing changed. So did his. The fire in his blood became an inferno of need that totally shut off his thought process. This was what he wanted, what they both wanted.

And it was time.

But Maggie pulled away. "No. Wait. Stop." She gulped in air, obviously trying to get her bearings. "Everything's happening so fast."

It was true. Even through his passionate haze he could see her fear. And why not? They might have been lovers fifteen years ago, married fifteen years ago, but they were now interacting as two new people. And the new person he'd become barely bore any resemblance to the boy she'd loved.

He stepped back.

She blinked up at him. "So now what?"

"I'm not sure." He wasn't. He'd never even considered a permanent relationship with any woman but Maggie. Part of him wanted to pick up where they'd left off. The other part knew that couldn't happen. No one can really pretend fifteen years hadn't happened. Worse, Nick Andreas didn't have permanent relationships.

"We can't just ride off into the sunset."

"No. We can't." He peered over at her, chuckled. "Maggie, I'm way different from the guy you married."

"I know."

"I've done my share of running around."

"I guessed that."

"The thing is…I'm not sure I can settle down."

Her head tilted. Then she laughed. "Maybe that's our problem. Maybe we look at each other and don't see a potential partner, we see instant marriage. Maybe what we need to do is pull back, sort of start over." She walked over and slid her hands around his neck. "Actually date."

"We never did date."

"No. We didn't."

"We went right from friends to lovers to a married couple in a few weeks."

She kissed him lightly. "Exactly."

He slid his hands around her waist. "So, what do we do?"

"Well, I'm going to kiss you good-night and you're going to leave."

He frowned. "I'm not sure I like this."

"Which is probably why we skipped the dating step." She kissed him again. "You can be very persuasive."

One more kiss.

"But good night."

CHAPTER ELEVEN

Two minutes before nine o'clock on Saturday morning, Maggie found the downstairs office and slipped inside, trying to appear cool, calm and efficient. She was here to be an assistant. So what if she could have easily made love with Nick the night before? So what if she and Nick hadn't just cleared the air, they'd cleared a path to be together? She was just about certain neither one of them wanted to announce that to his brothers. At least not until they themselves understood what they were doing.

Plus, she still had to take notes.

She knew her calm attitude was the right choice when Nick said a pleasant, but restrained, "Good morning," and introduced her to his brother Cade—a typical Andreas with dark hair, broad shoulders and shrewd dark eyes.

As soon as she was settled, Darius started the meeting.

The morning passed quickly in a flurry of discussions and the kind of arguments only brothers could have. Maggie was amazed at how close they'd become, considering that Whitney had told her they'd only decided to be brothers for real the past January.

They broke for lunch and then picked up where they left off for another two hours of discussion.

When the meeting was over, Maggie went to her room,

intending to begin inputting the minutes in her laptop but she fell asleep. She didn't awaken until someone knocked on her door. Fearing it was Nick, she fixed her hair when she passed a mirror and raced to the sitting room.

"Come in," she said as she opened the door, only to find Whitney on the other side.

She held out a simple gold necklace with a small diamond pendant and diamond earrings. "I brought these for you to wear."

Maggie gasped. "I couldn't."

"Don't worry." She smiled. "You're only borrowing them. Besides, you have to. If you wear anything else with that dress, you'll overpower it. These are perfect."

Staring at them, Maggie had to admit they were perfect. And she did want to look good for Nick. "Okay."

"Okay." Whitney turned away, then faced Maggie again. "And breathe. Darius said the meeting went well, you were a star and Nick told them he'd already given you the general manager's job."

"Really?" In everything that had happened, she'd forgotten about the job, about the fact that Nick wanted to move to New York.

"Really. You're set. So just relax and enjoy."

When Whitney was gone, Maggie pressed a hand to her stomach. Relax? Enjoy? They weren't even officially dating and already she had to face a problem. She'd finally, finally come home and he was leaving. Moving to New York.

Ten minutes after the official start time of the ball, Nick headed for Maggie's suite. He knew what he was doing. When he and Maggie walked into that ballroom together tonight, they'd be a couple. But that was good. He didn't want to give himself any way out or any way to finagle himself and Maggie into something less than what she needed. She wanted to date for real. To give them a real shot. And he agreed.

Still, nerves jangled. His tie felt too tight. Hell, his skin felt too tight.

Two seconds before Nick would have knocked on Maggie's suite door, she opened it. The scent that was so uniquely Maggie greeted him first, nearly paralyzing him with wicked thoughts. Then he looked at her.

Her long red hair had been pinned up in a bundle of curls. Some hung loose and danced along her neck, pulling Nick's gaze there, then to her shoulders. The sleeves of her pale yellow gown draped to her biceps, leaving her shoulders and chest bare, taking his gaze to her breasts. They peeked out over the satiny yellow material, but not a lot. Just a peek. Just enough to whet a man's appetite and maybe even make him thank his maker.

He took a step back. The gown skimmed her trim, toned body and glided over her baby bump. It hugged her hips and caressed her thighs and fell to the floor with a loose grace that made it all at once sexy and elegant.

"Wow."

She smiled sheepishly. "Your sister-in-law has good taste."

Though he let himself be a little mesmerized, something inside his gut told him to stop. To hold back. Because he was sure it was the playboy inside him, he ignored it. He'd loved this woman and she was working her way back into his life. This was the thing he could do with Maggie that he hadn't been able to do with any other woman. Be smitten. Charmed. Hypnotized. It was the first step to being able to commit and he told his panicky feeling to settle down, and he just let himself enjoy.

"No. You have one hell of a body. I think you could make sack cloth and ashes look good."

He held out his arm and she slid her hand into the crook of his elbow.

"Shall we?"

She drew in a quick breath. "Yeah. I'm as ready as I'll ever be."

"You'll dazzle them."

"Right. I'm a small-town girl who really wasn't all that successful in the big city. I was lucky to get a job with you, Nick."

Her voice was so soft, so serious, that he stopped. Guilt welled inside his chest. They'd screwed up their lives royally. Her by leaving. Him by letting her go. Not finding her once he'd refused the money. Not realizing she'd been in no state to make their big decision. They'd talked this all out the night before. He wouldn't let it hold her prisoner.

"We were lucky to find each other."

As soon as the words were out of his mouth, he realized how true they were, but that itchy little shadow of doubt nudged at him again. Again, he ignored it.

They glided down the spiral staircase into the front foyer where they were greeted by Darius and Whitney. Dressed in a pale blue strapless gown, Whitney was the kind of beautiful that could stop traffic. But to Nick she didn't hold a candle to Maggie.

"You look fabulous!" Whitney said, bussing a kiss on Maggie's cheek. "I told you you would be fine."

Maggie laughed. Darius kissed her cheek, told her she looked fantastic and more or less handed her and Nick off into the ballroom.

Within three seconds Cade was at their side. He pulled at the collar of his white tuxedo shirt. "I hate these things."

Nick laughed. "They're not so bad."

"Not to you, Mr. Party Guy." He yanked on his collar again. "I live on a ranch, spend time on oil rigs. I don't do things like this."

Once again, Nick felt a nudge of something that made him feel odd, uncomfortable. Cade hadn't necessarily meant anything by his comment. But it gave Nick that too-tight skin feeling again. He was well-known for dating starlets, sophisticates and even a princess or two. He didn't commit. Yet, here he was with a pregnant woman—a woman he shouldn't hurt—

That's when he understood. The feeling racing through him wasn't about his fear that he couldn't commit, it was the knowledge that he shouldn't even try this unless he was sure. Because if he wasn't, Maggie was the one who would be hurt.

But, knee-deep in the conversation with Cade, Maggie laughed. "Well, if it's any consolation you look great. I'll bet all the available women are salivating at the possibility of dancing with you."

"Was that an offer?"

Maggie froze, but Nick stepped between her and Cade so quickly she wouldn't have had a chance to answer anyway. "She's spoken for."

"So what? She's not dancing."

Taking her hand, Nick turned to the dance floor. "She is now."

They twirled out onto the floor in a waltz. Her gown flowed around them. He caught her gaze and she smiled at him. This was right. This was what he wanted. He twirled her until they reached the French doors, then he twirled her one more time, taking them out to an empty terrace.

Silver moonlight enveloped them. Her skin glowed. Her eyes sparkled. Contentment settled over him. They moved around the terrace to the waltz, gazing into each other's eyes. Happy. When the song ended, Maggie stepped fully into his embrace, but before Nick could kiss her, Cade appeared in the doorway.

"Darius sent me to find you. Dinner's about to be served. We're on the head table with him."

Nick took Maggie's hand and led her to the door. Cade slapped his back. "I hope you brought your checkbook because I'm not even going to tell you how much Whitney hit me up for."

Nick laughed, too. *This* he understood. "My checkbook's at home. But I was thinking of doing a wire transfer anyway."

Cade laughed. "Always one-upping everybody."

A weird sensation stole through him. It was as if Cade's words turned him back into Nick Andreas. "I don't one-up."

"Of course, you do." Cade casually headed into the ballroom. "We all do. It's part of being an Andreas."

They found the head table and Nick pulled out Maggie's chair. Dinner was served. Whitney made a sweet plea for money from the nearby podium. And the band began to play again.

A few minutes later, Darius returned to the table where Nick and Maggie sat, lingering over dessert.

"Cade, Whitney and I are going upstairs to say goodnight to Gino. Would you like to come along?"

Maggie all but jumped out of her chair. "I'd love to."

Nick laughed. "I'd also love to."

They met Cade and Whitney in the foyer, eased up the circular stairway and back a long hall to the nursery. Darius opened the door.

Baby cries, toddler shouts and laughter poured out like the roar of a lion. Chaos reigned.

"Come in!" Working hard to be heard above the noise, Gino's nanny, Liz, a pretty blonde who looked to be about twenty, motioned them inside.

Whitney and Maggie entered first, then Cade and Darius.

Nick followed his brothers in. Two little boys about Gino's age played on a mat on the floor. Three little girls who looked to be a year or two older than Gino sat at the small plastic table and chairs having a tea party. A baby lay in a bassinette.

"Who are all these kids?"

"Play date," Liz answered simply. "When the parents party, I volunteer to hold a play date for Gino."

Whitney laughed. "I tell her she's crazy."

"But the kids love it," Liz insisted. "They always sense when their parents are out for the evening and it makes them unhappy. This way they feel like they're part of things."

Nick noticed Cade looking uneasily at the three little girls currently arguing over a teapot, as if the noise of their argument slithered like a rattlesnake along his skin.

He felt the same weird pressure building up in him. Kids were cute. He was around them all the time at his mom's daycare. He'd simply never gotten this close to them. He was always kind of looking at them through a doorway. Or waving as he drove past his mom carrying one. He wasn't accustomed to being with kids who weren't old enough to play Wiffle Ball.

Liz continued talking. "After they've run out of steam, I read a story and they fall asleep."

"Maybe we should take Gino into another room to say good-night?" Whitney suggested, pointing to a door to the right.

Darius scooped Gino off the mat, but he immediately leaned out of Darius's arms, begging Nick to take him.

Nick beamed and realized that his former thought process was incorrect. He *had* gotten very close to a kid who wasn't old enough to play Wiffle Ball. Gino. He adored this little boy. He couldn't define or describe the feelings that welled up in him every time Gino sought him out. Or hugged him. Or gave him one of those sloppy kisses only a baby could give. He wasn't quite sure why the other kids scared him, except maybe there were so many of them.

They trooped toward the master bedroom door, but suddenly the baby in the bassinette began to yelp. The tea party girls' fight intensified. The two abandoned boys on the mat burst into wails.

Everybody but Liz and Maggie froze.

"I've got this," Liz insisted.

But Maggie pulled the baby from the bassinette. "I'll take him. You settle the others and I'll bring him back when we bring Gino."

Liz said a quick, "Okay, thanks," as she headed over to break up the tea party scuffle.

They walked through the sophisticated brown and aqua master bedroom into the sitting room in front of it. Nick sat on the sofa with Gino, who playfully slapped his face.

"I think you have too much energy to go to sleep."

Gino yelped.

Everybody laughed. Cade snagged him from Nick's lap. "Hey, kid. I'm going downstairs to see if I can't find a little entertainment tonight with a willing woman. So I'm going to kiss you and hug you and bug out of here."

"That's not something you tell a baby," Darius scolded.

But Whitney laughed. "It's fine." She turned to Cade. "But next year it won't be."

Cade said, "Yes, ma'am," kissed Gino's cheek noisily and handed him back to Nick before he left the room.

Nick also gave him a quick kiss. The nursery noise had fallen off to almost nothing, which probably meant story time was in progress. He wasn't surprised when Darius hoisted Gino off his lap.

"I hear Liz reading. It's best for Gino to already be in his crib for this."

Nick rose. "Right."

Whitney faced Maggie. "You can bring little Bruce in, too, now."

"Can I have two more minutes?"

Whitney's eyes softened with love, but something puckered in Nick's chest. In a few short weeks, Maggie would give birth to a little one like that.

Whitney and Darius took Gino into the nursery and Nick rose from the sofa. He walked over to Maggie.

"Let me see Bruce."

She handed the baby over with a smile and Nick looked down at the kid. Because he was a baby, just a little younger than Gino had been when he came into their lives, Nick expected to feel the rich, deep emotion he'd felt the first time he'd held Gino, but he felt nothing. No surge of love. Or joy. Or even slight happiness.

He supposed it made perfect sense. He loved Gino. He was his blood. He could do no wrong. Nick didn't have that connection to any of the other kids here so he didn't feel the love.

It wasn't a big deal. It certainly wasn't something he'd even mention now that he'd figured it out. But even as he thought that, his gaze fell to Maggie's growing belly. And suddenly he realized this horrible feeling wasn't just about some nameless kids attending his half brother's birthday party.

What if he didn't feel anything for Maggie's baby?

CHAPTER TWELVE

When they returned to Ocean Palms, Maggie could feel the change in Nick. He was lighter. Happier. So much like the old Nick that sometimes it was hard to believe fifteen years had passed since they were married as kids.

With the bid in, her training period began, and so did their dating. They went to movies, concerts, took walks on the beach. Though Nick began spending two days a week at Andreas Holdings headquarters, they never discussed his moving to New York. And soon Maggie realized why. He wouldn't talk about anything permanent because no matter how much she loved him or how much he seemed to love her, there were no guarantees. So he wouldn't make any specific plans. That way if things didn't work out between them, moving away could be his fallback position.

Which was fine. Great actually. If things didn't work out between them personally, she'd still have a job and he could get far enough away that each could get over the breakup. But Maggie was supremely confident things would work out. She and Nick had always fit like two puzzle pieces. And they definitely still had sizzle.

Recognizing the change in their situation, her dad shamelessly asked Nick for help getting in his hay. Since he was spending half his weekend at the farm anyway,

Charlie figured he might as well work. And Nick happily agreed.

Friday in the second week of August, when the air was thick with late summer heat, the town kids chatted about going back to school, and her training period was coming to an end, Maggie arrived at work feeling like the boss.

Driving up to her private parking space in her shiny new red SUV, the work and rewards finally came together for her. Nick was returning from two days in New York and she'd been running the show for over a month. People respected her. She knew the ropes. She had some experience, not just theory.

"Good morning, Janette," she said, smiling at *her* new assistant, a thirty-something single mom, who wasn't afraid to get her hands dirty or dig in and do difficult work.

"Good morning, Maggie. Mail is open and on your desk."

Maggie said thanks and breezed through to her office. She plopped into the chair and immediately began returning phone calls.

Though Nick was supposed to fly home that morning and come to Andreas Manufacturing in the afternoon, he strode into the office about twenty minutes after she did. His hair was still wet from the shower. He wore jeans and a big sloppy T-shirt. He walked around the desk, spun her chair around, leaned in and kissed her.

Delight danced through her. "Thought you were flying back this morning."

He kissed her again. "I flew home last night."

"At?"

He winced. "About midnight. We finished up at ten and by the time I got packed and to the airstrip, it was... late."

She laughed.

"Hey, I missed you."

"I missed you, too."

And she hadn't forgotten that tonight was supposed to be *the* night. They'd had several close calls with making love, but for one reason or another it had never actually happened. Pretty soon she'd be too big and too tired to even consider it and she wanted it to be special, perfect. So when he'd left on Tuesday, she'd promised and he'd made her pinky swear that tonight would be the night.

"My dad's driving to Ohio today."

"Oh, yeah?"

"Yep. Gonna go see Charlie Jr."

"Really?"

"So now we don't have to worry about asking his permission for me to spend the weekend."

He laughed. "It's just like when we were kids."

Framing his face with her hands, she laughed. "Not quite. This time we know what we're getting into."

A shadow passed across his face. Quickly. But she'd seen it. Something serious was troubling him. "What's wrong?"

He pulled away. "Nothing."

"There's something."

He shook his head. "Yeah, we have to work eight hours before we can go home."

Though his answer was meant to reassure her, he was having doubts. Big or small, it sent a warning spiraling through her.

She told herself to forget it. They'd make love tonight and maybe another time or two over the next week, but soon she'd have to abstain. She didn't want to lose this chance by pushing him to talk about something that might be nothing.

* * *

At five o'clock, Nick listened for the sounds of Janette leaving. Drawers closed. Her computer wound down. She popped her head inside the office.

"See you on Monday, Maggie." She glanced at him. "See you Monday, Nick."

Maggie said, "Good night."

Nick smiled and waved.

One. Two. Three.

The door closed.

He leaped off the sofa. "I thought she'd never leave."

Leaning back in the tall chair behind the desk, Maggie laughed. "It's actually two minutes till five." She rose. "You're impatient."

"Not arguing that." He grabbed his keys and cell phone from the coffee table, motioned for her to precede him. "Let's go."

"Wait!" She laughed. "We haven't even discussed logistics yet."

His brow furrowed. "Logistics?"

"Do you want to come with me to my house while I pack a bag so you can drive me to your house?"

"Yes." Sheesh. He was a moron. If he were any more eager, he'd take her right here on the sofa.

He sucked in a breath. Smiled. "We'll both drive to your dad's house. You can pack a bag and leave your car, and life will be good."

"Great."

She drove to the farm and he followed a safe distance behind her. In the car, he reminded himself that she was a pregnant woman. Perhaps not physically delicate, but certainly not agile. And let's not forget emotional. Tonight had to be special.

He pulled the Porsche in beside her new SUV, jumped out and headed up the porch steps like a calm, sane man.

Walking into the dark foyer, he assumed she was upstairs and he went into the kitchen for a glass of water. But he stopped dead in the doorway. Her dad sat at the kitchen table, head in his hands.

"What's up?"

Maggie sent him a pleading look, as Charlie said, "I can't go."

"You can't?"

"He's missing Vicki."

"Not just missing Vicki," Charlie corrected. "I'm having trouble with the whole situation. Every time I get to the highway, I remember driving to Charlie Jr.'s with her and somehow or another that takes me back in time to when I found her."

Nick eased over to the table, pulled out a chair and sat. "I think that's probably normal."

Charlie dragged his fingers through his hair. "I was so lonely after your mom died and Vicki walked into my life and suddenly I wasn't alone anymore."

Nick's gaze shot to Maggie's face. The way Charlie was talking it was as if Maggie hadn't even existed. He could see from the question in her eyes that Maggie felt it, too.

Still, she patted her dad's arm and said, "I know. Vicki coming into your life was a good thing."

"And Charlie Jr., too." He shook his head. "Man, she loved that baby. She was such a great mom."

Maggie stiffened. She said, "Yes, she was," but Nick could see the hurt on her face.

"She loved doing school things with him, loved taking him to the beach. And bake? Every time he sneezed she baked him cookies."

Maggie swallowed, but she quickly pulled herself together and snuggled against her dad's shoulder, comforting him. "I know. She was great."

But Nick wasn't a daughter struggling to comfort her dad, and he knew the truth. Vicki hadn't been a great mother. At least not in Nick's memory. She might have been mother of the year to her own child, but the child who'd come to her by default, Maggie, had largely gone ignored. Maggie had felt like an outsider in her own home. Worse, her father had never noticed. And maybe Vicki hadn't, either. They were both nice people, good people. Especially Charlie. He wouldn't deliberately ignore anyone. Yet, he hadn't noticed that his second wife had never taken to the child from his first marriage.

Maggie rose to get her dad a drink and Nick glanced at her protruding stomach. Fear skittered through him. He felt nothing for her baby. Except maybe jealousy. Nick might have been the first man to make Maggie pregnant, but another man had given her the child she'd hold. Another man had given her the baby she'd become a mother to. How could he not be jealous?

How could he guarantee he wouldn't be like Vicki, not quite able to love her child?

How could he say he wouldn't unintentionally hurt Maggie's baby the way Vicki had hurt Maggie?

Nick stayed another twenty minutes and helped Maggie start supper. But when she asked him to set the table, he rubbed his hand across the back of his neck. "I think I'm going to head home. Let you and your dad have some privacy."

She nodded, walked over and brushed his lips with a kiss. "As soon as he's sleeping, I'll come over."

Nick smiled before he left, but the seeds of discord that had been growing inside him had begun to sprout into full-blown doubt. No matter how much he loved Maggie, if he put her baby into the same kind of home life that she'd had, she'd never forgive him.

Hell, he'd never forgive himself.

He had to figure out a way to fix this.

Maggie finally got her dad into bed at about nine. She hastily packed a bag, showered, dressed in a pretty, airy sundress and headed to Nick's.

As was her practice, she didn't knock. She parked her SUV in the garage beneath the house and headed up the stairway into the butler's pantry and to the kitchen.

"Nick?"

"I'm out here."

She turned to face the French doors, which were open. But the deck light wasn't on. Confused, she set her bag on a close counter and walked outside.

"Hey."

He didn't turn from the railing. "Hey."

So she met him there, mimicking his position by leaning her forearms on the wooden rail and looking out into the darkness. "What's up?"

"The stars are pretty tonight."

She glanced up. "They are." The stars were bright, the ocean nothing more than a comfortable roar a hundred yards or so beyond Nick's house. Only the white foam of an occasional wave was visible in the darkness.

Nick stayed silent and the odd, unnamed fear she'd had that morning resurrected. She'd seen the shadow cross his face while they were chatting in the office. He'd also left her to deal with her dad alone. Normally he stayed around. Talked her dad through his sadness. Tonight, he'd gone.

She bumped his shoulder. "So why'd you leave me all alone with my dad?"

He still didn't look at her, didn't say anything and the unnamed fear took hold, took meaning. All along it had seemed too good to be true that they could pick up where they had left off. And she knew—she just knew—he was having second thoughts. Making love the first time had taken them from friends to a married couple. It had been a lightning-fast change. No chance to think things through or look back.

And today they were going to make love again. For the first time in this portion of their relationship. Undoubtedly he knew there'd be no turning back. And maybe he wasn't ready?

She eased away from the railing. "If you don't want me to stay—"

He pivoted to face her. "No. God. No. I'm sorry." He scrubbed his hand across his mouth. "It's just—I just…" He sucked in a breath. "I've been having some weird thoughts lately."

"What kind of weird thoughts?"

"You know how I—you—" He stopped, huffed out a breath. "All that talk about Vicki being a good mom tonight floored me."

"She was a good mother."

"To Charlie Jr."

She laughed as relief rippled through her. "I told you all that was resolved."

He took her upper arms in his warm hands and caught her gaze. "That's not what I saw on your face tonight."

"A momentary lapse."

"Really?" He studied her eyes. "Because it's been fifteen years since you and Vicki supposedly found your footing, yet thinking about your childhood hurt you."

"A bit." She might as well admit it. Nick had been her best friend through that time. He knew how alone she'd felt. How abandoned. She might not have thought about it in a while, but being home had brought a lot of it back. And, tonight, her dad's words had cut like a knife. "But I've decided to treat it as only a momentary lapse. She might not have been there for me. But she had been for Charlie Jr." Unconsciously she rubbed her hands along her swollen tummy. "But I now understand why it happened. I wasn't her blood child."

She stopped herself because the color had drained from Nick's face and his gaze had fallen to her stomach.

And suddenly his fears made sense.

He didn't love her baby. Didn't *want* to love her baby.

"Oh, my God."

She turned to go but Nick stopped her. "Wait! Wait!" He shook his head in regret. "It's not what you think. Things are just confusing for me right now."

She searched his eyes. "How confusing?"

"I'm involved with a woman who's pregnant with another man's child. But I've also seen the life you've led, being that child, the child from a different relationship. I didn't just see Vicki ignore you. I saw the end result. I saw you cry." He raked his fingers through his hair. "I know how you hurt."

She stepped back, out of his reach. "You don't want my baby."

It was a statement, not a question.

"I don't want to *hurt* your baby and I feel—"

"Feel what?" she demanded as the blood in her veins chilled to just above freezing. She now had proof Nick didn't want her baby. Nick Andreas never stammered. He didn't get confused. He always knew what he wanted. If he thought he was confused now, it was because he was arguing with the answer he already knew.

"That's just it. I don't know."

She squeezed her eyes shut.

"I'm afraid we're going to do to your baby what Vicki did to you."

She took another two steps back. "I'm not. I'm not even close to fearing that. You know why? Because I know you and I know the huge capacity you have to love. If you're worried that you can't love my baby…it's because you don't, because you know you won't."

She spun away and headed for the French doors. She grabbed her overnight bag and raced down the stairs.

"Wait! Maggie!" Nick was on her heels. "Damn it, Maggie! I thought you said we could talk about anything. We have to talk about this."

She jumped into her SUV. "We just did."

And Nick watched her go. Once again, she'd made a decision for them. He wanted to talk. She ran. And maybe that was what was fundamentally wrong with their relationship.

CHAPTER THIRTEEN

"LET me get this straight. You're working on a Monday?"

Nick rolled his eyes and headed for the silver coffee service in his New York office. "Maggie's trained now. She doesn't need me."

"She's about to give birth. I think she needs you."

"She has six weeks."

"So you're here?"

"Yes. Full-time."

Darius just stared at him. But Nick gave him a look. The look. The one that said *don't cross this boundary*.

Darius shrugged. "Fine." He tossed a stack of papers on Nick's desk. "That's the email trail for my discussion with the group of private investors in London who want to buy into Andreas Holdings. They know there's another shareholder."

"And you want me to…do what?"

"Just familiarize yourself with the backstory. Because if we don't find that shareholder before the people in London do, we may be going to war."

Darius left and Nick settled down at his desk. Picking up the papers Darius had left him, he forced himself not to think about Maggie. Half of him understood why she'd balked, been appalled, about his worry over not being able to love her baby. The other half was angry. He was only human. He hadn't asked for the weird feelings, for the fear. Yet, she'd acted as if he'd calmly, rationally decided not to love her child.

He ran his hands down his face. She'd been hurt.

Hell, he'd been hurt!

But he'd tried to call her. Had tried to see her. And she wouldn't answer the phone or see him. Maybe that's why he hadn't gone after her the first time. She was stubborn.

Pain rippled through him at the thought. She wasn't stubborn…well, maybe a little… She was hurt. He knew she was hurt and she wouldn't let him help her, wouldn't let him try to fix this.

Of course, he'd been the one to make the problem.

Which took him back to the fact that he hadn't asked for his feelings.

He just had them.

He still had them.

And maybe she was right not to want to see him. Maybe there was no way to work this out.

The only thing he could do was work. Get his mind off this. So he put his attention on the email trail Darius wanted him to read and started in. He worked until five o'clock, then realized he hadn't even taken a break for lunch. Without a word to anyone, he left Andreas Holdings and went straight to Darius's penthouse apartment. Normally he'd stay at the house in Montauk, but he wasn't ready for that yet. Whitney would know he and Maggie had split. If she didn't know today, she'd know soon because she and Maggie had become friends. And then Nick would face a million questions that he'd prefer not to answer right now.

How would he explain to Whitney, lovable Whitney, who'd lost a baby, that he didn't have an ounce of feelings for Maggie's little one? He'd tried. He'd honest-to-God tried to feel something for Maggie's baby. But when he did, the only emotion that registered was horrible jealousy. Maggie had no trouble carrying this baby. But she'd lost theirs. He wasn't pointing fingers. He knew nature was nature. Maggie was not at fault. So, he supposed he was railing at nature. Angry with fate. Disgusted with destiny. Why had his baby died?

A million emotions washed through him as he entered the penthouse. Rich buttery hardwood floors and a sky-line view of the city greeted him as he entered. He barely noticed them. One minute he shook with rage. The next he was a puddle of sadness, of loss.

He grabbed a bottle of twelve-year-old Scotch and headed for the TV room, where he planned to drink him-self to sleep.

It took two weeks before Maggie stopped crying herself to sleep. Nick no longer came to the plant. He stayed in New York. Every Friday morning, he called Janette who filled him in on any phone calls or correspondence that needed his attention. But he never spoke to Maggie.

She could think that he was still angry and didn't want anything to do with her, but she had a feeling that, like her, he knew talking would only be painful and slow their recovery from their breakup.

Which meant he wanted to recover. He wasn't coming home so there'd be no risk that seeing her would make him long for what they'd had. What they had was deficient. He really and truly believed he couldn't love her child and if he couldn't love her child, then there was no future for them. Because he was right. She would not let her child be raised by a parent who couldn't love him.

Him.

Her baby could be a boy. And if it was he would need

a male influence. Not someone who loved his mom, but didn't love him. But someone to teach him. Someone to guide him along the road to being a man. She'd learned firsthand from Vicki that if the same sex parent had no interest in a child, there'd be no teaching. There'd be no bonding. And that would leave a huge hole. A void. Her child would live a loneliness that couldn't be described.

She wouldn't do that to her baby.

So she spent the next three weeks telling herself that Nick walking away had been the right thing.

That Friday, she hadn't even watched the door hoping Nick would stroll through, as she had the first few Fridays of her tenure as general manager. She didn't linger until six, thinking he might pop in after he thought she was gone, so that she could catch him, and if nothing else see him.

She was beyond all that. Strong now. Getting ready for her baby.

As she drove home, a storm began rolling in. Dark clouds gathered, filling the blue sky with inky blackness.

Dressed in a suit and a crisp white shirt, her dad glanced over her head as she walked inside. She could see from the worried expression that clouded his eyes that he didn't like the look of the sky.

"Are you sure you don't mind me going?"

She set her briefcase on the kitchen table and smiled. "Positive."

This time, the expression on his face said he didn't believe her. He shrugged out of his jacket. "You know what? I don't really need to go to bereavement group tonight."

"You do!" Maggie crossed the room, picked up his jacket and handed it to him. "I'm fine."

He laughed. "Okay. Okay. I get it. I'm a mess without the group. I'm going."

Walking across the kitchen to the door, he shrugged into his jacket again. One foot on the back porch he hesitated. "Wow. That storm's going to be a beaut."

She glanced at the dark, angry clouds. "You know what? I think you'd better take my SUV."

"The truck's fine."

"The truck is a piece of junk." She laughed and for the first time in weeks actually felt human. Normal. Grabbing her keys from the counter by the door, she said, "Take the SUV."

He smiled as if hearing her laugh had been worth the insult to his beloved truck. But he glanced worriedly at her belly and set her keys on the counter again. "You can't drive the truck. It's a standard. If I take your car, you're stranded."

She pointed at the sky. "As if I'm going out in this."

"Right."

"So go."

Still, he hesitated.

Impatience crawled up her spine. She was tired, achy and just wanted to be alone. Specifically, she wanted a nice shower and two hours of mindless television so she could forget her backache, forget that she had another week of carrying this baby, forget that she and Nick weren't really a match.

He looked down at the keys, then back up at her. He studied her face for several seconds. "Okay. Fine. I'm going."

Though it was difficult, she mustered a smile.

He stepped out into the wind.

Grateful for the reprieve and knowing she had at least twenty minutes before the storm actually broke, she climbed the stairs, turned on the shower and stepped into the warm spray. Her back had ached all day. Her feet thumped with the weariness of having to support her burgeoning weight. But most of all her heart hurt.

She might have spent the day not looking for Nick, but now that she was alone, in the quiet, quiet house, she couldn't get him out of her mind. Losing Josh had been nothing compared to losing Nick. She should have known that. She should have realized that getting involved with the man who'd stolen her heart at six and let her leave him at eighteen, would end in the kind of heartbreak that tore through her soul, leaving tattered, unmendable pieces in its wake.

She forced her head under the spray as tears pooled in her eyes. She wasn't feeling sorry for herself. She was angry with herself. She'd been through this before. And though she'd been the one to leave Nick the first time, she'd always known she wasn't quite right for him. He was smart, strong, gorgeous. She had to force herself to do things, push herself to be bold. She wasn't even sure how to behave in the world he now lived in. And she certainly wasn't gorgeous.

Hell, today she looked more like a whale than a woman.

The tears in her eyes spilled over and ran down her cheeks. Again, she didn't try to stop them. Her entire body ached, but her broken heart shimmered with misery. Because she hurt so badly she decided not to fight it. She'd take this night and grieve the loss of her one true love, then tomorrow morning she'd be fine. There would be no more reason for her dad to worry about her. She'd pull herself together and no matter how intense the pain that sneaked up on her, no matter how lonely she'd get for the one person who'd ever made her genuinely happy, she would put on a smile and she would get through her life as if she were the luckiest, most blessed woman in the world.

Actually, once she had her baby she would be the luck-iest, most blessed woman in the world. She'd have her dad. She'd have her baby. She would have the family she'd always longed for as a child but never quite fit into.

When she knew her skin would prune if she spent any more time under the spray of water, she hauled herself out and wrapped herself in a towel.

The first swipe of lightning raced across the sky. Were she in a better mood, she would have smiled at her timing. Instead she groaned when pain filled her back. This was awful. She'd known she'd be uncomfortable the last week of her pregnancy, but she hadn't expected this kind of torture.

Another flash of lightning streaked through the thick black clouds as she waddled to the bedroom. This was not looking good.

Still, what did she care? She had four hours till mid-night. Four hours left in her self-declared night of mourn-ing. She intended to use them.

But the next lightning bolt hit close. Her room filled with light, and a crack and boom immediately followed. She didn't even get seconds to count in between the lightning and the thunder. They were almost simultaneous, which meant the strike had been within a mile of her home.

The bedroom light flickered.

No. No. No! She could not lose the electricity. If she had to grieve in a dark house, she'd be beyond pathetic. Just let her keep the lights.

They flickered again then blinked off completely.

Light from the candles she'd left in the bathroom sent a wink of a glow into the hall. With a groan and a hand on her aching back, she made her way to the bathroom. She picked up the two scented candles she'd had sitting on the vanity and carried them back to her bedroom.

She really wasn't in the mood to wrestle into pajamas, so she drew a nightgown over her head. Her plan had been to make herself some hot cocoa, sit on the porch and cry. But the storm had brought a heavy humidity, making it too hot and humid for cocoa. The wind was too strong for her to sit on the porch. The lightning too close.

And as for crying, she could do that in her bedroom. On her bed.

She lay down. Suddenly the ache that had been in her back, raced around her sides to her tummy.

Dear God. What if she was in labor? A week early. With no car.

She settled herself. She'd simply call 9-1-1. It wasn't a big deal.

Except that her purse with her cell phone was downstairs and she now ached so badly she didn't think she could move.

Nick's lightweight shirt blew in the wind whipping across his deck that overlooked the ocean. Normally he loved to watch storms wreak havoc miles out over the water and wait for the resultant crash of the waves on his shore. But this storm was here. Any second now sheets of water would drench the happy little tourist town and anyone foolish enough to be standing on his deck.

Yet he didn't feel like going inside.

He ached so much he pressed his hand to his chest and rubbed the spot where he believed his heart to be.

Lightning streaked through the billowing black clouds, followed by a roar of thunder. Only an idiot tempted fate by making himself a target for lightning, no matter how awful he felt. He turned to go inside and found himself face-to-face with his brothers. Darius looked worried. Cade carried a case of beer.

His spirits lifted, and for the first time since discovering he wasn't the only Andreas son, he was abundantly glad he had siblings.

"Are we in a hurricane?"

Cade laughed at Darius. "Greenhorn, where I come from this isn't even a really big storm."

With his hands on both of his brothers' shoulders, Nick turned them and urged them inside. "This might not be a big storm where you come from but where you *are* it's a dilly. So move."

He closed the French doors behind them, two seconds before the first wave of rain hit. It pelted the glass like a million tiny diamonds. A continuous clicking sound filled his kitchen, as the lights flickered then went out.

"Great."

"Well, since there's no power for the refrigerator, it looks like we'll have to drink this beer."

Nick couldn't help it. He laughed. Cade was nothing if not pragmatic. A night with two stupid brothers was exactly what he needed to forget that he'd lost Maggie again. And this time it was his fault.

"Toss me a can."

"It's bottles. Walk over and get one."

Nick first went for the flashlight he kept in the top drawer of the cabinets. He hit the button and illuminated the room in an eerie beam of light.

Darius took a beer from Cade. "Too bad we can't sit outside and watch this."

"Yeah." Cade cast a longing glance out at the ocean. "That's some storm."

"Thought you were used to bigger?" Nick said, also accepting a beer from Cade.

"I am. But I'm also landlocked. I don't get to see anything like this on the water."

"We can go downstairs. Sit under the house."

Cade was already on his way to the stairs. "I forgot about that."

In two minutes, they were under the house, on rickety lawn chairs, drinking beer, watching the storm.

"I hope Maggie's not out in this."

And with those words from Darius, Nick suddenly realized why his brothers had come. He'd thought they'd noticed his apprehension when he'd left Andreas Holdings that afternoon. He had to be at the plant on Monday and he would see Maggie for the first time in six weeks. They knew he still hurt over her. They also knew he believed he'd made all the right choices. But he still hurt. And he still worried about seeing Maggie.

So he'd suspected they'd hopped on Cade's plane and followed him. To support him. But they weren't here for him. They were worried about Maggie.

"She's fine. She has her dad. Her friends. People at the plant took to her like bees to honey. She's got at least eight mother hens who fawn all over her."

Darius took a slug of beer. "She doesn't want her dad or a mother hen. According to Whitney, she's probably curled up in a ball of despair, wondering what the hell she did wrong."

"She didn't do anything."

Cade leaned around Darius and nudged Nick's arm. "Yeah. We get that part, genius."

"So, what? You're mad at me, too?"

"More like confused." Always calm and in control, Darius spoke with the air of authority. "You can't tell us that you don't love her. We see it on your sappy face. Yet you walked away when she needs you the most."

"She doesn't need me."

Cade barked a laugh. "Ah, poor, Nick. The love of his life doesn't need him."

"Shut up."

Darius turned to Cade. "Yeah, Cade. That's not helping."

Cade faced the ocean. "Okay. Fine. I'll just drink my beer and wait for waves to start splashing across our toes."

They were silent for a minute as the wind and rain, lightning and thunder put on a grand show.

Finally Nick said, "Power's probably going to be out all night." He sucked in a breath. "But Maggie's not alone." He told himself he'd only said that to alleviate his brothers' concerns. Not because a tiny spark of panic had welled up in his gut. "She's got her dad. And a car. And a cell phone."

"Right," Darius agreed. "She's probably fine."

"I mean…what could happen?" Nick took a quick drink of his beer, feeling odd tentacles of fear crawling up his spine with icy fingers. "She's due but not till next week." He sucked in a breath. "Though the last time I saw her she looked really big. So big that I'd wondered if she'd miscalculated her due date."

Darius groaned. "I hope you didn't tell her that."

He was digging, trying to get Nick to tell him about their fight, but horrible self-loathing and disappointment filled him. After the way they'd all taken to Gino, he'd never tell them. He couldn't tell them. They'd think him as crazy as Maggie did.

Instead he said, "I don't have a death wish."

Cade laughed, but much to Nick's relief didn't say anything.

Nick settled back in his chair. Rubbed his hand over the

day-old stubble of beard on his chin and cheeks. Maggie was fine. The power was out, but she was with her dad.

He squeezed his eyes shut. "Janette told me her dad has bereavement group every Friday night." Shooting out of his chair, he headed for the steps and his SUV keys. "She's alone in this."

He wasn't surprised that neither of his brothers argued when he bolted out into the night. He wasn't even surprised that he was going to check on her. He dialed her cell phone, but she didn't answer.

And suddenly he needed all his concentration for driving. Tree limbs had broken off. Water washed across the road. So he tossed his phone to the seat beside him and kept going.

He loved her. There'd never been any doubt in his mind that he loved her. He might be a fool who was so torn up about her baby that he couldn't accept him or her, but he'd never doubted his love for Maggie.

Ducking rain, he raced up the front porch steps to her house. He pounded on the door. "Maggie!"

She didn't answer. He tried several times and gave up. Though it wasn't late, she could be in bed, sleeping. And he was being foolish. So they were having a storm. She'd probably gone wherever she needed to go before it started. She might have driven her dad to bereavement group and decided to stay with him rather than ride home in the storm alone.

That was probably it.

Feeling foolish, he raced back to the SUV, accompanied by the roar of thunder, the pounding of the rain. His hand stalled above the door handle.

What if she was inside but just plain couldn't hear him?

What if she was afraid?

Lightning hit a nearby tree. Thunder roared like a hungry lion.

Hell, he was afraid.

He ran up the porch steps again, and, this time, tried the front door. It was unlocked. She wouldn't leave her house unlocked if she wasn't here.

He searched the downstairs first, calling her name. "Maggie! Maggie!"

But no answer.

He bolted upstairs, taking the steps two and three at a time as panic rolled through him.

Bursting into the room, he said only, "Maggie." She lay on the bed, curled up in a fetal position.

She turned to him. Tears streamed down her cheeks. Her eyes were glassy. "The baby's coming. I can't move. I couldn't even get to my cell phone."

Panic seized Nick. Trees and power lines were down. Even if she'd gotten to a phone, and called 9-1-1, there was no guarantee an ambulance could have gotten here.

He sat on the edge of the bed, trying to remember the books he'd read fifteen years before when she was pregnant with his child.

Sobbing, she said, "I'm so glad you came."

He blinked back his own tears. He was worthless. Ridiculously worthless. Always worthless when it came to Maggie.

He caught her hand. "I'm glad, too—"

She moaned suddenly and squeezed his hand. "Oh, God, Nick. This baby is coming right now."

Not giving himself time to think, he jumped up and grabbed the covers, tossing them off the bed.

She rolled to her back, her knees up, her legs spread, as if nature had taken over.

Which was good. He was going to need more than a

little help from Mother Nature, if they were going to get through this.

"Where are your scissors, towels and a basin for water?"

Grabbing her knees, she reared up and groaned through a pain that had to have been excruciating. "Towels are in the bathroom closet. Scissors are in the top drawer of the bathroom vanity. Basin is in the kitchen, beneath the sink."

"Okay. Hang on. I'll be back as soon as I can."

Taking one of her candles with him, he raced to the kitchen and found the basin. He flew back up the stairs, hurled himself into the bathroom and grabbed an armload of towels and the scissors.

When he returned to the room, Maggie was panting. Her gown had worked its way up her tummy.

Sweat beaded on Nick's forehead, but he didn't stop or take time to think. He grabbed two towels and slid them under her before taking the basin to the bathroom and filling it with hot water. While there, he grabbed some alcohol.

He pulled out his phone to call 9-1-1, hoping they'd reach the farm before the baby was born, but Maggie groaned.

"He's coming!"

Nick doused his hands in alcohol then rinsed them in the water before he raced to the foot of the bed. As she'd said, the baby was coming. He watched the head crown, then the shoulders ease through one at a time and caught the baby before it hit the bed. He grabbed another towel and wrapped the baby, laying him on Maggie's stomach so he could cut the cord.

Maggie's eyes filled with tears. "Oh, my God, Nick. It's a boy! Look at him. He's beautiful."

Nick paused. Actually looked at the baby. A boy. He swallowed. Tears filled his eyes. "He is beautiful."

"So tiny."

He glanced at the absolutely perfect miniature fingers and toes. An unexpected smile formed. "He's probably the smallest person I've ever seen."

Unnamed emotions skittered through him. He blamed it on coming down from the adrenaline that had spiked in his blood. After handling the rest of the birth, he washed his hands and called 9-1-1. He explained the situation to the dispatcher and she said she'd send an ambulance immediately.

When he disconnected the call, the silence in the room was deafening. He didn't know what to say. What to do. He'd known Maggie was in trouble and raced to her. But now that the trouble was over, they were still the same people.

She patted the bed beside her. "Sit."

He ambled over. Sat on the bed. Glanced at the baby. "He's so beautiful."

She smiled. "Yes. He is. Thank you. I don't know what would have happened without you."

His chest ached. He pictured her on the bed, alone, scared, not able to handle the situation for herself. Still, he said, "You would have been fine. It was a very easy delivery."

She gaped at him. "Do you not get it yet? Nick, I need you. Everybody needs somebody sometime and every time I've really needed somebody you have been there."

He smiled reluctantly. "Sort of like fate."

"Sort of like destiny."

He looked at the baby again. So tiny. So perfect. Then he glanced at Maggie. So content. So perfect. "I can be an ass."

"Or maybe it just takes you a while to think things through and come to terms with it all."

Wrapping his fingers around the baby's middle, he lifted the towel-clad bundle from Maggie's tummy. "Welcome to the world, kid."

Maggie laughed.

"My God. I thought Gino was small when we got him at six months. This kid is like one-tenth his size." He caught her gaze. "He really needs us."

"Yes, he does." She smiled slowly. "And I really need you."

The joy of hearing that enveloped his heart, warmed it enough that he could take a risk. "I need you, too."

She caught his fingers and squeezed. "I'm so sorry I got angry that you were afraid you couldn't love him."

"Shh. It's fine. We're fine." He glanced at the baby. "Maybe better than fine. My God. He's so adorable. I can't believe I was afraid."

"I can understand. I—"

"No, Maggie. I was jealous." He closed his eyes in misery. "My brothers and I made a pact when we decided to become brothers for real. No secrets. So no secrets here, either. I was jealous." He swallowed. "You had lost our baby. Another man had given you this child…this child that you'd get a chance to hold and love. I couldn't get past that."

"Nick—" His name whispered to him as she slid her hand across his. "Have you ever really grieved our baby?"

He sucked in a breath. "I'm not sure."

"You need to do that. You need to let yourself feel all the pain of his loss and put him in a special place in your heart."

"I wonder what he would have looked like."

"Well, seeing how the Andreas genes seem to dominate, I'd guess he'd have been dark-haired with dark eyes."

Nick smiled.

"And a devil. Ornery, but fun."

This time Nick laughed. "Yeah. That's how I saw him, too."

"So keep him in your heart."

He swallowed hard and nodded.

"And take care of me and Egbert."

His head snapped up. "Egbert?"

"Sure. It's an old family name that no one's used in decades."

He rose, rocking the brand-new baby boy. "There's a reason it hasn't been used in decades. As names go, it sucks."

She laughed.

The noise of the ambulance pulling into the farm rolled into the room a few seconds before red and blue lights flashed through.

"So, you don't like Egbert. What do you think we should name him?"

He looked down, love filled his heart until he thought his chest would explode from it.

He caught her gaze. "Michael Nicholas Andreas."

She smiled. "That's a great name."

"He's a great kid."

"He is."

He paced to the window, saw the ambulance crew getting out and faced her again. "And you'll marry me."

"Well, I'll have to if you're adopting my son and giving him your last name."

He laughed. The ambulance crew hustled in. Took the baby. Cared for Maggie.

And Nick leaned against the windowsill. For fifteen years he'd cursed fate. Now suddenly he didn't hate the old bat so much. He had Maggie back. For real. For good.

And he had a son.

EPILOGUE

Whitney and Darius had insisted on bringing Gino to North Carolina for the baptism. While the waters had become too cold to swim in New York, the beach in North Carolina was still warm and sunny.

Still, they'd held the baptism dinner at Maggie's dad's house. *He'd* insisted.

"All right. All right," Charlie yelled, calming the noisy group. He'd gotten out Vicki's good china and her crystal for wine and set the big table in the formal dining room. "Turkey will be carved in about two minutes. There's no reason to get restless."

Gino yelped, pointing at the mashed potatoes and gravy on Whitney's plate.

"Yes, they're yours," Whitney said with a laugh.

"What's his?"

All eyes turned toward the arched entryway, when Cade walked in.

Maggie was about to jump up and give him a hug since he'd said he wouldn't be able to make it, but Nick said, "You missed the actual baptism."

He strolled to a seat at the table. "Had to fly myself over," he said, pulling out a chair and straddling it. "Can't fly in a suit, can't go to church in jeans."

Charlie harrumphed. "Lots of people go to church in jeans."

"That's just an excuse," Whitney said, handing him a plate and some silver.

Darius shook his head. "I just think he's so accustomed to being with cattle that he sometimes forgets how to be human."

Cade threw a fresh dinner roll at him. "At least I'm not so pampered that I use bath salts."

Whitney gaped. "Bath salts are good for the skin."

And so it went. Charlie passed out slices of juicy turkey. Nick, Cade and Darius teased. Gino ate his mashed potatoes. Maggie and Whitney talked about caring for infants as Maggie cuddled her newborn baby.

Things weren't perfect. But life rarely was. But, finally, finally, she had a family. The family she'd always longed for. The family Nick had promised at eighteen that he would give her.

BABY ON
THE RANCH

BY
SUSAN MEIER

CHAPTER ONE

SUZANNE CALDWELL SHOVED against the spot in the door of the Old West Diner where the Waitress Wanted sign filled the glass. The scent of fresh apple pie greeted her, along with a rush of noise. Though there were no more than ten people at the counter and in the booths, the place was as rowdy as a party. Women wearing jeans and tank tops sat with men dressed in jeans, T-shirts and cowboy hats.

She didn't get two steps into the room before the noise level began to drop. As if noticing the stranger, people stopped talking midsentence.

She clutched her six-month-old baby, Mitzi. There was nothing like walking into a roomful of staring strangers to make you realize how alone you were in the world. And she was definitely alone. She'd run out of gas about a mile out of Whiskey Springs, Texas, and, literally, had no one to call for help.

No family. Her grandmother had died six months ago and her mom had died when Suzanne was six. Her dad, whoever he was, had never acknowledged her.

Her mom and grandmother were both only children, so she had no aunts, no uncles, no cousins.

And no friends. The wonderful sorority sisters who'd vowed to be her ally for life had dumped her when she got pregnant by a popular university professor. It was her fault, they'd said, and had accused her of trying to ruin Bill Baker's career. As if. The guy had gone on a campaign to seduce her and had wormed his way into her life because of her grandmother's fortune. When Martha Caldwell made some major mistakes in money management and lost the bulk of her wealth, Professor Baker suddenly didn't want to see Suzanne anymore. And he most certainly wanted no part of their baby.

So, yeah. She was alone. Alone. Broke. Desperate to make a home for herself and her baby. And she'd left Atlanta bound for Whiskey Springs, hoping to find some help.

But after walking the last mile on a hot June day, her heels ached in her black stiletto boots. Mitzi squirmed in her arms. Her heavy diaper bag was dislocating her shoulder. Still, she kept her head high as she made her way to the first empty booth. By the time she got there, the diner was dead silent.

A waitress shuffled over. "Help you?"

She cleared her throat. "I'd like a piece of the apple pie I can smell, a cup of coffee, a glass of milk and some pudding, please."

"What kind of pudding?"

She swallowed. Not one person had turned back to his or her coffee or food. They just stared as if she were a zombie or vampire or some other mythical creature they'd never seen before. "What kind do you have?"

"Vanilla or chocolate."

"Mitzi loves vanilla."

Without so much as a word of acknowledgment, the waitress scurried away.

"You're not from around here."

Knowing the man could only be talking to her, she

followed the voice and found herself staring into a pair of the shrewdest eyes she'd ever seen. Cool, calculating, so black the pupils were almost invisible, his eyes never blinked, never wavered as they held her gaze.

Toto, we are not in Kansas anymore.

"No, I'm not from around here."

"What's your business?"

"None of yours." She turned away from the penetrating, unsettling eyes and shifted Mitzi on her lap.

To her horror, the man walked over and plopped down on the bench seat across from hers. His full lips pulled upward into a devilish smile. His dark eyes danced with pleasure. "Now, see. That's not just a bad attitude. It's also wrong."

She should have been scared to death. He was big. Not fat, but tall and broad-shouldered. The kind of guy who could snap a little five-foot-five girl like her in two. But instead of fear, a very unladylike shiver of lust rippled down her spine.

"Everything that happens in Whiskey Springs is my business because this is my town."

Not at all happy with herself for even having two seconds of attraction to an ill-mannered stranger, she said, "*Your* town? What are you, the sheriff?"

He chuckled. The people at the counter and in the booths around them also laughed.

"No. I'm Cade Andreas. I own this town. I bought all the buildings last year. I lease the businesses back to their proprietors, but I still own every square inch, including the one you're sitting on."

Oh, good God. *This* was Cade Andreas?

Fear and confusion immediately replaced attraction. Wasn't the Andreas family broke? She owned one-third of Andreas Holdings stock and hadn't been able to sell it because the company was on the skids. What was he doing buying a town?

"And I'd like to know what brings you to my town."

She raised her gaze to his face. A day-old growth of beard covered his chin and cheeks, giving him a sexily disreputable look. His lips were full, firm, kissable. His nose had been broken—undoubtedly in a fight—but it wasn't disfigured, more like masculine. Definitely not dainty. There was nothing dainty about this man. He was all male. One hundred percent, grade A, prime specimen sexy.

Finally, their eyes connected. Her chest tightened. Her breathing stalled. She could have blamed that on her unwitting attraction, but refused. A guy who bought a town had to be more than a little arrogant. Definitely past vain. Maybe even beyond narcissistic. And she'd learned her lesson about narcissistic men with Mitzi's father. It would be a cold, frosty day in hell before she got involved with another self-absorbed man. So she refused to be attracted to Cade Andreas. Refused.

But she still needed a job. She might own stock worth millions of dollars, but nobody wanted to buy it. Potential didn't sell stock these days. Dividends did. And in the past two years Andreas Holdings hadn't paid any. So she was hoping that since she owned one-third of the company they could at least let her work there. The choice to approach Cade Andreas, the youngest of the three brothers who owned controlling interest of Andreas Holdings stock and ran the company, was simply a matter of practicality. Texas was driving distance. New York City, the headquarters for the corporate offices, wasn't. Still, if they gave her a job, she'd get there somehow. She'd go anywhere that she could put down roots and make a home. Maybe find some friends.

"What brings you to my town?"

This time the words were harsh. Not quite angry, but definitely losing patience.

She glanced at the waitress who stood behind the counter, balancing a coffeepot and Suzanne's piece of pie, obviously holding them hostage until she answered Cade.

She looked back at him. His already-sharp eyes had narrowed in displeasure, and she had the sudden, intense intuition that if she told him who she was—in front of his adoring friends and the frozen waitress—he would not jump for joy. She would bet her last dollar that none of these people knew how much trouble Andreas Holdings was in and Cade would not be happy with the person who announced it.

There was no way she could say who she was and why she was here without talking about something he would no doubt want kept private, and no way she could explain her presence in this two-bit town so far from a major highway that no one was ever just passing through.

She glanced around, saw the sign in the door advertising for a waitress and grabbed the first piece of good luck that had come her way in over a year.

"I heard about the job for a waitress, so I came."

"In your fancy boots, with your baby all dolled up?"

"We put on our best stuff," she said, making herself sound as if she fit the part of a waitress. She regretted the deception, but if anybody ever deserved to be played, this guy did. Owned a town, huh? She potentially held the future of his family's company in her hands just by choosing whom to sell her stock to, yet he'd never once considered that she might be somebody worthy of his time. "For the interview."

A short, round dark-haired woman wearing an apron scampered out of the kitchen. "You're looking for a job?"

"Yes." The truth of that brought her back to reality. Her purpose for coming to Whiskey Springs *had been* to get a job—from Andreas Holdings. Now that plan was on hold. She wasn't exactly here to be a waitress, but money was money. And she needed some. Now. Today. She had enough cash to pay for her piece of pie and even buy extra milk for Mitzi, but after that she and Mitzi were sleeping in her car.

"I'm Suzanne Caldwell." Because her grandmother had held the stock in a trust, her name wasn't mentioned on any documents, so she could give it without worry. "This is my baby, Mitzi."

Mitzi picked that exact moment to cry. The little brunette scrambled over. "I'm Amanda Mae and if you want a job, you've got it." She shot Cade an evil look, causing Suzanne to immediately love her. "Real men don't make babies cry."

Cade held up his hands innocently. "Hey, I was on my own side of the booth the whole time. I didn't touch her."

"You're threatening her mama."

His face fell. "I never threatened her!"

"Just your voice is threatening."

He sighed. "Yeah. Right. Whatever."

She took the baby. "Would you like a bottle, little Mitzi?"

Suzanne said, "I ordered some milk and pudding for her."

Amanda Mae looked horrified. "June Marie, where are you with this baby's food?"

The waitress hustled over, set Suzanne's pie in front of her and poured her a cup of coffee before she rushed away and got both the pudding and the milk.

Eyes narrowed, Cade studied the woman across the booth from him. She was a pretty little package. Eyes so blue they bordered on the purple color of the wildflowers that grew on his pasture in the spring. Black hair cut in a straight, blunt line at her chin, giving her a dramatic look that didn't fit with a woman who needed a job as a waitress. And those boots. Black stilettos. The kind a man envisioned on his chest, pinning him to a bed.

He stopped those thoughts. She might be a pretty with her perfect nose and full, tempting lips, but he wasn't interested.

Still, he had no doubt that he had to keep an eye on her. Something wasn't right with her. It wasn't just her city-girl clothes. Her demeanor didn't fit. Waitresses didn't have smooth hands, perfect posture, an unblinking stare.

He rose from the booth. "Well, seeing as how you seem to have gotten the job you wanted, I guess we'll be running into each other from time to time."

She only smiled. A cool, remote smile that heated his blood and all but challenged him to turn on the charm and see how long it would take to get that smile to thaw. Luckily, he was smarter than that.

Amanda Mae said, "Do you have someplace to stay, honey?"

She faced the diner owner. "I— No. Actually, I need a place to stay."

"Hotel's in the next town over," Cade said, striding back to his seat at the counter and his now-cold coffee.

Amanda Mae shot him another evil glare. "Or she could use the apartment upstairs until she gets on her feet."

"I'd like that." Suzanne pressed her fingers to Amanda Mae's hand in a gesture of appreciation that stopped Cade cold. Maybe she was in need of a little help? Her crisp white blouse and fancy jeans could be the last good things she owned. He hadn't heard a car drive up. He glanced out the big front window into the street. He didn't see a car. She could be dead broke—

Nope. His business sense wouldn't accept that. Something about her screamed money. Big money. If she was pretending she didn't have any, there was a reason.

Damn. He was going to have to keep an eye on her.

Immediately after Cade left, Amanda Mae took Suzanne upstairs to look at the little furnished apartment.

"One of the waitresses always lives here," she said, leading Suzanne into the tiny bedroom that barely had enough space for a crib and a double bed. "So we keep it furnished."

Gratitude weakened Suzanne's knees. At least they wouldn't have to sleep in her car tonight. She turned to Amanda Mae with a smile. "Thanks. I appreciate it."

Amanda Mae stuffed a few bills into her palm. "And here's some money to go to the secondhand store down the street and buy some sheets and towels."

Her face reddened. This time last year she was telling her grandmother she was three months pregnant and that her baby's daddy wanted no part of her. Her wonderful, loving grandmother had taken her hand and told her not to worry. That everything would be okay. Even though she'd made some bad investments, they still had the Andreas Holdings stock.

A couple of months hadn't just changed everything; they'd taken away her home, her only family. Instead of being a well-loved granddaughter, she was a broke single mom. So alone her only contacts had been lawyers and accountants, until her grandmother's estate was settled. Then even they didn't call.

Tears welled up. She caught Amanda Mae's gaze. "I'll pay you back."

Amanda Mae squeezed her hand. "In good time. For now, I'm just happy to have some help for the breakfast crowd."

Driving back to his ranch, Cade speed-dialed the number for his assistant.

"Hey, Cade."

"Hey, Eric." He'd hired Eric right out of grad school because he was sharp and educated, but also because he had total recall. If someone mentioned an aunt, cousin, sister, brother or long-lost friend even once in a conversation, Eric would remember him or her. "Have you ever heard of Suzanne Caldwell?"

"Can't say that I have."

Damn.

"Who is she?"

"Just a woman who came into the diner today. She took the waitress job, but something just didn't seem right about her."

"Ah. I'm guessing your business sense kicked up."

He scowled at the phone. "Don't poke fun at my business sense. It's made me rich enough that I'd never have to work another day in my life. While you, on the other hand, still work for me."

He disconnected the call. But when he thought of Suzanne, the hair on his nape snapped up. Damn it! Why would a waitress activate his business sense? And why was he going back to his ranch when his instincts were screaming that he should be checking into this?

Slamming on the brakes, he manipulated his truck through a fishtail and headed back into town. He pulled it into a parking space at the diner, but when he walked by the huge front window, he saw that the new waitress wasn't inside.

His instincts calmed, his intuition quieted and he cursed himself for being the suspicious fool that Eric hinted he was. But before he could turn around and go back to his truck, he saw Suzanne coming down the outside steps from the second-floor apartment, carrying her baby.

A hot rush of desire whooshed through him. Luckily, the hair on his nape also prickled the way it always did right before a negotiation went sour. The first reaction might have been attraction. But the nape prickle? That was what told him he was about to get into a fight. Not a fistfight, but a disagreement, or maybe a battle to protect what was his. He slid into the alley between the general store and the hardware and watched her head up the street.

Unfortunately, the view from behind was every bit as stunning as her front profile. Her straight black hair fringed the collar of the crisp white blouse that hugged a trim, toned back. It slid along the indent of her small waist to an absolutely perfect behind that swayed ever so slightly with every step of her long legs—legs made to look longer and sexier by her stiletto boots.

Attraction hit him like a warm ocean wave and left him drowning in sensation. This time he had to admit it was only attraction. He tried to blink it away but failed. There was just so much about her that was geared to appeal to a man. No male alive could resist that kind of shapely body. Especially when the pretty little package had a face to match. Dramatic hair. Eyes that could very well glow in the dark.

He shook his head to clear the haze. Fantasizing would not do either one of them any good. He needed to figure out why she set off his business alarms or it would drive him crazy. Yes, that might make him a control freak. But he was a rich, successful control freak. And if his business sense said jump, his answer was always how high.

When he was sure she was far enough ahead that she wouldn't see him, he followed her. When she ducked into the secondhand store, he stopped. He waited for her to get deep enough into the building that she wouldn't notice him hovering beyond the display in the big glass front window.

Judy Petrovic, proprietor of Yesterday's Goods, ambled over to her.

Suzanne turned and offered her a sweet, sincere smile, which nearly knocked Cade off his feet. He'd never seen her smile. Well, he'd seen her sassy imitation smile, but never a genuine smile until now. And he was glad. Had she smiled at him like that in the diner he worried he would have stuttered.

She handed her baby to Judy, then her heavy-looking diaper bag. Judy bounced the little girl as Suzanne dipped down and rummaged through a table of what looked to be sheets, maybe towels. Walking back and forth from the display to the cash register, she made a pile of linens before she grabbed a pair of secondhand jeans and a T-shirt, and several things for her baby. After Judy rang up her purchases, she paid with crumpled-up bills that she'd been clutching in her left hand.

Cade pulled back and slid around to the side of the building, his chest tightening with regret. She'd said she'd come to Whiskey Springs for the job as a waitress and she'd asked for it without a hint of regret. Now she was buying somebody's old, worn sheets to fit on the old, worn mattress on a bed that had seen more years than most of the people in this town.

She really was broke.

And here he was spying on her like some old goof.

He was a goof. The truth was he wasn't entirely sure that his sixth sense about her really was his business sense. It could be nothing but attraction. Lord knew it had been so long since he'd been naturally overwhelmingly attracted to a woman that he might have forgotten the signs. He'd botched his first marriage so much that he stayed away from any woman who might inspire anything more than lust. And a woman with a baby wasn't somebody a man should be fooling around with. Since he didn't want to be attracted to Suzanne, he could be trying to kid himself into thinking it was his sixth sense. Rationalizing so he didn't have to admit to anybody that he virtually tripped over his tongue when he looked at her.

A dry dusty breeze swirled around him, reminding him that he was hiding in an alley, spying on a waitress.

Good God. What was he doing?

CHAPTER TWO

CADE RAISED HIS ARM TO WAVE hello, but it slid across silk sheets, and the wonderful dream he was having burst like a bubble.

He bounced up in bed and scrubbed his hand across his mouth. It was the same dream he always had. It began with him riding up to the main corral, watching his deceased wife, Ashley, as she tended the long strip of flowers she'd planted along the road to the barns, stables and corrals. No matter how many times he'd told her that barns did not need flower beds, he'd never been able to get it through her head.

But when he had the dream, the chance to see her, he didn't want to argue about flowers. Even in sleep, his heart knocked against his ribs, and he wanted to hold her, to kiss her, to tell her how much he missed her.

He squeezed his eyes shut. He didn't get the chance to do any of those. Just like always, he hadn't even gotten to say hello. His subconscious wouldn't even give him hello, forget about a hug, a light kiss....

Knowing he couldn't give in to the sadness, he tossed back the covers and headed for the shower. He'd gotten beyond losing Ashley. She'd died two years ago and he wasn't an idiot. She was gone. He couldn't deny that there was a hole in his chest where his heart should have been, but that part of his life was over.

He ducked his head under the spray and let the water beat down on him, remind him he was real, remind him he had satisfying work, a huge ranch, oil wells, a town that depended on him. There wasn't a man in the state of Texas more fulfilled than he was.

It was enough.

He shoved his legs into jeans, wrestled a T-shirt over his head and jogged downstairs. Though it was only 4:00 a.m., Mrs. Granger, the cook, would have coffee in the kitchen. Still, he didn't turn toward the warm scent. He also didn't go to his office. It was hours before the New York Stock Exchange opened, so there was no point going to his desk. Instead, he found an old pair of boots, jumped in his truck and headed for the stables.

That was what he usually did after the dream. Not just because he needed something to occupy his mind, but because the dream left him hungry, angry, and he wouldn't inflict himself on anybody until he settled down.

He hadn't expected lights to be on in the long red stable, but he wasn't surprised to see his foreman and father-in-law, Jim Malloy, cloistered in his office.

"What are you doing up so early?"

Jim's chair creaked as he leaned back. "Me? This is my normal starting time. My guys will be here in an hour or so. I need to get caught up on paperwork. Better question is what are you doing up so early? Stock exchange doesn't open for hours."

He flopped to the chair in front of Jim's desk. Shrugged.

"You had that dream again."

Cade said nothing.

"Pain's probably never going to go away."

"I'm fine. I have my work."

"A lot of work," Jim said with a laugh.

They were quiet for a few seconds then Jim rose. "Coffee?"

"Is it fresh?"

"Come on. I haven't been here *that* long. Of course it's fresh."

"Then I'll have some."

Jim poured two mugs of coffee and handed Cade's to him before he sat on the edge of the desk. "You were a good husband to Ashley and you're still a good son-in-law."

Cade snorted in derision. His father-in-law had known about the time Cade had spent away from Ashley. The times business had taken him to other cities for weeks at a clip. It was kind of him to tell Cade he'd been a good husband, but Cade wasn't so easily buffaloed.

Jim patted his knee. "You *were* a good husband. Just because you don't get to talk to Ashley in your dream, it doesn't mean you're being punished."

Jim was wrong again. He'd been out of town the day Ashley died. Not with her. Not holding her hand, but sweet-talking an oil baron into selling his company. And Ashley had died alone. That, he believed, was what his subconscious was telling him every damn time he had the dream. Just as she hadn't gotten to say goodbye to him, his subconscious wouldn't let him say goodbye to her. Not even symbolically.

Still, he didn't argue with Jim. He took a sip of coffee then choked it out. "My God. Sludge tastes better than this."

"Oh, yeah? And when, exactly, have you tasted sludge?"

Cade laughed. Jim went back to his seat behind the desk. They occupied themselves talking foals and fences, the price of beef and which animals they'd breed. Seconds turned to minutes and minutes to an hour and with every tick of the clock, the tightness in Cade's chest loosened. The residual sadness from the dream receded. He'd never get a chance to say goodbye to Ashley. He had to accept that and move on.

Suzanne woke a little after five o'clock and actually showered before Mitzi even stirred. She dressed quickly in the little pink uniform Amanda Mae had given her for her first day as a waitress, then just as quickly dressed Mitzi. She grabbed her cereal and a fresh bottle on her way out the apartment door.

As expected, she found Amanda Mae in the diner kitchen, kneading a batch of bread.

"Make room on the prep table for me," she said, sliding Mitzi into the seat of the swing they'd set up in the corner. She and Amanda Mae had already decided Mitzi could be in the diner with Suzanne while she worked. When the diner got busy and the kitchen heated from all the cooking, they could move the swing and Mitzi to the little alcove between the dining room and kitchen. But now, the kitchen was a quiet, homey place, suitable for a baby.

"As soon as I feed Mitzi, I'm going to bake a batch of my grandmother's cinnamon rolls."

Amanda Mae's eye brows rose. "Oh, yeah?"

"It's my way of saying thank you for giving me a job."

"Hey, it's no skin off my nose. I know you're probably only temporary, but I need the help. I'm happy for any amount of time you can give me."

Even though Amanda Mae understood, guilt took up residence in Suzanne's chest. She had no idea how things would turn out when she actually spoke with the Andreas brothers about her shares of stock, but she hoped they'd give her a job. She needed to make a home for her baby and waitress pay wasn't as good as working for a shipping conglomerate.

So she fought through the guilt. Not only would she give Amanda Mae a good day's work every day she waitressed, but she'd found a tangible way to pay her back for her kindnesses. The Caldwell cinnamon roll recipe was a family secret, passed down from one Caldwell woman to the next. It was an honor to have it. But it was an even bigger joy to actually eat the cinnamon rolls.

She thought of Cade, hoping a good cinnamon roll might mellow him out, so she could confess who she was on day one of her charade as waitress. Then he could confess that his family didn't have the money to buy her out. So that she could ask for a job before Amanda Mae got accustomed to having her here. It was a long shot. But right now it was all she had.

When Mitzi was fed, she walked around the kitchen gathering the ingredients for the cinnamon rolls. Amanda Mae made room on the prep table for Suzanne and she went to work.

She began with warm water and yeast. When the yeast was ready, she added the other ingredients until she had a nice dough. As the dough rose, the first customers of the morning filtered in and back out again. But while the rolls were baking, the customers in the dining room began asking what was filling the air with the wonderful scent. Some waited long after they'd finished their breakfasts just to get one of the first rolls as they came out of the oven. By seven-thirty, over half were gone.

"Good Lord, girl," Amanda Mae said, staring at the second empty cinnamon roll tray. "We could sell three dozen of these a day."

"People will tire of them," Suzanne said, dusting her hands on her apron before she lifted Mitzi from the swing. She'd just finished putting the last pan into the oven.

"I'm not so sure."

Suzanne worried her bottom lip. "So you think they're good enough to soften a grouchy guy?"

Amanda Mae laughed. "Maybe. But if I were you, I'd try being nice to Cade instead of sniping at him the way you did yesterday."

"You noticed."

"Honey, two polecats fighting over table scraps make fewer sparks."

She winced. "I just don't know what it is about him, but he brings out the worst in me."

Amanda Mae laughed. "Or the best."

"Oh, come on. You're not saying we're attracted."

"Stranger things have happened."

"I can't be attracted to him."

"Figured as much. Figured you've got business with him. The only reason city slickers come to Whiskey Springs is because they have business with Cade."

She sucked in a breath. "I do."

"Then forget all about your hormones and be nice to the guy. At least until you get a chance to tell him what you need."

A little after eight, Cade was lost in work and didn't hear Eric come into the room until he said, "Have you even had coffee yet?"

Pulling away from the computer, he stretched his arms above his head and glanced at the clock.

"If you call the sip of the sludge I had in Jim's office coffee, then yes. But if you're talking about real coffee. No. I haven't even been to the kitchen yet. Did you get some?"

Eric waved a tall mug. "My first stop is always for coffee. But if you want, I can go back and get a cup for you, too."

He leaned back in his chair. "I'm fine."

Eric sat on one of the two chairs in front of Cade's desk. "So did you find out anything interesting yesterday from Suzanne Caldwell?"

He'd forgotten all about the waitress he'd met the day before. But now that Eric mentioned her, he was back to being curious again. She was too pretty, too sophisticated, too coolly elegant to be a real waitress.

Glad to have his mind off his failure as a husband, he rose from his desk and began to pace. "The thing is I have no idea how she got into town since she didn't have a car. Plus, she didn't have any luggage. Even a poor woman would have had luggage, if only one suitcase." He faced Eric again. "She could be running from something. Or someone. And that could be trouble."

"If this woman worries you so much why not go into the diner for breakfast? Maybe you can get some answers by turning on the charm."

The last thing he wanted to do was turn on the charm. He was way too attracted to her to tempt fate. Still, he didn't like people who kept secrets. His whole town was an open book. Everybody knew everybody else and they liked it that way. He couldn't tolerate somebody coming in and stirring up the pot.

That in and of itself was reason enough that he

probably should try to cuddle up to her a little. Show her he was a nice guy. A great guy. And maybe she'd tell him her story?

Convinced this was the right thing to do, he gave Eric enough work to keep him busy for the morning and jumped into his truck. He slid it into an empty parking space on Main Street and shut down the ignition. Oddly, he peered into the rearview mirror and checked his hair, which was sticking up on one side. He patted it down then scowled at himself.

What was he doing? He wasn't here to ask her on a date. He didn't want a date. He wanted information.

He rammed the truck door to open it and all but stormed into the diner. And there she stood. Order pad in hand. Pencil behind her ear. Crisp white apron covering the pink candy-striped waitress uniform Amanda Mae insisted that all her girls wear.

As the little bell above the door tinkled announcing his arrival, she glanced over at him. Their gazes caught. Her pretty violet eyes widened and his heart flip-flopped.

He held back a curse. Hadn't he already gone over all of this in his head? He'd had the love of his life, and he'd botched that relationship. So he wasn't interested in trying again. And even if he was looking for a fling, something discreet and purely for sex, Suzanne Caldwell was not the woman he would choose. She might be pretty. Very pretty. *Dramatically* pretty. But she had a baby and he was certain she was holding back information about herself. He was not interested, except to make sure she wasn't a threat to the peace of his people.

He ambled to the counter, slapped Marty Higgins on the back and sat on the stool next to him. "Morning, Marty."

"Morning, Cade."

He and Marty were the only two patrons left from the morning rush, but that might be good. In a quiet diner, the waitresses sometimes had nothing better to do than talk to the customers.

As casually as possible, he slid his gaze to Suzanne's again. "Morning, Ms. Caldwell."

"Good morning, Mr. Andreas."

"It's Cade," Marty corrected before he took a sip of his coffee.

Cade pulled out his most charming smile. "He's right. Everybody calls me Cade."

"Is that an order?"

His eyes narrowed. "It's not an order and it's also not a reason for you to be so prickly. Especially when I haven't even had coffee yet."

She pulled the pencil from behind her ear. "So you want a coffee."

"And eggs over easy, bacon, home fries, rye toast and two blueberry pancakes."

She stopped writing and glanced at him again. Her gaze rippled from his face down his chest and probably would have gone the whole way to his toes had he been standing.

"You got a problem?"

"You're awfully fit for a guy who eats like a horse."

Hormones bubbled up in him. He had always been proud that he was in shape as a result of hard work, not some sissy gym. But he didn't like the way his gut tightened or his hormones awoke like a bunch of cowboys at the scent of morning coffee. "Believe me. I'll use it all up before noon." He made a quick shooing motion with his hand. "Just go get it."

She smiled sweetly. "No reason to be prickly."

His hormones spiked. Damn she was sassy!

She turned and sauntered away and he watched every sway of her hips, cursing himself in his head for not looking away as he should have.

"She is a pretty little filly, isn't she?" Marty whispered, leaning in so only Cade could hear.

"Yeah, but she's pretty like a cactus. Nice to look at but a man had better not touch."

Marty chuckled. "See, now I hadn't even gotten to the thinking-about-touching stage. You must have it bad. Especially if you're coming into the diner for breakfast when you've got a damn fine cook at your ranch."

Cade glowered at Marty. "I'm here for information." He stopped himself. Why was he explaining himself to the guy who ran the hardware? Since when did he explain himself to anybody?

Marty slapped a five-dollar bill on the counter and rose. Leaning across toward the kitchen, he yelled, "See you tomorrow, Amanda Mae." He smiled at Suzanne. "You too, sugar."

Suzanne strolled back to the counter, pot of coffee in one hand, cup and saucer in the other. Placing them in front of Cade, she addressed Marty, "You leave me a halfway decent tip?"

Marty laughed. "Yep."

"Okay, then, you can go."

Marty left, chuckling to himself and shaking his head. Cade's blood pressure rose. The woman knew she could wrap most men around her little finger because of her looks alone. Well, he was not going to be so easy to manipulate as old Marty.

"Cream?"

"No. I drink my coffee black."

"Wow. Alert the media."

She turned to go, but he snagged her wrist. His fingers wrapped around skin so soft they felt pillowed by it. Her scent drifted over to him. Her gaze swung to his.

He fought the urge to swallow. Her eyes were so beautiful it was enough to stop a man's heart. But he was stronger than this. Smarter than to get caught in a woman's web. And he was also a man on a mission. Figure out who she was so he could get rid of her or just get rid of these odd feelings he had every time he was with her.

"How the hell did you ever succeed as a waitress with that attitude?"

She smiled sweetly. "Maybe I didn't? Maybe that's why I had to travel the whole way here to be able to find someone who'd hire me?"

It was the first thing she'd said to him that made perfect sense. He dropped her wrist and let her go. She returned a few minutes later with his food.

Just then her baby let out with a squawk. Seated in a swing set up in the alcove between the dining room and the kitchen, she slapped a rattle against the white tray.

Cade wasn't surprised that her baby was there. Whiskey Springs was a very laid-back town and Amanda Mae was a very sweet, helpful employer. But it had been so long since he'd seen a baby that curiosity overwhelmed him. Gino, his third half brother, had been six months old when their father had died and passed off Gino's care to the adult Andreas sons. But in the eighteen months that had passed, Gino had become a two-year-old, a toddler. He wasn't a baby anymore.

He peeked at the little girl with her big blue eyes and shiny black hair just like her mother's, and an achy pain circled his heart. Because he had black hair and Ashley had had blue eyes, he'd always imagined that at least one of their kids would have dark hair and Ashley's pale blue eyes. But he and Ashley couldn't have kids.

The reminder made his heart hurt a little more. Not only would he spend the rest of his years without the woman he adored, but also he'd never have kids. Being a father had been the one goal in life he'd wanted more than success. His own father had been a poor excuse for a dad and Cade knew in his heart he could do better. Lots better. If only because he knew exactly what a kid longed for from a father, because he hadn't had it.

He studied the little girl. Her plump cheeks. The spit bubbles she blew as she sputtered and chattered, trying to form words. She was so cute. So happy.

She *was* happy. That had to mean Suzanne was a good mom. But that only brought him back to the same question. Why would a single mom take her baby so far from home for a job that barely paid minimum wage?

When Suzanne walked back to refill his coffee, he caught her hand again. "What are you doing here, really?"

"Maybe I'm running?"

Cade scowled. Now she was teasing him.

But she sighed and said, "Look, I'm not trying to hide my past. It's just kind of embarrassing. I got involved with a college professor who took advantage of my innocence. I was a bit of a starstuck puppy."

Surprised by her easy admission, he leaned back and felt a tad foolish for constantly questioning her motives.

"When I told him I was pregnant, he told me he didn't want anything to do with me or our baby. Eventually I had to quit school. Then my grandmother died and now I'm alone and broke."

Foolishness morphed into regret. His father, the

great Stephone Andreas, had done the same thing to his mom—and him. Stephone had gotten his mom pregnant then barely acknowledged Cade's existence until he was eighteen. Then he'd sent a lawyer to offer the trust fund that became Cade's grubstake to make himself a very rich man. But through his entire childhood, his mom had busted her butt to make a life for them. He had a soft spot for single moms.

So why did he continually harass this one?

But before he could apologize, Suzanne caught his gaze and very quietly said, "Where I come from, people share. I just told you my big embarrassing secret. Seems to me you should reciprocate by telling me yours."

Any bit of sympathy he had for her disappeared and was replaced by a swell of annoyance. His biggest life secret was that he'd never gotten the chance to say good-bye to his wife. And that was none of Suzanne's business. Especially since he found her attractive. Ashley was the love of his life. She was a sweet, wonderful woman who would have never talked to him—to anyone—the way Suzanne just had, nosing into personal business.

"Hey, Cade!"

To Cade's complete horror, his mother, Virginia Brown—Ginny for short—walked into the diner and over to him. A tall brunette with sharp green eyes and a perpetual grin on her face, she took the seat Marty had just vacated.

"What are you doing here? Don't you have a cook?"

"Yes, I have a cook." He faced his mother with a warning glare.

She only laughed. "So why are you at the diner?"

She asked the question as Suzanne wiped down the counter in front of them, cleaning away Marty's crumbs.

Cade didn't have to reply because Suzanne said, "What can I get for you?"

His mother smiled, but she sniffed the air. "What is that wonderful smell?"

Suzanne straightened with pride. "Cinnamon rolls. I gave Amanda Mae my grandmother's recipe as a thank-you for hiring me."

Even as Suzanne spoke, Cade picked up on the scent himself. Because it had mixed in with the aromas of coffee and pancakes, he'd almost missed it. But the second he homed in on it, his mouth watered.

"I showed her how to make them this morning."

"Are there any left?" Ginny asked hopefully.

Suzanne shrugged. "Maybe a dozen or so."

"I'll have one of those and a cup of coffee."

Cade said, "And I'll have one to go."

Suzanne suddenly became very busy dusting a napkin holder. "Want another cup of coffee?"

"Yeah."

As Suzanne walked away, Ginny burst out laughing. "You don't have to answer my question about why you're here. I think I figured it out on my own."

"You figured wrong."

Ginny laughed again. "Really? Did you miss how she blushed when you said you wanted a cinnamon roll? I think she thinks the way to your heart is through your stomach."

With a deep breath for patience, he faced his mother again. Rolling his eyes in Suzanne's direction to let his mom know he couldn't talk in front of the new waitress, he said, "You've got it all wrong."

She laughed. "Really? You're here when you shouldn't

be and she's serving up old family recipes? If you don't see the signs in that then you're the one who's got it all wrong."

Suzanne didn't really hear the exchange, though she caught enough of it to ascertain that the woman sitting next to Cade was his mother. There wasn't much family resemblance. His hair was black. His mother's sable. His eyes were dark. His mother's pale. Their only common trait was that they were both tall and fit.

In his gray T-shirt and tight jeans, Cade looked especially fit. And that was why Suzanne had been thrown off her game and forgot to be nice to him when she waited on him. But she'd tried to rectify that by telling him about Mitzi. She'd even tried to get him to tell her about himself, hoping for an opening to explain she was the owner of the trust that held one-third of his family's company's stock.

But he hadn't bitten and now he wasn't alone at the counter anymore. Worse, he was taking his cinnamon roll out. He wouldn't eat it in the diner, swoon with ecstasy and be open to anything she told him. By the time he ate the thing, he could even forget who'd made it. She needed to come clean with him about who she was. If she could just get fifteen minutes of his time, in private, she could end this blasted charade.

One cinnamon roll in a take-out box and another on a dessert plate for Cade's mom, she walked over to the counter, poured Cade's mom's coffee and set a cinnamon roll in front of her. As she set Cade's take-out box in front of him, his mom very sweetly said, "I didn't catch your name."

Hoping to get him to stay, Suzanne refilled Cade's cup. "It's Suzanne. Suzanne Caldwell."

"I'm Ginny Brown. I used to be the town librarian, but since my son struck it rich, I now own the bookstore."

As Suzanne said, "It's nice to meet you," she noticed the burn of embarrassment crawl up Cade's neck to his face.

Ginny patted his arm. "He hates it when I mention his being rich."

Cade caught her gaze as if pleading for mercy, a move so unexpected that something soft and warm cradled Suzanne's heart. It was sweet that he couldn't be angry with his mom. But it was also curious that Ginny believed he was still rich.

Unless even she didn't know about the Andreas Holdings troubles?

Cautious, she ran the damp cloth along the counter again. "You should be happy your mom is proud of you."

"There's such a thing as being too proud."

She shrugged. "Maybe. But I think I would have liked to have known what that felt like. My mom died when I was six."

Ginny gasped. "I'm so sorry."

She shrugged again. "I had a good grandmother to raise me." Even as she said that, she glanced back at the kitchen. In a lot of ways Amanda Mae reminded her of her grandmother. Except younger. Probably about her mom's age. Ever since she'd arrived the day before, Amanda Mae had been nothing but kind. This morning's customers had accepted her, as well. And she liked them. If she didn't have other business to attend to, this would be a perfect place to make home.

But she did have other business.

She faced Cade and his mom. "Anyway, it's from my gram that I learned how to make the cinnamon rolls."

"Well, if they taste as good as they smell, the people of this town are going to love you forever."

Warmth filled her heart at the possibility. Wouldn't it be nice to have a whole town of friends?

Finished with his breakfast, Cade rose. He tossed a twenty-dollar bill on the counter and picked up his take-out container. "This should cover it and the tip."

With that he left, and she'd missed her chance to tell him who she was.

After about thirty seconds of staring at the door, Suzanne realized she'd watched him go. What female over the age of fifteen wouldn't? He had a strong, broad back, exquisitely outlined by his tight gray T-shirt. And a perfect backside in well-worn jeans. Add boots and a Stetson to that combo and the mouths of women in three states were probably watering right now.

"Could I have some more coffee?"

Shaking herself out of her daze, Suzanne smiled down at Cade's mother only to see that Ginny was smiling up at her. Shrewdly. Craftily.

"You know, we're having a party at Cade's ranch on Saturday night. I'd love it if you'd come."

CHAPTER THREE

BECAUSE CADE DIDN'T VENTURE into the diner the rest of the week, Suzanne knew she had to go to his party.

She had Amanda Mae drive her to her car to get her two suitcases on Saturday afternoon. The diner owner's eyebrows rose when she saw the powder blue Mercedes, but she said nothing. In the four days they'd worked together, an odd kind of bond had grown between the two women. Since her grandmother's death, Suzanne had felt alone, adrift, and she sensed Amanda Mae didn't often get close to people, either.

But though their growing friendship bolstered Suzanne's courage enough that she knew she could talk to Cade that night, she also realized that she was growing attached to Amanda Mae. If she stayed much longer and got a job at Andreas Holdings, she'd have to move away. Then she'd feel a real loss and so would Amanda Mae. Tonight had to be the night she talked to Cade.

That evening she dressed in the only cocktail dress she'd kept—a little red sheath—her grandmother's pearls and red stiletto sandals. When Amanda Mai's sixteen-year-old neice, Gloria, arrived to babysit, she gave detailed instructions on caring for Mitzi, then carefully guided herself down the outside stairway in the waning light.

Using the directions Amanda Mae had written out
for her, she confidently drove to Cade's ranch. But ma-
neuvering down the long lane that led to his house, she
was so confused she nearly stopped her car. Though
the house was huge, it was simple. Plain white with
black shutters and a black front door with a silver door
knocker. There was no valet parking. Cars had just
stopped on each side of the lane, but even more cars
had been parked in the grass of what should have been
his front yard.

She frowned. This was different.

As she opened her car door, music greeted her,
making her think the party was outside. Which was
fine. She liked garden parties. She especially loved a
gorgeous sit-down dinner outside in the early evening.
The only problem was an outdoor party sort of screwed
up her plan. Because she knew she had to tell Cade who
she was, she'd decided to ask him for a few minutes
alone. She'd envisioned him saying yes, then herself
leading him to his office, where she'd explain who she
was in that businesslike environment behind closed
doors. First, so no one could overhear. Second, so his
reaction would be more professional than personal.

She walked up the cobblestone sidewalk to the front
door and rang the bell. But after two minutes and two
more bell rings, no one had answered. She tried the silver
knocker but that brought no one to the door, either.

With a sigh, she walked around the side of the house.
If they were outside, she would just join them.

But when she rounded the corner, she stopped dead
in her tracks. Long buffet tables were piled high with
food. The music she'd heard was a country band playing
a square dance. Couples moved around in a circle under
the canopy of a gazebo. Lights circled a swimming pool

where kids and teenagers were actually swimming. There were no lily pads decorating the pretty blue water. No careful row of flower pots strategically placed to preclude anyone getting to close to the edge. Nope. This pool was in use.

The urge to turn and run enveloped her, but before she could move, Cade's mom hurried over. "Suzanne! You look exquisite."

"Thanks." She took in Ginny's jeans and bright yellow T-shirt, her cowboy boots. "I didn't realize this was a—"

"Barbecue." Ginny winced. "Sorry. I just assumed you'd realize that in Texas *party* usually means *barbecue*."

Cade picked that precise second to walk over. Dressed in jeans and a chambray shirt with a bolo tie and a Stetson, he looked like a man who could own a town. Sleek, sexy, sharp and just country enough to remind a woman she was on his turf.

The crackle of attraction that raced through her competed with a rumble of warning. *Tell him. Get him alone and tell him who you are. Do not waste another second.*

Before she could utter a peep, though, Cade's eyes made a quick sweep from her sandaled feet up her dress to the top of her head and sent another burst of attraction through her.

He smiled slyly. "Come on. Surely you knew this was a barbecue. Everybody in the other forty-nine states knows barbecue is Texas's middle name."

But Cade wasn't one bit sorry she hadn't dressed for a barbecue. Her sexy little sheath was just short enough to show off her great legs. Her super-high-heel sandals sent the blood humming through his veins. The pearls gave her a classy, elegant look.

What if she'd dressed like this deliberately? Wanting him to notice her?

"Let me introduce you around before dinner." Ginny took Suzanne's arm and turned her to the crowd. "You've met most of these people at the diner. Still, there are a few you haven't."

"But I—" Suzanne protested, but it was as if his mom didn't hear. And just like that, Suzanne had been spirited away.

He watched them go. His eyes narrowed as his gaze honed in on the back—or should he say lack of back—in Suzanne's dress. It was literally open from her neck to her hips…another inch and it would have been illegal in some states.

But it wasn't. It was simply mind-numbingly sexy.

Eyes narrowed, he watched as his mother introduced her to Jeb and Caroline Hunter, the couple who owned the ranch next to his. She smiled politely and shook hands with Jeb, but her gaze wandered over to his.

Before he had a chance to react, his mom took her to Tom Calhoun, Bruce Murphy, Danny Jones and Joshua Turner. All four were recent university graduates. Tom worked at the bank with his father. Bruce had taken over the local car repair shop. Josh was a freelance certified public accountant and Danny was still looking for a job.

He stiffened a bit. Any one of those men was more suited to her. They were her age. Just starting out like she was.

But, once again, after shaking hands, Suzanne's gaze ambled back to his.

He smiled. Well. Well. Maybe she wasn't interested in men her own age? And maybe he'd been playing this all wrong. She might have a baby, but she'd been burned by that child's daddy. Maybe she wasn't interested in another long-term relationship? Maybe she wasn't interested in a relationship at all? Maybe she was a young, healthy, sexy woman looking for a little fun, a little romance.

And from the way her gaze kept streaming back to his, maybe she was looking for that fun with him?

His eyes never left her as his mother trotted her through the group, introducing her to all the guests. Even the kids in the pool. But every few seconds, her gaze would wander back to his and he'd smile.

Until finally, *finally,* his mother got her a glass of wine from a passing waiter and left her with Missy Jo Johnson and Amanda Mae. This time, when her gaze ambled over to his, he nudged his head to indicate she should break away, come to him.

It was a test. If she came over, he'd know she was interested. If she didn't…well, he had other guests to pursue.

Just as he expected, she excused herself and walked over.

Playing with her pearls, she cleared her throat. "Um, Cade, could you and I go somewhere private to talk?"

Sweet success sparked through him. He didn't mind leaving the party. His guests were entertained and probably no one would miss him. More important, no one would be so foolhardy as to come looking for him.

She glanced up at him hopefully.

He smiled down at her. In ten minutes the charcoal beneath the beef wouldn't be the only thing sizzling.

"Sure, sugar."

With his hand at the small of her back, he guided her through the French doors into the formal dining room. The velvet skin of her back tickled his palm with every step she made. Little beads of sweat formed on the back of his neck.

She peeked back at him. "Do you have a den?"

"Den?"

"You know, sort of an office. Someplace private?"

He'd intended to simply take her to his bed. But he wasn't about to argue over logistics. In the marble-tile foyer with the huge crystal chandelier, he pointed straight ahead. He let her get a few steps in front of him so he could take in the view of her gorgeous back, her nicely rounded bottom caressed by the soft material of her perfect red dress. He pressed his hand to his chest to still his beating heart. She was absolutely perfect.

Whoever said money didn't buy happiness was a complete liar.

"Second door down."

She stepped into the room ahead of him. He closed the door and locked it.

Apparently hearing the click, she turned and frowned at him. "You're locking the door?"

"Well, you don't want to get caught do you?"

She frowned. Her full lips turned down prettily, creating a dimple in her right cheek. Cade all but rubbed his hands together with glee.

"No. I don't."

She sipped her wine. Realizing she might be nervous, he didn't immediately pounce, but ambled to the bar and poured himself two fingers of Scotch. They might have to get back to the party, but the beef wouldn't be done for another hour. They had plenty of time.

He motioned to the black leather sofa. "Seat?"

She smiled nervously. "I think I'd rather stand."

His brow puckered. Confusion eclipsed the heat sparking in his blood stream.

"I...um..." She glanced down at her wine, then back up at him with a hesitant smile. "Well, there's something that I have to tell you."

That didn't quite compute. "Tell me?"

"Yes." She sucked in a breath. "I'm Suzanne Caldwell."

His eyes narrowed.

"You don't recognize the name because my grandmother never had her name on any documents. She held everything in trust."

His hormones stilled. "Held what in trust?"

She cleared her throat. Swallowed again. "The one-third interest in Andreas Holdings that your father had given her."

His hormones died. His muscles tensed and his brain went to red alert.

"*You're* the missing shareholder?"

She nodded.

Cade swayed a bit, downed his Scotch and fought the urge to fall to the sofa. "Well, this is a hell of a time to tell me."

"I couldn't think of a better time—or way. The times I saw you in the diner there were people around. I know your father's company has fallen in hard times because I couldn't sell my shares—"

His face fell in horror. "You tried to sell your shares?"

"What else was I to do? My grandmother's estate— furniture, art, everything—went to pay off debts I didn't realize Gram was accumulating. I have no money."

"At least there's one thing you weren't lying about."

She gaped at him. "I never lied at all! I told you the truth. I had come here to Whiskey Springs looking for a job. In fact, that's why I'm here right now."

"You want a job?"

"Why not? I own one-third of the company. Surely, there's something I can do at Andreas Holdings. Something that pays enough that I can support my baby."

He squeezed his eyes shut, counted to a hundred and still couldn't control his temper. He didn't know who he was more angry with, her for not telling him who she was the day she arrived, or himself for being such an idiot. Attracted to the enemy. Because that's what she was. Whether she knew it or not, she held more shares of his father's company than any of the Andreas brothers. Yes, united they owned controlling interest, but if they ever had a fight or came down on different sides of an issue with the company, *she'd* rule.

They needed to get those shares back. But even though he could afford to buy her out, his brothers couldn't. They were rich but didn't have that kind of money to spare. And he wouldn't buy her shares because, added to his own, they'd give him controlling interest. Then he and his brothers wouldn't be equals anymore. As it stood, everybody knew he had about ten times the money his brothers had. But when it came to owning their family's company, they were all equals. His buying her out would ruin that.

He took off his Stetson and tossed it across the room.

"I need time to think."

"To me there's nothing to think about. I need a job. I own one-third of a company. It's a no-brainer."

"No, it isn't. The company isn't here. It's headquartered in New York."

"So you're telling me you can't give me a job?"

No. He was stalling for time, trying to figure out how to arrange this so her stock didn't ruin the relationship that had finally been forged between the four Andreas half brothers.

He glanced over at her pretty, pouty expression and his hormones jumped again. This was so not how he'd expected to be spending the next hour.

"Do you have any skills?"

"I was an art history major. One semester away from getting a degree."

He groaned. Like Darius had any use for an art history major.

"My brothers are going to kill me."

She walked over, stood directly in front of him. The scent of her cologne combined with the shear force of her femininity and sent his hormones scurrying to life again.

"Why? I'm the owner of the stock, not you."

He scrubbed his hand across his mouth. "Greeks have a long tradition of killing messengers."

She laughed and he fought the urge to squeeze his eyes shut. He needed twenty minutes alone to think this through, but he couldn't send her back to the party unescorted. God only knew what she'd tell his guests.

"All right." He strode around the desk and flopped into the tall-back black leather chair. Whether he liked it or not, he could not make this decision alone. He pointed at the captain's chairs in front of his desk. "Sit."

She ambled to the desk. "What are we doing?"

"We're calling my brother."

"Ah."

Ah? Even the way she'd said that was cute. Sexy. He had to get rid of her. This was what he got for sniffing around a woman who, according to his very accurate business instincts, was trouble.

Dialing the number from memory, Cade sat back in his chair. Darius's house manager, Mrs. Tucker answered. "Andreas residence."

"Hey, baby. How's it going in the money capital of the world?"

Hey, baby? This was how he talked to staff?

Suzanne sniffed and tried to yank her skirt to a more proper place on her legs. Too late, she realized Cade would notice the action and that would only draw his gaze where she didn't want it.

She wanted to be taken seriously. Given a job. Yet this whole meeting had a weird feel to it, almost as if something had been going on that she'd missed.

"Can you get Darius for me?"

She pursed her lips. Straightened her spine. Tried to look like a woman with something to offer a huge shipping conglomerate. She knew her "almost" art history degree hadn't given her a marketable skill, but she could type. She could organize. There were a million things she could do. Plus, she wasn't picky, or proud. She'd take what she could get.

Just then Cade's gaze met hers. Intense heat filled her. He was so good-looking that for a few seconds there, when they'd found themselves alone, before she'd told him about her shares of Andreas Holdings, she'd wondered what it would be like if they'd gone to find someplace to be alone for an entirely different reason than business....

She swallowed. Oh, good grief. Now she got it. In those few seconds, he'd been wondering, too. Or maybe planning.

That's why he'd locked the door!

Oh, no! He might have actually thought she'd brought him to his office to seduce him.

Well, too bad. She needed a job more than she needed a boyfriend—no, lover. He'd never be anybody's boyfriend, but she'd bet he'd happily be her lover.

Heat filled her. Her insides constricted then blossomed.

She had to stop thinking about that.

"Hey, Darius, it's me. I've got good news and bad news." A pause. "Well, the good news is I've found our mystery shareholder. The bad news is she wants a job. I'm going to put the phone on speaker." He hit a button on his phone then replaced the receiver.

"Darius, our shareholder is Suzanne Caldwell. She's across the desk from me."

"It's a pleasure to meet you, Ms. Caldwell."

Darius's voice was deep and smooth and had the tone of someone accustomed to being diplomatic. With Cade Andreas as a brother, he probably had to be.

"It's a pleasure to meet you, too, Mr. Andreas. I'm sorry to be trouble, but my grandmother died only a few months ago and the estate was a mess. She had spent more money than was coming in for the past several years—"

"Probably because Andreas Holdings stopped paying dividends."

"Maybe," Suzanne agreed. She sucked in a soft breath. "Anyway, I have a child. A baby girl, Mitzi, and I—we—"

"Of course, you need money. Perfectly understandable. You do understand, though, that Andreas Holdings isn't in a position to buy your shares."

Cade leaned back in his chair. Crossed his arms.

Gave her one of those looks that could have melted butter.

Having realized where his mind had been when he locked the den door, Suzanne didn't get a shiver of fear from "that" look. Instead, her blood simmered.

She licked her lips. "I understand. I'm not approaching you to sell my shares."

Cade sat forward and leaned his arms on his desk. "She wants a job, Dar."

"As?"

Again Cade answered. "I know you can't drop her into a vice president position, but she's fairly smart."

Suzanne glanced up sharply. *He thought she was smart?*

"And," Cade continued, "I'm sure there are a lot of things she could do for us on an executive level. Something that would pay her enough to get a nice condo and a nanny for her baby."

Wow. He was being so kind. So considerate. So generous. Almost as if he liked her.

Her stomach filled with butterflies.

What if he liked her? What if this strong, sexy, smart man hadn't harassed her at the diner because he was the bossy overlord of the little piece of heaven he called Whiskey Springs, but because he'd been…interested… and his flirting skills were a little rusty?

She swallowed.

"There's got to be something she can do."

"Why don't you both fly up to New York City tomorrow morning so we can discuss it? You can be my guests at the house in Montauk Sunday night. Gino will be thrilled to see you, Cade. And Whitney loves company. Bring your daughter, Ms. Caldwell. It will be our pleasure."

With that Darius disconnected the call and silence reigned in Cade's office.

He leaned back in his chair. Rubbed his fingers across his forehead. Closed his eyes.

This wasn't at all what she'd had planned. And the thought that he might "like" her only added confusion to the mix. He was a gorgeous, sexy guy and she was attracted to him. But was she ready for anything to happen between them? After having been dumped only a little over a year ago?

No. She wasn't.

"I'm sorry."

"You didn't make the royal proclamation that we had to go to New York together. Darius did."

"I know, but your having to go to New York is my fault. I'd be happy to go by myself." She winced. "Except I don't have plane fare."

"I have an actual plane."

"Really?"

"Seven."

Her eyes widened. For a family that was broke, they certainly had more assets than she did.

"We'll leave at six. That should get us to the house in Montauk before noon, considering we'll have to drive from the airstrip."

He rose from the desk. "Now, I have guests to attend to."

He walked out of the den without another word. Suzanne folded her hands on her lap not quite sure what she should do.

She was about to fly to New York City with a man who'd thought she'd brought him into his office to seduce him. A man who plainly had been willing to be seduced.

And he'd left before they could clear the air about their feelings.

Could she have botched this any worse?

CHAPTER FOUR

WHEN SUZANNE'S CELL PHONE alarm woke her at four o'clock the next morning, she pulled the covers over her head. Explaining who she was to Cade had been a disaster. Now she had to fly to New York with him. That is, after she told Amanda Mae she couldn't work for the next few days—and might not be coming back to work at all.

Staying in bed sounded like a really good plan.

Unfortunately, Mitzi had heard the alarm, too, and her soft cries filled the room.

"I'm coming," she said, sliding out of bed. She fed the baby a bottle, dressed her in a happy yellow sundress with pink, blue and green ladybugs circling the hem, then took a shower and dressed herself in the blue suit she'd kept for interviews. Because, technically, she was going for an interview.

Ten minutes later, balancing a baby, a diaper bag, a suitcase packed with extra clothes for both her and Mitzi, and a car seat, she carefully walked down the outside stairway and into the diner.

Amanda Mae harrumphed. "What are you all dolled up for?"

She set the empty car seat on the floor. Walking to the cupboard where they now kept Mitzi's cereal, Suzanne avoided Amanda Mae's gaze. "I'm going to New York City with Cade Andreas."

She turned just in time to see Amanda Mae's big brown eyes pop and her mouth fall open. "What?"

"Oh, Amanda Mae. I am so sorry, but I have a confession to make."

"Look, honey, there isn't a woman in the world who could fault you for quitting a job as a waitress and running away with Cade Andreas. Even I'd let him put his boots under my bed and I haven't done the nasty in over a decade."

Thank God that made her laugh. "No. I'm not… He's not… We're…" She stopped. She had no idea what they were. He'd taken her part in the discussion with his brother. He'd made inroads with the company she couldn't have made for herself. And he was taking her to New York.

"Oh, come on. I told you I saw that spark between you. I think our boy Cade is sweet on you."

She swallowed, ignoring the heat that shimmered through her at the thought that Cade might actually feel something for her. Hadn't she thought the same thing herself the night before?

"We're going to New York to talk with his family. I own one-third of the company he and his half brothers inherited when their dad died."

Amanda Mae's eyes narrowed. "You're an heiress?"

Busying herself with preparing Mitzi's cereal, she said, "If you call someone who actually doesn't get any money from the estate they inherit an heiress, then, yes, I'm an heiress."

"You had an estate but didn't get any money?"

"My gram made some bad investments." She slid Mitzi into the swing and stooped down to begin spoon-feeding her. "Really bad. And she stopped getting dividends from the one company she thought she could always depend on." She didn't say from whom she stopped getting dividends to protect Cade and his brothers. "Three years went by with her losing money, but she never stopped her outrageous spending. So when she died I had to sell our home, our furniture, the art collections." She glanced down at her simple blue suit. "Even most of my clothes."

Crossing her arms on her chest, Amanda Mae said, "What does that have to do with going to New York?"

Scooping another spoonful of cereal into Mitzi's eager mouth, she cleared her throat. "I'm hoping that since I own one-third of their company, they'll give me a job."

Amanda Mae blew her breath out in disgust. "No matter how you slice it, you're leaving, and from what you're saying I don't even get any good gossip out of it."

"I'm not a hundred percent sure I'm leaving for good. They might not give me a job." She fed another bite to Mitzi as she continued in a rush. "So I may have to come back and continue working for you."

With a sad sigh, Amanda Mae turned away. "Yeah, well, I've still gotta call someone to come in to handle your shift this morning."

Suzanne's throat tightened. She liked Amanda Mae. There had been a click of something between them, an instant bond. It didn't feel right to be hoping to get another job. It felt even worse to have saddened her friend.

"I talked to your niece last night. She'll do the breakfast crowd."

The diner door opened and Suzanne's gaze swung

over as Cade walked in. He wore his usual jeans and T-shirt. But today, remembering Amanda Mae's comment that he was sweet on her, the little zing of attraction she always felt for him morphed into a breath-stealing whoosh. He could have any woman on the face of the earth. If he was interested in her, it was equal parts of flattering and confusing. She really wasn't ready for another relationship. But how did anybody turn down a man like Cade Andreas?

Amanda Mae glanced sideways and saw him, too. Still, she didn't turn around and face Suzanne. Her voice was gruff when she said, "Okay. Thanks for taking care of that. You scoot now."

Suzanne's heart turned over in her chest. Even with Cade waiting for her in the dining room, she couldn't get her feet to move. Still she had to follow through with her stocks. If owning one-third interest gave her enough clout to get her a good job she owed it to Mitzi to take it.

She scooped Mitzi out of the swing. "I'll stop in when we get back." She smiled ruefully. "To let you know if I'm still your waitress."

Amanda Mae didn't turn around. "Sure."

With that, Suzanne walked into the dining room.

Cade didn't say a word, simply motioned for Suzanne to follow him outside. At the door, he took the car seat and diaper bag from her and she carried Mitzi.

He opened the back door of his extended cab truck and slid the car seat inside. "I know this thing gets buckled in but I don't know how to do it." He held out his hands. "So give me the baby while you install it."

She slid Mitzi to him, careful to keep from accidentally brushing hands, and efficiently installed the car seat. When she turned to take Mitzi from him she noticed he was studying her. "Haven't you ever seen a baby before?"

He smiled ruefully and handed Mitzi to her. "Yes and no. Yes, I've seen a baby. But it's been a while." He paused, then added, "She's cute."

If that was a peace offering for leaving her in his office the night before, or a way for them to get back to a natural footing with each other, it worked. "Thanks. I like her."

He chuckled. "No kidding."

Once Mitzi was buckled in, he ushered her up to the passenger seat then rounded the hood and climbed in himself.

Emotionally confused after her talk with Amanda Mae and not wanting to break the fragile peace between herself and Cade, Suzanne stayed quiet. But the silence in the truck became oppressive, nudging her to say something—anything—to break it. Blessedly, his phone rang.

Wearing an earpiece, he didn't have to pick up. He said simply, "Hey, Eric, isn't it a little early for you and monster dog?"

As he spoke, her gaze strayed over to him. It wasn't often that he was occupied and she grabbed the opportunity to study him without worry. She took in the stretch of the denim across his strong thighs. The way his T-shirt hugged the well-defined muscles of his chest. His easy competence driving.

What would it be like to be dating this man?

Her breath stalled in her chest. The blood in her veins crackled to life. He was, without a doubt one of the sexiest men she'd ever seen. But date him?

Okay. It would probably be fun, since she guessed he'd never be boring. But she didn't know him. And she didn't even really know that he liked her. All she had were suspicions based on Amanda Mae's observation and the guess she'd made the night before that he thought she'd brought him back to his office to seduce him. That was trouble enough. She had to stop thinking there was more to it.

When they arrived at a private airstrip, she jumped out of the truck and immediately grabbed Mitzi and headed for the plane. Though she'd flown in private planes before, Cade's was one step beyond what she was accustomed to. Five butterscotch leather seats were arranged throughout the cabin. Two sat across from a shiny yellowish wood entertainment unit with a big-screen TV. Two sat by a bar made of the same shiny wood. One in the back was connected to a desk.

Cade strode to the one in the back and tossed a black leather briefcase on the desk.

Ten seconds later, the pilot jogged up the steps, followed by a female copilot.

"I'm Dave. This is Jenny." The pretty red-haired copilot nodded. "The weather looks good. We should be in New York in a few hours." He smiled at Suzanne. "Buckle yourselves in."

With that he and Jenny entered the cockpit. Cade pulled two files out of his briefcase, opened them and never looked up again.

She suppressed a sigh. She understood he was ignoring her. She supposed that could actually work to their advantage. If they were both on their best behavior, they wouldn't risk another misunderstanding. But, sheesh, it was going to be a long, boring ride if they didn't talk.

Hours later, Suzanne almost cheered when they landed. From the plane's window, she could see a man in tan pants and a white dress shirt standing by a long black limo, holding a toddler. A woman in capris and a frilly blouse stood beside them. All three wore sunglasses. The toddler squirmed.

The captain and cocaptain said goodbye as Cade walked down the three steps to the tarmac, then took the big diaper bag from Suzanne and caught her hand to help her down the steps. When his fingers closed around hers, their eyes met. The hot June breeze drifted around her. Warmth radiated from their joined hands.

Okay. He might be ignoring her but they were still attracted to each other and last night they'd both jumped to some bad conclusions. She had to do something about the awkwardness between them. And quickly before they weren't alone anymore.

"Look, I'm sorry I gave you the wrong impression last night."

Dropping her hand, he turned to walk to the limo. "What wrong impression? You own one-third of my family's company. No way I could get the wrong impression about a fact."

"So you're not mad about the other?"

He stopped and faced her, his expression shuttered. "What 'other'?"

Ah, so he wasn't ignoring her. He was pretending the beginning part of their conversation, the click of the lock on the den door, the hot look in his eyes never happened?

Actually, that would be one way for them to get beyond the awkwardness.

"I was just pleased you took my part with your brother last night."

He huffed out a breath, propped his hands on his hips and looked up at the blue sky. "It was the right thing to do. The fair thing."

Her pulse stilled. Her battered ego fluttered to life. Fairness might be commonplace for him, but she couldn't remember the last time anyone had truly treated her fairly. Except Amanda Mae. Still, there was no way to explain that to him without getting maudlin or too personal. And after her last attempt at a personal conversation with this guy—well, she knew better.

So she simply said, "Thanks. I appreciated it."

As they approached the limo, the man Suzanne assumed was Darius stepped forward. He took the diaper bag from Cade. "Nice to see you, brother." He turned to Suzanne. "And this must be Suzanne and Mitzi."

From his welcoming smile, it was easy for Suzanne to see Darius was a nice guy. With black hair and dark eyes similar to Cade's, he definitely had a family resemblance to his half brother. "Yes. I'm Suzanne Caldwell. It's nice to meet you."

"This is Whitney, my wife, and our son, Gino."

Whitney grinned and pointed at Mitzi. "Can I hold her?"

Suzanne laughed. "Yes. She gets a little heavy after hours and hours on a plane."

After a quick scowl at Cade, as if chastising him for not helping with the baby, Whitney took Mitzi. "Well, hello there, Miss Mitzi."

Mitzi immediately began to cry.

"I'll take her back."

Whitney returned the baby to Suzanne. "She'll get used to me, but now's not the time to force the issue."

"Cook has made lunch," Darius said, motioning for everyone to enter the limo when the driver opened the door.

When they were settled, they took off toward Darius and Whitney's home. Suzanne spent most of her time entertaining Mitzi, while Darius, Whitney and Cade made small talk.

Out of the corner of her eye, she studied their interaction. A brother and his wife, teasing another brother who gave as good as he got. He wasn't rude, the way he'd been the day she'd met him. He wasn't overbearing, as he'd been the day he'd come into the diner. He was nice.

Normal.

Huh! She almost snorted a laugh. Normal? He owned a ranch, a town and seven planes. And a big chunk of a shipping conglomerate. He might wear boots and jeans, but he was savvy, sharp. Sophisticated.

A sizzle of excitement sparked through her. She wasn't just attracted by his looks. She liked that he was smart. She liked that he was savvy.

She almost groaned. Being around him must be making her brain soft because it didn't matter if she liked him or not. She'd been burned by the last man she'd been involved with and now had a baby to raise. She needed a job. Those were the things she should be thinking about. Not how attractive he was. Or even how smart.

The "house" in Montauk was actually an oceanside estate. They stepped out of the limo to the sounds of waves crashing on the shore. Whitney showed Suzanne to the suite of rooms she would be using during her stay and then escorted her and Mitzi to the dining room where Gino ate macaroni and cheese and the four adults ate spinach salads with crusty homemade bread.

After lunch, Whitney suggested they leave Gino and Mitzi with the nanny for an afternoon nap, while she and Suzanne took a stroll on the beach.

Darius led Cade to the office, and he plopped down on a seat in front of Darius's desk. "Okay. So you've met her. What are we going to do?"

Before the question was fully out of his mouth, the office door opened and Nick, the other Andreas half brother, walked in. "Mrs. Tucker sent Michael to the nursery and Maggie to the beach where Whitney and Suzanne are walking," he said, referring to his fiancée and her nine-month-old son. "She told me the men were meeting in the office."

Darius gestured to the empty chair in front of his desk. "Take a seat. We're talking about shareholder number five."

Wearing cutoff jeans and flip-flops, Nick plopped down on the seat beside Cade. "Ah, the mysterious Suzanne Caldwell, the one who technically owns the most stock."

"Individually." Cade snarled. "Together we still own two-thirds."

Nick laughed and addressed Darius. "Touchy."

"Did you see Ms. Caldwell?"

Nick shook his head. Darius laughed. "Just wait. One look and you'll know why our brother is behaving like a bear with a thorn in his paw."

"I'm not behaving like a bear." Cade popped out of his seat and began to pace. "I'm just concerned. She tried to sell her stock. Nobody wanted it, but once our annual statement comes out and everybody sees profits are up, she'll get offers. And Andreas Holdings isn't in a position to be one of them."

"Cool your jets, Cade. Nick and I decided we shouldn't wait for the company to have enough money to purchase the stock. We should buy it as individuals." Darius leaned back in his chair. "We know you could have your share of the money tomorrow. Unfortunately, Nick and I aren't that lucky. It will take us some time to get that kind of cash together."

Cade turned. "How much time?"

"I think eighteen months. After you called last night, I called Nick and we ran some numbers and we both think we can have our portions in eighteen months."

Cade groaned. "That's not good enough. She's broke. Seriously broke."

"That's why we've come up with some other ideas. First, I think you should take a look at her finances. Maybe she has assets she doesn't know about?"

He shook his head. "From what she told me accountants and attorneys pretty much pillaged every asset in her grandmother's estate to pay debts. I don't think I'm going to find anything they didn't."

Nick shrugged. "Look anyway. You never know. Her grandmother might have put some things in Suzanne's name alone. Things that might not have turned up on a search of her grandmother's assets."

Darius picked up a pencil and tapped it against his desk blotter. "Second, because we won't be solvent enough to buy her out for at least another year, we're going to have to strike a deal to buy her shares eighteen months from now when we have the cash."

"What kind of deal?"

"We'd set the purchase price of her stock at its value the day her grandmother died. We'll offer a million dollars as a holding fee. Then in eighteen months we'll pay the balance."

Relieved, Cade nodded, but Darius continued. "The job of persuading her to take the deal falls to you, Cade. Nick and I are running the company. We never pushed you to do any more than what you could squeeze in. So it's your turn to step up."

Nick grinned. "Suzanne Caldwell is all yours."

"And you talk to her today," Darius said. "As soon as you get a private minute with her, so she can stop worrying and enjoy her time here."

Suzanne, Whitney and Maggie returned from their walk on the beach chatting like three long-lost friends. Whitney had explained that Gino was actually Darius, Nick and Cade's half brother and that their father had been killed in an accident with Gino's mother. So Whitney and Darius had adopted him.

Maggie had explained that she had been married to Nick at eighteen. She'd left him when the brothers' absentee father, Stephone Andreas, had offered him five million dollars to divorce her, and now they were back together, planning a wedding in four weeks.

Suddenly Suzanne's story of having been taken advantage of by a sleazy university professor didn't sound all that crazy. And when Maggie and Whitney gasped in horror then sympathized, Suzanne actually felt wanted. Normal. Just like one of the girls.

They entered the nursery talking about how much alike Darius, Nick and Cade were even though they were entirely different. Darius had grown up working for Andreas Holdings and had stayed on as CEO and Chairman of the Board after their father died. Nick owned a manufacturing plant in North Carolina. And Cade was a billionaire. He'd taken the five million dollars their dad offered and he'd made himself a very wealthy man. Knowing he didn't depend on Andreas Holdings for cash explained a lot about his life in Whiskey Springs.

Both women also admitted it had been Cade who'd more or less nudged Nick and Darius into seeing the truth about their relationships. Which struck Suzanne as interesting. For a guy who wasn't married himself, he certainly seemed to have a high opinion of marriage.

By dinnertime, she was totally comfortable—until she saw the seating arrangement, which put her beside Cade. She knew his family wasn't matchmaking. Darius sat at the head of the table with Gino's high chair at his right. Whitney sat across from him, at the other end of the table. Nick, Maggie and Michael took up the entire left side. With Mitzi in the nursery with the nanny, she and Cade were the only two people left and there were only two chairs remaining. Both on the right side. It was simple math, not matchmaking.

Cade politely pulled out her chair. She accepted with a smile.

But after only five minutes of sitting beside him, a little hum of attraction set up housekeeping in her bloodstream, if only because of proximity. He was so close she could touch him if she wanted. So close he could touch her.

She told herself it was ridiculous to be plotting an accidental elbow brush. Told herself to stop being attracted to a guy she shouldn't want. But the truth was, after hearing Whitney and Maggie talking about Cade that afternoon, she didn't believe he was half the narcissist she'd originally thought. And what was the deal with him encouraging his brothers to marry Whitney and Maggie? She'd thought for a sure a rich, handsome guy like Cade would push a playboy lifestyle. Not just for himself but for his brothers, so he'd have guys to go to Vegas with. The fact that he hadn't made him seem like a whole different person to her.

A likable person.

A person very different from the professor who had dumped her.

And maybe she shouldn't be as afraid of this attraction as she thought.

The dinner of honey-lemon rack of lamb and red potatoes, served with good wine and mocha cream pie for dessert, was delicious and the conversation pleasant. Nick was a charming Southern gentleman who loved horses and enjoyed a good story. Darius was a businessman to the core, but Whitney easily mellowed him out, got him to laugh and talk about things other than employee disputes and prospective customers.

But the entire time Suzanne was aware of Cade. His size. His sexy Southern drawl. The times he joined in the conversation. The times he didn't.

She'd never felt as curious about a man before. She knew the attraction was to blame. Still, no matter how many times she told herself to stop wondering about him, she couldn't.

When dinner was through, Darius tapped his knife to his wineglass and said, "I'd like to propose a toast, but you'll notice my wife isn't having wine tonight."

Suzanne blinked. She glanced at Whitney, who had pinkened endearingly and the realization hit her the same time that it hit Maggie. Both gasped and simultaneously said, "You're pregnant!"

Whitney clapped with glee. "Yes! I'd wanted to tell you this afternoon but Darius and I had decided to make the announcement to everyone at once."

From there pandemonium broke out. Nick congratulated Darius and kissed Whitney. Maggie and Suzanne continued talking simultaneously. Cade held back, but only for a second. *He'd* wanted a baby. He'd wanted a black-haired, blue-eyed little boy. Or a blond-haired, brown-eyed little girl. They'd never figured out if it was he or Ashley who couldn't conceive because they'd found her cancer as soon as her testing began. Not wanting to upset her, he hadn't even gone for tests. So he didn't even know if he could have kids.

Now Nick had a son and would have more children. Maggie was an earth-mother. She'd happily tend to six kids. Go to soccer games. Be a den mother for Boy Scouts.

Darius had Gino...plus a new baby on the way.

And Cade would probably never have kids. No sons. No daughters. He was the one who hadn't pretended to be a big, bad playboy, as his two older brothers had. He was the one who had married his high school sweetheart, tried to start a family, longed to be the dad Stephone Andreas never was to him. He'd had visions of coaching Little League, visions of watching his daughter dance in recitals, visions of rocking babies in the rocking chair his mom had kept in her bedroom until he'd built his big house. Then she'd given it to him as a housewarming gift. Only to have it sit empty in an unused nursery.

Still, he swallowed back the injustice of it all and rose. He walked over to Darius, slapped him on the back and said all the right things.

When the commotion died down, Darius and Whitney excused themselves to get Gino ready for bed, and Nick and Maggie drifted away. Cade knew exactly what they were doing. He'd been ordered to take Suzanne under his wing and tell her the brothers' plan.

Talking to her was the last thing he wanted to do. Were the choice his, he'd grab one of Darius's best bottles of whiskey, amble down to the beach and get himself drunk enough that he wouldn't care that all his plans for a family had been snatched away from him.

Instead, he had to handle Andreas brothers' business.

Knowing that Mitzi was in the nursery with the nanny, he turned to Suzanne. "How about a walk on the beach?"

She faced him with a surprised look.

Because that sounded a little too much like a romantic overture, he cleared up any misunderstanding. "My brothers want me to tell you what we've decided about your stock."

"Oh." Her eyes clouded with something he couldn't quite identify. Disappointment, maybe? "Okay."

Pretending not to notice the expression in her eyes, he led her out the French doors, past the shimmering pool and down the path to the shore.

"I'm so happy for Darius and Whitney," she said, facing Cade with a grin. "They're wonderful parents to Gino."

He sucked in a breath. The lonely, empty feeling of loss returned, but he shut that down and forced himself to be happy for his brother. "Yes. They're great parents."

"And little Michael. What a scamp! He crawls everywhere." She peeked over at him again. "I can understand why Nick and Maggie decided to wait a few months to get married." She kicked the sand with the toe of her sandal. "Not only is he big enough now to stay with Nick's mom while they honeymoon, but they really wanted a summer wedding. On the beach." She glanced at him again. "Nick lives at the beach, too. In North Carolina. They grew up together at the beach, you know?"

He and Ashley had grown up together, too, so, yes, he knew. He knew all about first loves and how wonderful they could be. But for once he wasn't thinking about Ashley. He was thinking about Suzanne. He'd never heard that lilt in her voice before. She'd obviously had a good time with Maggie and Whitney. And even as he wanted to wallow in misery, he felt an odd stirring in his chest. Almost as if he'd been hoping for her to be happy and now that she was it made him happy. Proud. As if he'd had some part in it.

He scowled. He did not want her happiness to matter to him. It was bad enough he was in charge of her welfare. He didn't want to be manager of her happiness, too. He might have been forced to help her, but he refused to get involved with her. She was a pretty, sexy thorn in his side. A temptation he didn't want nor need.

"Are you going to stop talking long enough for me to tell you what my brothers decided this afternoon?"

She stepped back as if he'd slapped her. "I was just making conversation."

Okay, now he'd hurt her. He hadn't meant to. He'd just wanted this over with.

He stopped, ran his hand along the back of his neck. "Some of this you're going to like. Some of it you might hate."

"Just say it."

The hurt that wobbled through her voice hit him right in the heart and froze it. He hated to see women hurt or, worse, cry.

He sighed. "Look, I'm sorry. I know I'm gruff sometimes. It's just the way I am. But the bottom line is we want to buy back your stock. We can't afford it now, but we're willing to give you a holding fee."

Her eyes widened, lit with joy, and his heart began to beat again.

"You're going to give me a holding fee?"

"Yes, a million dollars."

Her mouth fell open. "A million dollars!"

"The company is improving. Once our annual statement comes out, you'll have real suitors who will be after your stock. Which is why we intend to be able to buy you out in eighteen months."

"Eighteen months!"

"We'll pay you the prevailing price on your grandmother's date of death."

She pressed her hand to her chest. "Oh, my gosh!"

"So you won't have to worry about the holding fee. Though it will be deducted from the amount you get for the stock, it'll be a drop in the bucket compared to the hundred million dollars or so you'll get in the sale."

Her face lit with so much joy that he relaxed.

"A hundred million dollars! I can get a house! A new car. Not worry about—"

But suddenly the joy faded, her eyes narrowed and she frowned. "Wait."

"What?"

"Does this mean I don't get a job?"

"This means you don't need a job."

"The hell, I don't! You're telling me you 'believe' you'll be able to buy my stock in eighteen months, but you don't know. All the agreements in the world mean nothing if you can't get the money together when you think you will. *Nothing* in life is certain."

He couldn't argue that.

"So you can't tell me for sure you'll be buying the stock. Your holding fee is more of a hope that you'll be able to buy the stock in eighteen months."

"Why don't we cross that bridge when we come to it? A million dollars is a lot of money—"

"Yes. And I appreciate it. But I watched my grandmother lose *hundreds* of millions of dollars in a few short years when the stock market began to crumble and Andreas Holdings quit paying dividends." She sighed. "I don't trust easy money. I'd like a job. Then I'd have the security of earning a steady salary, no matter how long it takes you to pull together the cash for my shares."

"Yeah, well, you don't have a marketable skill."

"I can type! I can research. I could even be a receptionist. I'm not picky—"

Something inside of Cade snapped. As he watched her pretty mouth telling him things that didn't actually seem unreasonable—but had to be unreasonable because they were not the plan he and his brothers had worked out—his frustration combined with the futility of arguing with this woman, who was too darned pretty for his own good, and he totally lost his hold on common sense.

All he wanted was for her to stop talking, and the quickest route to that, his hormones assured him, was to kiss her. Before he really thought the plan through, his arm snaked around her waist and hauled her to him as his head descended until his mouth met her soft, sweet lips.

Every muscle in his body tensed. He'd intended to surprise her into silence, instead *his* breathing stuttered, *his* chest tightened, *his* gut squeezed. Her soft lips drew him in, causing him to forget his mission. Especially when her lips seemed to invite him to taste more, take more.

Temptation and desire met and merged. She wasn't stopping him. And she tasted so good. So perfect—

Perfect?

For what?

She was a single mom. A business associate now. A woman he couldn't love then leave.

He knew better than to kiss her.

He *knew* better!

He jerked away, breaking the kiss, and stepped back. Shocked by his behavior, he ran his hand along the back of his neck. Suzanne stared up at him with wide eyes and lips dewy from his kiss.

"Okay, look. I'm sorry. That shouldn't have happened."

She simply continued to stare at him. And he knew he'd given her the wrong idea. Romantic ideas. Damn. Why did he always behave like an idiot around her?

He took another step back, away from her. "Here's the deal. I was married."

She blinked, as if absorbing that, then said, "And she hurt you, right?"

"No. She died." He said it gruffly, angrily. He'd learned long ago that anger was the best way to keep the other, more dangerous emotions at bay. "But even before she got sick, I proved to both of us that I wasn't any great shakes as a husband. She was the love of my life and I treated her shabbily."

He sucked in a breath, wished she'd stop looking at him with big blue eyes that had gone from sharp with desire to soft with sadness. For him. God, he hated pity.

"Get any romantic ideas you might have out of your head because I'm not in the market for a relationship and you shouldn't want me."

When she only blinked, Cade knew he wasn't getting through, so he pushed harder. "Okay, let me tell you a few things that never made it to the diner gossip because they're things I don't tell anyone." He held up his index finger. "Number one, I spent the first two years of my marriage traveling to build my fortune."

His second finger snapped up. "Number two, you'd have thought that after she got sick I would have settled in, settled down, but no. I wanted Beacher's Oil so bad that I pursued it like the Holy Grail and one night while I was sweet-talking my way into a deal, she faded away. She was gone when I got back."

When he stopped, the salty air rang with the sound of the waves. He scrubbed his hand down his face, surprised he'd admitted so much, but knowing he'd had to to make it abundantly clear to her why she shouldn't feel sorry for him. Shouldn't feel *anything* for him.

"Cade, I'm so sorry."

At her soft apology, he realized that even his expanded explanation hadn't worked because now her big blue eyes were rimmed with tears.

"Forget it. Just understand I was no good as a husband and stay the hell away from me."

CHAPTER FIVE

HE TURNED AND BEGAN STRIDING up the beach. Suzanne watched him bound away, an achy pain squeezing her heart. He hadn't fooled her with the gruff voice and the straightforward proclamations. She could see from the tortured look on his face that his wife's death had been brutal on him. It was no wonder he behaved oddly around her. He was attracted to her and didn't want to be.

He stopped, faced her. His dark hair blew in the breeze off the ocean. His dark eyes bored into her. "Are you coming? I'm not going to stand here all night. If you want to walk up by yourself that's fine. But it's dark and I don't generally leave women alone in the dark."

She scrambled across the shifting sand to catch up with him, confusion warring with the sympathy she felt for him. Losing her grandmother had changed her life, filled her with grief, filled her with *anger*. She couldn't even imagine how hard it would be to lose a spouse.

At the French doors off the patio into the den, Cade paused, waiting for her to get to the door before he opened it for her.

They stepped into the dimly lit den only to discover Nick and Maggie sat on the brown leather sofa, Whitney sat on a wing chair and Darius was behind the bar.

"Drink?"

Suzanne's gaze swung back to Cade, as if looking for his preference, but he walked away without a glance in her direction.

"I'll have a beer and I'll get it myself."

Carrying two beers and a glass of wine, Darius walked to the conversation group. He handed the wine to Maggie and one of the beers to Nick then sat on the chair beside Whitney's. "Great. I love it when someone wants to play bartender. Suzanne, just give your request to Cade."

"I'm fine. Thanks." Not exactly sure what to do, she hovered near the door.

Whitney waved her over, motioning to the empty love seat. "Please. Sit."

Suzanne glanced at the love seat then back at Cade. The only seat left in the room would smash them against each other.

It didn't matter. He'd made himself perfectly clear. He wasn't interested. He'd had the love of his life. He'd been a bad husband. And after her ordeal with Mitzi's dad, she was also smart enough not to want to get involved with a guy who boldly admitted he wasn't husband material...

Except that kiss had been amazing. Her breathing had stopped and all her senses had intensified. He'd drawn her in, clouded her brain, liquefied her limbs with one soft press of his mouth to hers.

They weren't just attracted. They were smokin' hot attracted.

But they were also smart. Too smart to get involved. He was a bad bet as a romantic partner. With her life in total chaos, she wasn't exactly looking for a romance, let alone a guy who might be attracted to her but didn't want to be. They had more than enough motivation to stay away from each other, even squished together on a couch.

She ambled to the love seat. Cade slid from behind the bar with his opened bottle of beer. But he didn't come over to sit with her. He headed for the cold fireplace.

Really? He was going to be that petty?

But a little voice inside her head cautioned her not to be so sure he was being petty. That kiss had knocked her socks off. Surely it must have had the same effect on him.

What if he didn't trust himself to control himself?

What if *that* was really why he was angry?

"So, I'm guessing Cade told you about our plans for you."

Something about the authoritative tone of Darius's voice raised her hackles, but she told herself not to be so sensitive. Even though the Andreas brothers hadn't offered a job, their suggested holding fee had been generous and she needed to think it through. Though she'd popped off with Cade, she couldn't simply turn down a million dollars because it wasn't what she'd expected.

"I thought your offer was very generous, but—"

"But she's a bit miffed that we didn't pony up a job."

When Cade interrupted her, Suzanne could have sighed. His interpretation of her reaction might have been correct, but now that things were sinking in, she wasn't quite so adamant. Besides, she could speak for herself.

"I don't think *miffed* is the right word. *Cautious* is better. I never expected to be offered a holding fee and I need—"

"You were like a bull snorting fire out on the beach. You're not happy with our offer."

Suzanne scorched him with a look. She might not have been happy with the offer, but that was her gut reaction. Not a real decision. Plus, his way of shutting her up had been to kiss her.

How would he like her telling his brothers that?

Darius quietly broke into her stare down with Cade. "What concerns you?"

"I asked for a job because I want some security. What happens in eighteen months if the company doesn't rebound the way you think it should?"

"It will," Nick put in, as calm and serious as Darius. "But that doesn't matter. The company itself isn't buying your shares. We're buying them from our personal accounts. And we'll easily have the money in eighteen months."

"And once you get that money, you're back to being a very wealthy woman," Darius reminded her. "If we employ you, you'll need to move to New York. You'll have to get a condo and a nanny. And just when you have yourself settled, we'll have pulled the money together to buy you out and you'll have to fire your nanny and sell your condo when you move back to Atlanta. If you take the holding fee, you can simply go back now, reenroll in school."

He had a point. With a million dollars she could go back to school....

She frowned. The thought of returning to the same university where Bill Baker taught was not a pleasant one. But her old school wasn't the only university in the country. With a million dollars she could enroll just about anywhere.

She could finish her degree and then take a year

of more practical classes. Like accounting. Or maybe business management. This rough patch in her life had proven she needed to be employable. If nothing else, somehow or another at the end of these eighteen months she intended to have a job.

Nick smiled. "We won't let you down."

"Plus, you might just discover you're not as broke as you think," Darius added. "You could find assets you didn't know about when Cade takes a look at the big picture of your finances."

Her eyes narrowed. "Cade's taking a look at my finances?"

Darius smiled. "Your grandmother could have opened accounts for you that she forgot. Accounts that wouldn't show up when her estate ran a check because they'd have your name and social security number on them, not hers. So I've assigned Cade to look into that."

Just when things started to fall into place in her head, she somehow ended up connected to Cade again. She shifted on the love seat. "I don't want Cade poking into my finances."

Cade snorted as if the idea didn't please him, either.

Whitney shook her head, rose and sat beside Suzanne. "I'm going to apologize for my husband and his brothers." She caught both of her hands. "I know Darius has a tendency to bulldoze situations and I'm guessing Cade didn't explain this well." She glared at Cade.

He shrugged. "I actually never got a chance to make much of an explanation."

"The way Darius explained this to me," Whitney said, "Cade himself wouldn't be looking at your books. He's got a staff of accountants who would be examining the records, searching for lost accounts, that kind of thing."

"Maybe I should hire some accountants myself."

Cade huffed out a laugh. "Why waste money on accountants when I have them at my disposal?"

She licked her lips. That was true. She might be getting a lot of money eventually. But right now she was getting only a portion of that money and she couldn't be reckless. If she was careful now, in a few short months she and Mitzi would be financially secure.

"Okay."

Whitney's eyebrows rose. "Okay?"

"I'll take the money. I'll take the help of Cade's accountants. I'll spend the next semester finishing my degree and the year after that I'll take classes that might lead me to a real job."

From across the room Cade said, "You won't need it."

But she ignored him. Just as he'd said, he wasn't right for her. *They* weren't right for each other. Sure, they were sexually attracted, but she absolutely, positively did not want to be involved with him. She understood he was sad and angry about his wife's death, but why he thought he could take that out on her was a total mystery. If she ever got romantically involved again, it would be with someone who would really love her and appreciate her.

And Cade Andreas did not fit that bill.

A few minutes after midnight, Cade was running chalk along the tip of his pool stick when Whitney and Maggie pleaded tiredness. Suzanne had long ago gone upstairs to check on Mitzi and simply hadn't returned. But now Darius and Nick also said their good-nights and strolled off to bed with Whitney and Maggie.

Perfectly happy to have a few minutes by himself,

Cade decided to have one last beer before he went to his suite upstairs. Unfortunately, he only got halfway through before Nick returned.

"I thought you were all snuggled up with the future Mrs. for the night."

"She's showering." Nick ambled into the room and fell to the seat on the sofa beside Cade. "I think you and I need one of those little talks like the one we had when you told me I had to pick up my end of the slack for Andreas Holdings."

"Not hardly, bud. You and Darius already had your little talk with me about helping Suzanne for the good of Andreas Holdings, and you see how well that went over."

Nick went on as if he hadn't spoken. "Tonight when Darius and I were trying to persuade her to take our money, we dangled going back to school in front of her."

Cade shrugged. "It worked a hell of a sight better than the talk I had with her." He vividly remembered how that ended. With a kiss. His intention had been to get her to stop talking and all he'd done was awaken his own damned hormones. "Our offer might have surprised her at first, but now she seems happy to take it."

"Yeah," Nick said, drawing out the one syllable into a long, skeptical word. "The problem is Maggie has some concerns about Suzanne going back to Atlanta."

"Maggie has some concerns?"

"Apparently they had some long talks today. From the things Suzanne said, Maggie believes Suzanne returning to her old school isn't a good idea. Mitzi's father is a professor there and apparently he made her life miserable enough that she had to quit. The guy's a snake and

Maggie thinks it wouldn't be good for Suzanne to even see him."

"And you want me to...what?" For the love of God, had Nick not already noticed that he was *not* the person to talk to Suzanne?

"Pour on some of your rich Texan charm and persuade her to stay at your ranch with you. There has to be a university near Whiskey Springs that she can attend, somewhere she can transfer her credits."

He gaped at his brother. Now he knew Nick was insane...

Except Nick hadn't actually seen the discussion he'd had with Suzanne. He hadn't seen how Suzanne had gotten her back up. He hadn't seen Cade lose his head and kiss her.

And it would be a cold day in hell before Cade told him.

He snorted a laugh. "Right. We've already nudged her into thinking about going home. It's too late to change her mind. She wants to return to Atlanta."

"Maybe not. Just because that's where her school was, it doesn't mean she wants to go to Atlanta. She might have simply been happy at the thought of having a plan and somewhere to go."

"There are lots of good schools. In other cities."

"She has no family, Cade. Even if she stays away from the creep who fathered her baby and moves to another city, she's still got a boatload of problems. Who's going to watch Mitzi? Who's going to answer baby questions? At the very least, your staff could babysit while she attends classes." He shook his head. "It just doesn't feel right to send her off into the world alone. Not when she's one of us."

"One of us?"

"As long as she owns Andreas stock, she's one of us."

Cade sucked in a breath. If there was one thing their father's death had instilled in them, it was loyalty. With that reminder, he felt a brush of guilt. But just a brush because there was one very good reason Nick and Maggie's plan wouldn't work. "And how am I supposed to persuade her to transfer to a university near Whiskey Springs and stay with me? We might see her as 'one of us' but she barely knows us."

"You could tell her you need her close in case your accountants have questions."

The collar of Cade's shirt suddenly got too tight. That idea might actually work.

"She's one of us, Cade." Nick rose. "And Maggie believes she's lost. Alone. We want her to be comfortable. Not to be struggling through her last year of school with no one to help her with her baby, when you've got a whole town at your disposal."

He left the room and Cade flopped back on the sofa. He could picture having Suzanne living in his home. He'd vacillate between behaving like an angry bear and a hungry panther, slithering through his house, following her scent, itching to touch her. Hadn't that kiss on the beach proven he couldn't control himself around her?

Damn straight it had.

He was not—absolutely was not—inviting her to live with him.

Except…

What if she was alone? What if she really would be struggling to go to classes and care for her baby? What if she had no one to talk to? No one to call if Mitzi got sick. No one to even ask questions about raising her baby.

He told himself to stop obsessing. Suzanne was a smart, independent woman who would be fine. She *wanted* to be on her own. Hadn't she said as much at least three times?

Monday afternoon, after a round of goodbyes at the limo Darius had sent to take them to the airport, Suzanne and Cade made the ride to the airstrip in total silence. When they boarded the plane, Cade again sat at the desk in the rear, his head down, his focus on the papers in three open files.

Closing her eyes, Suzanne made herself comfortable on her seat. But after they were in the air, Cade's voice drifted over to her.

"I know this weekend didn't turn out the way you'd hoped. But my brothers are genuinely trying to help you. They're nice guys. Even if you don't like me, there's no reason to be suspicious of them."

She glanced at Mitzi, who slept in her carrier, then back at Cade. She hadn't been able to sleep the night before. Not just because she'd agreed to take a million dollars to hold her stock and now had a direction for her life. But because she'd begun to remember some of the things Whitney and Maggie had told her about Cade. Things that had caused her to see him in a different light.

Like how he'd helped his two brothers see they were crazy about Whitney and Maggie and it was time to settle down. After her little tiff with Cade on the beach, she now knew he'd done that because he'd been married and understood a little more about life and love than his older brothers. But that didn't diminish the fact that he'd come to Whitney's and Maggie's aid. Just as he'd come to her aid the night she'd told him she was the missing shareholder, explaining to Darius that she needed a job.

He loved Gino. He loved little Michael. He teased and bantered with his brothers and their wives, but in a fun, brotherly sort of way.

If it hadn't been for that little tiff on the beach and the way he'd treated her after, she'd probably like him right now. And not just as a friend, but...well, romantically.

"I'm not suspicious of your brothers."

"Really?"

She shook her head and laughed softly. "Why would you think that when I took their offer?"

"Because you're quiet."

She pointed at the open files on his desk. "Yeah, well, you have work to do."

"And I've got plenty of time to get to it. Right now, I just want to make sure you're clear about our offer. That you don't have questions. That you're okay with everything."

Before this weekend she might have thought he was goading her, or thought she was too dumb to understand a simple deal. Today she knew he wasn't like that. If he was asking, it was out of genuine concern. Her heart got a little tug, but she ignored it. He'd made himself perfectly clear. He wasn't interested. And she had too many things on her plate right now to regret his choice.

"I understand everything your brothers told me this weekend."

"Good."

"Good..." She paused. Actually, she might understand everything about their deal, but there was one little bitty thing she didn't get about the Andreas brothers themselves. It was none of her business, but the truth was, with all the nice things Cade did for his brothers, his one omission seemed odd, out of character.

"Actually I have thought of something I might need to have cleared up."

"Like what?"

Marshaling her courage, she said, "Like you probably have five times the money your brothers have—"

"More like ten."

"So why don't you just buy me out? If you're all so worried about my stock getting into the wrong hands, why not just buy my stock and be done with me?"

He didn't even hesitate. "Because you own one-third of the company. My brothers and I each own one-sixth. If I buy you out and add my one-sixth to your one-third, I own half the company. We'd no longer be equals. I won't do that to them."

She blinked. Wow. If she had any questions about how he felt about his brothers they'd all just been answered. Their bond meant more to him than the possibility of losing her stock. Their connection meant more to him than money.

Maybe his wife's death had taught him a lesson?

Silence reigned again. But in a few seconds, Cade cleared his throat, bringing her attention back to him. "There is one more thing you and I need to discuss."

His sudden nervousness didn't fit with the straightforward conversation they were having and she tensed. "What?"

"Nick and Maggie think you should live with me at the ranch."

Positive he was joking, she laughed. "Right."

"Hey, I don't want you to. But I figured I'd better tell you just in case it somehow gets back to you that I was supposed to ask, but didn't."

Confusion wrinkled her brow. "Why would they want me to live at your ranch? What would I do so far out in God's country?"

He peeked over at her, clearly relieved that she thought the idea as crazy as he did. "Exactly." But when he caught her gaze with his sincere brown eyes, her heart stuttered a bit in her chest. "I mean, I'm sure we could find a university nearby...but you're probably eager to get on with your life."

She did want to get on with her life. She truly did. But something about this man called to her. It was more than sexual attraction. More than empathy for his loss and his suffering. A click of connection sparked in her every time she as much as looked at him.

But he didn't feel the same thing for her. And she had money now. Plans.

"I am eager to move on. I have to enroll in the next semester of classes." She paused. She'd already figured out she wasn't going back to her old school. There was no way she'd risk seeing Bill Baker. "Except I'm not quite sure what university I'll go to. With a whole country full of schools to choose from, it could take me months to figure out where I should go."

He skewered her with a look. "There is no perfect plan, Suzanne. But the bottom line to this is neither one of us wants you to live with me."

Considering how she'd begun to soften to him, he was right. It probably wasn't a good idea. She shook her head. "No. We don't."

"Okay, then don't overthink it."

She settled back in her seat, convinced they'd made the right choice. But the thought of living at his ranch lingered and then morphed into something she hadn't expected. It might not be a good idea to live with Cade, but she had to admit it would be nice to stay in Whiskey Springs. Nice to see if she and Amanda Mae could have the kind of close relationship she'd suspected from the day they'd met. Nice to see all the people she'd met at the diner again, make them friends.

Nicer still to have roots.

A place to raise her baby.

A home.

CHAPTER SIX

WHEN THEY FINALLY ARRIVED at Cade's private airstrip, he shoved Suzanne's diaper bag and suitcase into his truck while she buckled sleeping Mitzi's baby carrier in the rear seats and they headed to Whiskey Springs.

It was, at best, a fifteen-minute drive to her temporary apartment above the diner, but to Cade it seemed to take forever. First, he was eager to get to town. Because the land was flat, he could see Whiskey Springs off in the distance and tonight it had a weird red glow. Something he'd have to investigate once he got there. He couldn't believe one of the residents would be so foolish as to start a fire on a scorching hot June night in a drought. This time of the year, the land was sometimes so dry it was a wonder it didn't spontaneously combust. But there was no other explanation for the red glow. It had to be a fire.

Second, he needed to get away from the woman in the truck with him. He understood her desire to make her own way with her million dollars. To find a university, finish her degree, have a skill so she'd know she and her baby would never go hungry. Hell, he'd been equally determined to prove himself when he turned eighteen and his dad dumped five million dollars in his lap. He'd wanted the money—needed the money—but he'd wanted to be his own man, too. So he'd learned to invest, to build his dad's peace offering into a real pile of money he could use to make more money, and then more money and more money. Until his dad knew that even without the five-million head start, he would have made it.

So he and Suzanne were a lot alike. Enough alike that he realized he might be attracted to her for a little more than just her cute little butt. That's what had scared him the night he'd kissed her and why he'd been so determined to scare her off. He thanked God she'd decided to take her money and run. Otherwise, they might actually become friends.

He nearly snorted a laugh. Friends? If they spent more than an hour alone, getting along, he'd have her in bed. And that wouldn't do either one of them any good.

Mitzi squeaked, then moaned slightly before she burst into genuine tears and everything inside of Cade stilled. Since meeting Gino, he was accustomed to squeaking and crying and even an occasional mess. Like spit-up. Having a baby brother had acclimated him to kids. Plus, it had taken some of the sting out of his own childlessness. True, he'd had a moment of regret when he'd heard about Whitney's pregnancy, but he'd sucked himself back out of that black hole. He would not ever have a child of his own. Period. He accepted that.

But hearing Mitzi, up close and personal, did the strangest things to his chest. It tightened. It sort of tingled. He wanted to turn around and comfort her.

"Shh! Mitzi, sweetie. We're almost there. Then Mama will take you out of that tight little car seat, kiss your sweet cheeks and tickle your belly."

Clearly not appeased, Mitzi only cried harder.

"Please, sweetie." This time Suzanne's voice held a note of pleading that clenched Cade's gut.

"Don't worry about her on my account."

Suzanne peeked at him. "The fussing's going to get worse the longer it takes us to get into town."

"I know. But we only have another five minutes." And the red glow hovering around the town got redder the closer they got. "She's a baby. She's been strapped in that seat for hours. I don't blame her for being uncomfortable."

Suzanne turned from trying to entertain Mitzi. "I know that and Mitzi knows that. I just didn't think you did."

"What? I look like some kind of baby monster?"

"No, but you can sometimes be a grouch."

He leveled his best watch-your-step look at her and realized he'd just proved her point. "Yeah, well, when it comes to kids I'm a lot more understanding than I am with adults."

The red skyline finally caught Suzanne's eye. She pointed out the windshield. "Is that normal?"

He shifted uncomfortably on the seat. "No."

"Oh, Lord."

He levered his foot on the gas pedal, pushing it to the floor. With Mitzi screaming and Suzanne's gaze glued straight ahead, Cade barreled the truck into town. He got only a third of the way down Main Street before Bob Patterson stopped him.

Dressed in the heavy-duty gear of a volunteer fireman, he motioned for Cade to lower his window.

Cade didn't waste time on greetings. "What's going on?"

"I'm sorry, Cade. It's the diner."

Suzanne gasped. "Oh, no."

Bob blew his breath out. "Total loss. Amanda Mae is beside herself."

Suzanne shoved her door open. "Is she down there?"

"Yeah, crying her heart out."

Cade watched in amazement as Suzanne blinked back her own tears. She jumped out of the truck and fumbled with the door of the extended cab and the catch on Mitzi's car seat.

Cade stopped her by grabbing her hand. "I'll take care of Mitzi. You go to Amanda Mae." He glanced out his window at Bob. "You take her down there."

"Yes, sir."

He caught Suzanne's gaze again. "And you stay with him. It won't do Amanda Mae any good to have you getting hurt rushing to her side."

With that, Suzanne scooted around the truck. Oddly, she did exactly as Cade wanted for once. She paused by Bob, who took her arm and directed her through the gathered crowd.

Mitzi squawked.

He opened the door and then the back door so he could reach in, unbuckle Mitzi and pull her out.

Holding her at eye level, he said, "All right. Here's the deal. Your mom had to rush down there, but we're going to take it a little slower. It's not going to help matters if you continue to squawk."

As if understanding, Mitzi stopped crying.

There. See? Everybody made too much of this whole parenting thing. Babies loved him because he was straightforward and honest with them. And he loved babies. If only because they didn't try to con you. The way he understood it, that particular bad behavior didn't present itself until junior high.

He settled Mitzi on his arm. But a thought occurred to him and he spun her around, holding her at eye level again. "Are we okay in the diaper area?"

She only looked at him. Her blue eyes as bright as her mom's. Her dark hair sticking up in all directions.

"What? I'm trying to see if you need a diaper. If you do, I'll handle it."

She still only looked at him.

Since she wasn't giving him any hint, his options were to check—which was not at all appealing—or take his chances. Hoisting her to his chest, he decided to take his chances.

She snuggled into his neck, nuzzling in as if she planned to go back to sleep—or as if she liked him, trusted him.

Wonderful feelings bubbled up inside him. But he told himself not to be ridiculous. Babies trusted anybody who kept them warm and dry.

Still, he couldn't stop himself from kissing her cheek before he began picking his way through the crowd. Most stepped aside as he ambled through. A few offered their regrets for his loss, since, technically, everything in town was his. But he didn't give a flying fig about the loss of one building. He'd created his plan to buy all the buildings in town so he could give people like Amanda Mae a break. He paid the taxes, took care of repairs, did renovations. A little town like Whiskey Springs didn't support its own pharmacy or diner or Laundromat. Hell, they barely supported a convenience store. So he'd bought them all, subsidized them, so the people who worked on his ranch or for the corporate offices of his oil company had the things they needed without having to drive forty miles to the closest city.

But though the building was his, everything inside that building had belonged to Amanda Mae, and he hoped to heaven she had insurance.

The closer he got, the more chaos surrounded him. Firemen worked diligently to ensure the fire didn't spread, but the diner was engulfed. Red flames leaped from the roof. The windows had already exploded out.

When Suzanne reached Amanda Mae, the diner proprietor was sobbing softly. Tears immediately sprang to Suzanne's eyes. She raced over to Amanda Mae, who was surrounded by townspeople. But the minute Suzanne appeared, she stepped away from them and threw herself into Suzanne's arms.

"I don't know what I'm going to do."

Suzanne stroked her hair. "I'm sure Cade will come up with something."

She shook her head fiercely. "No reason for Cade to care about my equipment and supplies. That's my doing."

"Well, insurance will—"

"I let my insurance lapse…"

All Suzanne could say was, "Oh."

Suddenly, Amanda Mae pulled away. "Oh, my gosh! I forgot. All your things were in the apartment."

Suzanne shook her head. "I didn't really have much."

"Which makes it all the worse that you lost it!"

"Let's not worry about me," Suzanne said, sliding her arm across Amanda Mae's shoulder. Inside, her heart was breaking. Not only had Amanda Mae lost everything, but she had no insurance. God only knew how Cade would handle this.

As if thinking him made him appear, he stepped through the crowd and walked over. Miraculously, Mitzi was sound asleep on his shoulder. The tears rimming her eyelids spilled over. It was probably the sadness of the moment that had her thinking this way, but she couldn't help seeing how adorable Mitzi looked with a man. A father.

Where had that come from? He'd warned her he was a terrible husband, not because he'd felt the need to unburden himself, but because they were attracted. He didn't want her to get ideas. She'd agreed. He would really be upset if he knew she'd seen him as a father for Mitzi.

Patting Mitzi's back, Cade walked over. "I'm sorry, Amanda Mae."

After blowing her nose, she batted a hand. "Don't worry about me. I think this might be the good Lord's way of telling me it's time to retire."

Suzanne gasped, but Cade said, "You're too ornery to retire. You need the diner. It's your lifeline to the people of this town. I've got another building—"

"I don't want another building." Fresh tears sprouted in Amanda Mae's eyes. "I didn't have insurance, so I don't have the money to buy all new equipment. I'm old. I'm tired. I can't start from scratch."

"I have money."

The words popped out of Suzanne's mouth before the thought even fully formed in her head.

"It'll take a hundred thousand dollars at least just for the kitchen. Then there's the dining room. I'd need booths, tables, chairs, plates, cups—" She ran her fingers through her hair. "And supplies. Every piece of meat, every jar of mayonnaise, every egg is gone."

"I've got money to replace it all," Suzanne said, her

voice slowing down as she really thought this through. She'd wanted to finish her degree, but she could delay that. Especially for a friend. Plus, if she invested most of her money in the diner, she could also work there. Except not as a waitress, but a partner.

"We'll be partners."

Amanda Mae blinked. "Partners?"

"I'll put up whatever it takes for new equipment, etcetera. You provide the expertise."

Amanda Mae sniffed.

"Cade's said he's got a building—"

"Yeah, but where are you gonna live? Your apartment's gone."

She glanced over at Cade. This was the part where it got tricky. He'd said his family wanted her to live with him. But in the plane they'd more or less decided that was a bad idea. Still, Amanda Mae needed her and she didn't so much want to finish school as she wanted a job. A place. Some security. Surely she could find an apartment once everything settled down with the diner. She'd only need to stay with him a week or so…

"Cade's brother wants me to live at his ranch."

Cade's mouth dropped open in dismay.

Amanda Mae gasped. "You can't give me your money and go live with Cade!"

"Sure I can. Cade and his brothers gave me a holding fee to buy my shares of their father's company's stock. And they were generous." She pressed her hand to her chest. "I can afford to do this."

Cade's deep voice drifted into their conversation. "Suzanne, can I talk to you for a second?"

Suzanne faced Cade with a hopeful smile. "Sure."

He dragged her away from Amanda Mae, who was

immediately swallowed up in the comforting arms of the townspeople again.

"I thought the plan was to go find a school and finish your degree?"

"Look, I know what's really bugging you is that I told Amanda Mae I would stay with you. But I only said that so she wouldn't worry about me for the next few days. I won't stay with you long. As soon as we get the new diner started, I'll find a place and move out."

He rolled his eyes to the heavens as if seeking strength. "Suzanne, this is going to be a lot of work."

"I know, but I want to work. I also want to do this." She glanced back at the diner owner. "Do you know that in one month of being virtually homeless while I tried to figure out what to do, Amanda Mae was the only person who helped me?"

He sucked in a breath, patted Mitzi's back. "No."

"Even you ushered me out of town, suggesting that I go to the next town over for a hotel room."

He looked away.

"Nobody saw that I was struggling, putting up a good front but drowning, except Amanda Mae."

She caught his arm to get his attention, but sparks of electricity crackled up his biceps. And Cade knew exactly why it was a bad idea for them to live together.

Still, Suzanne kept talking as if nothing were amiss. "This is my chance to pay her back. I want it."

He squeezed his eyes shut. Technically, what she was suggesting made perfect sense. Plus, it would appease his brothers. But he knew in real life it was going to be a disaster.

Why did he have to be so attracted to this woman? What was it about her that made him forget that he wasn't interested? Because even if he was looking for a woman in his life, this particular woman needed a husband and a father for her baby. And he'd vowed he'd never marry again. Didn't his hormones realize he could not be a husband? He could not hurt another woman.

"Come on. It won't be so bad to have me and Mitzi around. Look how you like her."

His heart turned over in his chest. He did like Mitzi. In a matter of a few days, he'd come to adore this baby girl. But that was actually another problem. He'd be with this child twenty-four-hours-a-day some days. He'd grow attached. Maybe long for something he couldn't have. His own kids. His well-ordered life would turn into chaos. Not because a child made a mess of things, but because he'd remember those plans, those dreams he'd had with Ashley. A houseful of kids. Christmas Eves beside a fireplace with little girls and boys wide-eyed with expectation. Little League. Dance lessons. Being a proud papa in the audience when *his* little girl danced a solo.

He swallowed.

Those dreams were gone.

And this child would only make him long for things he couldn't have. She'd already more than halfway stolen his heart. Her pretty mom would make him think that maybe, just maybe, he should try again.

But that wouldn't just be a betrayal of Ashley. It would be a betrayal of Suzanne. He couldn't ever love as completely, as wondrously, as innocently as he'd loved Ashley. And anything less would be cheating Suzanne.

He handed Mitzi to her mom. "You have two weeks." He turned to go, but faced her again. "And while you're at my house you keep the baby quiet."

"I thought you said you didn't mind her fussing—"

"Driving in a car with a baby and living with one are two different things. Especially since my office is in the house. Keep her quiet and out of my way."

CHAPTER SEVEN

AT TEN O'CLOCK THAT NIGHT, Cade's mom volunteered to take the baby. Because his truck already had the car seat, he and Ginny decided to exchange vehicles. Suzanne listened to their discussion without comment as they walked down Main Street to Cade's truck and stopped at the driver's side door.

"Take Mitzi to the ranch and put her in the room with the crib."

Ginny raised one eyebrow in response, as if questioning that. But he said nothing, only handed her his keys.

She gave her keys to him, saying, "My SUV is on Third Street."

Buckling Mitzi into her car seat, Suzanne gasped. "Oh, my gosh! I forgot about my car. It could be toast!"

"Where'd you have it parked?"

"There weren't any spaces behind the diner, so I parked it about a block away."

Ginny winced. "You might be lucky."

Cade said, "We'll check up on it after the fire's out."

When Mitzi was settled, Ginny opened the driver's side door. "I'll see you when you're done here."

"I think it might be pointless to wait up. You might as well stretch out on the bed. We could be here all night."

Suzanne gave Mitzi one last kiss on the cheek. When she hesitated over the baby, Cade caught her elbow and pulled her away from the truck.

"She'll be fine with my mom. We need to make sure Amanda Mae is settled, and right now you seem to be the person she's listening to. *Partner.*"

She winced at his tone, but hustled with him over to Amanda Mae. At least three times the diner owner pulled herself together, then broke down and cried some more. When the fire was out, the firefighters told her they would stay behind to ensure no residual sparks reignited, but she should go home.

Cade and Suzanne walked her to her sister's house, where her niece Gloria met them at the door. Doc came by with something to help Amanda Mae sleep. Holding the two pills, she hugged Suzanne and Cade then excused herself to get a shower and go to bed.

Suzanne and Cade found her Mercedes, which, aside from a bit of soot, was fine. She drove him to his mom's SUV and then followed him to the ranch. In the echoing marble-floored foyer of his big house, he tossed his mom's keys to the cherrywood table beneath a huge mirror.

"Since my mom is in the suite I'd planned to give you, I'll show you to a room you can use tonight."

"I'd rather be by Mitzi."

"My mom's a light sleeper. She'll get up with Mitzi if she cries." He headed up the stairs. "But if it will make you feel any better, I'll put you in the suite beside hers."

"It would."

"Great."

She didn't miss the sarcasm in his voice. She knew he wasn't happy she'd told Amanda Mae she was staying at his ranch, but she didn't want Amanda Mae to worry. Plus, she would be out of his house as quickly as she could find an apartment. There was no reason for him to be snippy.

They walked the length of a long hall and he opened the door on a pretty blue suite for her.

"Thank you. It's lovely."

He said, "Peachy," then turned, took the three steps across the hall and opened the door.

"That's your room?"

"Yep. You're right across the hall."

Memories of their kiss on the beach trembled through her. Though she was absolutely positive he wanted nothing to do with her, she also knew they were attracted to each other. And though this bedroom was only for one night, the room he would put her into for the next week or so until she found her own place was only a few more feet down the hall. They weren't so close as to be able to hear the rustle of sheets, but they were close enough that, if temptation arose, either one of them could take a short walk to find the other.

A little crackle sparked through her bloodstream.

This was ridiculous. They didn't want to be attracted. Still, there was no denying chemistry. Look what they'd done on the beach. Shared a kiss so hot they could have raised fog off the ocean. It wasn't wise to tempt fate.

"Don't you have another room you can put me in?"

"Thought you wanted to be by the baby?"

"Don't you have another room to put me and the baby?"

He opened his door with a small shove of his shoulder.

"Nope. That's the only one with a crib. I'm not running a day care here."

With that he stepped inside his room and closed the door. Foreboding rustled through her like the wind rustles through leaves before a storm, but she straightened her shoulders and went into her temporary suite.

He might be attracted, but he wasn't interested. Except maybe sexually. But neither she nor Cade would be stupid enough to play with fire.

Still, she intended to be out of his house long before it became an issue. And while she was here she could simply downplay their attraction.

Tired from staying up past four, and without Mizti to wake her, Suzanne slept until nine o'clock the next morning. When she woke, she panicked until she remembered Cade's mom had Mitzi. She sprang out of bed to find them, but realized she had nothing to wear but the filthy, smoky clothes she'd taken off the night before when she'd showered.

After a quick search, she found a fluffy white robe in the closet, and, using the comb in her purse, she managed to tidy her hair.

But she didn't waste time on makeup. She raced from her room and knocked on the door of the suite beside hers, the room Cade's mom had shared with Mitzi. But no one answered. Realizing they were probably already up and about, she ran down the wide spiral staircase, through the echoing marble foyer and to the hall, where she stopped.

She had no idea where Ginny and Mitzi were. The house was huge and it wasn't the only place they could be. There were barns, stables, a swimming pool, ponds. They could be anywhere.

Still, going to the only room she knew—the big office where she'd had her fateful conversation with Cade—didn't seem wise.

Except, he'd probably know where his mother was with Mitzi.

With a deep breath, she strode to the office and found him sitting behind the massive desk. Color suddenly warmed her cheeks. Not only did she remember what he'd been planning the last time they were in this room, but also she was practically naked beneath this robe. And he would know that.

This was not the way to downplay their attraction.

A dark-haired man in a suit sat on one of the chairs in front of the desk. Seeing her, he rose.

Cade rose, too. His eyes made a quick trip down her robe-covered body. "Suzanne."

She clutched the collar more tightly together. "Where is everybody?"

"If you mean Mitzi," Cade said, pretending great interest in something on his desk, as if using his search as a way to keep his eyes off her, "my mom is feeding her breakfast on the patio by the pool."

She turned to race away, but Cade stopped her. "Hey, before you go, I want you to meet Eric."

She stopped, faced them again. "Eric?"

The young man in the dark suit nodded slightly. "Nice to meet you, ma'am."

"Eric is my personal assistant. I just gave him the rundown on your situation. He'll lead the search for accounts your grandmother might have set up for you that you don't know about."

She'd forgotten about that. "Oh."

"You authorized it."

She swallowed. "Yes. I remember."

"Don't scowl as if you've made a deal with the devil. Using my staff is just a way to save you some money." His voice shifted, changed, and laughter filled it as he said, "Money which you need, since you're now partner in a restaurant."

"Diner," Suzanne corrected, straightening her spine. Did he think she was going to bail? Or, worse, did he think she and Amanda Mae were going to fail? "And I'm fine with the promises I made last night."

"Then you'd better get a hitch in your get-along because I'm meeting Amanda Mae in an hour to talk specifics about a lease for the new building."

"An hour?"

"And it takes fifteen minutes to get into town." He sat behind the desk again, pointed at her robe. "By the way, I had someone get the suitcase you took to New York from the truck. It should be outside your bedroom door by now."

Suzanne spun around and headed upstairs. She dressed in jeans and a clean T-shirt then ran to the patio, where she found Ginny sitting at an umbrella-covered table with Mitzi beside her in the high chair.

Shielding her eyes from the sun with one hand, Ginny said, "Cade told me the two of you are going into town."

"Yes. We're meeting with Amanda Mae to talk about a lease for the new diner." Suzanne pulled Mitzi out of the high chair, hugged her and kissed her. "Hey, baby. Your mama's here now."

Drinking deeply of Mitzi's freshly bathed baby scent, she let her gaze fall on the high chair and her brow furrowed in confusion. Why would a single man have a room with a crib and a high chair?

Then she remembered Cade had a half brother. Gino.

The little boy wasn't Darius and Whitney's son. But a half brother.

She hugged her baby again. "Oh, gosh. I missed you."

Ginny laughed. "She missed you, too. She had a screaming fit at about five this morning."

"Why didn't you get me?"

"Because we were fine. And you'd probably just gotten to bed. She took a bottle. I sang her a lullaby and she went right back to sleep."

Reaching over, Ginny tweaked Mitzi's cheek. "You are a precious little princess, aren't you?"

Mitzi giggled.

Surprised, Suzanne caught Ginny's gaze. "She likes you."

"She adores me and we will be fine all day without you."

"All day?"

"You're going into town, remember?"

"Seeing the building and signing the lease shouldn't take more than two hours."

"Honey, there'll be insurance reports for Cade's insurance claim and investigators to deal with. Not to mention an internet search for the new equipment and then there's the time you'll spend with Cade and his lawyer."

She bit her lower lip. "I'd better get going."

She handed the baby back to Cade's mom, but before she could pull away, Ginny caught her hand. "You've never really left her for a whole day before, have you?"

She shook her head.

"We're fine." Ginny's voice softened. "Seriously. This is like a playdate for me, too."

Suzanne laughed and said, "Thanks," before she

walked into the house again. Today she couldn't take Mitzi with her. But pretty soon she would be able to. She already knew Amanda Mae didn't mind having Mitzi in a swing nearby. Plus, as half owner of her own business, she called the shots.

Realizing that if the Andreas brothers had given her a job she would have had to leave her baby like this every morning, she raced up the stairs, grateful that her initial plan had failed.

Maybe she wasn't a jinx after all? Things might go wrong in her life, but good things always seemed to come of them. Her affair with the wrong man had produced a beautiful baby. The Andreas brothers' decision to give her a holding fee for the purchase of her stock rather than a job had resulted in her becoming a business owner.

A business owner!

She had a place.

She belonged somewhere.

Cade kept the meeting at his lawyer's office cool and professional. Amazingly, when it came time to make any decisions, Amanda Mae deferred to Suzanne. At first, Suzanne hesitated. Then Cade watched something shift in her pretty lilac-colored eyes. Her shoulders straightened imperceptibly, as if she'd realized she had to be the stronger partner in her deal with Amanda Mae while she recovered from the shock of losing her business.

As a professional negotiator Cade could have balked over some of Suzanne's suggestions, but as an Andreas brother his priorities were different. He sent his lawyer a quiet signal that whatever Suzanne and Amanda Mae wanted, it was to be done—including that Cade would pay for the construction to turn the empty building into a diner.

Let Nick tell him he wasn't taking care of Andreas family business now. He'd all but handed Suzanne and Amanda Mae a sparkling new building. And—God help him—she was living with him. Just as Nick and Maggie wanted.

They returned to the ranch about three that afternoon and Suzanne headed upstairs to see Mitzi. He didn't follow her. Spending the day watching her eyes light with joy every time he met one of her conditions had turned his nervous system inside out. She glowed as she took the reins of her partnership with Amanda Mae. And every time she grew stronger, more confident, his chest tightened with a strange kind of happiness. Gooey, sappy, it spread from his chest and made him want to strut with pride for being able to help her.

It was just wrong.

Wrong.

He had no intention of getting close to her even though she was about to live with him for the next few weeks while she apartment or house hunted.

Knowing she could find his mom and Mitzi on her own, he walked back to the office where Eric was using his laptop for the search of assets.

"Anything?"

"Nothing so far. Even though I have her social security number, I hit the wall with the banks. I need to have Suzanne sign some releases. Then I'll go to the banks Martha Caldwell used most often, releases in hand, and we'll see what's what."

He fell to the sofa. "Sounds like a plan." But after only ten minutes of listening to Eric catch him up on things that had happened that day, he began to twitch, and he realized he was listening for Suzanne. Had she found the baby? Was the baby all right? Had his mom been okay watching her all day?

He sighed and hoisted himself off the couch. Convinced it was the good host in him that was making him feel odd that he'd simply walked away from his guest, he headed out of the office. Damn his mother for drilling manners into him.

"I've gotta go check on Suzanne."

Eric grinned stupidly. "Sure. Fine. The rest of this can wait."

He nearly sighed again. Did *everybody* think he had a crush on Suzanne?

Taking the steps two at a time, he scowled. Of course they did. Because he was acting like a ninny about her. And after that earth-shattering kiss he might as well admit it. He *did* have a crush on Suzanne. A stupid crush. *Crush.* Infatuation. Not serious emotional attachment. They hadn't known each other long enough for him to have anything more than a sexual attraction. Sure, he'd realized they had something in common when he recognized her desire to make something of herself matched his own, but that was just one thing. There were too many good reasons to stay away from her to fall victim to an itty-bitty attraction.

Of course, there was the weird happy feeling he'd gotten watching her that day….

He scowled again. Seriously. Was even he going to question himself?

When he reached her door, he knocked twice. Knowing there was a small sitting room before the bedroom—so he wouldn't inadvertently catch her naked, but also she might not hear his knock—he turned the knob and opened the door.

Suzanne was halfway to the door, smiling from ear to ear. "Hey."

"Hey." He nodded at the baby she held. "Everything okay?"

"Yeah. She's great." She hugged Mitzi to her. "She loves your mom."

He hovered in the doorway. "Room okay?"

"It's lovely. Perfect." She glanced around at the comfy yellow sofa draped with a white angora afghan, the big-screen TV that could be hidden in the cherrywood armoire, the plush Persian rug on the floor grounding the grouping. "Actually, it's huge. My grandmother had some fancy suites, but this one is spectacular. That bathroom is to die for. And a baby bath? Whoever thought of that was just a genius."

He leaned against the doorjamb, hating the male pride that bubbled up in him at seeing how happy she was, and pretending he didn't feel it. "Yeah, it's nice."

"It's like the nursery is part of the suite." She frowned and gave him a puzzled look. "Do you sleep in here when Gino is here with you?" Her frown deepened. "Oh, wait. He has a nanny who probably sleeps here...." She stopped again. "Gino's only two and this house is older than two years old." She glanced around, as if disoriented. "Was Gino even born when you built this house?"

He cleared his throat. "No. Putting a nursery in was just a commonsense thing at the time. If you're okay, I'm going to go back to Eric. We have tons of work to do. I eat at seven. If you want to join me, fine. If you want to eat sooner or later just tell the cook."

With that he left, cursing himself for being an idiot. Suzanne was a smart woman, who, as her confidence grew, was getting smarter by the minute. He could not have a crush on her. She'd figure it out…and then what? They'd be awkward around each other; that's what.

She had to live here for at least two weeks—maybe longer if she decided to buy a house and had to wait to take possession. He could not let her realize he was beginning to like her. So he had to get rid of the crush. Dismiss it. Pretend it had never happened. Because it was foolish. Ridiculous.

He was better than this, smarter than this, stronger than to fall victim to some idiotic crush.

Suzanne joined him for dinner that night, but Mitzi was fussy so she didn't get through the salad before she had to take the baby and run. Cade alerted the staff and finished his meal, but with every course he got more and more antsy. Mitzi wasn't a fusser. What if there was something wrong?

Telling himself he was simply concerned, he tossed his napkin to the table and made his way to Suzanne's suite. He hesitated. But knowing he wasn't about to walk away, he rolled his eyes and knocked on the door. If he didn't do this now, he'd just come up again later. Might as well indulge his curiosity and get it over with.

Within seconds Suzanne answered, holding naked Mitzi, who was wrapped in a terry cloth blanket.

"Everything okay?"

"Everything's fine." She turned and headed for the nursery. "Mitzi's a baby. She doesn't believe in anybody's schedule but her own. Right now she wants a bath and to go to bed. I don't get a say in it."

Following her into the bright green room with a matching white crib and changing table, and his mother's old oak rocker, he grunted. "What's with the blanket?"

"You mean the towel? Would you hold a naked baby without some protection against an accident?"

He laughed.

She paused and nudged her head in the direction of the baby's bathroom. "Come on. I'm serious. We have only seconds here before she does something we could potentially regret."

He followed. Slowly. For a guy who was determined not to have a crush on this woman, following her was equal parts of smart and stupid. It was stupid because every second he spent in her presence meant possible discovery. But smart because there was no room in this house that reminded him of his thwarted life plan with Ashley more than this suite. And maybe he needed a reminder of what a man was really supposed to feel for a woman. This sexual thing he had going for Suzanne was only part of a relationship. It would be wrong to make a fool of himself over a crush that was based on very little more than the fact that she had a hot little body.

His heart sort of hiccuped when he entered the bathroom that had been built off the nursery of the master suite—the bathroom his wife had designed—and everything fell into place in his head again. This room had been built for his babies. Having a stranger use it was a potent reminder that he'd never have a child. Especially not with Suzanne. Because he didn't love her. He *wouldn't* love her. He'd never again love the way he'd loved Ashley and he hadn't been a good husband to her, so how could he expect he'd treat Suzanne any better? She deserved more.

She *did* deserve more. She was a nice woman who had a baby who needed a daddy. Not some jaded old cowboy.

Suzanne lowered Mitzi into the waist-high baby tub that had been installed beside the sink. "I'm telling you, this place is a mother's dream."

Happiness swam through him at her praise, but at least this time he understood it. It wasn't wrong to be glad to see the bathroom put to good use. It was pragmatic. For the past two years he'd felt this part of his house was a waste. It was good to see a baby in the tub. Good to see the well-designed space making a mom happy.

Mitzi splashed in the water.

Suzanne gently tweaked her nose. "You love this, don't you?"

He cleared his throat. Now that he had his priorities straight, he could actually converse with her without feeling like his hormones were going to take him down all the wrong roads.

"Gino loves a bath, too."

"Oh, so you've bathed him here!"

"Actually, he's never even been to Texas, let alone to the house. I've had the honor of bathing him when I visit him in Montauk."

She laughed. "Ah, building memories with your little brother."

"That's what Whitney and Darius call it. I call it more like survival of the fittest."

"He's a splasher?"

"Yeah, he is."

She ran a small pink sponge along Mitzi's body as the baby slapped her hands in the water and babbled, not paying any attention to her mom. It seemed Suzanne was bathing the baby without Mitzi noticing.

Cade smiled. This was good. Really good. The little reminder that Suzanne deserved better than him seemed to have turned off all his unwanted feelings. He only felt positive, happy things.

He pushed away from the door frame. "Well, if you don't need anything…"

She peeked back at him. "We don't. We're fine."

"Okay, then I've got to catch up on the rest of what I missed today."

"Eric is still here?"

"No. He goes home at six. Sharp. Every day. He'll come back if I want him to. He'll work seven days a week if I need him to. But he's got a big dumb dog who has to be let out to pee at six-fifteen."

Suzanne laughed. The sound filled the bathroom like music. "That's adorable."

Panic fluttered in Cade's stomach. He wasn't supposed to love her laugh. "Dog's ugly as sin."

She shook her head and went back to rinsing Mitzi. "Those are the best."

He swallowed. Sucked in a breath. Reminded himself that getting involved with her would be cheating her, so he wasn't allowed to have these feelings.

It didn't work. One glance at her bathing the baby and the fluttery feeling in his stomach intensified.

So maybe it was time to suck it up and spend a few minutes talking, so he could grow accustomed to her voice, her laugh…everything. Then there'd be nothing new about her to resurrect emotions he didn't want to have.

"He named the damned thing Ostentatious."

For that Suzanne turned and grinned at him. "Eric named his dog Ostentatious?"

There. See? That wasn't so hard.

"He says the dog always makes a grand entrance, but I'm guessing what he makes are big messes."

Satisfied that his crush was losing some of its power, he turned to go, but Suzanne said, "Cade?"

He stopped, faced her again.

"Thanks. I know you did me and Amanda Mae some favors today."

He grunted. He had billions of dollars, using a few of those dollars to make sure two women got a chance with a new business shouldn't feel like a favor. It should be common sense. So why had his chest just swelled with pride once more?

"Don't mention it."

She smiled. And his heart did a silly flip-flop.

Damn it! The crush was still very firmly in place.

It looked like he had two choices. Option one? Ignore her. Now that their business was done and he knew her suite was adequate, he didn't even have to be in the same room with her.

Option two? Spend so much time with her that she stopped being special. Attractive. Unique. Fun.

Mitzi dropped the plastic ball she was gnawing on and it fell to the floor. Suzanne bent to scoop it up and Cade's eyes followed the smooth flow of her back and the rounding of her bottom as she reached to retrieve it.

He turned and scooted away.

For now, ignoring seemed like the better plan.

Though Cade avoided Suzanne all day Wednesday, the pull that night was too strong to defy. Still, he'd refused to go to her room. Instead, he asked Mrs. Reynolds, his house manager, if Suzanne had eaten.

"Miss Suzanne and Miss Mitzi ate around five-thirty. Mrs. Granger made a special pudding for Mitzi, which the baby gobbled up." She laughed lightly. "Then they played by the pool for an hour before retiring to their suite."

Hearing that stodgy Mrs. Reynolds hadn't been able to resist watching them either, Cade didn't feel nearly so foolish when he had to fight himself to keep from climbing the stairs to check on them.

What was it about babies and new moms that brought out the protective instincts?

God only knew. Not only were Nick and Maggie overly concerned about her, but his staff also had it bad. Mrs. Reynolds kept tabs on her. The cook made special food for them. If Eric started acting all sappy and mushy, Cade would know his entire household had gone around the bend.

He forced himself to stay in the family room, playing video football for two hours, absolutely positive Suzanne and baby would be asleep by the time he went to his room. But when he walked upstairs, the door to Suzanne's suite was slightly ajar.

He sighed.

Don't do it! Do not check on her! Every person on the staff has checked on her. Your own mother called to be sure they were okay. They are okay. You do not need to check!

Of their own volition, his feet wandered to her door. His knuckles tapped twice. The door creaked open a bit more, and there were Suzanne and Mitzi watching TV.

"Hey."

"Hey!" Suzanne rose from the sofa, bringing Mitzi up with her. "You have some timing. Last night you hit bath time. Tonight I'm just about to feed her a bottle and rock her to sleep."

"I was only going to ask how things went today with

Amanda Mae. I'm guessing the shock has worn off and reality is setting in. I wanted to make sure you were dealing okay." How he'd come up with such a reasonable explanation for his presence on such short notice, Cade didn't know. But he was proud of himself. "Seeing as how you're busy, I'll go."

"No." She motioned him to follow her. "I can talk while I'm feeding her."

"Won't that defeat the purpose?"

"What purpose?"

"Aren't you trying to get her to fall asleep?"

"She's already dead on her feet. Once she starts drinking her bottle, there won't be enough noise on the planet to keep her awake. One conversation won't bother her."

They talked about Amanda Mae while Mitzi guzzled her milk. She burped, then Suzanne let her have the bottle again. This time, she drank slower. Her eyelids drooped until she fell asleep.

When Suzanne glanced up, Cade was staring longingly at Mitzi.

The whole situation confused her. She knew Cade was attracted to her, but didn't want to be. His way of dealing with her seemed to be ignoring her. She'd decided that was as good a plan as any and she'd given him a wide berth. But this was the second night that he'd come into their suite.

To see Mitzi.

He'd told her that he wanted her to keep the baby out of his way, but he was the one who kept finding them because he clearly liked the baby. Which was so cute she couldn't really fault him for it.

"Wanna lay her in the crib?"

He caught her gaze. "I'll wake her."

"I told you. She's a heavy sleeper."

He swallowed.

Suzanne saw such raw emotion, such raw pain in his eyes that things fell into place for her. "You built this suite of rooms for yourself and your wife, didn't you?"

"It doesn't matter."

"Sure it does. I don't think you get this, but I can see you're drawn to Mitzi…drawn here. To this suite. I think because you're curious."

He turned away. "A bit."

"There's no shame in that."

He snorted a laugh. "Suzanne, let it go."

"No. Just give in to the feelings. Everybody loves a sweet baby and Mitzi's one of the sweetest. Why don't you let yourself admit you enjoy having a baby around?"

This time, when he faced her he was not laughing. "Let…it…go."

She laid Mitzi in her crib and walked over to Cade. "You think you scare me?" She snickered. "Seriously. Only a little over a week ago, I was facing the possibility of sleeping in my car. You're going to have to do a little better than scowl."

"Okay, how about this?" He stepped closer, so close she could feel the heat of his body. "The reason I keep coming in here is because I have a crush on you."

She blinked. "What?"

"A crush. The hots. Call it what you want but I'd love to sleep with you."

She stepped back. Cleared her throat. She already knew that. He'd warned her off the night he'd kissed her. She just didn't think discussing it would do either of them any good. Still, she had to say something. "So you're telling me you're not coming in to see Mitzi?"

"No. I'm telling you that everything in my well-ordered life has been tossed in the air because of you." He turned away. Ran his fingers through his thick dark hair, spiking it. Then he spun to face her again. "I accepted my wife's death. I accepted that I'd never have kids. That my fate was to take care of my town. The people. And then you popped up and now everything's confused."

Suzanne frowned, backtracking to the most important thing he'd buried in his rant. "You can't have kids?"

"Don't know. We'd just begun tests to see why Ashley hadn't gotten pregnant in eight years of marriage when we found her cancer." He turned away. "Never seemed to be a reason to get myself tested after that."

"So you might actually be able to have kids?"

He shrugged. "Maybe."

"So don't torture yourself. Go get tested."

He spun to face her. "I think you're missing the big picture here. It doesn't matter. I was a bad husband. I'm not going to remarry. And I'm certainly not going to have kids with no mama."

"Why does that makes you mad at me?"

He took her chin, lifted her face until she caught his gaze. "I want to look at you only as somebody to sleep with. Then I could deal with you. Then I could get you in my bed or decide against it."

Her eyebrow arched skeptically. "I have no say."

He laughed softly. "If I decided I wanted you in my bed you would be there."

His tone made her swallow.

"But you have a baby. A little girl who reminds me how much I wanted to be a dad. To have sons. Boys to teach. Children to leave my legacy. And I'm not clear about anything anymore. Ashley was the love of my life. The woman I wanted to be the mother of my children. Without her, these rooms aren't supposed to tempt me."

"Maybe it's not the room." She didn't know how she got so bold, but the answer seemed glaringly easy to her. She stepped closer, mimicking his movement when he'd tried to intimidate her, showing him she wasn't afraid. "Maybe it's the situation. Since I'm as tempted by you as you are by me, then I don't see your problem."

He gaped at her. "I told you. I was a crappy husband."

That made her laugh. "You know what? I'm starting to think that's just an excuse. You're a nice guy. I see it every day. You bought a whole town so nobody would have to pay property taxes. You gave me and Amanda Mae more than a couple of breaks on our deal and you won't one-up your brothers and buy my stock. Face it, Cade. You're a nice guy."

He took a step closer, putting them so close they were just about touching. "You wanna test that, little girl?"

Her voice shook the tiniest bit when she said, "Yes," because she'd seen his kindnesses not just to her but to Amanda Mae, and his brothers. And he liked Mitzi. Wanted to be a dad. No matter how he saw himself, he was a good guy. He might have been a crappy husband to his wife, but it appeared her death had changed him. "I like you and you like me. Why shouldn't we do something about how we feel?"

"Because I'm being kind to you. Smart in the way I treat you."

"What if I don't want you to be smart?"

"You'd better. I don't intend to ever marry again and

you need a husband. But if you push me, I might not be able to walk away from what you're offering."

Her breath stalled. No man had ever worried that he wouldn't be able to resist her. The mere thought sent a shiver of excitement down her spine, liquefied her knees. He stood so close that if she lifted her hand she could touch the stubble on his chin and cheeks. If she rose to her tiptoes she could kiss him.

Renewed boldness blossomed in her, along with an incredible need. What would it be like to make love with a man who desperately desired her?

Heaven?

Or maybe hell. He'd been very clear that he didn't intend to remarry. And just as he'd said, she needed more from a relationship than just sex. She wanted a husband. She couldn't get into a relationship with another man who didn't want forever. She needed someone to cherish her. Love her. Be her partner.

And maybe that was the real bottom line. She wanted a partner and he was offering a roll in the hay.

She stepped back, away from him. "You're right."

"Damn straight, I'm right."

He left quickly and Suzanne fell to her bed in dismay. Wonderful sensations still rumbled through her. Longing she'd never felt before. But fool me once, shame on you. Fool me twice, shame on me. She'd never again fall for a man who didn't want her.

Completely.

For good.

One Bill Baker was enough to last a lifetime.

CHAPTER EIGHT

THURSDAY MORNING AS SUZANNE drove up to the brand-new building that she and Amanda Mae had leased from Cade, everything about her new project suddenly became real for her.

She wasn't just a diner owner on paper. She was a diner owner for real. She sat in her car, staring at the building, with realizations knocking into each other like dominoes. By partnering with Amanda Mae she'd made decisions beyond offering money and agreeing to work. She was creating a life here, in this town. About to buy a house or find an apartment. About to interact with most of the people who lived in Whiskey Springs, if only because the diner was the only place to eat out. About to be an active resident of the town owned by Cade.

She laid her head on the steering wheel in dismay. No wonder he had been so skittish, so agitated when she offered Amanda Mae a partnership. She had, without consciously deciding to, edged herself into his world.

She pressed her fingers to her temples, thinking it through and decided it was too late to call back her choices. She would simply have to learn to coexist with Cade.

And he'd have to learn to coexist with her.

Once she moved out of his house that should be more

than possible. In the five days she'd worked as a waitress, he'd only come into the diner once. Surely, they
could handle seeing each other once a week.

Shoving her shoulder against her car door, she got
out, bounded into the building and discovered Amanda
Mae was already inside.

"So, Joey, I want the kitchen to be right here."

A man Suzanne had never met jotted notes on a small
pad of paper. Wearing a pair of brown coveralls and big
work boots, he had to be a representative of one of the
construction companies they'd chosen to ask for bids
on the work required to turn an empty building into a
diner.

Suzanne handed Amanda Mae a cup of coffee she'd
picked up for her at the convenience store. "Is this one
of the people who will be bidding on the renovations
for the diner?"

The man looked up sharply, as if startled by Suzanne's
question.

Amanda Mae popped the lid on her coffee. "He's the
guy who'll actually be doing the work."

"I thought we'd agreed with Cade to go out for
bids?"

"Yes, but my niece Jennifer's husband called last
night saying Joey needed a job."

So many facts assaulted Suzanne that she didn't know
which one to focus on. She understood Amanda Mae
wasn't herself. Her entire world had gone up in smoke.
She had a right to do things that were a little impulsive,
even irrational. But they'd promised Cade they'd go out
for bids, and after the conversation the night before, she
did not want to cross him.

"But the agreement we signed with Cade—"

"It's irrelevant. I've seen Joey's work. He's the best in town. Cade will want the best."

Joey glanced at her and smiled sheepishly.

"I'm sure he will. But a bidding process—"

"Would be a waste of time since the guy who is the best is available." Amanda Mae turned to Joey. "So, how long will this take?"

"If I get the right crew, I can probably have this done in six weeks, maybe a month."

Amanda Mae gasped. "Six weeks! I can't go that long without an income."

In all the confusion, Suzanne had forgotten Amanda Mae needed money, so her rushing to get this moving faster made perfect sense. It was an argument she could give to Cade for why she'd broken their agreement. But more than that, Suzanne had a resolution for that problem, too.

She tapped Amanda Mae's arm. "Actually, I have an idea. In the city a lot of vendors provide breakfasts, lunches and snacks with carts. I thought we'd try our luck on the internet and see if we could find a cart for a reasonable price—"

"Or I could make you a small stand in front of the building here," Joey said. "No charge except for materials," he added, catching Suzanne's gaze, as if telling her he appreciated her letting him have the job. "And you could sell your things from that. Right outside the new building that you want customers to come to anyway."

Suzanne brightened. Not just because he was building it for nothing, but because he'd thought it through. Her confidence in the town's best builder grew. "That's great."

Amanda Mae was not quite so enthusiastic. "Yeah, but where are we going to cook the food?"

"We can't "cook" anything. We'll have to sell things like sandwiches that we can put together in the stand." She smiled at Amanda Mae. "Plus, I'm sure Mrs. Granger will let me use her kitchen to make a batch of cinnamon rolls every morning."

"Thought you said people would grow tired of them."

"Thought you said they wouldn't."

Amanda Mae sighed. "Okay."

Suzanne frowned. She might have agreed but her tone was dull, listless. Selling sandwiches from a stand outside the future diner was a fantastic idea. Amanda Mae should be jumping for joy. But she wasn't.

She glanced over at her partner, genuine concern squeezing her heart. If getting a substitute income from a sandwich stand hadn't perked her up, then Suzanne was going to have to think harder, be smarter, figure out ways to show her everything was going to work out.

They spent the rest of the day on the internet, using Gloria's laptop to begin looking for appliances, pots and pans and utensils for the diner, as well as supplies to equip their interim sandwich stand. Needing the things for the stand immediately, they ordered those items that day, and actually got an overnight delivery on most of them. It was expensive, but they would be back in business on Monday morning.

By the time Suzanne returned to the ranch, she was exhausted. But she knew she had to go to Cade's office to tell him she and Amanda Mae had hired a contractor.

With a deep breath for courage, she turned and walked down the hall. As always, Cade sat at the huge mahogany desk. When she knocked on his door frame, he glanced up.

"Yes?"

"We hired a contractor today."

Obviously annoyed, he put down his pen. "I thought you were going out for bids?"

"Joey Montinegro was available."

Cade picked up his pen again. "Oh, well, okay, then."

She took a step into his office. "I take it this guy is good?"

"The best."

"Thank goodness. Amanda Mae hired him this morning without telling me." She took another step into the room. She knew he wanted to avoid her, but he was the closest thing she had to a mentor and she was worried about Amanda Mae. Maybe he'd have some advice. "It was the weirdest thing. All day long she behaved oddly. Not like herself at all."

"She just lost her business. She's bound to have a few moody days."

"This went beyond moody. She seems really sad."

He sucked in a breath, but didn't look up. "She probably is. Creating a new diner and even having a partner are risky. She has to be worried that you guys could fail."

"She did mention not having an income until we open, but we're opening a sandwich stand right outside the new building. In a few days we'll have an income."

He busied himself with the work on his desk again. "Just give her some time. She'll rebound. People have nowhere else to go to eat but that diner. Soon she'll remember that and she'll be fine."

"Okay."

She waited for him to say something else, but he didn't. She tried to think of something else to say, anything to make her presence less awkward, and couldn't.

"Okay, then. I'll just go to my room and play with Mitzi."

She turned to go, but he said, "Suzanne?"

"Yes?"

"Will you be joining me for dinner?"

There wasn't one spark of anything in his dark eyes. No attraction. No recognition. No interest. He'd made up his mind, shored up his defenses. There'd be no more personal conversations, no getting to know each other. That was how he intended to coexist.

She could probably eat with him that night, but they'd be like two awkward strangers.

Her heart tweaked a little in disappointment, but deep down inside she knew it was for the best.

"No. I'll get something after I have Mitzi settled."

But Mitzi wouldn't settle that evening and the once-comfortable suite became unbearably cramped. Because she'd come home early, she'd already spent hours stuck in three rooms and suddenly she couldn't do it anymore. Glancing out the window, she saw a series of sidewalks and trails that led to stables and corrals off in the distance. She changed Mitzi's diaper, put on her scruffy tennis shoes and headed out for a walk.

Her "walk" ended up taking twenty minutes. By the time she arrived, she was breathless. Hindsight was always twenty-twenty, but she wished she'd thought far enough ahead not to sell her stroller in the big sale she'd had to earn money to pay off her grandmother's debts and taxes.

She paused, admiring the flower beds that skirted the thin concrete road, pleased that someone had taken the time to make the place pretty.

"See these?" she said to Mitzi. "They're petunias."

"Sweet Williams, up by the barn."

She glanced around, confused because she hadn't actually seen anybody as she walked up. She still didn't see anyone.

"Down here."

An older man, probably in his late fifties, rose from behind a huge flowering bush. "Jim Malloy. I'm foreman here. And you're—"

"Suzanne Caldwell." Because he'd pulled off his gloves, she extended her hand to shake his.

He shook his head and smiled broadly. "Hands are still a little too dirty for shaking. Can't say I recognize your name."

"I'm partnering with Amanda Mae Fisher on the diner. Cade's letting me live here."

"Ah, you're the heiress."

She snorted a laugh. "If that much gossip has reached you here back at the barns, then you also know I didn't inherit any money."

"But you did get a big block of stock." He grinned. "Andreas Holdings stock. That probably put a burr in Cade's shorts."

She laughed. It wasn't funny that her being a shareholder of Andreas Holdings stock made Cade angry, but she loved the slang of this area. It provided a vivid, probably accurate picture of how Cade felt. She also loved the people of Whiskey Springs. Warm. Friendly. Genuine. Sometimes painfully honest. But she'd had so much dishonesty in her life lately that, even painful, the honesty was refreshing.

He pointed at Mitzi. "So who is this?"

She proudly presented her baby. "This is my daughter, Mitzi."

"Well, aren't you just the sweetest little thing?" He glanced at Suzanne again. "How old?"

"Six months…heading toward seven. It's really hard to keep up with baby ages. At first we counted in weeks, which was a dilly to try to figure out. Now counting months is nearly as hard."

"Yeah, it is." He glanced down at his dirty hands. "Wish I could hold her."

The regret in his voice hit Suzanne right in the heart. With his gray hair and kindly weathered face, he looked and acted like a well-loved grandfather. The sort of grandfather she'd always dreamed about but never had. She'd been so happy to have at least one living relative that she'd never told anyone about her secret longing for a granddad.

But suddenly that dream morphed and took a different shape. Because she had no relatives, her baby wouldn't ever have a grandmother or grandfather. No cousins. No aunts. No uncles. No father. She wished for a grandfather just like Jim Malloy for Mitzi, then stopped herself. She had to stop connecting herself to Cade. This guy was his ranch foreman. For both of their sakes, once she got a house in town, she'd have to stay away from anything connected to Cade.

"I guess I'd better get back. If Cade comes up to my room to say good-night, he might worry if I'm not there."

"You didn't tell him you were leaving the house?"

"No. I sneaked out. You could say he's really not happy to have me underfoot."

Jim peered over at her. "It's not like Cade to be unhappy about having a pretty girl around."

"We sort of bring out the worst in each other." Feeling odd talking about Cade with one of his employees, she changed the subject. "It doesn't matter." She nodded at the flowers at their feet. "By the way, I think it was a great idea to pretty up the area with flower beds."

He sighed, looked skyward. "It wasn't my idea. It was my daughter's." He caught her gaze. "I tend them for her now that she's gone."

It took a second, but only a second, for that to sink in. "You're Cade's wife's father? Ashley's dad?"

His eyes narrowed. "So he told you about her?"

She cleared her throat, made a mental note never to walk to the barns again and quietly said, "He spoke very highly of her. He loved her...I think he still does love her. She must have been a wonderful person."

"She was."

Suzanne saw tears fill his eyes and took a step back. "I should probably return to the house."

He said nothing, simply knelt down again and went back to weeding.

Walking beside flower beds that wound along a road that led almost to Cade's house, she suddenly understood why he couldn't consider another relationship. Reminders of his deceased wife were all around him... and so was her father. A father who'd never move on from the death of his daughter. A father who would mourn the loss forever.

A father who might also remind Cade he hadn't been such a wonderful husband.

The following Monday, Suzanne woke early, made her cinnamon rolls and headed for the sandwich stand. This was the day they would open for business. After stocking the stand on Friday and Saturday, she'd spent all day Sunday at the ranch, avoiding Cade, so it felt blissfully wonderful to have somewhere to go.

When she arrived, Amanda Mae was already there. "Give me those beauties," she said, taking a tray of cinnamon rolls from Suzanne's hands. "People are lining up."

Suzanne laughed. "And you've been worried that we'd fail."

Amanda Mae sighed. "All right. I get it. I know I was a bit of trouble last week, but I'm okay now and we need to get selling. So I'll say I'm sorry I was a grouch and we can get to work."

She turned to leave but Suzanne caught her arm, refusing to let her go without really talking this out. "You weren't a grouch. You were concerned about the future. I understand. I've been through a loss or two myself. I'm guessing I was probably a little hard to get along with after my grandmother died. Maybe even when I first came to Whiskey Springs."

Amanda Mae chuckled. "So, we're even?"

Suzanne smiled. "I think we're better than even." But as Amanda Mae carried her tray of rolls to the stand, Suzanne said, "Actually, I could use your help with something else."

Setting the tray of rolls in the front of the display case so everyone could see them, Amanda Mae said, "What?"

"Finding someplace to live."

For that Amanda Mae turned around. "You're leaving Cade's?"

"I was only supposed to stay there until I found a place. But we've been so busy I haven't even started looking for a house or an apartment. Now I've got to get moving."

"You have any money?"

"They gave me a nice chunk of change to hold my

stock. Lots of it went for diner equipment and things for this stand. Lots more is going for taxes. But I have a bit left. As long as I don't get carried away, I'll be fine."

"And pretty soon we should be making enough that we can both take a salary."

"Yeah. That's right. Pretty soon I'm going to get a salary!"

Amanda Mae laughed. "Okay, then I'll make a few calls."

Cade left the office that afternoon at three. He was tired of working, and one of the perks of being rich was that if he didn't feel like doing anything, he didn't have to.

He headed outside to the pool house, intending to change into trunks and enjoy what was left of the gorgeous day. The sky was blue. The sun was hot. And he owned a swimming pool he rarely used. So today was the day.

But when he stepped onto the patio, he found his mom and Mitzi. He'd almost forgotten about them.

He ambled over. "Hey."

His mom peered up at him over her sunglasses. "Hey. What are you doing out here?"

"Don't feel like working." He stooped down in front of Mitzi who sat in a pack-and-play under a huge umbrella. "How's it going for you today, kid?"

She gurgled a laugh.

"Does she go into the pool?"

"She loves the pool." She pointed to a small box past the pack-and-play. "See, she has two floaties and a turtle."

"What the devil is a turtle?"

"It's a one-piece suit that's a life jacket for a baby. I saw one on the internet and couldn't resist buying it."

She held up the garment that looked like it was stuffed with foam blocks. "See? It's padded enough and covers so much that it sort of looks like a tortoise shell when she puts it on."

He laughed. "Great. Give me two minutes to change and I'll take her in the pool with me."

"Actually, Cade, I'd appreciate if you could finish watching her for the day. I made dinner plans with Mary Louise Marks and I'd sort of like to slide by the beautician for a trim before I go."

Cade laughed. "Let me change into a suit and I'll give you your freedom."

He ran to the pool house and put on trunks. By the time he came out, his mom had not only stuffed Mitzi into the one-piece swimmer, she'd also gathered her things and was ready to go.

"You're not getting tired of this, are you?"

"No. But I have been neglecting the bookstore. Babysitting for Suzanne came up so quickly I never had time to look at my calendar. There may be more days I can't babysit."

Cade waved a hand in dismissal. "We have a staff here. You don't need to be here every hour of every day. From now on, just come and go as you want. The staff and I will work it out."

"Thanks." She kissed his cheek then scampered off.

He carried Mitzi toward the shallow end of the pool. "You know that outfit makes you look fat, right?"

Mitzi giggled.

He grinned. "Finally, a woman who doesn't obsess about her weight."

Mitzi laughed again.

Cade waded into the pool, then, holding Mitzi

under the arms, he skimmed her over the surface of the water.

She giggled with delight. A fluffy feeling invaded his chest. He let her dip a little deeper and she screeched.

He pulled her out of the pool and examined her face. "Is that good or bad?"

She giggled.

"Okay. Good."

He dipped her again. They played in the pool for at least an hour then Cade took her out and sat down with her on the chaise lounge. She was so small, so soft and so sweet. Part of him couldn't help longing to take care of her. To be the one to teach her to ride a pony. To be the one to teach her to swim. To be the one to pace the floor when she went on her first date.

But he couldn't. He knew he couldn't. Soon Suzanne would move out, taking Mitzi with her.

Still, he cuddled the baby closer. What was the harm in enjoying the few minutes or days he might get with her? None.

Mitzi fell asleep on his chest and he slid his arm over her, making sure she stayed put, before his own eyelids began to droop.

And that was how Suzanne found them. Her baby girl cuddled up to Cade, sleeping soundly. For several minutes she just stood staring at them, her own wishes and yearnings floating through her. It was so hard to believe Cade thought he was a bad person that at times like this she wanted to shake him silly and make him see he wasn't. But she also knew herself. She sometimes saw the good in people when there was none. And she couldn't be fooled a second time.

Still, he looked so cute with a baby. And Mitzi looked so cute with a daddy.

With a sigh of longing, she walked over to the chaise and as carefully as possible lifted Mitzi from his chest.

He immediately woke. "Hey—" He blinked, recognized who she was and said, "Sorry about that."

"What? I'm the one who should be sorry for not being here with my own child." She glanced around. "Where's your mom?"

"She had an appointment this afternoon. So I took over the job as babysitter."

Suzanne gasped. "I'm so sorry!"

He shifted on the chaise. "We have a staff. It's not like you're putting anybody out. In fact, my mom told me today she has a few things she needs to do at the bookstore and I told her not to worry. We'll handle Mitzi."

She caught his gaze. "You don't mind?"

He nonchalantly rose from the chaise. There was no way he'd let her see how much he'd enjoyed the afternoon. He didn't want her to get ideas again. He'd play this off as a duty. A task he could assign to his staff. "No. We'll be fine. You just go to work at your regular time and I'll instruct Mrs. Reynolds to be available if my mom needs her."

Wide-awake now, Mitzi squirmed. Full of energy she leaned toward the pool, screeching as if demanding to go back in.

Cade winced. "That's my fault. I let her play in the pool until she pooped out. Now that she's rested, it looks like she wants in again. Sorry."

But Suzanne laughed. "You're sorry you got time to take my little girl for a swim? Right about now I envy you."

She chuckled and headed for her suite, and he ran his hand down his face. She might envy him his free time, but he envied her more. Even with a job that took most of her day, a partner struggling to regain her footing and no home, Suzanne had everything he wanted.

CHAPTER NINE

THE FOLLOWING DAY, SUZANNE came home to find
Ginny with Mitzi as usual. Ginny told her about the
dinner engagement and needing to go to the beautician
and Cade's offer of staff to take care of the baby.

Grateful to both Ginny and Cade, Suzanne said,
"Thanks."

But Ginny brushed off her thanks. "We love her,
Suzanne. The staff actually groans when I come in and
take her."

Confident that no one felt put-upon taking care of
Mitzi, Suzanne didn't worry. The following two nights
she came home to find Mrs. Reynolds with Mitzi. But
the Saturday evening, when she returned home a little
later than normal and a lot more tired because there
had been an unexpected rush for sandwiches for quick
suppers, Cade was walking down the foyer stairway
with Mitzi. In spite of her exhaustion, she couldn't help
noticing how adorable they looked. The gorgeous dark-
haired man with the adorable dark-haired baby. They
could be father and daughter.

Longing tightened her chest, twisted her heart. She
knew it had to be exhaustion that caused that slip, so
she ignored it. "Hey."

"You look like hell."

After fourteen hours making sandwiches, she probably did. She wanted desperately to toss her purse to the foyer table and collapse on the floor. Her second-best desire was to go upstairs, shower and collapse on the bed.

Instead, she clapped her hands to Mitzi. "Come to Mama."

Cade held her away. "I'm serious. You look like hell. When was the last time you slept?"

"Last night."

"Don't try to buffalo me. I know she gets up at night. And I know you set your alarm for five every morning to make cinnamon rolls. When do you sleep?"

The urge to collapse against him and whine nearly overtook her. She'd been a spoiled college student when her grandmother died. Now suddenly she was a single mom, half owner of a diner, and she felt like she was drowning.

But he was not the person to tell. He didn't want to get involved with her. But his kindnesses to Mitzi sometimes had her forgetting that.

"I'm fine." Embarrassed, she took Mitzi from his arms. "I can be a mom and work. Millions of women do it." She shifted to the left, so she could walk around him up the stairs.

"Suzanne—"

She turned, tears pooled in her eyes. She wasn't just tired, she was beginning to see him in ways that weren't right. A father for her child. A confidant for herself. He might think he was a bad person but every day she saw evidence that he wasn't and she was beginning to like him. A lot.

"I'm sorry. I didn't mean to insult you. I was just saying I could keep Mitzi a while longer."

"I'm fine."

But she wasn't. She was tired and swimming in confusion. But she couldn't tell him that. She didn't want to get any closer to him than she already was, like him any more than she already did. And that's all talking would do. Make her like him even more than she already did.

Not wanting to spend another Sunday avoiding Cade, she packed Mitzi in her car. They took a long drive, and eventually drifted over to Amanda Mae's house. She made hot dogs on a grill and they sat on lounge chairs under a tree.

"So are you going to tell me what's bothering you?"

She couldn't really tell Amanda Mae she was exhausted. The woman was twenty years older than she was and not even slightly winded by the amount of work they were doing. Besides, this was her first job and they'd only been working a few weeks. Surely things would get better?

"Nothing. I'm fine."

"No, you're not." Amanda Mae studied her face for a second. "Okay, now I'm gonna go to meddling, but since we haven't been able to find you an apartment I think I know what's troubling you." She paused, sucked in a breath. "I've seen this thing that's been going on between you and Cade."

Suzanne stiffened. "There's nothing going on between me and Cade."

Amanda Mae laughed. "I saw your chemistry with the guy before you did." She laughed again. "Anyway, I'm guessing that has something to do with your sudden appearance at my house today."

Since that was the truth, she couldn't deny it. "Because I'm gone so much, he spends a lot of time with Mitzi." She swallowed. "He's awfully cute with her and she loves him." Her throat suddenly became unbearably tight, but she trudged on because it felt good to finally be able to admit some of this. "After I see them together, I get weird feelings. Like how he'd make a really good dad. But even though he likes me, he's said he doesn't want anything to do with me. So now, when we're both home, I feel like I have to hide from him."

Amanda Mae's face softened. "Oh, honey. Don't take it personally. He was so in love with Ashley. So young when he met her and so young when he married her. I don't think he even dated anybody else. After she died, he dated a bit for fun and company, but not looking to replace her. He can't replace her." She shook her head. "No, he *won't* replace her. And there's a bunch of us in town who respect that. But—" she sucked in a breath and caught Suzanne's hand "—that doesn't help you. Especially when we can't seem to find you an apartment so you can move into your own place."

"I'll figure something out."

Amanda Mae shook her head. "Actually, I've thought this through and I don't want you to stay in Whiskey Springs because of me. I appreciate you sticking by me through my sulk over losing the diner, but things are going well now. I ran the business myself before our partnership. I can run it again. If you think you need to go, go. Take a week, take a month, take a year. Just know that I'd like to see you come back." She shrugged. "You know. Be my partner. There's no man worth losing a friend over."

Suzanne's throat tightened even more. Amanda Mae might have run the diner, but she'd had help. Waitresses.

Busboys. The sandwich stand was a totally different animal and Suzanne couldn't abandon her. "Thanks, but I'll be fine."

Amanda Mae considered that. "And if you're not?"

"Then I'll take some time." She caught Amanda Mae's forearm. It had been so long since anybody really cared about her that she swallowed back a bucket of tears. "Thanks."

Amanda Mae groaned and batted a hand. "Don't go getting all mushy."

Suzanne laughed, as she fought her tears. She and Amanda Mae really had formed a bond. That was why she didn't want to leave. Whiskey Springs was the home she'd always wanted. Amanda Mae was quickly becoming the stand-in for her mom, who had died too young. The only fly in the ointment was her longing for a man who didn't want her.

It was dark when Suzanne returned home, but she felt better. Relaxed. But Wednesday night she was exhausted again. There was another rush on the stand just before supper time. Apparently, no one in Whiskey Springs felt like cooking on Wednesday and Saturday nights.

Done in, she melted onto the seat of her Mercedes, drove the fifteen minutes to Cade's ranch, rolled out of the car and went in search of her baby. When she found no one in the nursery, she groaned. She'd hoped only to have to walk up the stairs, bathe the baby, feed her and then shower herself before she could fall into bed.

But no such luck.

At the top of the stairs, she was so tired she considered folding herself into a ball and rolling down rather than walking. But she managed the steps, a trip to the kitchen—which was empty—a trip to the office—equally empty—and finally she found Cade and Mitzi in the pool.

"We just got in," Cade said as she walked across the patio to them.

"Oh. I was kind of hoping to take her upstairs and get her ready for bed."

"And I was thinking some time in the water might make her sleepy."

He was suddenly very knowledgeable about the baby, but she didn't have the energy to dwell on that or even out-and-out ask him why. Instead, she headed for the chaise lounge, hoping she didn't fall asleep while she waited for them to come out.

Cade played with the baby for another minute or two then he said, "Why don't you come in, too?"

"I don't have a suit."

"We have at least thirty in the cabana. They're all new. Once someone uses one, we tell them to take it home."

After standing out in the Texas sun for twelve hours, her sweaty body almost wept at the thought of diving into the cool water. But that would mean spending time with Cade—with both of them half-naked. Not wise. "I don't know."

Holding Mitzi securely with one hand, Cade skipped the other along the water, sending a cold spray over Suzanne. Sputtering, she bounced off the chaise.

"Hey!"

"Now, you're wet. No reason not to come in."

Sighing, and too tempted by the prospect of a refreshing dip to refuse, Suzanne walked into the cabana. He'd made his feelings plain and she'd already decided not to be stupid. She might like him a little more every day. But he did not like her.

As Cade had said, there were plenty of swimming suits, all with tags. She found her size and cringed at the tiny bikinis. There was no way in hell she'd go prancing out to the pool in a little red two-piece number. She rummaged along the rack until she found a pretty aqua one-piece. It not only fit, it also covered everything but a spare inkling of cleavage.

It was fine.

Really.

A little self-conscious, she walked out of the pool house and ambled over.

Cade made a big deal out of not watching her walk to the pool. He admitted to a bit of disappointment that she'd chosen the one-piece suit, until he saw how pretty she looked. The color suited her dark hair and creamy skin. Plus, covered or not, her curves were very nicely outlined.

Still, knowing she was off-limits, he focused all his attention on skimming Mitzi along the top of the water as Suzanne dived off the diving board.

When she surfaced, water ran from her hair along her shoulders down the crevice between her breasts. It was everything he could do to keep from staring. So he skimmed Mitzi along the water again, making her giggle, taking his attention away from Suzanne.

"Come on, baby. Want to come to Mama?"

Cade skipped her along the water, out of Suzanne's reach. "We're okay."

Mitzi giggled and Suzanne said, "I see that."

"We actually go to the pool every day."

"Really?"

Because her voice vibrated with concern, he added,

"I love to swim, but laps can get boring. She gives me a reason to be out here."

Suzanne's eyes softened. Their pretty blue color always fascinated him but this evening's softness filled him with trepidation. He'd lured her out to the pool to relax because he'd been worried about her. Now he not only saw the flaw in his plan, he also remembered why he'd been ignoring her. She was gorgeous. And he was tempted.

"That's actually kind of cute."

Trying to bring back the light mood, he snorted in derision. "Yeah, well, don't go telling the people in town. I have a reputation to maintain."

She laughed and everything inside of Cade responded, except not out of attraction, out of something else, something stronger, something warmer. Pleasure. Though he knew he was skirting a dangerous line, something pushed him to keep going, to make her laugh again, to make her happy.

"I'm serious. Something like this gets out, every woman in a three-mile radius will be bringing her baby over."

She laughed, slid her hand through the water. "You'd love it."

His heart stumbled. His chest tightened. Lord, he loved it when she laughed. Groping for something to bring them back to normal, he said, "For about a day and a half. Then it would get old. Let's just let Mitzi benefit from this."

"Yeah. She deserves it." She skimmed her hand along the water again, suddenly avoiding his gaze. "I feel really bad that she doesn't have a daddy."

So did he, but he also knew the truth. Pretty girl like Suzanne wouldn't be alone long. Though that thought squeezed his chest even more, he softened his voice and said, "She will. Someday."

"I have every intention of being a good mom, a great mom. But I know what it's like not to have a daddy." She shrugged. "Or even a granddaddy. I know it's a longing she'll always have. I have to fix that."

He swallowed. "You will."

She finally glanced over at him. "I hope. Otherwise it will be the great failure of my life."

He sniffed a laugh, glad to be reminded of why she had to be off-limits for him. *His* great failure. "We all get a great failure in life. Why should you should be any different?"

"Because mine involves someone else. A baby who doesn't deserve to do without because I was a poor judge of character."

"And my wife didn't deserve to be the one to suffer because I spent so much time away." He shrugged. "Lots of life isn't fair." Knowing they'd already been over his feelings about his first marriage and not wanting to tread that path again, he changed the subject. "So how was work today?"

She didn't hesitate. "Exhausting. I had no idea fifty percent of the population of a small town could want sandwiches for supper every Wednesday."

"Your cash registers must be singing."

"Amanda Mae is in her glory."

He laughed. "But you're just tired."

"Don't make a big deal out of it. This diner is going to be the best thing that ever happened to me. Already, I'm making friends. I love this town. I love the people. I never would have met half of them had it not been for the diner."

He wanted to tell her that it wouldn't do any good to

know everybody in town if she died from exhaustion. But he said nothing because a little voice inside him reminded him that her love of the town caused another complication for him. All this time he'd envisioned her being out of the picture once she left his house. Instead, he realized that exactly the opposite would happen. As she made friends, she would be invited to barbecues, baptisms, weddings, swim parties…everything he would be invited to.

She was in his life for good now. Permanently.

And he was going to have to watch when she found the daddy she so desperately wanted for Mitzi.

Because Cade agreed with Suzanne—her baby did deserve a dad—he knew he couldn't be hanging around, playing with her baby, trying to make her smile, clouding the issue for her and himself. So he avoided Suzanne after that and let Mrs. Granger and Mrs. Reynolds care for the baby when his mom couldn't.

But two Thursday later he still couldn't quite put them out of his mind. He returned from a meeting at the bank and walked back to his office to find Eric happily occupied at his desk in the room next to Cade's, and his messages neatly stacked beside his phone. But he didn't care one whit about returning those calls. The urge to find Mitzi or drive into town to check on Suzanne was so strong he had to fight himself to plop down on his chair.

Then his phone rang.

Glancing at caller ID, he saw it was his brother, punched the button and said, "Hey, Nick."

"Hey, Cade. I've got you on speaker. Darius is with me in my office."

"What's up?"

"Maggie wants you to invite Suzanne to the wedding on Saturday."

"Are you serious?"

"Dead serious," Nick replied. "You're coming anyway. It shouldn't matter if you fly her over with you."

Cade groaned. After two weeks of not talking to her, he still thought about her way too often. Now they'd be alone for a three-hour plane ride. Then there was the twenty-minute drive in the limo to Nick's house. They'd be at the same table for lunch and dinner on Friday, as well as breakfast, lunch and dinner on Saturday. Not to mention the actual wedding itself. He wouldn't survive that.

"I'm not even sure what time I'm leaving."

"You can work that out with her," Nick said. "Come on, Cade. Maggie likes Suzanne. She wants her there. She's afraid she's lonely."

"And Whitney thinks she needs family," Darius added. "After her visit here, Whitney had expected her to call and chat but she hasn't. So Whitney called her cell phone but she didn't answer."

"She's busy all day with Amanda Mae's diner."

There was a pause. "Amanda Mae's diner?"

"Suzanne made friends with Amanda Mae, the local diner owner. So when we saw the diner burning the day we got back from Montauk, she got caught up in the moment and offered Amanda Mae as much money as she needed to get the diner up and running again."

Another pause.

Cade slid his hand across the back of his neck. "I know you probably think this is insane, but she's busy and I know she's happy working at the diner—even if she is exhausted. Plus, because the apartment she was using also burned, she's forced to live with me until she can find a house or a condo."

"Well, that's something," Darius said. "But it sounds like she could use a weekend off. Bring her to the wedding."

"Yeah," Nick said. "It's going to be great. Ceremony on the beach. Big reception afterward. She'll have fun."

"Plus," Darius chimed in, "Whitney will hound me to death if she thinks 'one of ours' is being left out. So bring her."

They talked only another minute before Darius and Nick clicked off. As Cade hung up the phone, the antsy, hungry feeling he usually had around Suzanne was superseded by real concern. He rose from his chair and paced to the window, scrubbing his hand across his mouth.

He couldn't stand to think of Suzanne as alone, but now that his family had forced him to see it, he realized she'd basically set it all out for him. Her mom had died. Her gram had died. Mitzi's father had dumped her.

She'd come to a town where she knew absolutely no one, looking for a job, and Amanda Mae had given her one. Now she and Amanda Mae were friends and she was also making friends with the locals. But he understood what concerned Maggie and Whitney because it suddenly concerned him, too. She had no family.

No one. She might have friends and customers and people to talk to on regular days but what about holidays? Days when the diner was closed? In the times when a person needed a family, she'd always be alone. That's what Whitney and Maggie sought to prevent.

He couldn't let his attraction to her stand in their way.

* * *

Suzanne was surprised to find Cade waiting for her in the front foyer when she returned to the ranch house that afternoon.

"You and I need to talk."

"Now? I haven't even seen Mitzi."

"She'll be fine with my mom for another few minutes."

Tired and sweaty from a day of selling sandwiches, cinnamon rolls and drinks, she wanted a shower and twenty minutes alone with her baby. But she knew determination when she saw it and right now it was written all over Cade's face.

"All right." She crossed her arms on her chest. "Let's get this over with."

"You're not going to the gallows."

"I know but I'm tired."

"Getting up at five-thirty to be in town by eight every day will do that to you."

She rolled her eyes. "Haven't we already been over this?"

He sighed. "All right. You're right. Let's just get to it. Nick and Maggie would like you to come to their wedding on Saturday."

Her heart stuttered. It was equal parts of wonderful and confusing to be invited to the wedding of people she barely knew.

"Please don't tell me you don't want to go."

"I do want to go." Desperately. She liked Whitney and Maggie. She'd thought they'd made a connection. True, she was making friends with people in town every day, but she had a different feeling around Maggie and Whitney. Almost like what she imagined having sisters would feel like.

"We're leaving Friday morning. We'll stay that night

and Saturday night and return Sunday afternoon. Can you leave Amanda Mae alone Friday and Saturday?"

She chewed her lower lip. "I suppose she could get Gloria to help her at the stand."

"Good. You need a break."

She couldn't argue that.

Cade took a step closer. "You and Amanda Mae also need to work out a plan for this stand of yours. It might be time for a new schedule or maybe even time to hire an employee or two. You can't go on like this. You're exhausted."

He was the only person who seemed to care about that. Even Amanda Mae didn't see that by the end of every day she was dragging. The fact that he did, coupled with his nearness, caused her to swallow hard.

"I know neither one of you wants to be doling out money right now, but—" his voice softened unexpectedly "—you have to think of your health, Suzanne."

A shiver of attraction worked its way through her. He didn't seem to notice how close they were standing or that he was worried about her, being kind to her. It amazed her that he didn't see himself as a good person. Because ever since their trip to Montauk all she saw was goodness in him.

Unable to help herself, she looked up, caught his gaze. "We'll work something out."

"I hope so."

She smiled in response, and though he didn't return her smile, he did hold her gaze. Silence stretched between them. She thought about their time in the pool—when he looked so cute with Mitzi, when he talked to her about getting a daddy for Mitzi—and wondered how he couldn't see that she didn't want just anybody to be a father for her child. She wanted him.

She *did* want him. In spite of the way he kept warning her off, she was falling in love with him. And he'd also shown her signs that he liked her more than he wanted her to believe. Maybe even more than he let himself believe.

Which meant, if she wanted this, then maybe she'd have to make the first move.

She rolled to her tiptoes and brushed her lips over his. Need tingled through her, along with an amazing power. He hadn't moved. He barely breathed. But he also hadn't run, stepped back, told her no.

Her heart jumped to her throat. He was actually giving her a chance.

She rose a little higher on her tiptoes and, balancing herself with her hands on his shoulders, pressed her mouth to his.

She expected at least a bit of resistance, so when his mouth relaxed under hers and his hands dropped on her hips, a swell of feminine hunger shot through her. The time for pretense was over. He was everything she wanted and if he wanted her, she wasn't going to let him pretend otherwise. She deepened the kiss, but he quickly took control, opening his mouth over hers, forcing her to open hers to him.

Time spun out as his mouth seared hers in a hot, passionate kiss. Achy needs rose like wildflowers. Everything she knew or thought she knew about passion redefined itself in one blistering kiss. Her bones liquefied. Her blood shimmered.

And then suddenly he pulled away and stepped back. Raking his fingers through his hair, he squeezed his eyes shut.

She worked to steady her trembling limbs, her thundering heart, her weak knees. But it was no use. If he'd been pleased with her kiss, his reaction would have been very different. No guy who was pleased to have been kissed would squeeze his eyes shut.

Oh, lord. What had she done? No matter how much she wanted him, she knew he didn't want her. Yet, she couldn't stop herself from forcing the issue.

Mortification replaced desire. She turned on her heel and raced up the stairs.

The drive to the airport for the trip to North Carolina was made in complete silence. For the better part of the night before, Suzanne had actually considered not going to Maggie and Nick's wedding, but in the end she couldn't stay away. She couldn't turn down the possibility of making friends of Whitney and Maggie. She'd liked them too much to let a little thing like personal humiliation keep her home. God knew, she and Cade had ignored each other for two weeks, they could certainly ignore each other for a three-hour plane ride.

The pilot and copilot said good morning and disappeared into the cockpit to start the engines.

As the plane took off, she put her head back and closed her eyes. She heard the sounds of Cade moving about, then his voice when he said, "Juice?"

Surprised by his consideration, she quietly said, "No. I'm fine."

He opened his juice with a quiet pop. "So are we going to talk about this or what?"

She remembered their last plane ride, how Cade hadn't wanted to talk about what had happened in his den before she told him she was Andreas's Holdings' missing shareholder, and decided to take a page from his book. Rather than face her humiliation, she would simply refuse to discuss it.

Not opening her eyes, she said, "I don't think we have anything to talk about."

"I shouldn't have kissed you—"

Unfortunately, she couldn't let him take the blame. "You didn't kiss me. I kissed you."

"I seem to remember being a party."

That almost made her smile, but she still didn't open her eyes. "Now you're just trying to make me feel better."

"Yeah, I am." He paused, then added, "I can't take you to Nick's house all quiet like this. The women will skin me alive first and ask questions later. We have to deal with this."

For that, she opened her eyes. Sitting in the back, with his boot-covered feet on the desk, Cade didn't look a thing like a billionaire businessman, though he did look like a man prepared to discuss a problem.

But her problem wasn't that they'd kissed again. It was that she was falling in love with him and he didn't want her, so there was no way she would discuss it. And if she'd stop wallowing in her misery he'd probably let her alone. "We're fine."

"Really?"

"Yes."

"Well, it's a long plane ride. If you change your mind, I'm here."

Cade took his feet off the desk and prepared to work, proud of himself. He might not have gotten her to talk, but he'd made the offer and now they were at least polite enough that they wouldn't raise any suspicions when they got to Nick and Maggie's.

He shouldn't have kissed her the day before, but this time he'd recovered more quickly than he had from the last kiss. He was proud of the fact that he was able to talk to her. To treat her like any other person. To forget she was gorgeous. Toss wanting to sleep with her to the back of his mind. Now, when they arrived at Nick and Maggie's they would be normal.

Still, what pleased him the most was that even after that blistering kiss, he could relegate his sexual feelings for her to the back of his brain and not let them rule him.

He opened a file to get a little work done, but his gaze wandered over to Suzanne. Her eyes were closed, her head back. Her long neck was exposed. Without warning, visions of nibbling that long slim throat filled his brain, his hormones awoke, his body tensed for action.

He banished the visions, subdued his hormones and told his body to settle down. His family considered Suzanne one of theirs. And though he might not have agreed at first, discovering how alone she was, he knew it would be selfish of him to keep her away from Maggie and Whitney when she needed a family. So he could not nibble her neck. Slide his hands along the sleek curve of her waist. Press her into a mattress with the entire length of his body…

He squeezed his eyes shut.

Damn.

Just when he thought he was doing so well.

He leaned back against his seat, mimicking Suzanne. This sexual thing he felt for her wasn't going away. He should have realized that when he couldn't turn away her kiss the day before. Even if he had been able to control himself, and he hadn't, now Suzanne was having trouble controlling her reactions to him. But that was only part of it. He didn't just have a sexual thing for her; he also didn't like to see her sad. He hated the idea of her baby needing a daddy and hated even worse that someday some other guy would be that daddy because that meant someday some other guy would be Suzanne's lover.

So maybe it was time to start thinking of alternatives?

He couldn't marry her. He wouldn't tic another woman to him. But he cared enough about Suzanne and was attracted enough that he knew this wasn't just going to disappear because they wanted it to. He had to fix it, even if it was with only a partial solution.

Carrying Mitzi, Suzanne stood behind Cade as he opened the front door of Nick's house without knocking. They stepped into a foyer that rang with the voices of people in the open-floor-plan family room and kitchen, and she glanced around in awe. The place was much bigger on the inside than it appeared from the outside. Pale orange tile led to a cherrywood staircase that spiraled up three stories, meaning there was plenty of space for family and she didn't have to worry about being too close to Cade.

It was cute that he'd wanted to talk in the plane. But that had only made things worse. He'd made her laugh when she'd wanted to crawl into a hole and die. He cared about her. He was attracted to her and she was attracted to him.

She just plain wanted to be allowed to love him and she wanted him to love her.

And as soon as her mind drifted in that direction, she knew she was in trouble. Luckily, Cade brought her back to reality by shouting, "We're here," as he set their suitcases on the floor beside the tall staircase.

When he didn't get an answer, presumably because

he hadn't been heard above the noise coming from the kitchen, he simply left their luggage on the foyer floor and walked into the family room off the kitchen.

"Daddy, you put in too much shrimp!" Maggie stood beside a man who looked to be in his fifties. With his red hair and green eyes so much like Maggie's, it was easy to see he was her father.

"There can never be too much shrimp in jambalaya." Maggie's dad noticed them standing in the door and grinned at them over a huge pot on the six-burner stove in the center island of a pale oak kitchen with black granite countertops. "Hey! Nice to see you, Cade."

"Nice to see you, too, Charlie." He nodded in Suzanne's direction. "This is Suzanne Caldwell and her daughter, Mitzi."

"Your missing shareholder."

Maggie came from behind the stove and hugged Suzanne. "I'm so glad you could come. Let me take Mitzi."

She slid the baby out of Suzanne's arms as Cade motioned to Mr. Forsythe. "This is Maggie's dad, Suzanne, Charlie Forsythe."

"Nice to meet you, kiddo."

"Nice to meet you, too, Mr. Forsythe."

"Everybody calls me Charlie."

Just then the French doors opened. Whitney walked in carrying Maggie's son, Michael. Liz, the nanny, walked in behind her, holding Gino.

"Is that Mitzi?" Whitney cried then she spotted Suzanne. "It is Mitzi!" She raced over and hugged Suzanne. "You're just in time for lunch." She released Suzanne and hugged Cade. "Darius and Nick are on the deck grilling. You might want to join them."

"First, tell me what rooms we're in and I'll take the bags up."

Charlie waved him out the door. "I'll take the bags up. You go see your brothers."

Suzanne followed Charlie as he took her bags upstairs and directed her to a bedroom with a crib and a bathroom. It wasn't a suite, but a simple, comfortable room with access to the gorgeous upstairs deck that looked out over the ocean.

"It's beautiful."

"Yeah, Nick's got good taste," Charlie said, grinning. "Lunch in ten minutes. You don't want to miss my jambalaya." With that he left. Suzanne took a minute to unpack a few things and wash her face before going back downstairs to the noisy kitchen.

Whitney and Maggie immediately bombarded her with questions about the diner. Suzanne answered them, only to be rewarded with another round, until her nervousness disappeared as it had on her weekend in Montauk with these two women. As they set the long table in front of a huge window with a view of the Atlantic, Suzanne remembered thinking that being with Whitney and Maggie made her feel like she had sisters, and for a few seconds she let herself wonder what it would be like to be part of this big, noisy group.

Considering that only family owned shares of Andreas Holdings, owning one-third of the company did make her family of a sort. As long as she owned her shares, she really was one of them. And maybe in the eighteen months it would take for the brothers to come up with the money to buy her out she really could make friends with Maggie and Whitney—then she'd always be a part of their group.

But even as she thought that, Cade came inside and

she knew that wasn't true. Every time he was nice to her, she grew to like him just a little more and pretty soon her feelings might not be so easy to hide. And then what? Every time Maggie or Whitney would invite her somewhere Cade would be there. And some of those times he'd probably have a woman with him. How could he not? He was too gorgeous to be alone. And some women wouldn't want what Suzanne wanted. They'd settle for a one-night stand or a weekend here or there....

She nearly gasped. Dear God. What was she thinking? That she should marry him? She'd only known him a few weeks!

But in her heart of hearts she knew she wasn't wrong.

She wanted to marry him. And he wanted nothing to do with her.

CHAPTER TEN

NICK AND MAGGIE'S WEDDING took place at two o'clock Saturday afternoon on the beach right behind Nick's house.

Wearing a white gauze sundress and a big white sun hat, Maggie came out of the beach house and descended the deck stairs. Charlie walked her down a short path to the beach, where—two feet away from waves that crawled ever closer to their flip-flops—Nick, Darius and Cade stood with the minister. All three of them wore cutoff jeans and a T-shirt.

Nick's mom, Becky, a pretty blonde, stood near them. Suzanne and Whitney's parents, a wealthy New York lawyer and his wife, stood behind Becky. To the left, wearing sundresses and floppy sun hats, Whitney and a friend of Maggie's served as bridesmaids. And in front of them was a small group of Maggie's friends and employees from the manufacturing plant she managed for Nick.

It was the oddest wedding Suzanne had ever seen, but she wasn't really experienced with weddings. Most ceremonies she'd attended had been held in churches. Most grooms wore tuxes. Most brides wore a gown. But Nick and Maggie wanted the beach. They wanted to be comfortable. To declare their love.

Just the thought brought tears to Suzanne's eyes. Their love story had been a beautiful one. It was wonderful to see Maggie walk up to Nick, take his hand, declare her love in front of the minister, then cry softly as Nick read the vows he'd written.

Suzanne's tears brimmed over, and her gaze strolled to Cade. He held himself casually, as if he were unaffected by this ceremony, but he wasn't grinning the way Darius was. The way a brother would be. And Suzanne understood why. Darius could be silly and make jokes about Nick losing his freedom because he was with the love of his life, too. Cade had found and lost the love of his life. The memories brought to him by this ceremony were probably bittersweet.

Tilting her head to one side, she studied him, amazed that a woman could inspire that much devotion in a man. But, getting to know his family, she was beginning to understand it. The entire Andreas family was loyal, but Cade was loyal to a fault. If he'd fallen in love it had been forever. For good.

It was part of why she loved him. Even though he hadn't wanted her around, he was good to her. Fairness and honesty weren't just words for him; they were a code to live by. After the way she'd been treated by her friends and Bill Baker, was it any wonder she admired those qualities? Any wonder she admired Cade himself? He was a good man, somebody she *desperately* wanted to love because he embodied all the qualities she would look for in the next man she gave herself to.

Halfway through Nick's vows, Whitney's mom handed a tissue to Suzanne who began crying in earnest when the minister pronounced Nick and Maggie husband and wife. They were a gorgeous couple who would be bountifully happy for the rest of their lives. It was a beautiful thing to experience.

Still, that was only part of the reason she wept. She also wept for Cade. For his loss. For her loss. Because of his past, he'd never want her the way she wanted him, and a man she considered to be just about perfect was lost to her.

She scrambled back to her room, telling Whitney that Mitzi needed a diaper change. She stayed there while Mitzi napped, taking a long bath before she dressed in her red cocktail dress for the semiformal reception being held at a hotel a thirty-minute drive away.

Just before she would have been ready to walk downstairs to join the group, there was a knock at her bedroom door.

Adjusting her grandmother's teardrop pearl earrings, she raced to answer, worried that she was behind schedule and Nick or Maggie had sent someone to get her.

When she opened the door to find Cade, she gaped in amazement. Accustomed to seeing him in jeans and a Stetson, seeing him in a tuxedo rendered her speechless. With his dark, shiny hair combed in a respectable way, he was so good-looking he could have posed for magazine ads.

Praying she wouldn't stutter, she said, "Hey. Am I late?" Then turned around and pressed her hand to her chest. He would tempt a nun out of the convent. So it was not odd or surprising that she was having trouble steadying her breathing and hoping her knees could support her.

"No. I was sent to make sure you knew which limo you were riding in." He ambled into her room. "We're sharing one, by the way."

They were sharing a limo? Lord, she hoped there

was another couple or even another person riding with them. Let it be Charlie. Or Whitney's quiet parents.

"I'm ready. I just need to take Mitzi downstairs to Liz."

Cade led her down the spiral staircase. After they deposited Mitzi with the nanny, and Suzanne fussed over her long enough to ease her guilt over leaving, he guided her to the only limo left in front of the house.

She turned around in horror. "I *was* late!"

"Only a bit." He put his hand on the small of her back, where there was no dress, and pin pricks of excitement danced up her spine. "We're fine. Ten minutes behind them at most."

He directed her into the empty limo and her heart galloped. She was so late there was no other couple to ride with them. They were alone! Alone! She was going to make a colossal fool of herself.

She sat on the sofalike seat, shifting over as far as she could, basically hugging the wall.

Rather than sit beside her, Cade sat across from her.

She wrestled back a sigh of relief, not wanting to embarrass herself. But she knew that he knew she'd worked to put space between them.

"Drink?"

"God, no." If she was this nervous and antsy now, imagine what alcohol would do to her. She'd probably drool on him.

The limo pulled out, started off toward the hotel. Suzanne pretended great interest in the scenery.

"Relax. I'm not going to eat you."

She swallowed and tried to laugh. The sound came out strangled.

"Although I have to admit, the first time I saw you in that dress I considered it."

She smiled shakily. "The dress is dramatic. I bought it for the effect."

"Well, you got your money's worth." He leaned back, unbuttoned his jacket and lounged against the seat.

Looking so tempting she could have happily snuggled up to him, he smiled. "You know when you asked me for a few minutes alone that night at the barbecue, I thought you were going to seduce me."

"I know." Dear God, had her voice actually squeaked?

He shook his head. "I had some plans for you that night."

That sent a shaft of heat directly to her womanhood. They had to change the subject or she'd start to shiver. "I saw the look in your eyes. That was why I didn't waste time before I told you about my stock."

He chuckled. The rich, warm sound filled the air around her and seemed to wrap her in the essence of him.

"Yeah, well, if you could have read my mind you probably would have run for the hills." He paused, cocked his head and smiled sexily. "Or maybe not."

After a few seconds' pause, he kicked the toe of her stiletto-heeled sandals and caught her gaze. "You wouldn't have been sorry."

"Now it sounds like you're propositioning me."

He shrugged. "Maybe I am?" He smiled. "We're attracted. And we can't seem to control our chemistry. Or ignore it. Or avoid it. Because we're normal, healthy people. But we're also adults who should be able to discreetly enjoy what's between us."

"I have a baby."

"I have a ranch. What difference does it make?"

"It makes a lot of difference and you know it. I've already told you I want a father for Mitzi."

"And you know I already love Mitzi. You know I would be a good daddy to her for as long as we would be together. We'd just avoid the mess of promises of happily ever after. We both know that doesn't exist. So if we don't get married, just—" he nonchalantly lifted a shoulder "—live together, and you get tired of me and my work schedule, you'd have a get out of jail free card."

"Get out of jail free?"

"You could leave. No hassle. No questions."

She sucked in a quiet breath, not liking his idea. She already knew she was in love with him. She'd never leave. Never. "And what if you got tired?"

He grinned. "Tired? Of making love to you?" He laughed. "I don't think you're going to have to worry about that one."

Just then the limo door opened. Suzanne hadn't even realized they'd stopped moving. Cade stepped out then leaned in again. Offering his hand to help her out, he grinned at her.

She sucked in a breath, urging her heart and lungs to function normally, but the second he grasped her fingers, both her pulse and breathing went haywire again.

He tugged gently and she stepped out of the limo, but she struggled a bit to get her footing and he steadied her with a hand at the small of her back.

Arousal exploded inside her. She fought to suppress a shiver.

He smiled, slowly, knowingly. "See? We'd be very good together. And we'd probably last longer than you think."

"But you don't love me."

"I wouldn't be asking you to live with me if I didn't have feelings for you."

But not love. He didn't say it. He didn't have to. He'd already told her he'd had the love of his life. If she took his offer she'd be second-best. Always second place in his heart and his life. But would that be so bad? They'd be together. He'd help raise Mitzi. She'd be part of his wonderful family.

He said, "Just think about it a bit," before he turned them in the direction of the hotel ballroom.

Nick and Maggie greeted them at the door. Wearing a tux like Cade's, Nick looked almost as handsome as his younger brother. Maggie was breathtaking in a floor-length ivory sheath. It was, after all, their second wedding. She hadn't wanted to wear white or something too youthful. So she'd settled for classy and looked the part of a millionaire's sophisticated wife.

Cade guided her to the table reserved for family. Throughout the meal, Nick's mom, Becky, kept them entertained with stories from Maggie's and Nick's past—especially how they'd loved each other from childhood—until Suzanne's heart swelled with longing. She glanced over at Cade. There was no doubt he was gorgeous. The kind of man who could sweep a woman off her feet in seconds, not even minutes. But the love Becky had described was so pure and so innocent...so perfect, that she knew that was what she wanted—no, it was what she needed.

If she agreed to what Cade was offering, he might always want her sexually but she'd never have the all-consuming, innocent, wonderful love that she wanted. The kind that would steal her breath, wrap her heart in warmth, take her through the rest of her life.

Could she live without it?

With dinner over, the band played a soft romantic song for Nick and Maggie. The way they put their heads together and whispered caused Suzanne's heart to squeeze. They were more than attuned to each other; they were a matching set, two halves to a whole.

And Suzanne had her answer for Cade. She so desperately wanted the kind of closeness Maggie and Nick had. No matter how much she loved Cade, he didn't love her. She couldn't settle for second-best.

When Cade asked her to dance, she rose automatically, but hesitated as they walked to the dance floor. She'd been falling in love with him since the day she met him, but he had not been falling in love with her. With his offer, he'd put all his cards on the table and she had no more excuses, no starry-eyed hopes. She knew what he wanted from her. And it wasn't what she wanted from him.

They reached the dance floor and Cade slid his hand to the small of her back. Tingles formed. Everything female in her responded. To his touch. His scent. His very presence.

He pulled her close and the desire to rest her head on his shoulder nearly overwhelmed her. So she looked away. Unfortunately she saw Whitney and Darius dancing. Saw the closeness. Saw the intimacy of their glances. The way they danced like people who knew each other's next move long before it was made.

Her heart stuttered.

She wanted that.

She so desperately wanted that. So what was she doing with a man who couldn't give it to her?

"Relax."

She swallowed and looked up into Cade's face. His eyes were bright, alert, like a cat waiting to pounce.

She had absolutely no doubt that he desired her. But she couldn't let that muddy the waters. She'd made up her mind. It was time to be strong.

She stepped back. "I think I need some air."

His arms dropped away, but he immediately caught her hand. "There's a patio." He nudged his head in the direction of open French doors. "Come on."

Oh, great. If they were going outside, alone, she might have actually made things worse.

But he didn't seem to notice her hesitation. He led her across the crowded dance floor to a slight breach in the crowd then guided her to doors that opened onto a patio.

She gulped in air as he pulled her along the stone floor to a cobblestone path that wound through a tropical garden. When they'd walked past the reach of the outdoor lights, he stopped.

"Is this air enough for you?" He slid his hands to her back and pulled her close. "I sort of like it out here myself."

She should have told him she'd thought about his offer and had decided to decline. Instead, instinct took over and she leaned in against him. He was solid and warm and very, very real. True, he could never love her, but she did love him. A chance to be with him like this would never come along again. She wanted this minute, this one minute, to at least be held by him.

His hands inched up her spine, along her bare flesh, raising goose bumps. When they reached her shoulders, he pulled her closer still, lowered his head and kissed her.

The bottom dropped out of her world. His lips moved over hers possessively, taking not asking, because they'd kissed before. Twice.

And she answered just as passionately because if this was her last chance to kiss him she was going to make it good. She might never have seen herself as being assertive, but she had changed. She owned half a business. She had good ideas. And maybe that was the problem. She was no longer the frightened young woman who winced and ran away. She stayed and fought.…

Maybe she should be fighting to win him?

He pulled her closer still, bringing her body against his. Even through the folds of his tuxedo jacket she could feel the strong beat of his heart and thrilled to the realization *she* was doing this. His heart was beating for her.

He was everything she wanted. Sexy. Smart. Savvy. Strong.

But that was the kicker. He was strong. Much stronger than she was, even with her newfound confidence. He wouldn't tame easily. If he tamed at all.

And if she didn't step away now, she'd never step away.

With a sigh of regret, she pulled back. "Stop."

He chuckled. "I don't have to. You just did."

She sucked in a breath of air. "Okay. Here's the deal. I like you."

He put his hands on her hips and dragged her back to him. "I like you, too."

She shook her head. "No. I *like* you." She winced. This was not the time to be pussyfooting around. This was the time to be real. Honest. "I *love* you. You might be able to get involved like this." She motioned with her hand between them, indicating their physical relationship. "But I want more."

"That's why we're out here away from everybody."

Panic raced through her. "No. Not *that* more. I mean

more as in a relationship, a real relationship, not a tryst in the dark. Not a secret affair." She swallowed. If she was doing this, she had to go the whole way. "I want you to love me."

His hands fell to his sides. "Oh?"

She squeezed her eyes shut as disappointment flooded her. Deep down inside she'd almost hoped he'd say he did love her or, at the very least, that he believed that someday he could love her. Instead, he'd confirmed her worst suspicions. He wasn't interested in love. Only sex.

She licked her lips, savoring the taste of him, a taste she'd never get again, and stepped back. "Come on, Cade. I've been saying it all along. I have a child. I need a home. A real home. I'm just starting to build my life again and I want to do it right."

"And living with me would be wrong."

"What Whiskey Springs man in his right mind would ever approach me after we'd lived together? You employ nearly everyone. I'd be a pariah."

He combed his fingers through his hair as if he knew she was right.

She shook her head sadly. "Did you think we could live together for a few months or maybe even years with no consequences?"

"I don't know."

"There'd be consequences. They are always consequences." Like her currently shattering heart that still, God help her, held on to the hope that he wouldn't let her go.

He put another two feet of distance between them. "I get it."

And by the fact that he'd taken another step back, she

knew that he did understand. He wouldn't argue and give her false hope or make promises he couldn't keep.

She turned and walked away. Up the garden path alone.

Pain rolled through her in a trembling wave. Her throat closed. Still, she fought the tears. She had at least another hour of this reception and there was no way she'd let anybody know Cade had broken her heart.

She was done being the person everybody pitied. She'd do her crying in private.

She rode home in a limo with Darius and Whitney, silently packed her things and ordered a cab that took her to the airport, where she used her one-and-only credit card to get a commercial flight. She found a late flight and climbed aboard the nearly empty plane. When she arrived in Texas, she called Amanda Mae to pick her up and by noon next day, she was at Cade's gathering the last of her few belongings.

"So what are you going to do?"

Having already cried herself out on the dark plane, she shrugged. "Not sure."

"Where are you going to go?"

Longing for her grandmother tightened her chest, brought tears to her eyes again. "I think I'd like to visit my gram."

Amanda Mae frowned. "Oh, honey, you're sad enough. Don't go to the cemetery."

"No. No cemetery. I thought I'd spend some time outside our old house. Just soak myself in the memory of what it felt like to be loved."

"If you don't stop, you're going to make me cry."

"I just need a little bit of something to hold on to. I came here looking for a job and found friends." She squeezed Amanda Mae's hand. "But I think I might have let go of my past too soon."

"Because it sucked."

She laughed in spite of herself. "No. It's more than that. I was so wrapped up in meetings with lawyers and accountants that I never really mourned my gram." She sat on the bed beside her friend. "I wonder now if that wasn't part of why I was so quick to fall for Cade. So quick to see him as a husband. A daddy."

Amanda Mae squeezed her hand. "You saw what he is. A good man. Don't fault yourself. Fault him. He's the one who can't move on."

And with that, they left her suite, her pathetic suitcase in Amanda Mae's hand, Mitzi in her carrier. They said goodbye on the driveway of Cade's big house and Suzanne promised she'd be back soon. But she didn't think she would be. She'd rather entice Amanda Mae to visit in Georgia. Maybe start a bigger diner. Or a bakery. Or anything Suzanne wanted because in another seventeen months she'd be a very wealthy woman.

Still a sad woman…but a very wealthy one.

CHAPTER ELEVEN

MONDAY MORNING, CADE headed for the stables, resisting the urge to drive to town to check on Suzanne to make sure she was okay. He'd gotten the skinny from his staff that Amanda Mae had brought Suzanne home and they'd packed up her belongings. He knew she'd probably gone to Amanda Mae's to live. Which was fine. Probably for the best.

He'd made a fool of himself with her. He thanked his lucky stars no one had been within hearing distance in that garden at Nick's wedding because his foolishness was only his own personal embarrassment.

Oh, he got what she was saying. She wanted what he didn't. Marriage. But the real underlying sentiment was much simpler. She wanted him to love her, and he simply couldn't risk it.

So he'd let her walk away, let her go back to Nick's beach house in the limo with Darius and Whitney. When she wasn't around on Sunday afternoon he'd correctly assumed she'd taken a commercial flight back to Texas.

He stopped his truck in front of the main stable and jumped out.

Standing with one foot hooked over the fence and

his black Stetson shielding his eyes from the sun, Jim greeted him. "Hey, Cade. How was the wedding?"

"Great." That wasn't exactly a lie, but he certainly wasn't going to tell his father-in-law that he'd propositioned Suzanne and she'd rejected him. "Nick's house at the beach is a paradise. And it's always fun to jag around with my brothers, make 'em feel like losers for settling down."

Jim laughed.

Cade relaxed and continued on into the stable. This was what he needed. Not just a quiet trot around the ranch to check things out, but a little time with Ashley's dad to remind himself that he was doing the right thing by stepping away from Suzanne.

He pulled a saddle from the hook on the wall as Jim said, "Heard that little girl from Georgia went with you."

His face heated but he kept walking toward his Appaloosa. "I couldn't exactly leave a houseguest alone while I went off gallivanting. Besides, Maggie and Nick wanted her there."

"She's a pretty little thing."

"I hadn't noticed."

"So what's this? You blind now?"

Cade laughed. "All right. She's pretty. But you know I'm not interested."

Jim opened the corral door. "Cade, it's been *years*."

"Two. Hey, Sugar," he crooned, approaching his horse. "I think you and I need to spend a little quality time together." Sugar lifted his head and whinnied. Cade grunted as he hoisted the saddle to his horse's back.

"Two long years," Jim said, helping Cade cinch the saddle.

"What? You think I have no concept of the passage of time?"

"I'm just saying it seems odd is all. We all loved Ashley. Her mom and I talk about her every day. But you're young. You should be moving on."

"I have moved on. Hell, I've got more work now than I ever had. And more people depending on me." Which was what he wanted—association with people but from a distance. This way he didn't hurt anyone.

He led Sugar out of the stable and spent the afternoon riding the fence until it ended, and just plain exploring the land beyond that.

Now both Ashley and Suzanne were gone. And he would have to deal with it.

That night Cade didn't sleep. He went to his office where he spent hours poring over reports for the new division of his oil conglomerate, even though he didn't absorb a word he read. At seven Eric arrived, took one look and simply headed into his office without comment.

But two days later, when he still hadn't slept, Jim wasn't as polite as Eric. "You look like hell."

"I haven't been sleeping."

"Word got back from town that your little girl from Georgia hasn't been showing up at the sandwich stand."

His heart stopped. He'd thought she'd gone to Amanda Mae's, maybe slept on her couch. He'd thought she was working the stand, surrounded by people who were growing to like her. "Her choice."

"So where'd she go?"

"She didn't tell me."

Jim sighed, fell to a chair in front of Cade's desk. "Are you slow or are you just plain crazy?"

"What I am is tired. Say what you came in here to say then leave."

To his surprise, Jim rose from his chair and walked to the door that separated Cade's office from Eric's. He closed it.

"Okay, I'll say my piece then I'll be gone. Suzanne was a cute little gal with a heart of gold and a very good head on her shoulders. And you liked her. Maybe even loved her. Yet you chased her away."

"I did not love her!"

"Really? You're not eating. You're not sleeping. You didn't even behave this badly when Ashley died."

The reality of that hit Cade like a punch to the chest. He couldn't sleep. He couldn't eat. He couldn't even work. Even after Ashley died, he could work.

"Oh, God." He pressed his fingers to his eyes. He did love her. "This is so wrong."

"How can you say that?"

"Because I wasn't a very good husband to the last woman I married." He sucked in a breath. "You know as well as I do that I left her alone. Lots. It hurt her."

Jim shook his head. "You were building a business. She always understood. Besides, you were there when it counted most."

Jim might believe that but Cade didn't. He put a business deal ahead of his dying wife. He wasn't around when she drew her last breath. The very second she needed him the most, he was gone.

"Cade?"

"I don't want to talk about it."

"This is about you not being there when she died, isn't it?"

He said nothing.

"Oh, Cade. She'd rebounded. That morning she was

happy as a lark. As I recall, she shooed you out. Because you'd been there every day for weeks." He sucked in a breath. "How can you not remember this? How can you not remember the vacations? The long weekends? The days when you only owned stocks and the ranch...when every other day was a holiday for you?"

Cade swallowed. Every time he thought of his marriage, he only remembered himself leaving. He remembered all the times he wasn't home as if they ran in a long unbroken stream. He'd forgotten the weeks he'd been able to take long vacations with Ashley because he worked for himself. He'd forgotten the days he'd stayed home just because he could. He'd forgotten the two weeks before she died, when he hadn't left her side, when he'd slept on a couch by the hospital bed they'd set up in a room near the kitchen.

When Cade said nothing, Jim tossed up his hands in defeat. "All I'm saying is you're a fool to let a good woman walk away. A fool not to take a second chance when the good Lord decides to give you one."

He rose and headed for the door. "That's it. That's my piece. I said it. What you do with it is your business."

The first night after Suzanne left Whiskey Springs, she'd gotten a hotel room for herself and Mitzi. The second night, having arrived in Georgia, she got another hotel room and bought some newspapers so she could begin house hunting.

But the third night, even in the familiar hotel room, she felt alone and cold. So lonely she could have happily curled in a ball and cried for hours. But she didn't. She couldn't. She had a child.

So she called Amanda Mae. "Hey."

"Hey. It's pretty damned late to be calling a woman

who has to get up at five to make your cinnamon roll recipe."

"Sorry about that."

"I hate making those blasted things. Can't I persuade you to come home?"

Home. Whiskey Springs had become home, but she'd made the mistake of falling for Cade and she couldn't live there anymore. "I thought you said you were fine on your own."

"I thought I would be, but I'm not. I'm used to your company. Can't we just ban Cade from the diner when it opens next week?"

Just the thought made Suzanne laugh. Still, she didn't want to talk about Cade. Every time she even thought of him, her chest hurt. Her eyes filled with tears.

"You visit your gram yet?"

She sucked in a breath. "No. Maybe tomorrow. I'll sit outside the gates, look at the house, remember some things."

"Makes sense. Just don't stay too long or think too much."

"I won't." Because things were getting too sentimental, she changed the subject. "Amanda Mae, I think it's finally sinking in that in eighteen months I'm going to be rich."

"I know."

"And I have to figure out how to manage that money so I don't lose most of it the way my grandmother did."

"Personally, I don't think you should have sold the stock. You should have waited around for the company to rebound and then been a real thorn in the Andreas brothers' sides."

Suzanne laughed in spite of the pain that crushed her

heart when she thought of the Andreas brothers, their wives, their babies. People who should have been her friends. They were lost to her now. "I don't want to be anything to them."

"Of course you do. I think that's the problem. You'd be part of their family if that stubborn old mule Cade wasn't such an idiot."

Suzanne smiled at the motherly tone in Amanda Mae's voice, even as the tears in her eyes spilled over. This time she didn't try to stop them. Mitzi was finally asleep so she wouldn't hear. And maybe a good cry was what she needed to get herself out of this maudlin mood?

"Look. I've gotta go. I'm really tired."

Amanda Mae sighed. "I should take a piece of that boy's hide."

"No. Let it go, Amanda Mae."

Suzanne clicked off, but Amanda Mae's eyes narrowed. Everybody in this town kowtowed to Cade Andreas, but Amanda Mae Fisher had long ago realized a woman had to fight for what she wanted.

She shrugged off her robe and threw it to her bed before she put on blue jeans and a T-shirt. It might be late, but she was mad.

When his doorbell rang after eleven, Cade cursed. He stormed up the hall, thinking the blooming idiot ringing his bell would wake Mitzi. Then he remembered Mitzi no longer lived with him. Sadness seeped into his soul, but he stopped it. Regardless of what his father-in-law thought, he couldn't get over leaving Ashley the day she died. Couldn't drag Suzanne into his life when his past relationship had been such a disaster.

He yanked open the door only to find an angry Amanda Mae Fisher on his front step.

"You are a freaking pain in my butt."

Cade stifled a long-suffering sigh. "Look, I know you're miffed. I know you want your partner back but—"

"I don't give a flying fig about having a partner. I ran that diner alone for fifteen years. I can run it alone another fifteen. But I do miss my friend." She stopped, sucked in a breath. "Cade, you know I haven't got any kids. And she was like my kid. In here—" she patted the spot where her heart would be "—I felt a connection. You know what it's like to be alone. Why would you force me to live without the chance to be somebody's mama, even if it is unofficial?"

Cade squeezed his eyes shut then popped them open again. Everybody was blaming him for Suzanne leaving, but it had been her choice. And didn't anybody see he was suffering, too?

"I don't know what you want me to do—"

"Go after her," Amanda Mae said, not giving him a chance to make any of his excuses. "It's you she wants. Sometime tomorrow she's going back to the estate she shared with her gram. She can't get inside, but she intends to spend some time sitting outside the gates, thinking about her past, remembering her gram. That poor kid's been through enough. Don't let her go on suffering just because you think you don't want her here."

The truth of that hurt his heart. He did want her here. He did love her. He'd realized that talking to Jim. But things between him and Suzanne were not as simple or cut-and-dried as Jim or Amanda Mae thought.

He'd had a great love and he hadn't been there for her when she needed him the most. Despite Jim's kind reassurances that haunted him. Hurt him. Held him back. Who was he to get a second chance at love?

He didn't deserve it and Suzanne deserved better.

Cade went to bed that night feeling cold and lonely. He crawled under the covers of the big bed that had been his and Ashley's, the only thing he'd brought from the master suite into his new room after her death.

Because he hadn't been able to sleep since Suzanne had gone, he didn't think he'd sleep that night, either. But he laid his head on the pillow and didn't have another thought. He immediately drifted off.

But it was a fitful sleep. A sleep filled with worry for Suzanne. He didn't know how much money she'd spent on the diner. How much money she had left. He hoped she'd have enough for a house but what if she didn't? What if she could only afford to rent a shabby apartment in a run-down section of the city? She'd be in an area potentially filled with drugs and gangs. And it would be his fault. His brothers would kill him. His sisters-in-law would skin him alive when they found out.

In his dreams they yelled at him. In his dreams, he didn't blame them. He worried about her. Feared for her. Chastised himself.

Then suddenly he was on his Appaloosa, riding. The wind billowed around him. Sun beat down on him. He knew the dream, knew that Ashley waited on the other side of this ride.

He gently nudged Sugar, urging him on.

As he approached the corral, he could see Ashley tending the flowers. He wouldn't get to talk to her. He wouldn't get much more than a few seconds to see her, still he nudged Sugar to go faster.

At the corral, he slid off the horse and stopped. He

raised his hand to wave the way he always did, and this time he didn't feel the silk pillow case. He didn't awaken.

Joy trembled through him.

"Ashley?"

She turned and smiled. His heart tripped over itself.

"Cade."

The sound of her voice was nearly his undoing. Joy and sorrow buffeted him like a ray of sunlight and an angry wind. He wanted to see her, talk to her, but he knew he didn't deserve it.

He took two steps over, but stopped, worried that if he got too close she'd vanish.

She smiled again, a warm, gentle smile that reminded him of just how young she was. How young she'd been when they'd married. How shy. How timid. By now, Suzanne would have come over, asked him a million questions. Maybe even kissed him. Ashley stayed where she was.

He swallowed. There was a gulf between them. Not just distance. Not even life and death. A real gulf. He knew her. He loved her. But not the way he knew Suzanne. Not the way he loved Suzanne.

She smiled again. Her head tilted to the side as if she were studying him, figuring something out. Then she raised her hand and waved slightly. "Goodbye, Cade."

Tears filled his eyes. "No." He stopped. He couldn't keep her. He knew he couldn't keep her. He swallowed once. Then whispered, "Goodbye, Ash."

When he woke, his room was totally silent. His weary body was relaxed. His weary mind sharp, alert.

He'd finally gotten to say goodbye.

* * *

The next morning, Suzanne awoke determined to find somewhere to live. Hotel rooms weren't cheap and, though she had money, she knew she couldn't stay in a hotel room forever. She wanted a house.

She woke Mitzi, fed her, bathed her and dressed her for the day. After checking out of the hotel, she took her meager possessions, mostly secondhand things she'd bought while in Whiskey Springs, and drove to a department store.

In a few months, she'd be filthy rich. She wouldn't squander what she had but, by God, she and Mitzi could at least not look like refugees.

In the store, she bought clothes for Mitzi, a stroller, a walker and two teddy bears. She bought shirts and jeans, shorts, skirts, tennis shoes and flat sandals for herself. And some makeup. She even found a salon and was lucky enough to get a walk-in appointment to have her hair trimmed.

With her hair coiffed, she asked for directions to the ladies' room and changed into a stylish skirt with a ruffled blouse very much like the one Whitney had worn the day she met her. As fascinated Mitzi watched, she put on makeup, fluffed out her hair and headed out to the parking lot.

Her Mercedes sat waiting. She stuffed all the bags she'd hung on the handles of Mitzi's new stroller into the trunk. Then she buckled Mitzi into her car seat.

Her intention had been to head for a real estate office to begin her search for a house, but when she reached a familiar off-ramp for the Interstate, she took it. She'd told Amanda Mae she wanted to say goodbye to her gram. And this morning she would.

Three turns got her on the road to her grandmother's

estate and twenty minutes later, she sat in front of the locked wrought-iron gate, staring at it.

She missed her grandmother. In all the hubbub of straightening out Martha Caldwell's beleaguered estate, she hadn't taken the time to grieve her loss. Looking past the gate to the big house beyond the long, well-tended lawn and flower beds, she couldn't actually see the small front stoop, but she could picture her grandmother sitting on the rocker beside the front door.

She snorted a laugh as tears filled her eyes. Her grandmother loved her front porch rocker, even though she was too far from the street to see anybody or for anybody to see her.

God, she was alone again. And she didn't want to be. She also didn't want to live in Georgia. She wanted to live in Whiskey Springs.

A soft tap on her window brought her out of her haze. She glanced over to see Cade. She didn't know how he'd known where she'd be, but he had. Joy filled her, then sadness. He might have found her, but she guessed Amanda Mae had sent him because he'd made it perfectly clear that he didn't want her.

She wasn't going back to the town where the true love of her life lived…especially since he didn't want her.

"Open the window."

"Go home, Cade."

"I can't go home. Amanda Mae has murder in her eyes. She blames me for you leaving."

Since she couldn't argue that. She didn't. She stared straight ahead.

He groaned noisily. "Come on."

She refused to even look at him.

"Please. We need to talk."

She still stared straight ahead.

"I talked with Ashley last night."

One of her eyebrows rose. Her curiosity was piqued.

Given that Ashley was no longer with them, at the very least, this would be a good story.

With a sigh, she opened her car door. He stepped aside and let her out.

"We had a busy morning. Mitzi's sleeping. I don't want to wake her."

She closed the door softly and faced him. Bad move. Not just because every hormone in her body sprang to aching life. But because he looked awful. Instead of his usual T-shirt and jeans, he wore pleated pants and a dress shirt. He had no hat so his hair blew in the slight breeze created by the overhang of rich green trees that surrounded her grandmother's property. His eyes were dull. Listless.

Talking to a ghost must not be pleasant.

"So?"

He peered over at her. "So?"

"How does a man talk to a wife who passed away?"

He winced. "I had a dream."

Her eyebrows rose.

"You don't understand." He swallowed. "Ever since Ashley died, I'd have this dream. In the beginning, I had it every day, then every week, then once a month."

She said nothing, only studied him. Birds chirped on the quiet street. A rare car drove by, forcing them to step off the road and to the sidewalk.

"I had the dream again last night. And this morning I realized I hadn't had the dream the entire time you were in town."

"Oh?"

He forked his fingers through his hair. "And last night the dream was different. I got to talk to her."

Gazing at her grandmother's house, a wave of empathy for him washed through her. What she wouldn't give for ten minutes with her gram. Just ten minutes to be able to say I love you and maybe hear the words again herself.

"Every time I have the dream, I walk over to her, hoping to say hello." He cleared his throat. "Hoping to get to say goodbye."

Her senses perked up. Things about his grief began to fall into place for her. "You never said goodbye, did you?"

He turned to her, his eyes flashing. "Don't feel sorry for me. I traded the chance to say goodbye for a business deal."

"No, you didn't. At least not on purpose. There was no way you could have known she would die that day."

He dragged in a breath. "She'd rebounded. She was happy. She shooed me off, saying I needed to get out of the house."

"Sounds to me like she was a really great wife." She shook her head. "Also sounds like you were around a little more than you thought."

"Maybe. Jim says I was. But I'm still something of a workaholic."

She laughed, stepped closer, put her hands on his shoulders to comfort him. She knew none of this had been easy for him. And the important thing was he'd come after her. "You could always change. A person who has billions of dollars doesn't have to work 24/7. He could take a day or a week or maybe even a few months off now and again."

He laughed, draped his hands around her waist. "Maybe." He swallowed. "I used to. Jim sort of reminded me of that, too."

She smiled softly, stepped closer. He felt so good, so strong, so real. "Maybe? There doesn't have to be a debate about it. You should just say yes." She shook her head. "You are a bit of a stubborn mule."

"So Amanda Mae says."

"You're also high-handed. Bossy. Arrogant."

"You think you can handle me?"

She laughed. "I left you, didn't I?"

His hands suddenly lifted from her waist. Slid up her back. Fell down again. "Yes. You did."

"I'm not sorry."

He laughed. "I didn't expect you would be."

"But I am coming back to Whiskey Springs." She peeked at him. "I like owning the diner. I like having my own things. A place in the world."

"I thought you wanted a place with me."

"I thought you didn't want me."

He leaned in, bumped his forehead to hers. "I do."

"You do what?"

"I do want you around."

"Are you asking me to live in sin?"

His head snapped up. His eyes narrowed. "You'd forgive me that easily?"

"Depends on what you say next."

He laughed, yanked her against him. "You're a smart, sassy, sometimes bossy woman who I think I love."

"Think?"

"Who I definitely love. I don't think I can live without you." He frowned. "No. I don't want to live without you."

Her chest tightened. It amazed her that he recognized the nuance of difference in those two statements. He was choosing her. Not being forced or compelled to love her. But choosing to.

A light, airy feeling invaded her.

"You've gotta say the words, Cade."

He brought her a tad closer. "What words?"

"Fooling around will not get you what you want."

"Fooling around is what I want."

She laughed. "Say the words."

He sobered. "I love you. I do. I want to raise your daughter have six more kids—"

"Six?"

"Maybe seven."

Realizing he was giddy, she laughed. "Amanda Mae will shoot me."

"Only if you force her to be the one to bake the cinnamon rolls every morning." He paused, but only slightly. "Marry me?"

Her eyes filled with tears. "Really? You don't want an adjustment period."

"I hear it takes over a year to plan a wedding these days."

"It does, if you want to do it right."

"I want to do it right."

She pressed her lips together as the tears in her eyes spilled over. "So do I."

Then he kissed her.

EPILOGUE

DARIUS HAD MARRIED WHITNEY in the ballroom in the mansion of the Andreas family estate on Montauk. Suzanne had seen pictures of the elaborate, but quiet, event. Nick had married Maggie on the beach. She'd been there with them. She'd seen the sandals. Raised an eyebrow over the cutoff jeans Nick had worn.

So it seemed only fitting in Suzanne's eyes that she and Cade have a big church wedding, with a minister, Nick and Darius as groomsmen, Whitney and Maggie as bridesmaids and Gino as ring bearer.

In the bride's room of the huge old gray-stone church that looked more like a cathedral with its vaulted ceilings and regal pillars, Whitney fussed with Suzanne's hair while Maggie straightened the long train of her frilly white gown.

Suzanne sucked in a breath. "How's Liz holding up?" There were four kids now. Three-year-old Gino and toddlers Michael and Mitzi. Plus a baby, since Whitney had given birth to Elizabeth. Dressed in a tiny tux, Gino sat on a fancy Queen Anne chair, his little legs swinging, the pillow for the rings sitting on the counter beside him. But Liz still had three kids to watch until the formal ceremony was over.

"She's fine. She's got plenty of help from Mrs.

Reynolds and Mrs. Granger. Cade's den looks like a day care. I'm sure they're having a high old time. Stop fretting!"

She pressed a hand to her stomach. "I can't help it."

Maggie eyed her shrewdly. "Nerves or cold feet?"

"Just nerves."

Whitney laughed. "Afraid of marrying a multibillionaire?"

She groaned. "I'm more afraid of marrying somebody so good-looking every woman in the world is going to try to steal him."

Maggie chuckled merrily. "Right. Cade only has eyes for you."

As if to confirm that, Cade caught Suzanne's gaze the second she and Marty Higgins stepped into the doorway of the big church and the organist began the chords of "Here Comes the Bride." A longtime friend of Cade's, constant diner customer and now the man dating Amanda Mae, Marty had volunteered to walk Suzanne down the aisle. His request for the honor had been every bit as sweet and sincere as Cade's proposal.

But at this second, she only saw Cade. As her designer gown swished softly on the silk runner that led her to the altar, she held his gaze, loving the way his eyes first skimmed her possessively, then softened with love when they locked with hers.

As she neared the end of the aisle, she looked over at Amanda Mae just in time to see her sobbing into a dainty pink hankie. She glanced at Jim and Audra Malloy and Jim winked at her, a private, special signal and she smiled, then she looked at Ginny, who sat in the seat in front of Jim and Audra. Ginny flashed her a grin before she too burst into tears. Audra Malloy tapped her on the shoulder and handed her a pristine white handkerchief. Sniffing softly, Ginny took it.

Suzanne finished her walk, nervously taking the hand Cade extended. The preacher opened his book and said, "Who gives this woman to be married?"

Marty choked out, "I do," then bussed a kiss across her cheek before he turned and took his seat with Amanda Mae.

She swallowed back her own tears. She'd entered this town a homeless orphan, a woman with no family, no friends. Now, almost one year to the date, she had a partner who acted more like a mom than a business associate. She had two best friends in Maggie and Whitney, and Nick and Darius, who would become real family when she married Cade.

Cade. The love of her life. Her reason to breathe. Her life partner. The man who'd given her a family and who would soon give her more children. Their house would be a noisy, happy place.

She couldn't ask for anything more.

No woman could.

MILLS & BOON®

Want to get more from Mills & Boon?

Here's what's available to you if you join the
exclusive **Mills & Boon eBook Club** today:

- ✦ *Convenience – choose your books each month*
- ✦ *Exclusive – receive your books a month before
  anywhere else*
- ✦ *Flexibility – change your subscription at any time*
- ✦ *Variety – gain access to eBook-only series*
- ✦ *Value – subscriptions from just £1.99 a month*

So visit **www.millsandboon.co.uk/esubs** today
to be a part of this exclusive eBook Club!

MILLS & BOON®
By Request

RELIVE THE ROMANCE WITH THE BEST OF THE BEST

A sneak peek at next month's titles...

In stores from 20th February 2015:

- **Royal and Ruthless** – Robyn Donald, Annie West and Christina Hollis

- **At the Tycoon's Service** – Maya Banks

In stores from 6th March 2015:

- **He's the One** – Cara Colter, Barbara Hannay and Jackie Braun

- **The Australian's Bride** – Alison Roberts, Meredith Webber and Marion Lennox

---

0215/05